PERTH & KINROSS COUNCIL
EDUCATION & CHILDREN'S SERVICES 9 NOV 2013
LIBRARIES & LIFELONG LEARNING

This book is due for return on or before the last date indicated on
the label. Renewals may be obtained on application.

2 0 NOV 2013

PERCY JACKSON

AND THE
LAST OLYMPIAN

Books by Rick Riordan

PERCY JACKSON AND THE LIGHTNING THIEF
PERCY JACKSON AND THE SEA OF MONSTERS
PERCY JACKSON AND THE TITAN'S CURSE
PERCY JACKSON AND THE BATTLE OF THE
LABYRINTH
PERCY JACKSON AND THE LAST OLYMPIAN

percyjackson.co.uk

PERCY JACKSON

AND THE
LAST OLYMPIAN

RICK RIORDAN

PUFFIN

573102

To Mrs Pabst, my eighth-grade English teacher,
who started me on the road to Camp Half-Blood

PUFFIN BOOKS

Published by the Penguin Group
Penguin Books Ltd, 80 Strand, London WC2R ORL, England
Penguin Group (USA) Inc., 375 Hudson Street, New York, New York 10014, USA
Penguin Group (Canada), 90 Eglinton Avenue East, Suite 700, Toronto, Ontario, Canada M4P 2Y3
(a division of Pearson Penguin Canada Inc.)
Penguin Ireland, 25 St Stephen's Green, Dublin 2, Ireland (a division of Penguin Books Ltd)
Penguin Group (Australia), 250 Camberwell Road, Camberwell, Victoria 3124, Australia
(a division of Pearson Australia Group Pty Ltd)
Penguin Books India Pvt Ltd, 11 Community Centre, Panchsheel Park, New Delhi – 110 017, India
Penguin Group (NZ), 67 Apollo Drive, Rosedale, North Shore 0632, New Zealand
(a division of Pearson New Zealand Ltd)
Penguin Books (South Africa) (Pty) Ltd, 24 Sturdee Avenue, Rosebank, Johannesburg 2196, South Africa

Penguin Books Ltd, Registered Offices: 80 Strand, London WC2R ORL, England

puffinbooks.com

First published in the USA by Hyperion Books for Children 2009
First published in Great Britain in Puffin Books 2009

1

Copyright © Rick Riordan, 2009

The moral right of the author has been asserted

Set in 13/16.5 pt Centaur MT
Typeset by Palimpsest Book Production Limited, Grangemouth, Stirlingshire
Made and printed in England by Clays Ltd, St Ives plc

British Library Cataloguing in Publication Data
A CIP catalogue record for this book is available from the British Library

HARDBACK
ISBN: 978–0–141–38294–4

TRADE PAPERBACK
ISBN: 978–0–141–38293–7

www.greenpenguin.co.uk

Penguin Books is committed to a sustainable future
for our business, our readers and our planet.
The book in your hands is made from paper
certified by the Forest Stewardship Council.

CONTENTS

1 GO CRUISING WITH EXPLOSIVES

The end of the world started when a pegasus landed on the hood of my car.

Up until then, I was having a great afternoon. Technically I wasn't supposed to be driving because I wouldn't turn sixteen for another week, but my mom and my stepdad, Paul, took my friend Rachel and me to this private stretch of beach on the South Shore and Paul let us borrow his Prius for a short spin.

Now I know you're thinking, Wow, that was really irresponsible of him, blah, blah, blah, but Paul knows me pretty well. He's seen me slice up demons and leap out of exploding school buildings, so he probably figured taking a car a few hundred metres wasn't exactly the most dangerous thing I'd ever done.

Anyway, Rachel and I were driving along. It was a hot August day. Rachel's red hair was pulled back in a ponytail and she wore a white blouse over her swimsuit. I'd never seen her in anything but ratty T-shirts and paint-splattered jeans before, and she looked like a million golden drachmas.

'Oh, pull up right there!' she told me.

We parked on a ridge overlooking the Atlantic. The sea is always one of my favourite places, but today it was especially nice – glittery green and smooth as glass, as though my dad was keeping it calm just for us.

My dad, by the way, is Poseidon. He can do stuff like that.

'So.' Rachel smiled at me. 'About that invitation.'

'Oh . . . right.' I tried to sound excited. I mean, she'd asked me to her family's vacation house on St Thomas for three days. I didn't get a lot of offers like that. My family's idea of a fancy vacation was a weekend in a rundown cabin on Long Island with some movie rentals and a couple of frozen pizzas, and here Rachel's folks were willing to let me tag along to the Caribbean.

Besides, I seriously needed a vacation. This summer had been the hardest of my life. The idea of taking a break even for a few days was really tempting.

Still, something big was supposed to go down any day now. I was 'on call' for a mission. Even worse, next week was my birthday. There was this prophecy that said when I turned sixteen, bad things would happen.

'Percy,' Rachel said, 'I know the timing is bad. But it's *always* bad for you, right?'

She had a point.

'I really want to go,' I promised. 'It's just –'

'The war.'

I nodded. I didn't like talking about it, but Rachel knew. Unlike most mortals, she could see through the Mist – the magic veil that distorts human vision. She'd seen monsters. She'd met some of the other demigods who were fighting the Titans and their allies. She'd even been there last summer when the chopped-up Lord Kronos rose out of his coffin in a terrible new form, and she'd earned my permanent respect by nailing him in the eye with a blue plastic hairbrush.

She put her hand on my arm. 'Just think about it, okay? We don't leave for a couple of days. My dad . . .' Her voice faltered.

'Is he giving you a hard time?' I asked.

Rachel shook her head in disgust. 'He's trying to be *nice* to me, which is almost worse. He wants me to go to Clarion Ladies' Academy in the autumn.'

'The school where your mom went?'

'It's a stupid finishing school for society girls, all the way in New Hampshire. Can you see me in finishing school?'

I admitted the idea sounded pretty dumb. Rachel was into urban art projects and feeding the homeless and going to protest rallies to 'Save the Endangered Yellow-Bellied Sap Sucker' and stuff like that. I'd never even seen her wear a dress. It was hard to imagine her learning to be a socialite.

She sighed. 'He thinks if he does a bunch of nice stuff for me, I'll feel guilty and give in.'

'Which is why he agreed to let me come with you guys on vacation?'

'Yes . . . but, Percy, you'd be doing me a huge favour. It would be *so* much better if you were with us. Besides, there's something I want to talk –' She stopped abruptly.

'Something you want to talk about?' I asked. 'You mean . . . so serious we'd have to go to St Thomas to talk about it?'

She pursed her lips. 'Look, just forget it for now. Let's pretend we're a couple of normal people. We're out for a drive, and we're watching the ocean, and it's nice to be together.'

I could tell something was bothering her, but she put on a brave smile. The sunlight made her hair look like fire.

We'd spent a lot of time together this summer. I hadn't exactly planned it that way, but the more serious things got at camp, the more I found myself needing to call up Rachel and get away, just for some breathing room. I needed to remind myself the mortal world was still out here, away from all the monsters using me as their personal punching bag.

'Okay,' I said. 'Just a normal afternoon and two normal people.'

She nodded. 'And so . . . hypothetically, if these two people liked each other, what would it take to get the stupid guy to kiss the girl, huh?'

'Oh . . .' I felt like one of Apollo's sacred cows – slow, dumb and bright red. 'Um . . .'

I can't pretend I hadn't thought about Rachel. She was so much easier to be around than . . . well, than some other girls I knew. I didn't have to work hard, or watch what I said, or wrack my brain trying to figure out what she was thinking. Rachel didn't hide much. She let you know how she felt.

I'm not sure what I would've done next, but I was so distracted I didn't notice the huge black form swooping down from the sky until four hooves landed on the hood of the Prius with a WUMP-WUMP-CRUNCH!

Hey, boss, a voice said in my head. *Nice car!*

Blackjack the pegasus was an old friend of mine, so I tried not to get too annoyed by the craters he'd just put in the hood, but I didn't think Paul Blofis would be real stoked.

'Blackjack,' I sighed. 'What are you –'

Then I saw who was riding on his back, and I knew my day was about to get a lot more complicated.

''Sup, Percy.'

Charles Beckendorf, senior counsellor for the Hephaestus cabin, would make most monsters cry for their mommies. He was huge, with ripped muscles from working in the forges every summer. He was two years older than me and one of the camp's best armour-smiths. He made some seriously ingenious mechanical stuff. A month before, he'd rigged a Greek fire bomb in the bathroom of a tour bus that was carrying a bunch of monsters across country. The explosion took out a whole legion of Kronos's evil meanies as soon as the first harpy went *flush*.

Beckendorf was dressed for combat. He wore a bronze breastplate and war helm with black camo pants and a sword strapped to his side. His explosives bag was slung over his shoulder.

'Time?' I asked.

He nodded grimly.

A lump formed in my throat. I'd known this was coming. We'd been planning it for weeks, but I'd half hoped it would never happen.

Rachel looked up at Beckendorf. 'Hi.'

'Oh, hey. I'm Beckendorf. You must be Rachel. Percy's told me . . . uh, I mean he mentioned you.'

Rachel raised an eyebrow. 'Really? Good.' She glanced at Blackjack, who was clopping his hooves against the hood of the Prius. 'So I guess you guys have to go save the world now.'

'Pretty much,' Beckendorf agreed.

I looked at Rachel helplessly. 'Would you tell my mom –'

'I'll tell her. I'm sure she's used to it. And I'll explain to Paul about the hood.'

I nodded my thanks. I figured this might be the last time Paul loaned me his car.

'Good luck.' Rachel kissed me before I could even react. 'Now get going, half-blood. Go kill some monsters for me.'

My last view of her was sitting in the shotgun seat of the Prius, her arms crossed, watching as Blackjack circled higher and higher, carrying Beckendorf and me into the sky. I wondered what Rachel wanted to talk to me about, and whether I'd live long enough to find out.

'So,' Beckendorf said. 'I'm guessing you don't want me to mention that little scene to Annabeth.'

'Oh, gods,' I muttered. 'Don't even think about it.'

Beckendorf chuckled, and together we soared out over the Atlantic.

It was almost dark by the time we spotted our target. The *Princess Andromeda* glowed on the horizon – a huge cruise ship lit up yellow and white. From a distance, you'd think it was just a party ship, not the headquarters for the Titan lord. Then, as you got closer, you might notice the giant figurehead – a dark-haired maiden in a Greek chiton, wrapped in chains with a look of horror on her face, as if she could smell the stench of all the monsters she was being forced to carry.

Seeing the ship again twisted my gut into knots. I'd

almost died twice on the *Princess Andromeda*. Now it was heading straight for New York.

'You know what to do?' Beckendorf yelled over the wind.

I nodded. We'd done dry runs at the dockyards in New Jersey, using abandoned ships as our targets. I knew how little time we would have. But I also knew this was our best chance to end Kronos's invasion before it ever started.

'Blackjack,' I said, 'set us down on the lowest stern deck.'

Gotcha, boss, he said. *Man, I hate seeing that boat.*

Three years ago, Blackjack had been enslaved on the *Princess Andromeda* until he'd escaped with a little help from my friends and me. I figured he'd rather have his mane braided like My Little Pony than be back here again.

'Don't wait for us,' I told him.

But, boss —

'Trust me,' I said. 'We'll get out by ourselves.'

Blackjack folded his wings and plummeted towards the boat like a black comet. The wind whistled in my ears. I saw monsters patrolling the upper decks of the ship — *dracaenae* snake-women, hellhounds, giants, and the humanoid sea-lion demons known as telkhines — but we zipped by so fast none of them raised the alarm. We shot down the stern of the boat and Blackjack spread his wings, lightly coming to a landing on the lowest deck. I climbed off, feeling queasy.

Good luck, boss, Blackjack said. *Don't let 'em turn you into horsemeat!*

With that, my old friend flew off into the night. I took my pen out of my pocket, uncapped it, and Riptide sprang to full size – one metre of deadly celestial bronze glowing in the dusk.

Beckendorf pulled a piece of paper out of his pocket. I thought it was a map or something. Then I realized it was a photograph. He stared at it in the dim light – the smiling face of Silena Beauregard, daughter of Aphrodite. They'd started going out last summer, after years of the rest of us saying, 'Duh, you guys like each other!' Even with all the dangerous missions, Beckendorf had been happier this summer than I'd ever seen him.

'We'll make it back to camp,' I promised.

For a second I saw worry in his eyes. Then he put on his old confident smile.

'You bet,' he said. 'Let's go blow Kronos back into a million pieces.'

Beckendorf led the way. We followed a narrow corridor to the service stairwell, just like we'd practised, but we froze when we heard noises above us.

'I don't care what your nose says!' snarled a half-human, half-dog voice – a telkhine. 'The last time you smelled half-blood, it turned out to be a meatloaf sandwich!'

'Meatloaf sandwiches are good!' a second voice snarled. 'But this is half-blood scent, I swear. They are on board!'

'Bah, your *brain* isn't on board!'

They continued to argue, and Beckendorf pointed downstairs. We descended as quietly as we could. Two floors down, the voices of the telkhines started to fade.

Finally we came to a metal hatch. Beckendorf mouthed the words, *Engine room.*

It was locked, but Beckendorf pulled some chain cutters

out of his bag and split the bolt like it was made of butter.

Inside, a row of yellow turbines the size of grain silos churned and hummed. Pressure gauges and computer terminals lined the opposite wall. A telkhine was hunched over a console, but he was so involved with his work he didn't notice us. He was about a metre and a half tall, with slick black sea-lion fur and stubby little feet. He had the head of a Dobermann, but his clawed hands were almost human. He growled and muttered as he tapped on his keyboard. Maybe he was messaging his friends on uglyface.com.

I stepped forward and he tensed, probably smelling something was wrong. He leaped sideways towards a big red alarm button, but I blocked his path. He hissed and lunged at me, but one slice of Riptide and he exploded into dust.

'One down,' Beckendorf said. 'About five thousand to go.' He tossed me a jar of thick green liquid – Greek fire, one of the most dangerous magical substances in the world. Then he threw me another essential tool of demigod heroes – duct tape.

'Slap that one on the console,' he said. 'I'll get the turbines.'

We went to work. The room was hot and humid, and in no time we were drenched in sweat.

The boat kept chugging along. Being the son of Poseidon and all, I have perfect bearings at sea. Don't ask me how, but I could tell we were at 40.19° north, 71.90° west, making eighteen knots an hour, which meant the ship would arrive in New York Harbor by dawn. This would be our only chance to stop it.

I had just attached a second jar of Greek fire to the control panels when I heard the pounding of feet on metal steps — so many creatures coming down the stairwell I could hear them over the engines. Not a good sign.

I locked eyes with Beckendorf. 'How much longer?'

'Too long.' He tapped his watch, which was our remote control detonator. 'I still have to wire the receiver and prime the charges. Ten more minutes at least.'

Judging from the sound of the footsteps, we had about ten seconds.

'I'll distract them,' I said. 'Meet you at the rendezvous point.'

'Percy —'

'Wish me luck.'

He looked like he wanted to argue. The whole idea had been to get in and out without being spotted. But we were going to have to improvise.

'Good luck,' he said.

I charged out of the door.

Half a dozen telkhines were tromping down the stairs. I cut through them with Riptide faster than they could yelp. I kept climbing — past another telkhine who was so startled he dropped his Li'l Demons lunchbox. I left him alive — partly because his lunchbox was cool, partly so he could raise the alarm and hopefully get his friends to follow me rather than head towards the engine room.

I burst through a door onto deck six and kept running. I'm sure the carpeted hall had once been very plush, but over the last three years of monster occupation the wallpaper, carpet and stateroom doors had been clawed up and slimed so it looked like the inside of a dragon's throat (and, yes, unfortunately I speak from experience).

Back on my first visit to the *Princess Andromeda*, my old enemy Luke had kept some dazed tourists on board for show, shrouded in Mist so they didn't realize they were on a monster-infested ship. Now, I didn't see any sign of tourists. I hated to think what had happened to them, but I kind of doubted they'd been allowed to go home with their bingo winnings.

I reached the promenade, a big shopping mall that took up the whole middle of the ship, and I stopped cold. In the middle of the courtyard stood a fountain. And in the fountain squatted a giant crab.

I'm not talking 'giant' like $7.99 all-you-can-eat Alaskan king crab. I'm talking 'giant' like bigger than the fountain. The monster rose over three metres out of the water. Its shell was mottled blue and green, its pincers longer than my body.

If you've ever seen a crab's mouth, all foamy and gross with whiskers and snapping bits, you can imagine this one didn't look any better blown up to billboard size. Its beady black eyes glared at me, and I could see intelligence in them – and hate. The fact that I was the son of the sea god was not going to win me any points with Mr Crabby.

'FFFFffffff', it hissed, sea foam dripping from its mouth. The smell coming off it was like a garbage can full of fish sticks that had been sitting in the sun all week.

Alarms blared. Soon I was going to have lots of company and I had to keep moving.

'Hey, crabby.' I inched around the edge of the courtyard. 'I'm just gonna scoot around you so –'

The crab moved with amazing speed. It scuttled out of the fountain and came straight at me, pincers snapping. I dived into a gift shop, ploughing through a rack of T-shirts. A crab pincer smashed the glass walls to pieces and raked across the room. I dashed back outside, breathing heavily, but Mr Crabby turned and followed.

'There!' a voice said from a balcony above me. 'Intruder!'

If I'd wanted to create a distraction, I'd succeeded, but this was not where I wanted to fight. If I got pinned down in the centre of the ship, I was crab chow.

The demonic crustacean lunged at me. I sliced with Riptide, taking off the tip of its claw. It hissed and foamed, but didn't seem very hurt.

I tried to remember anything from the old stories that might help with this thing. Annabeth had told me about a monster crab – something about Hercules crushing it under his foot? That wasn't going to work here. This crab was slightly bigger than my Reeboks.

Then a weird thought came to me. Last Christmas, my mom and I had brought Paul Blofis to our old cabin at Montauk, where we'd been going forever. Paul had taken me crabbing, and when he'd brought up a net full of the things he'd shown me how crabs have a chink in their armour, right in the middle of their ugly bellies.

The only problem was getting to the ugly belly.

I glanced at the fountain, then at the marble floor, already slick from scuttling crab tracks. I held out my hand, concentrating on the water, and the fountain exploded. Water sprayed everywhere, three stories high, dousing the balconies and the elevators and the windows of the shops.

The crab didn't care. It loved water. It came at me sideways, snapping and hissing, and I ran straight at it, screaming, 'AHHHHHHH!'

Just before we collided, I hit the ground baseball-style and slid on the wet marble floor straight under the creature. It was like sliding under a seven-ton armoured vehicle. All the crab had to do was sit and squash me, but before it realized what was going on, I jabbed Riptide into the chink in its armour, let go of the hilt and pushed myself out the back side.

The monster shuddered and hissed. Its eyes dissolved. Its shell turned bright red as its insides evaporated. The empty shell clattered to the floor in a massive heap.

I didn't have time to admire my handiwork. I ran for the nearest stairs while all around me monsters and demigods shouted orders and strapped on their weapons. I was empty-handed. Riptide, being magic, would appear in my pocket sooner or later, but for now it was stuck somewhere under the wreckage of the crab, and I had no time to retrieve it.

In the elevator foyer on deck eight, a couple of *dracaenae* slithered across my path. From the waist up, they were women with green scaly skin, yellow eyes and forked tongues. From the waist down, they had double snake trunks instead of legs. They held spears and weighted nets, and I knew from experience they could use them.

'What isss thisss?' one said. 'A prize for Kronosss!'

I wasn't in the mood to play break-the-snake, but in front of me was a stand with a model of the ship, like a YOU ARE HERE display. I ripped the model off the pedestal and hurled it at the first *dracaena*. The boat smacked her in the face and she went down with the ship. I jumped over her, grabbed her friend's spear and swung her around. She slammed into the elevator and I kept running towards the front of the ship.

'Get him!' she screamed.

Hellhounds bayed. An arrow from somewhere whizzed past my face and impaled itself in the mahogany-panelled wall of the stairwell.

I didn't care – as long as I got the monsters away from the engine room and gave Beckendorf more time.

As I was running up the stairwell, a kid charged down. He looked like he'd just woken up from a nap. His armour was half on. He drew his sword and yelled, 'Kronos!' but he sounded more scared than angry. He couldn't have been more than twelve – about the same age I was when I'd first arrived at Camp Half-Blood.

That thought depressed me. This kid was getting brainwashed – trained to hate the gods and lash out because he'd been born half-Olympian. Kronos was using him, and yet the kid thought I was his enemy.

No way was I going to hurt him. I didn't need a weapon for this. I stepped inside his strike and grabbed his wrist, slamming it against the wall. His sword clattered out of his hand.

Then I did something I hadn't planned on. It was probably stupid. It definitely jeopardized our mission, but I couldn't help it.

'If you want to live,' I told him, 'get off this ship *now*. Tell the other demigods.' Then I shoved him down the stairs and sent him tumbling to the next floor.

I kept climbing.

Bad memories: a hallway ran past the cafeteria. Annabeth, my half-brother Tyson and I had sneaked through here three years ago on my first visit.

I burst outside onto the main deck. Off the port bow, the sky was darkening from purple to black. A swimming pool glowed between two glass towers with more balconies and restaurant decks. The whole upper ship seemed eerily deserted.

All I had to do was cross to the other side. Then I could take the staircase down to the helipad – our emergency rendezvous point. With any luck, Beckendorf would meet me there. We'd jump into the sea. My water powers would protect us both, and we'd detonate the charges from a quarter of a mile away.

I was halfway across the deck when the sound of a voice made me freeze. 'You're late, Percy.'

Luke stood on the balcony above me, a smile on his scarred face. He wore jeans, a white T-shirt and flip-flops, like he was just a normal college-aged guy, but his eyes told the truth. They were solid gold.

'We've been expecting you for days.' At first he sounded normal, like Luke. But then his face twitched. A shudder passed through his body like he'd just drunk something really nasty. His voice became heavier, ancient and powerful – the voice of the Titan lord Kronos. The words scraped down my spine like a knife blade. 'Come, bow before me.'

'Yeah, that'll happen,' I muttered.

Laistrygonian giants filed in on either side of the swimming pool as if they'd been waiting for a cue. Each was two and a half metres tall with tattooed arms, leather armour and spiked clubs. Demigod archers appeared on the roof above Luke. Two hellhounds leaped down from the opposite balcony and snarled at me. Within seconds, I was surrounded. A trap: there's no way they could've got into position so fast unless they knew I was coming.

I looked up at Luke and anger boiled inside me. I didn't know if Luke's consciousness was even still alive inside that body. Maybe, the way his voice had changed . . . or maybe it was just Kronos adapting to his new form. I told myself it didn't matter. Luke had been twisted and evil long before Kronos possessed him.

A voice in my head said: *I have to fight him eventually. Why not now?*

According to that big prophecy, I was supposed to make a choice that saved or destroyed the world when I was sixteen. That was only seven days away. Why not now? If I really had the power, what difference would a week make? I could end this threat right here by taking down Kronos. Hey, I'd fought monsters and gods before.

As if reading my thoughts, Luke smiled. No, he was *Kronos.* I had to remember that.

'Come forward,' he said, 'if you dare.'

The crowd of monsters parted. I moved up the stairs, my heart pounding. I was sure somebody would stab me in the back, but they let me pass. I felt my pocket and found my pen waiting. I uncapped it and Riptide grew into a sword.

Kronos's weapon appeared in his hands – a two-metre-long scythe, half celestial bronze, half mortal steel. Just looking at the thing made my knees turn to Jell-O. But before I could change my mind I charged.

Time slowed down. I mean *literally* slowed down, because Kronos had that power. I felt like I was moving through syrup. My arms were so heavy I could barely raise my sword. Kronos smiled, swirling his scythe at normal speed and waiting for me to creep towards my death.

I tried to fight his magic. I concentrated on the sea around me – the source of my power. I'd got better at channelling it over the years, but now nothing seemed to happen.

I took another slow step forward. Giants jeered. *Dracaenae* hissed with laughter.

Hey, ocean, I pleaded. *Any day now would be good.*

Suddenly there was a wrenching pain in my gut. The entire boat lurched sideways, throwing monsters off their feet. Four thousand gallons of salt water surged out of the swimming pool, dousing me and Kronos and everyone on the deck. The water revitalized me, breaking the time spell, and I lunged forward.

I struck at Kronos but I was still too slow. I made the mistake of looking at his face – *Luke's face,* a guy who was once my friend. As much as I hated him, it was hard to kill him.

Kronos had no such hesitation. He sliced downward with his scythe. I leaped back and the evil blade missed by a millimetre, cutting a gash in the deck right between my feet.

I kicked Kronos in the chest. He stumbled backwards, but he was heavier than Luke should've been. It was like kicking a refrigerator.

Kronos swung his scythe again. I intercepted with Riptide, but his strike was so powerful my blade could only deflect it. The edge of the scythe shaved off my shirtsleeve and grazed my arm. It shouldn't have been a serious cut, but the entire side of my body exploded with pain. I remembered what a sea-demon had once said about Kronos's scythe: *Careful, fool. One touch, and the blade will sever your soul from your body.* Now I understood what he meant. I wasn't just losing blood. I could feel my strength, my will, my identity draining away.

I stumbled backwards, switched my sword to my left hand and lunged desperately. My blade should've run him through, but it deflected off his stomach like I was hitting solid marble. There was no way he should've survived that.

Kronos laughed. 'A poor performance, Percy Jackson. Luke tells me you were never his match at swordplay.'

My vision started to blur. I knew I didn't have much time. 'Luke had a big head,' I said. 'But at least it was *his* head.'

'A shame to kill you now,' Kronos mused, 'before the final plan unfolds. I would love to see the terror in your eyes when you realize how I will destroy Olympus.'

'You'll never get this boat to Manhattan.' My arm was throbbing. Black spots danced in my eyes.

'And why would that be?' Kronos's golden eyes glittered. His face – Luke's face – seemed like a mask, unnatural and lit from behind by some evil power. 'Perhaps you are counting on your friend with the explosives?'

He looked down at the pool and called, 'Nakamura!'

A teenage guy in full Greek armour pushed through the crowd. His left eye was covered with a black patch. I knew him, of course: Ethan Nakamura, the son of Nemesis.

I'd saved his life in the Labyrinth last summer and, in return, the little punk helped Kronos come back to life.

'Success, my lord,' Ethan called. 'We found him just as we were told.'

He clapped his hands and two giants lumbered forward, dragging Charles Beckendorf between them. My heart almost stopped. Beckendorf had a swollen eye and cuts all over his face and arms. His armour was gone and his shirt was nearly torn off.

'No!' I yelled.

Beckendorf met my eyes. He glanced at his hand like he was trying to tell me something. *His watch.* They hadn't taken it yet, and that was the detonator. Was it possible the explosives were armed? Surely the monsters would've dismantled them right away.

'We found him amidships,' one of the giants said, 'trying to sneak to the engine room. Can we eat him now?'

'Soon.' Kronos scowled at Ethan. 'Are you sure he didn't set the explosives?'

'He was going *towards* the engine room, my lord.'

'How do you know that?'

'Er . . .' Ethan shifted uncomfortably. 'He was heading in that direction. And he told us. His bag is still full of explosives.'

Slowly, I began to understand. Beckendorf had fooled them. When he'd realized he was going to be captured, he turned to make it look like he was going the other way. He'd convinced them he hadn't made it to the engine room yet. The Greek fire might still be primed! But that didn't do us any good unless we could get off the ship and detonate it.

Kronos hesitated.

Buy the story, I prayed. The pain in my arm was so bad now I could barely stand.

'Open his bag,' Kronos ordered.

One of the giants ripped the explosives satchel from Beckendorf's shoulders. He peered inside, grunted and turned it upside down. Panicked monsters surged backwards. If the bag really had been full of Greek fire jars, we would've all blown up. But what fell out were a dozen cans of peaches.

I could hear Kronos breathing, trying to control his anger.

'Did you, perhaps,' he said, 'capture this demigod near the galley?'

Ethan turned pale. 'Um –'

'And did you, perhaps, send someone to actually CHECK THE ENGINE ROOM?'

Ethan scrambled back in terror, then turned on his heels and ran.

I cursed silently. Now we had only minutes before the bombs were disarmed. I caught Beckendorf's eyes again and asked a silent question, hoping he would understand: *How long?*

He cupped his fingers and thumb, making a circle. *ZERO*. There was no delay on the timer at all. If he managed to press the detonator button, the ship would blow at once. We'd never be able to get far enough away before using it. The monsters would kill us first, or disarm the explosives, or both.

Kronos turned towards me with a crooked smile. 'You'll have to excuse my incompetent help, Percy Jackson, but it doesn't matter. We have you now. We've known you were coming for weeks.'

He held out his hand and dangled a little silver bracelet with a scythe charm – the Titan lord's symbol.

The wound in my arm was sapping my ability to think, but I muttered, 'Communication device . . . spy at camp.'

Kronos chuckled. 'You can't count on friends. They will always let you down. Luke learned that lesson the hard way. Now drop your sword and surrender to me, or your friend dies.'

I swallowed. One of the giants had his hand around Beckendorf's neck. I was in no shape to rescue him and, even if I tried, he would die before I got there. We both would.

Beckendorf mouthed one word: *Go.*

I shook my head. I couldn't just leave him.

The second giant was still rummaging through the peach cans, which meant Beckendorf's left arm was free. He raised it slowly – towards the watch on his right wrist.

I wanted to scream, *NO!*

Then down by the swimming pool one of the *dracaenae* hissed, 'What isss he doing? What isss that on hisss wrissst?'

Beckendorf closed his eyes tight and brought his hand up to his watch.

I had no choice. I threw my sword like a javelin at Kronos. It bounced harmlessly off his chest, but it did startle him. I pushed through a crowd of monsters and jumped off the side of the ship – towards the water thirty metres below.

I heard rumbling deep in the ship. Monsters yelled at

me from above. A spear sailed past my ear. An arrow pierced my thigh, but I barely had time to register the pain. I plunged into the sea and willed the currents to take me far, far away – fifty metres, a hundred metres.

Even from that distance, the explosion shook the world. Heat seared the back of my head. The *Princess Andromeda* blew up from both sides, a massive fireball of green flame roiling into the dark sky, consuming everything.

Beckendorf, I thought.

Then I blacked out and sank like an anchor towards the bottom of the sea.

2 I MEET SOME FISHY RELATIVES

Demigod dreams suck.

The thing is they're never just *dreams.* They've got to be visions, omens and all that other mystical stuff that makes my brain hurt.

I dreamed I was in a dark palace at the top of a mountain. Unfortunately, I recognized it: the palace of the Titans on top of Mount Othrys, otherwise known as Mount Tamalpais in California. The main pavilion was open to the night, ringed with black Greek columns and statues of the Titans. Torchlight glowed against the black marble floor. In the centre of the room, an armoured giant struggled under the weight of a swirling funnel cloud – Atlas, holding up the sky.

Two other giant men stood nearby over a bronze brazier, studying images in the flames.

'Quite an explosion,' one said. He wore black armour studded with silver dots like a starry night. His face was covered in a war helm with a ram's horn curling on either side.

'It doesn't matter,' the other said. This Titan was dressed in gold robes, with golden eyes like Kronos. His entire body glowed. He reminded me of Apollo, god of the sun, except the Titan's light was harsher, and his expression crueller. 'The gods have answered the challenge. Soon they will be destroyed.'

The images in the fire were hard to make out: storms, buildings crumbling, mortals screaming in terror.

'I will go east to marshal our forces,' the golden Titan said. 'Krios, you shall remain and guard Mount Othrys.'

The ram-horn dude grunted. 'I always get the stupid jobs. Lord of the South. Lord of Constellations. Now I get to babysit Atlas while *you* have all the fun.'

Under the whirlwind of clouds, Atlas bellowed in agony. 'Let me out, curse you! I am your greatest warrior. Take my burden so I may fight!'

'Quiet!' the golden Titan roared. 'You had your chance, Atlas. You failed. Kronos likes you just where you are. As for you, Krios: do your duty.'

'And if you need more warriors?' Krios asked. 'Our treacherous nephew in the tuxedo will not do you much good in a fight.'

The golden Titan laughed. 'Don't worry about him. Besides, the gods can barely handle our first little challenge. They have no idea how many others we have in store. Mark my words, in a few days' time, Olympus will be in ruins, and we will meet here again to celebrate the dawn of the Sixth Age!'

The golden Titan erupted into flames and disappeared.

'Oh, sure,' Krios grumbled. 'He gets to erupt into flames. I get to wear these stupid rams' horns.'

The scene shifted. Now I was outside the pavilion, hiding in the shadows of a Greek column. A boy stood next to me, eavesdropping on the Titans. He had dark silky hair, pale skin and dark clothes – my friend Nico di Angelo, the son of Hades.

He looked straight at me, his expression grim. 'You see,

Percy?' he whispered. 'You're running out of time. Do you really think you can beat them without my plan?'

His words washed over me as cold as the ocean floor, and my dreams went black.

'Percy?' a deep voice said.

My head felt like it had been microwaved in tinfoil. I opened my eyes and saw a large shadowy figure looming over me.

'Beckendorf?' I asked hopefully.

'No, brother.'

My eyes refocused. I was looking at a Cyclops – a misshapen face, ratty brown hair, one big brown eye full of concern. 'Tyson?'

My brother broke into a toothy grin. 'Yay! Your brain works!'

I wasn't so sure. My body felt weightless and cold. My voice sounded wrong. I could hear Tyson, but it was more like I was hearing vibrations inside my skull, not the regular sounds.

I sat up and a gossamer sheet floated away. I was on a bed made of silky woven kelp, in a room panelled with abalone shell. Glowing pearls the size of basketballs floated around the ceiling, providing light. I was underwater.

Now, being the son of Poseidon and all, I was okay with this. I can breathe underwater just fine, and my clothes don't even get wet unless I want them to. But it was still a bit of a shock when a hammerhead shark drifted through the bedroom window, regarded me and then swam calmly out the opposite side of the room.

'Where –'

'Daddy's palace,' Tyson said.

Under different circumstances, I would've been excited. I'd never visited Poseidon's realm, and I'd been dreaming about it for years. But my head hurt. My shirt was still speckled with burn marks from the explosion. My arm and leg wounds had healed – just being in the ocean can do that for me, given enough time – but I still felt like I'd been trampled by a Laistrygonian rugby team in studs.

'How long –'

'We found you last night,' Tyson said, 'sinking through the water.'

'The *Princess Andromeda*?'

'Went ka-boom,' Tyson confirmed.

'Beckendorf was on board. Did you find . . .'

Tyson's face darkened. 'No sign of him. I am sorry, brother.'

I stared out of the window into deep blue water. Beckendorf was supposed to go to college in the fall. He had a girlfriend, lots of friends, his whole life ahead of him. He couldn't be *gone*. Maybe he'd made it off the ship like I had. Maybe he'd jumped over the side . . . and what? He couldn't have survived a thirty-metre fall into the water like I could. He couldn't put enough distance between himself and the explosion.

I knew in my gut he was dead. He'd sacrificed himself to take out the *Princess Andromeda*, and I had abandoned him.

I thought about my dream: the Titans discussing the explosion as if it didn't matter, Nico di Angelo warning me that I would never beat Kronos without following his plan – a dangerous idea I'd been avoiding for over a year.

A distant blast shook the room. Green light blazed outside, turning the whole sea as bright as noon.

'What was that?' I asked.

Tyson looked worried. 'Daddy will explain. Come, he is blowing up monsters.'

The palace might have been the most amazing place I'd ever seen if it hadn't been in the process of getting destroyed. We swam to the end of a long hallway and shot upward on a geyser. As we rose over the rooftops, I caught my breath — well, if you can catch your breath underwater.

The palace was as big as the city on Mount Olympus, with wide courtyards, gardens and columned pavilions. The gardens were sculpted with coral colonies and glowing sea plants. Twenty or thirty buildings were made of abalone, white but gleaming with rainbow colours. Fish and octopi darted in and out of the windows. The paths were lined with glowing pearls like Christmas lights.

The main courtyard was filled with warriors — mermen with fish tails from the waist down and human bodies from the waist up, except their skin was blue, which I'd never known before. Some were tending the wounded. Some were sharpening spears and swords. One passed us, swimming in a hurry. His eyes were bright green, like that stuff they put in glow sticks, and his teeth were shark teeth. They don't show you stuff like that in *The Little Mermaid*.

Outside the main courtyard stood large fortifications — towers, walls and anti-siege weapons — but most of these had been smashed to ruins. Others were blazing with a strange green light that I knew well — Greek fire, which can burn even underwater.

Beyond this, the sea floor stretched into gloom. I could see battles raging — flashes of energy, explosions, the glint of armies clashing. A regular human would've found it too dark to see. Heck, a regular human would've been crushed by the pressure and frozen by the cold. Even my heat-sensitive eyes couldn't make out exactly what was going on.

At the edge of the palace complex, a temple with a red coral roof exploded, sending fire and debris streaming in slow motion across the furthest gardens. Out of the darkness above, an enormous form appeared – a squid larger than any skyscraper. It was surrounded by a glittering cloud of dust – at least I thought it was dust until I realized it was a swarm of mermen, trying to attack the monster. The squid descended on the palace and swatted its tentacles, smashing a whole column of warriors. Then a brilliant arc of blue light shot from the rooftop of one of the tallest buildings. The light hit the giant squid and the monster dissolved like food colouring in water.

'Daddy,' Tyson said, pointing to where the light had come from.

'*He* did that?' I suddenly felt more hopeful. My dad had unbelievable powers. He was the god of the sea. He could deal with this attack, right? Maybe he'd let me help.

'Have you been in the fight?' I asked Tyson in awe. 'Like, bashing heads with your awesome Cyclops strength and stuff?'

Tyson pouted, and immediately I knew I'd asked a bad question. 'I have been . . . fixing weapons,' he mumbled. 'Come. Let's go find Daddy.'

I know this might sound weird to people with, like, regular parents, but I'd only seen my dad four or five times in my life, and never for more than a few minutes. The Greek gods don't exactly show up for their kids' basketball games. Still, I thought I would recognize Poseidon on sight.

I was wrong.

The roof of the temple was a big open deck that had been set up as a command centre. A mosaic on the floor showed an exact map of the palace grounds and the surrounding ocean, but the mosaic moved. Coloured stone tiles representing different armies and sea monsters shifted around as the forces changed position. Buildings that collapsed in real life also collapsed in the picture.

Standing around the mosaic, grimly studying the battle, was a strange assortment of warriors, but none of them looked like my dad. I was searching for a big guy with a good tan and a black beard, wearing Bermuda shorts and a Hawaiian shirt.

There was nobody like that. One guy was a merman with two fish tails instead of one. His skin was green and his armour studded with pearls. His black hair was tied in a ponytail and he looked young – though it's hard to tell with non-humans. They could be a thousand years old or three. Standing next to him was an old man with a bushy white beard and grey hair. His battle armour seemed to weigh him down. He had green eyes and smile wrinkles around his eyes, but he wasn't smiling now. He was studying the map and leaning on a large metal staff. To his right stood a beautiful woman in green armour with flowing black hair and strange little horns like crab claws. And there was a dolphin – just a regular dolphin, but it was staring at the map intently.

'Delphin,' the old man said. 'Send Palaemon and his legion of sharks to the western front. We have to neutralize those leviathans.'

The dolphin spoke in a chattering voice, but I could understand it in my mind: *Yes, lord!* It sped away.

I looked in dismay at Tyson, then back at the old man. It didn't seem possible, but . . . 'Dad?' I asked.

The old man looked up. I recognized the twinkle in his eyes, but his face . . . he looked like he'd aged forty years.

'Hello, Percy.'

'What – what happened to you?'

Tyson nudged me. He was shaking his head so hard I was afraid it would fall off, but Poseidon didn't look offended.

'It's all right, Tyson,' he said. 'Percy, excuse my appearance. The war has been hard on me.'

'But you're immortal,' I said quietly. 'You can look . . . any way you want.'

'I reflect the state of my realm,' he said. 'And right now that state is quite grim. Percy, I should introduce you – I'm afraid you just missed my lieutenant Delphin, god of the dolphins. This is my, er, wife, Amphitrite. My dear –'

The lady in green armour stared at me coldly then crossed her arms and said, 'Excuse me, my lord. I am needed in the battle.'

She swam away.

I felt pretty awkward, but I guess I couldn't blame her. I'd never thought about it much, but my dad had an immortal wife. All his romances with mortals, including with my mom . . . well, Amphitrite probably didn't like that much.

Poseidon cleared his throat. 'Yes, well . . . and this is my son Triton. Er, my *other* son.'

'Your son and heir,' the green dude corrected. His double fishtails swished back and forth. He smiled at me, but there was no friendliness in his eyes. 'Hello, Perseus Jackson. Come to help at last?'

He acted like I was late or lazy. If you can blush underwater, I probably did.

'Tell me what to do,' I said.

Triton smiled like that was a cute suggestion – like I was a slightly amusing dog that had barked for him or something. He turned to Poseidon. 'I will see to the front line, Father. Don't worry. *I* will not fail.'

He nodded politely to Tyson. How come I didn't get that much respect? Then he shot off into the water.

Poseidon sighed. He raised his staff and it changed into his regular weapon – a huge three-pointed trident. The tips glowed with blue light and the water around it boiled with energy.

'I'm sorry about that,' he told me.

A huge sea serpent appeared from above us and spiralled down towards the roof. It was bright orange with a fanged mouth big enough to swallow a gymnasium.

Hardly looking up, Poseidon pointed his trident at the beast and zapped it with blue energy. *Ka-boom!* The monster burst into a million goldfish, which all swam off in terror.

'My family is anxious,' Poseidon continued, as if nothing had happened. 'The battle against Oceanus is going poorly.'

He pointed to the edge of the mosaic. With the butt of his trident, he tapped the image of a merman larger than the rest, with the horns of a bull. He appeared to be riding a chariot pulled by crawfish, and instead of a sword he wielded a live serpent.

'Oceanus,' I said, trying to remember. 'The Titan of the sea?'

Poseidon nodded. 'He was neutral in the first war of gods and Titans. But Kronos has convinced him to fight. This is . . . well, it's not a good sign. Oceanus would not commit unless he was sure he could pick the winning side.'

'He looks stupid,' I said, trying to sound upbeat. 'I mean who fights with a snake?'

'Daddy will tie it in knots,' Tyson said firmly.

Poseidon smiled, but he looked weary. 'I appreciate your faith. We have been at war almost a year now. My powers are taxed. And still he finds new forces to throw at me – sea monsters so ancient I had forgotten about them.'

I heard an explosion in the distance. About half a mile away, a mountain of coral disintegrated under the weight of two giant creatures. I could dimly make out their shapes. One was a lobster. The other was a giant humanoid like a Cyclops, but he was surrounded by a flurry of limbs. At first I thought he was wearing a bunch of giant octopi. Then I realized they were his own arms – a hundred flailing, fighting arms.

'Briares!' I said.

I was happy to see him, but he looked like he was fighting for his life. He was the last of his kind – a Hundred-handed One, cousin of the Cyclopes. We'd saved him from Kronos's prison last summer and I knew he'd come to help Poseidon, but I hadn't heard of him since.

'He fights well,' Poseidon said. 'I wish we had a whole army like him, but he is only one.'

I watched as Briares bellowed in rage and picked up the lobster, which thrashed and snapped its pincers. He threw it off the coral mountain and the lobster disappeared into the darkness. Briares swam after it, his hundred arms spinning like the blades of a motorboat.

'Percy, we may not have much time,' my dad said. 'Tell me of your mission. Did you see Kronos?'

I told him everything, though my voice choked up when I explained about Beckendorf. I looked down at the courtyards below and saw hundreds of wounded mermen lying on makeshift cots. I saw rows of coral mounds that must've been hastily made graves. I realized Beckendorf wasn't the first death. He was only one of hundreds, maybe thousands. I'd never felt so angry and helpless.

Poseidon stroked his beard. 'Percy, Beckendorf chose a heroic death. You bear no blame for that. Kronos's army will be in disarray. Many were destroyed.'

'But we didn't kill him, did we?'

As I said it, I knew it was a naive hope. We might blow up his ship and disintegrate his monsters, but a Titan lord wouldn't be so easy to kill.

'No,' Poseidon admitted. 'But you've bought our side some time.'

'There were demigods on that ship,' I said, thinking of the kid I'd seen in the stairwell. Somehow I'd allowed myself to concentrate on the monsters and Kronos. I'd convinced myself that destroying their ship was all right because they were evil, they were sailing to attack my city and, besides, they couldn't really be permanently killed. Monsters just vaporized and re-formed eventually. But demigods . . .

Poseidon put his hand on my shoulder. 'Percy, there

were only a few demigod warriors aboard that ship, and they all chose to battle for Kronos. Perhaps some heeded your warning and escaped. If they did not . . . they chose their path.'

'They were brainwashed!' I said. 'Now they're dead and Kronos is still alive. That's supposed to make me feel better?'

I glared at the mosaic – little tile explosions destroying tile monsters. It seemed so easy when it was just a picture.

Tyson put his arm around me. If anybody else had tried that, I would've pushed them away, but Tyson was too big and stubborn. He hugged me whether I wanted it or not. 'Not your fault, brother. Kronos does not explode good. Next time we will use a big stick.'

'Percy,' my father said. 'Beckendorf's sacrifice wasn't in vain. You have scattered the invasion force. New York will be safe for a time, which frees the other Olympians to deal with the bigger threat.'

'The bigger threat?' I thought about what the golden Titan had said in my dream: *The gods have answered the challenge. Soon they will be destroyed.*

A shadow passed over my father's face. 'You've had enough sorrow for one day. Ask Chiron when you return to camp.'

'Return to camp? But you're in trouble here. I want to help!'

'You can't, Percy. Your job is elsewhere.'

I couldn't believe I was hearing this. I looked at Tyson for backup.

My brother chewed his lip. 'Daddy . . . Percy can fight with a sword. He is good.'

'I know that,' Poseidon said gently.

'Dad, I can help,' I said. 'I know I can. You're not going to hold out here much longer.'

A fireball launched into the sky from behind the enemy lines. I thought Poseidon would deflect it or something, but it landed on the outer corner of the yard and exploded, sending mermen tumbling through the water. Poseidon winced as if he'd just been stabbed.

'Return to camp,' he insisted. 'And tell Chiron it is time.'

'For what?'

'You must hear the prophecy. The *entire* prophecy.'

I didn't need to ask him which prophecy. I'd been hearing about the 'Great Prophecy' for years, but nobody would ever tell me the whole thing. All I knew was that I was supposed to make a decision that would decide the fate of the world – but no pressure.

'What if *this* is the decision?' I said. 'Staying here to fight, or leaving? What if I leave and you . . .'

I couldn't say *die*. Gods weren't supposed to die, but I'd seen it happen. Even if they didn't die, they could be reduced to nearly nothing, exiled, imprisoned in the depths of Tartarus like Kronos had been.

'Percy, you must go,' Poseidon insisted. 'I don't know what your final decision will be, but your fight lies in the world above. If nothing else, you must warn your friends at camp. Kronos knew your plans. You have a spy. We will hold here. We have no choice.'

Tyson gripped my hand desperately. 'I will miss you, brother!'

Watching us, our father seemed to age another ten years.

'Tyson, you have work to do as well, my son. They need you in the armoury.'

Tyson pouted some more.

'I will go,' he sniffled. He hugged me so hard he almost cracked my ribs. 'Percy, be careful! Do not let monsters kill you dead!'

I tried to nod confidently, but it was too much for the big guy. He sobbed and swam away towards the armoury where his cousins were fixing spears and swords.

'You should let him fight,' I told my father. 'He hates being stuck in the armoury. Can't you tell?'

Poseidon shook his head. 'It is bad enough I must send you into danger. Tyson is too young. I must protect him.'

'You should trust him,' I said. 'Not try to protect him.'

Poseidon's eyes flared. I thought I'd gone too far, but then he looked down at the mosaic and his shoulders sagged. On the tiles, the mermaid guy in the crawfish chariot was coming closer to the palace.

'Oceanus approaches,' my father said. 'I must meet him in battle.'

I'd never been scared for a god before, but I didn't see how my dad could face this Titan and win.

'I will hold,' Poseidon promised. 'I will not give up my domain. Just tell me, Percy, do you still have the birthday gift I gave you last summer?'

I nodded and pulled out my camp necklace. It had a bead for every summer I'd been at Camp Half-Blood, but since last year I'd also kept a sand dollar on the cord. My father had given it to me for my fifteenth birthday. He'd told me I would know when to 'spend it', but so far I hadn't figured out what he meant. All I knew was that it didn't fit the vending machines in the school cafeteria.

'The time is coming,' he promised. 'With luck, I will see you for your birthday next week, and we will have a proper celebration.'

He smiled, and for a moment I saw the old light in his eyes.

Then the entire sea grew dark in front of us, like an inky storm was rolling in. Thunder crackled, which should've been impossible underwater. A huge icy presence was approaching. I sensed a wave of fear roll through the armies below us.

'I must assume my true godly form,' Poseidon said. 'Go – and good luck, my son.'

I wanted to encourage him, to hug him or something, but knew better than to stick around. When a god assumes his true form, the power is so great that any mortal looking on him will disintegrate.

'Goodbye, Father,' I managed.

Then I turned away. I willed the ocean currents to aid me. Water swirled around me and I shot towards the surface at speeds that would've caused any normal human to pop like a balloon.

When I looked back, all I could see were flashes of green and blue as my father fought the Titan and the sea itself was torn apart by the two armies.

3   I GET A SNEAK PEEK AT MY DEATH

If you want to be popular at Camp Half-Blood, don't come back from a mission with bad news.

Word of my arrival spread as soon as I walked out of the ocean. Our beach is on the North Shore of Long Island, and it's enchanted so most people can't even see it. People don't just *appear* on the beach unless they're demigods or gods or really, really lost pizza delivery guys. (It's happened – but that's another story.)

Anyway, that afternoon the lookout on duty was Connor Stoll from Hermes cabin. When he spotted me, he got so excited he fell out of his tree. Then he blew the conch horn to signal the camp and ran to greet me.

Connor had a crooked smile that matched his crooked sense of humour. He's a pretty nice guy, but you should always keep one hand on your wallet when he's around and do not, under any circumstances, give him access to shaving cream unless you want to find your sleeping bag full of it. He's got curly brown hair and is a little shorter than his brother Travis, which is the only way I can tell them apart. They are both so unlike my old enemy Luke it's hard to believe they're all sons of Hermes.

'Percy!' he yelled. 'What happened? Where's Beckendorf?'

Then he saw my expression, and his smile melted. 'Oh no. Poor Silena. Holy Zeus, when she finds out . . .'

Together we climbed the sand dunes. A few hundred metres away, people were already streaming towards us, smiling and excited. *Percy's back*, they were probably thinking. *He's saved the day! Maybe he brought souvenirs!*

I stopped at the dining pavilion and waited for them. No sense rushing down there to tell them what a loser I was.

I gazed across the valley and tried to remember how Camp Half-Blood looked the first time I saw it. That seemed like a bajillion years ago.

From the dining pavilion, you could see pretty much everything. Hills ringed the valley. On the tallest, Half-Blood Hill, Thalia's pine tree stood with the Golden Fleece hanging from its branches, magically protecting the camp from its enemies. The guard dragon Peleus was so big now I could see him from here – curled around the tree trunk, sending up smoke signals as he snored.

To my right spread the woods. To my left, the canoe lake glittered and the climbing wall glowed from the lava pouring down its side. Twelve cabins – one for each Olympian god – made a horseshoe pattern around the commons area. Further south were the strawberry fields, the armoury and the four-storey Big House with its sky-blue paint job and its bronze-eagle weathervane.

In some ways, the camp hadn't changed. But you couldn't see the war by looking at the buildings or the fields. You could see it in the faces of the demigods and satyrs and naiads coming up the hill.

There weren't as many at camp as four summers ago. Some had left and never come back. Some had died fighting. Others – we tried not to talk about them – had gone over to the enemy.

The ones who were still here were battle-hardened and weary. There was little laughter at camp these days. Even the Hermes cabin didn't play so many pranks. It's hard to enjoy practical jokes when your whole life feels like one.

Chiron galloped into the pavilion first, which was easy for him since he's a white stallion from the waist down. His beard had grown wilder over the summer. He wore a green T-shirt that said MY OTHER CAR IS A CENTAUR and a bow slung over his back.

'Percy!' he said. 'Thank the gods. But where . . .'

Annabeth ran in right behind him, and I'll admit my heart did a little relay race in my chest when I saw her. It's not that she tried to look good. We'd been doing so many combat missions lately she hardly brushed her curly blonde hair any more and she didn't care what clothes she was wearing – usually the same old orange camp T-shirt and jeans and once in a while her bronze armour. Her eyes were stormy grey. Most of the time, we couldn't get through a conversation without trying to strangle each other. Still, just seeing her made me feel fuzzy in the head. Last summer, before Luke had turned into Kronos and everything went sour, there had been a few times when I thought maybe . . . well, we might get past the strangle-each-other phase.

'What happened?' She grabbed my arm. 'Is Luke –'

'The ship blew up,' I said. 'He wasn't destroyed. I don't know where –'

Silena Beauregard pushed through the crowd. Her hair wasn't combed and she wasn't even wearing makeup, which wasn't like her.

'Where's Charlie?' she demanded, looking around like

I glanced at Chiron helplessly.

The old centaur cleared his throat. 'Silena, my dear, let's talk about this at the Big House –'

'No,' she muttered. 'No. *No.*'

She started to cry, and the rest of us stood around, too stunned to speak. We'd already lost so many people over the summer, but this was the worst. With Beckendorf gone, it felt like someone had stolen the anchor for the entire camp.

Finally Clarisse from the Ares cabin came forward. She put her arm around Silena. They had one of the strangest friendships ever – a daughter of the war god and a daughter of the love goddess – but ever since Silena had given Clarisse advice last summer about her first boyfriend, Clarisse had decided she was Silena's personal bodyguard.

Clarisse was dressed in her blood-red combat armour, her brown hair tucked into a bandanna. She was as big and beefy as a rugby player, with a permanent scowl on her face, but she spoke gently to Silena.

'Come on, girl,' she said. 'Let's get to the Big House. I'll make you some hot chocolate.'

Everyone turned and wandered off in twos and threes, heading back to the cabins. Nobody was excited to see me now. Nobody wanted to hear about the blown-up ship.

Only Annabeth and Chiron stayed behind.

Annabeth wiped a tear from her cheek. 'I'm glad you're not dead, Seaweed Brain.'

'Thanks,' I said. 'Me too.'

Chiron put a hand on my shoulder. 'I'm sure you did everything you could, Percy. Will you tell us what happened?'

I didn't want to go through it again, but I told them the story, including my dream about the Titans. I left out the detail about Nico. Nico had made me promise not to tell anybody about his plan until I made up my mind, and the plan was so scary I didn't mind keeping it a secret.

Chiron gazed down at the valley. 'We must call a war council immediately to discuss this spy, and other matters.'

'Poseidon mentioned another threat,' I said, 'something even bigger than the *Princess Andromeda*. I thought it might be that challenge the Titan mentioned in my dream.'

Chiron and Annabeth exchanged looks, like they knew something I didn't. I hated it when they did that.

'We will discuss that also,' Chiron promised.

'One more thing.' I took a deep breath. 'When I talked to my father, he said to tell you it's time. I need to know the full prophecy.'

Chiron's shoulders sagged, but he didn't look surprised. 'I've dreaded this day. Very well. Annabeth, we will show Percy the truth – all of it. Let's go to the attic.'

I'd been to the Big House attic three times before, which was three times more than I wanted to.

A ladder led up from the top of the staircase. I wondered how Chiron was going to get up there, being half horse and all, but he didn't try.

'You know where it is,' he told Annabeth. 'Bring it down, please.'

Annabeth nodded. 'Come on, Percy.'

The sun was setting outside, so the attic was even darker and creepier than usual. Old hero trophies were stacked everywhere – dented shields, pickled heads in jars from various monsters, a pair of fuzzy dice on a bronze plaque that read: STOLEN FROM CHRYSAOR'S HONDA CIVIC, BY GUS, SON OF HERMES, 1988.

I picked up a curved bronze sword so badly bent it looked like a letter M. I could still see green stains on the metal from the magical poison that used to cover it. The tag was dated last summer. It read: SCIMITAR OF KAMPÊ, DESTROYED IN THE BATTLE OF THE LABYRINTH.

'You remember Briares throwing those boulders?' I asked.

Annabeth gave me a grudging smile. 'And Grover causing a Panic?'

We locked eyes. I thought of a different time last summer, under Mount St Helens, when Annabeth thought I was going to die, and she kissed me.

She cleared her throat and looked away. 'Prophecy.'

'Right.' I put down the scimitar. 'Prophecy.'

We walked over to the window. On a three-legged stool sat the Oracle – a shrivelled female mummy in a tie-dyed dress. Tufts of black hair clung to her skull. Glassy eyes stared out of her leathery face. Just looking at her made my skin crawl.

If you wanted to leave camp during the summer, it used to be you had to come up here to get a quest. This summer, that rule had been tossed. Campers left all the time on combat missions. We had no choice if we wanted to stop Kronos.

Still, I remembered too well the strange green mist – the spirit of the Oracle – that lived inside the mummy. She looked lifeless now, but whenever she spoke a prophecy she moved. Sometimes fog gushed out of her mouth and created strange shapes. Once, she'd even left the attic and taken a little zombie stroll into the woods to deliver a message. I wasn't sure what she'd do for the 'Great Prophecy'. I half expected her to start tap dancing or something.

But she just sat there like she was dead – which she was.

'I never understood this,' I whispered.

'What?' Annabeth asked.

'Why it's a mummy.'

'Percy, she wasn't always a mummy. For thousands of years the spirit of the Oracle lived inside a beautiful maiden. The spirit would be passed on from generation to generation. Chiron told me *she* was like that fifty years ago.' Annabeth pointed at the mummy. 'But she was the last.'

'What happened?'

Annabeth stared to say something then apparently changed her mind. 'Let's just do our job and get out of here.'

I looked nervously at the Oracle's withered face. 'So what now?'

Annabeth approached the mummy and held out her palms. 'O Oracle, the time is at hand. I ask for the Great Prophecy.'

I braced myself, but the mummy didn't move. Instead, Annabeth approached and unclasped one of its necklaces. I'd never paid too much attention to its jewellery before. I figured it was just hippie love beads and stuff. But when Annabeth turned towards me, she was holding a leather pouch – like a Native American medicine pouch – on a cord braided with feathers. She opened the bag and took out a roll of parchment no bigger than her pinky.

[44]

'No way,' I said. 'You mean all these years I've been asking about this stupid prophecy, and it's been right there around her neck?'

'The time wasn't right,' Annabeth said. 'Believe me, Percy, I read this when I was ten years old, and I still have nightmares about it.'

'Great,' I said. 'Can I read it now?'

'Downstairs at the war council,' Annabeth said. 'Not in front of . . . you know.'

I looked at the glassy eyes of the Oracle, and I decided not to argue. We headed downstairs to join the others. I didn't know it then, but it would be the last time I ever visited the attic.

The senior counsellors had gathered around the ping-pong table. Don't ask me why, but the rec room had become the camp's informal headquarters for war councils. When Annabeth, Chiron and I came in, though, it looked more like a shouting match.

Clarisse was still in full battle gear. Her electric spear was strapped to her back. (Actually her *second* electric spear, since I'd broken the first one. She called the spear 'Maimer'. Behind her back, everybody else called it 'Lamer'.) She had her boar-shaped helmet under one arm and a knife at her belt.

She was in the midst of yelling at Michael Yew, the new head counsellor for Apollo, which looked kind of funny since Clarisse was so much taller. Michael had taken over the Apollo cabin after Lee Fletcher died in battle last summer. Michael stood a little over a metre tall with another half metre of attitude. He reminded me of a ferret, with a pointy nose and scrunched-up features – either because he scowled so much or because he spent too much time looking down the shaft of an arrow.

'It's *our* loot!' he yelled, standing on his tiptoes so he could get in Clarisse's face. 'If you don't like it, you can kiss my quiver!'

Around the table, people were trying not to laugh – the Stoll brothers, Pollux from the Dionysus cabin, Katie Gardner from Demeter. Even Jake Mason, the hastily appointed new counsellor from Hephaestus, managed a faint smile. Only Silena Beauregard didn't pay any attention. She sat beside Clarisse and stared vacantly at the ping-pong net. Her eyes were red and puffy. A cup of hot chocolate sat untouched in front of her. It seemed unfair that she had to be here. I couldn't believe Clarisse and Michael standing over her, arguing about something as stupid as loot when she'd just lost Beckendorf.

'STOP IT!' I yelled. 'What are you guys doing?'

Clarisse glowered at me. 'Tell Michael not to be a selfish jerk.'

'Oh, that's perfect, coming from you,' Michael said.

'The only reason I'm here is to support Silena!' Clarisse shouted. 'Otherwise I'd be back in my cabin.'

'What are you talking about?' I demanded.

Pollux cleared his throat. 'Clarisse has refused to speak to any us, until her, um, issue is resolved. She hasn't spoken for three days.'

'It's been wonderful,' Travis Stoll said wistfully.

'What issue?' I asked.

Clarisse turned to Chiron. 'You're in charge, right? Does my cabin get what we want or not?'

Chiron shuffled his hooves. 'My dear, as I've already

explained, Michael is correct. Apollo's cabin has the best claim. Besides, we have more important matters —'

'Sure,' Clarisse snapped. 'Always more important matters than what Ares needs. We're just supposed to show up and fight when you need us and not complain!'

'That would be nice,' Connor Stoll muttered.

Clarisse gripped her knife. 'Maybe I should ask Mr D —'

'As you know,' Chiron interrupted, his tone slightly angry now, 'our director Dionysus is busy with the war. He can't be bothered with this.'

'I see,' Clarisse said. 'And the senior counsellors? Are *any* of you going to side with me?'

Nobody was smiling now. None of them met Clarisse's eyes.

'Fine.' Clarisse turned to Silena. 'I'm sorry. I didn't mean to get into this when you've just lost . . . anyway, I apologize. To *you*. Nobody else.'

Silena didn't seem to register her words.

Clarisse threw her knife on the ping-pong table. 'All of you can fight this war without Ares. Until I get satisfaction, no one in my cabin is lifting a finger to help. Have fun dying.'

The counsellors were all too stunned to say anything as Clarisse stormed out of the room.

Finally Michael Yew said, 'Good riddance.'

'Are you kidding?' Katie Gardner protested. 'This is a disaster!'

'She can't be serious,' Travis said. 'Can she?'

Chiron sighed. 'Her pride has been wounded. She'll calm down eventually.' But he didn't sound convinced.

I wanted to ask what the heck Clarisse was so mad about, but I looked at Annabeth and she mouthed the words, *I'll tell you later.*

'Now,' Chiron continued, 'if you please, counsellors. Percy has brought something I think you should hear. Percy – the Great Prophecy.'

Annabeth handed me the parchment. It felt dry and old, and my fingers fumbled with the string. I uncurled the paper, trying not to rip it, and began to read:

'A half-blood of the eldest dogs . . .'

'Er, Percy?' Annabeth interrupted. 'That's gods. Not dogs.'

'Oh, right,' I said. Being dyslexic is one mark of a demigod, but sometimes I really hate it. The more nervous I am, the worse my reading gets.

'A half-blood of the eldest gods
Shall reach sixteen against all odds . . .'

I hesitated, staring at the next lines. A cold feeling started in my fingers as if the paper were freezing.

'And see the world in endless sleep,
The hero's soul, cursed blade shall reap.'

Suddenly Riptide seemed heavier in my pocket. A cursed blade? Chiron once told me Riptide had brought many people sorrow. Was it possible my own sword could get me killed? And how could the world fall into endless sleep, unless that meant death?

'Percy,' Chiron urged. 'Read the rest.'

My mouth felt like it was full of sand, but I spoke the last two lines.

*'A single choice shall . . . shall end his days.
Olympus to per — pursue —'*

'Preserve,' Annabeth said gently. 'It means "to save".'

'I know what it means,' I grumbled.

'Olympus to preserve or raze.'

The room was silent. Finally Connor Stoll said, 'Raise is good, isn't it?'

'Not raise,' Silena said. Her voice was hollow, but I was startled to hear her speak at all. 'R-a-z-e means "destroy".'

'Obliterate,' Annabeth said. 'Annihilate. Turn to rubble.'

'Got it.' My heart felt like lead. 'Thanks.'

Everybody was looking at me — with concern, or pity, or maybe a little fear.

Chiron closed his eyes as if he were saying a prayer. In horse form, his head almost brushed the lights in the rec room. 'You see now, Percy, why we thought it best not to tell you the whole prophecy. You've had enough on your shoulders —'

'Without realizing I was going to die in the end anyway?' I said. 'Yeah, I get it.'

Chiron gazed at me sadly. The guy was three thousand years old. He'd seen hundreds of heroes die. He might not like it, but he was used to it. He probably knew better than to try reassuring me.

'Percy,' Annabeth said. 'You know prophecies always have double meanings. It might not literally mean you die.'

'Sure,' I said. '*A single choice shall end his days.* That has tons of meanings, right?'

'Maybe we can stop it,' Jake Mason offered. '*The hero's soul, cursed blade shall reap.* Maybe we could find this cursed blade and destroy it. Sounds like Kronos's scythe, right?'

I hadn't thought about that, but it didn't matter if the cursed blade was Riptide or Kronos's scythe. Either way, I doubted we could stop the prophecy. A blade was supposed to reap my soul. As a general rule, I preferred not to have my soul reaped.

'Perhaps we should let Percy think about these lines,' Chiron said. 'He needs time –'

'No.' I folded up the prophecy and shoved it in my pocket. I felt defiant and angry, though I wasn't sure who I was angry with. 'I don't need time. If I die, I die. I can't worry about that, right?'

Annabeth's hands were shaking a little. She wouldn't meet my eyes.

'Let's move on,' I said. 'We've got other problems. We've got a spy.'

Michael Yew scowled. 'A spy?'

I told them what had happened on the *Princess Andromeda* – how Kronos had known we were coming, how he'd shown me the silver scythe pendant he'd used to communicate with someone at camp.

Silena started to cry again and Annabeth put her arm around her shoulders.

'Well,' Connor Stoll said uncomfortably, 'we've suspected

there might be a spy for years, right? Somebody kept passing information to Luke – like the location of the Golden Fleece a couple of years ago. It must be somebody who knew him well.'

He glanced at Annabeth. She'd known Luke better than anyone, of course, but Connor looked away quickly. 'Um, I mean, it could be anybody.'

'Yes.' Katie Gardner frowned at the Stoll brothers. She'd disliked them ever since they'd decorated the grass roof of the Demeter cabin with chocolate Easter bunnies. 'Like one of Luke's siblings.'

Travis and Connor both started arguing with her.

'Stop!' Silena banged the table so hard her hot chocolate spilled. 'Charlie's dead and . . . and you're all arguing like little kids!' She put her head down and began to sob.

Hot chocolate trickled off the ping-pong table. Everybody looked ashamed.

'She's right,' Pollux said at last. 'Accusing each other doesn't help. We need to keep our eyes open for a silver necklace with a scythe charm. If Kronos had one, the spy probably does too.'

Michael Yew grunted. 'We need to find this spy before we plan our next operation. Blowing up the *Princess Andromeda* won't stop Kronos forever.'

'No, indeed,' Chiron said. 'In fact his next assault is already on the way.'

I scowled. 'You mean the "bigger threat" Poseidon mentioned?'

He and Annabeth looked at each other like: *It's time.* Did I mention I hate it when they do that?

'Percy,' Chiron said, 'we didn't want to tell you until

you returned to camp. You needed a break with your . . . mortal friends.'

Annabeth blushed. It dawned on me that she knew I'd been hanging out with Rachel, and I felt guilty. Then I felt angry that I felt guilty. I was allowed to have friends outside camp, right? It wasn't like . . .

'Tell me what's happened,' I said.

Chiron picked up a bronze goblet from the snack table. He tossed water onto the hot plate where we usually melted nacho cheese. Steam billowed up, making a rainbow in the fluorescent lights. Chiron fished a golden drachma out of his pouch, tossed it through the mist and muttered, 'O Iris, Goddess of the Rainbow, show us the threat.'

The mist shimmered. I saw the familiar image of a smouldering volcano — Mount St Helens. As I watched, the side of the mountain exploded. Fire, ash and lava rolled out. A newscaster's voice was saying: — *even larger than last year's eruption, and geologists warn that the mountain may not be done.*

I knew all about last year's eruption. I'd caused it. But this explosion was much worse. The mountain tore itself apart, collapsing inward, and an enormous form rose out of the smoke and lava like it was emerging from a manhole cover. I hoped the Mist would keep the humans from seeing it clearly, because what I saw would've caused panic and riots across the entire United States.

The giant was bigger than anything I'd ever encountered. Even my demigod eyes couldn't make out its exact form through the ash and fire, but it was vaguely humanoid and so huge it could've used the Chrysler Building as a baseball bat. The mountain shook with a horrible rumbling, as if the monster were laughing.

'It's him,' I said. 'Typhon.'

I was seriously hoping Chiron would say something good, like *No, that's our huge friend Leroy! He's going to help us!* But no such luck. He simply nodded. 'The most horrible monster of all, the biggest single threat the gods ever faced. He has been freed from under the mountain at last. But this scene is from two days ago. *Here* is what is happening today.'

Chiron waved his hand and the image changed. I saw a bank of storm clouds rolling across the Midwest plains. Lightning flickered. Lines of tornadoes destroyed everything in their path – ripping up houses and trailers, tossing cars around like Matchbox toys.

Monumental floods, an announcer was saying. *Five states declared disaster areas as the freak storm system sweeps east, continuing its path of destruction.* The cameras zoomed in on a column of storm bearing down on some Midwest city. I couldn't tell which one. Inside the storm I could see the giant – just small glimpses of his true form: a smoky arm, a dark clawed hand the size of a city block. His angry roar rolled across the plains like a nuclear blast. Other smaller forms darted through the clouds, circling the monster. I saw flashes of light, and I realized the giant was trying to swat them. I squinted and thought I saw a golden chariot flying into the blackness. Then some kind of huge bird – a monstrous owl – dived in to attack the giant.

'Are those . . . the gods?' I said.

'Yes, Percy,' Chiron said. 'They have been fighting him for days now, trying to slow him down. But Typhon is marching forward – towards New York. Towards Olympus.'

I let that sink in. 'How long until he gets here?'

'Unless the gods can stop him? Perhaps five days. Most of the Olympians are there . . . except your father, who has a war of his own to fight.'

'But then who's guarding Olympus?'

Connor Stoll shook his head. 'If Typhon gets to New York, it won't matter who's guarding Olympus.'

I thought about Kronos's words on the ship: *I would love to see the terror in your eyes when you realize how I will destroy Olympus.*

Was this what he was talking about: an attack by Typhon? It sure was terrifying enough. But Kronos was always fooling us, misdirecting our attention. This seemed too obvious for him. And in my dream the golden Titan had talked about several more challenges to come, like Typhon was only the first.

'It's a trick,' I said. 'We have to warn the gods. Something else is going to happen.'

Chiron looked at me gravely. 'Something worse than Typhon? I hope not.'

'We have to defend Olympus,' I insisted. 'Kronos has another attack planned.'

'He did,' Travis Stoll reminded me. 'But you sank his ship.'

Everyone was looking at me. They wanted some good news. They wanted to believe that at least I'd given them a little bit of hope.

I glanced at Annabeth. I could tell we were thinking the same thing: what if the *Princess Andromeda* was a ploy? What if Kronos *let* us blow up that ship so we'd lower our guard?

But I wasn't going to say that in front of Silena. Her boyfriend had sacrificed himself for that mission.

'Maybe you're right,' I said, though I didn't believe a word of it.

I tried to imagine how things could get much worse. The gods were in the Midwest fighting a huge monster that had almost defeated them once before. Poseidon was under siege and losing a war against the sea Titan Oceanus. Kronos was still out there somewhere. Olympus was virtually undefended. The demigods of Camp Half-Blood were on our own with a spy in our midst.

Oh, and according to the ancient prophecy, I was going to die when I turned sixteen – which happened to be in five days, the exact same time Typhon was supposed to hit New York. Almost forgot that.

'Well,' Chiron said, 'I think that's enough for one night.'

He waved his hand and the steam dissipated. The stormy battle of Typhon and the gods disappeared.

'That's an understatement,' I muttered.

And the war council adjourned.

4 WE BURN A METAL SHROUD

I dreamed Rachel Elizabeth Dare was throwing darts at my picture.

She was standing in her room . . . Okay, back up. I have to explain that Rachel doesn't have a room. She has the top floor of her family's mansion, which is a renovated brownstone in Brooklyn. Her 'room' is a huge loft with industrial lighting and floor-to-ceiling windows. It's about twice as big as my mom's apartment.

Some alt rock was blaring from her paint-covered Bose docking system. As far as I could tell, Rachel's only rule about music was that no two songs on her iPod could sound the same, and they all had to be strange.

She wore a kimono and her hair was frizzy like she'd been sleeping. Her bed was messed up. Sheets hung over a bunch of artist's easels. Dirty clothes and old energy-bar wrappers were strewn around the floor, but when you've got a room that big, the mess doesn't look so bad. Out of the windows you could see the entire night-time skyline of Manhattan.

The picture she was attacking was a painting of me standing over the giant Antaeus. Rachel had painted it a couple of months ago. My expression in the picture was fierce – disturbing, even – so it was hard to tell if I was the good guy or the bad guy, but Rachel said I'd looked just like that after the battle.

'*Demigods*,' Rachel muttered as she threw another dart at the canvas. 'And their *stupid* quests.'

Most of the darts bounced off, but a few stuck. One hung off my chin like a goatee.

Someone pounded on her bedroom door.

'Rachel!' a man shouted. 'What in the world are you doing? Turn off that –'

Rachel scooped up her remote control and shut off the music. 'Come in!'

Her dad walked in, scowling and blinking from the light. He had rust-coloured hair a little darker than Rachel's. It was smushed on one side like he'd lost a fight with his pillow. His blue silk pyjamas had 'WD' monogrammed on the pocket. Seriously, who has monogrammed pyjamas?

'What is going on?' he demanded. 'It's three in the morning.'

'Couldn't sleep,' Rachel said.

On the painting, a dart fell off my face. Rachel hid the rest of the darts behind her back, but Mr Dare noticed.

'So . . . I take it your friend isn't coming to St Thomas?' That's what Mr Dare called me. Never Percy. Just *your friend*. Or *young man* if he was talking to me, which he rarely did.

Rachel knitted her eyebrows. 'I don't know.'

'We leave in the morning,' her dad said. 'If he hasn't made up his mind yet –'

'He's probably not coming,' Rachel said miserably. 'Happy?'

Mr Dare put his hands behind his back. He paced the room with a stern expression. I imagined he did that in the boardroom of his land-development company and made his employees nervous.

'Are you still having bad dreams?' he asked. 'Headaches?'

Rachel threw her darts on the floor. 'I should never have told you about that.'

'I'm your father,' he said. 'I'm worried about you.'

'Worried about the family's reputation,' Rachel muttered.

Her father didn't react – maybe because he'd heard that comment before, or maybe because it was true.

'We could call Dr Arkwright,' he suggested. 'He helped you get through the death of your hamster.'

'I was six then,' she said. 'And no, Dad, I don't need a therapist. I just . . .'

She shook her head helplessly.

Her father stopped in front of the windows. He gazed at the New York skyline as if he owned it – which wasn't true. He only owned part of it.

'It will be good for you to get away,' he decided. 'You've had some unhealthy influences.'

'I'm not going to Clarion Ladies' Academy,' Rachel said. 'And my friends are none of your business.'

Mr Dare smiled, but it wasn't a warm smile. It was more like, *Some day you'll realize how silly you sound.*

'Try to get some sleep,' he urged. 'We'll be at the beach by tomorrow night. It will be fun.'

'Fun,' Rachel repeated. 'Lots of fun.'

Her father exited the room. He left the door open behind him.

Rachel stared at the portrait of me. Then she walked to the easel next to it, which was covered in a sheet.

'I hope they're dreams,' she said.

She uncovered the easel. On it was a hasty charcoal sketch, but Rachel was a good artist. The picture was definitely Luke as a young boy. He was about nine years old, with a wide grin and no scar on his face. I had no idea how Rachel could've known what he looked like back then, but the portrait was so good I had a feeling she wasn't guessing. From what I knew about Luke's life (which wasn't much) the picture showed him just before he'd found out he was a half-blood and had run away from home.

Rachel stared at the portrait. Then she uncovered the next easel. This picture was even more disturbing. It showed the Empire State Building with lightning all around it. In the distance a dark storm was brewing, with a huge hand coming out of the clouds. At the base of the building a crowd had gathered . . . but it wasn't a normal crowd of tourists and pedestrians. I saw spears, javelins and banners – the trappings of an army.

'Percy,' Rachel muttered as if she knew I was listening. 'What is going on?'

The dream faded, and the last thing I remember was wishing I could answer Rachel's question.

The next morning, I wanted to call her, but there were no phones at camp. Dionysus and Chiron didn't need a landline. They just called Olympus with an Iris-message whenever they needed something. And when demigods use cell phones, the signals agitate every monster within a hundred miles. It's like sending up a flare: *Here I am! Please rearrange my face!* Even within the safe borders of camp, that's not the kind of advertising we wanted to do.

Most demigods (except for Annabeth and a few others) don't even own cell phones. And I definitely couldn't tell Annabeth, 'Hey, let me borrow your phone so I can call Rachel!' To make the call, I would've had to leave camp and walk several miles to the nearest convenience store. Even if Chiron let me go, by the time I got there, Rachel would've been on the plane to St Thomas.

I ate a depressing breakfast by myself at the Poseidon table. I kept staring at the fissure in the marble floor, where two years ago Nico had banished a bunch of bloodthirsty skeletons to the Underworld. The memory didn't exactly improve my appetite.

After breakfast, Annabeth and I walked down to inspect the cabins. Actually, it was Annabeth's turn for inspection. My morning chore was to sort through reports for Chiron. But since we both hated our jobs, we decided to do them together so it wouldn't be so heinous.

We started at the Poseidon cabin, which was basically just me. I'd made my bunk bed that morning (well, sort of) and straightened the Minotaur horn on the wall, so I gave myself a four out of five.

Annabeth made a face. 'You're being generous.' She used the end of her pencil to pick up an old pair of running shorts.

I snatched them away. 'Hey, give me a break. I don't have Tyson cleaning up after me this summer.'

'Three out of five,' Annabeth said. I knew better than to argue, so we moved along.

I tried to skim through Chiron's stack of reports as we walked. There were messages from demigods, nature spirits and satyrs all around the country, writing about the latest monster activity. They were pretty depressing, and my ADHD brain did *not* like concentrating on depressing stuff.

Little battles were raging everywhere. Camp recruitment was down to zero. Satyrs were having trouble finding new demigods and bringing them to Half-Blood Hill because so many monsters were roaming the country. Our friend Thalia, who led the Hunters of Artemis, hadn't been heard from in months, and if Artemis knew what had happened to them, she wasn't sharing information.

We visited the Aphrodite cabin, which of course got a five out of five. The beds were perfectly made. The clothes in everyone's footlocker were colour coordinated. Fresh flowers bloomed on the windowsills. I wanted to dock a point because the whole place reeked of designer perfume, but Annabeth ignored me.

'Great job as usual, Silena,' Annabeth said.

Silena nodded listlessly. The wall behind her bed was decorated with pictures of Beckendorf. She sat on her bunk with a box of chocolates on her lap, and I remembered that her dad owned a chocolate store in the Village, which was how he'd caught the attention of Aphrodite.

'You want a bonbon?' Silena asked. 'My dad sent them. He thought – he thought they might cheer me up.'

'Are they any good?' I asked.

She shook her head. 'They taste like cardboard.'

I didn't have anything against cardboard, so I tried one. Annabeth passed. We promised to see Silena later and kept going.

As we crossed the commons area, a fight broke out between the Ares and Apollo cabins. Some Apollo campers armed with fire bombs flew over the Ares cabin in a chariot pulled by two pegasi. I'd never seen the chariot before, but it looked like a pretty sweet ride. Soon, the roof of the Ares cabin was burning, and naiads from the canoe lake rushed over to blow water on it.

Then the Ares campers called down a curse and all the Apollo kids' arrows turned to rubber. The Apollo kids kept shooting at the Ares kids but the arrows bounced off.

Two archers ran by, chased by an angry Ares kid who was yelling in poetry: 'Curse me, eh? I'll make you pay!/I don't want to rhyme all day!'

Annabeth sighed. 'Not that again. Last time Apollo cursed a cabin, it took a week for the rhyming couplets to wear off.'

I shuddered. Apollo was god of poetry as well as archery, and I'd heard him recite in person. I'd almost rather get shot by an arrow.

'What are they fighting about anyway?' I asked.

Annabeth ignored me while she scribbled on her inspection scroll, giving both cabins a one out of five.

I found myself staring at her, which was stupid since I'd seen her a billion times. She was about the same height as me this summer, which was a relief. Still, she seemed so much more mature. It was kind of intimidating. I mean sure, she'd always been cute, but she was starting to be seriously beautiful.

Finally she said, 'That flying chariot.'

'What?'

'You asked what they were fighting about.'

'Oh. Oh, right.'

'They captured it in a raid in Philadelphia last week.

Some of Luke's demigods were there with that flying chariot. The Apollo cabin seized it during the battle, but Ares cabin led the raid. So they've been fighting about who gets it ever since.'

We ducked as Michael Yew's chariot dive-bombed an Ares camper. The Ares camper tried to stab him and cuss him out in rhyming couplets. He was pretty creative about rhyming those cuss words.

'We're fighting for our lives,' I said, 'and they're bickering about some stupid chariot.'

'They'll get over it,' Annabeth said. 'Clarisse will come to her senses.'

I wasn't so sure. That didn't sound like the Clarisse I knew.

I scanned more reports and we inspected a few more cabins. Demeter got a four. Hephaestus got a three and probably should've gotten lower, but with Beckendorf being gone and all, we cut them some slack. Hermes got a two, which was no surprise. All campers who didn't know their godly parentage were shoved into the Hermes cabin, and since the gods were kind of forgetful, that cabin was always overcrowded.

Finally we got to Athena's cabin, which was orderly and clean as usual. Books were straightened on the shelves. The armour was polished. Battle maps and blueprints decorated the walls. Only Annabeth's bunk was messy. It was covered in papers and her silver laptop was still running.

'*Vlacas*,' Annabeth muttered, which was basically calling herself an idiot in Greek.

Her second-in-command Malcolm suppressed a smile. 'Yeah, um . . . we cleaned everything else. Didn't know if it was safe to move your notes.'

That was probably smart. Annabeth had a bronze knife that she reserved just for monsters and people who messed with her stuff.

Malcolm grinned at me. 'We'll wait outside while you finish inspection.' The Athena campers filed out the door while Annabeth cleaned up her bunk.

I shuffled uneasily and pretended to go through some more reports. Technically, even on inspection, it was against camp rules for two campers of the opposite sex to be . . . like, *alone* in a cabin.

That rule had come up a lot when Silena and Beckendorf started dating. And I know some of you might be thinking: aren't all demigods related on the godly side, and doesn't that make dating gross? But the thing is, the godly side of your family doesn't count genetically speaking, since gods don't have DNA. A demigod would never think about dating someone who had the same godly parent. Like two kids from Athena cabin? No way. But a daughter of Aphrodite and a son of Hephaestus? They're not related. So it's no problem.

Anyway, for some strange reason I was thinking about this as I watched Annabeth straighten up. She closed her laptop, which she'd been given as a gift from the inventor Daedalus last summer.

I cleared my throat. 'So . . . get any good info from that thing?'

'Too much,' she said. 'Daedalus had so many ideas I could spend fifty years just trying to figure them all out.'

'Yeah,' I muttered. 'That would be fun.'

She shuffled her papers – mostly drawings of buildings and a bunch of handwritten notes. I knew she wanted to be an architect some day, but I'd learned the hard way not to ask what she was working on. She'd start talking about angles and load-bearing joints until my eyes glazed over.

'You know . . .' She brushed her hair behind her ear, like she does when she's nervous. 'This whole thing with Beckendorf and Silena. It kind of makes you think. About . . . what's important. About losing people who are important.'

I nodded. My brain started seizing on little random details, like the fact that she was still wearing those silver owl earrings from her dad, who was this brainiac military history professor in San Francisco.

'Um, yeah,' I stammered. 'Like . . . is everything cool with your family?'

Okay, really stupid question but, hey, I was nervous.

Annabeth looked disappointed, but she nodded.

'My dad wanted to take me to Greece this summer,' she said wistfully. 'I've always wanted to see –'

'The Parthenon,' I remembered.

She managed a smile. 'Yeah.'

'That's okay. There'll be other summers, right?'

As soon as I said it, I realized it was a bone-headed comment. I was facing the 'end of my days'. Within a week, Olympus might fall. If the Age of the Gods really did end, the world as we knew it would dissolve into chaos. Demigods would be hunted to extinction. There would be no more summers for us.

Annabeth stared at her inspection scroll. 'Three out of five,' she muttered, 'for a sloppy head counsellor. Come on. Let's finish your reports and get back to Chiron.'

On the way to the Big House, we read the last report,

which was handwritten on a maple leaf from a satyr in Canada. If possible, the note made me feel even worse.

'*Dear Grover,*' I read aloud. '*Woods outside Toronto attacked by giant evil badger. Tried to do as you suggested and summon power of Pan. No effect. Many naiads' trees destroyed. Retreating to Ottawa. Please advise. Where are you? — Gleeson Hedge, protector.*'

Annabeth grimaced. 'You haven't heard *anything* from him? Even with your empathy link?'

I shook my head dejectedly.

Ever since last summer when the god Pan died, our friend Grover had been drifting further and further away. The Council of Cloven Elders treated him like an outcast, but Grover still travelled all over the East Coast, trying to spread the word about Pan and convince nature spirits to protect their own little bits of the wild. He'd only come back to camp a few times to see his girlfriend Juniper.

Last I'd heard he was in Central Park, organizing the dryads, but nobody had seen or heard from him in two months. We'd tried to send Iris-messages. They never got through. I had an empathy link with Grover, so I hoped I would know if anything bad happened to him. Grover had told me one time that if he died, the empathy link might kill me too. But I wasn't sure if that was still true or not.

I wondered if he was still in Manhattan. Then I thought about my dream of Rachel's sketch — dark clouds closing on the city, an army gathered around the Empire State Building.

'Annabeth.' I stopped her by the tetherball court. I knew I was asking for trouble, but I didn't know who else to trust. Plus I'd always depended on Annabeth for advice. 'Listen, I had this dream about, um, Rachel . . .'

I told her the whole thing, even the weird picture of Luke as a child.

For a while, she didn't say anything. Then she rolled up her inspection scroll so tight she ripped it. 'What do you want me to say?'

'I'm not sure. You're the best strategist I know. If you were Kronos planning this war, what would you do next?'

'I'd use Typhon as a distraction. Then I'd hit Olympus directly, while the gods were in the west.'

'Just like in Rachel's picture.'

'Percy,' she said, her voice tight, 'Rachel is just a mortal.'

'But what if her dream is true? Those other Titans – they said Olympus would be destroyed in a matter of days. They said they had plenty of other challenges. And what's with that picture of Luke as a kid –'

'We'll just have to be ready.'

'How?' I said. 'Look at our camp. We can't even stop fighting each other. And I'm supposed to get my stupid soul reaped.'

She threw down her scroll. 'I knew we shouldn't have shown you the prophecy.' Her voice was angry and hurt. 'All it did was scare you. You run away from things when you're scared.'

I stared at her, completely stunned. '*Me?* Run away?'

She got right in my face. 'Yes, you. You're a coward, Percy Jackson!'

We were nose to nose. Her eyes were red, and I suddenly realized that when she called me a coward maybe she wasn't talking about the prophecy.

'If you don't like our chances,' she said, 'maybe you should go on that vacation with Rachel.'

'Annabeth –'

'If you don't like our company.'

'That's not fair!'

She pushed past me and stormed towards the strawberry fields. She hit the tetherball as she passed and sent it spinning angrily around the pole.

I'd like to say my day got better from there. Of course, it didn't.

That afternoon we had an assembly at the campfire to burn Beckendorf's burial shroud and say our goodbyes. Even the Ares and Apollo cabins called a temporary truce to attend.

Beckendorf's shroud was made out of metal links like chainmail. I didn't see how it would burn, but the Fates must've been helping out. The metal melted in the fire and turned to golden smoke that rose into the sky. The campfire flames always reflected the campers' moods, and today they burned black.

I hoped Beckendorf's spirit would end up in Elysium. Maybe he'd even choose to be reborn and try for Elysium in three different lifetimes so he could reach the Isles of the Blest, which was like the Underworld's ultimate party headquarters. If anyone deserved it, Beckendorf did.

Annabeth left without a word to me. Most of the other campers drifted off to their afternoon activities. I just stood there, staring at the dying fire. Silena sat nearby crying while Clarisse and her boyfriend Chris Rodriguez tried to comfort her.

Finally I got up the nerve to walk over. 'Hey, Silena, I'm really sorry.'

She sniffled. Clarisse glared at me, but she always glares at everyone. Chris would barely look at me. He'd been one of Luke's men until Clarisse rescued him from the Labyrinth last summer, and I guess he still felt guilty about it.

I cleared my throat. 'Silena, you know Beckendorf carried your picture. He looked at it right before we went into battle. You meant a lot to him. You made the last year the best of his life.'

Silena sobbed.

'Good work, Percy,' Clarisse muttered.

'No, it's all right,' Silena said. 'Thank . . . thank you, Percy. I should go.'

'You want company?' Clarisse asked.

Silena shook her head and ran off.

'She's stronger than she looks,' Clarisse muttered, almost to herself. 'She'll survive.'

'You could help with that,' I suggested. 'You could honour Beckendorf's memory by fighting with us.'

Clarisse went for her knife, but it wasn't there any more. She'd thrown it on the ping-pong table in the Big House.

'Not my problem,' she growled. 'My cabin doesn't get honour – I don't fight.'

I noticed she wasn't speaking in rhymes. Maybe she hadn't been around when her cabinmates got cursed, or maybe she had a way of breaking the spell. With a chill, I wondered if Clarisse could be Kronos's spy at camp. Was that why she was keeping her cabin out of the fight? But, as much as I disliked Clarisse, spying for Titans didn't seem like her style.

'All right,' I told her. 'I didn't want to bring this up, but you owe me one. You'd be rotting in a Cyclops's cave in the Sea of Monsters if it weren't for me.'

She clenched her jaw. 'Any other favour, Percy. Not this. The Ares cabin has been dissed too many times. And don't think I don't know what people say about me behind my back.'

I wanted to say, *Well, it's true.* But I bit my tongue.

'So what – you're just going to let Kronos crush us?' I asked.

'If you want my help so much, tell Apollo to give us the chariot.'

'You're such a big baby.'

She charged me but Chris got between us. 'Whoa, guys,' he said. 'Clarisse, you know, maybe he's got a point.'

She sneered at him. 'Not you too!'

She trudged off with Chris at her heels. 'Hey, wait! I just meant – Clarisse, wait!'

I watched the last sparks from Beckendorf's fire curl into the afternoon sky. Then I headed towards the sword-fighting arena. I needed a break, and I wanted to see an old friend.

5   I DRIVE MY DOG INTO A TREE

Mrs O'Leary saw me before I saw her, which was a pretty good trick considering she's the size of a garbage truck. I walked into the arena and a wall of darkness slammed into me.

'WOOF!'

The next thing I knew I was flat on the ground with a huge paw on my chest and an oversized Brillo-pad tongue licking my face.

'Ow!' I said. 'Hey, girl. Good to see you, too. Ow!'

It took a few minutes for Mrs O'Leary to calm down and get off me. By then I was pretty much drenched in dog drool. She wanted to play fetch, so I picked up a bronze shield and tossed it across the arena.

By the way, Mrs O'Leary is the world's only friendly hellhound. I kind of inherited her when her previous owner died. She lived at camp, but Beckendorf . . . well, Beckendorf *used* to take care of her whenever I was gone. He had smelted Mrs O'Leary's favourite bronze chewing bone. He'd forged her collar with the little smiley face and crossbones nametag. Beckendorf had been her best friend next to me.

Thinking about that made me sad all over again, but I threw the shield a few more times because Mrs O'Leary insisted.

Soon she started barking — a sound slightly louder than an artillery gun — like she needed to go for a walk. The other campers didn't think it was funny when she went to the bathroom in the arena. It had caused more than one unfortunate slip-and-slide accident. So I opened the gates of the arena and she bounded straight towards the woods.

I jogged after her, not too concerned that she was getting ahead. Nothing in the woods could threaten Mrs O'Leary. Even the dragons and giant scorpions ran away when she came close.

When I finally tracked her down, she wasn't using the facilities. She was in a familiar clearing where the Council of Cloven Elders had once put Grover on trial. The place didn't look so good. The grass had turned yellow. The three topiary thrones had lost all their leaves. But that's not what surprised me. In the middle of the glade stood the weirdest trio I'd ever seen: Juniper the tree nymph, Nico di Angelo and a very old, very fat satyr.

Nico was the only one who didn't seem freaked out by Mrs O'Leary's appearance. He looked pretty much like I'd seen him in my dream — an aviator's jacket, black jeans and a T-shirt with dancing skeletons on it like one of those Day of the Dead pictures. His Stygian-iron sword hung at his side. He was only twelve, though he looked much older and sadder.

He nodded when he saw me, then went back to scratching Mrs O'Leary's ears. She sniffed his legs like he was the most interesting thing since rib-eye steaks. Being the son of Hades, he'd probably been travelling in all sorts of hellhound-friendly places.

The old satyr didn't look nearly so happy. 'Will someone

– what is this *Underworld* creature doing in my forest!' He waved his arms and trotted on his hooves like the grass was hot. 'You there, Percy Jackson! Is this your beast?'

'Sorry, Leneus,' I said. 'That's your name, right?'

The satyr rolled his eyes. His fur was dust-bunny grey and a spider web grew between his horns. His belly would've made him an invincible bumper car. 'Well, of course I'm Leneus. Don't tell me you've forgotten a member of the council so quickly. Now call off your beast!'

'WOOF!' Mrs O'Leary said happily.

The old satyr gulped. 'Make it go away! Juniper, I will not help you under these circumstances!'

Juniper turned towards me. She was pretty in a dryady way, with her purple gossamer dress and her elfish face, but her eyes were green-tinted with chlorophyll from crying.

'Percy,' she sniffled. 'I was just asking about Grover. I *know* something's happened. He wouldn't stay gone this long if he wasn't in trouble. I was hoping that Leneus –'

'I told you!' the satyr protested. 'You are better off without that traitor.'

Juniper stamped her foot. 'He is not a traitor! He's the bravest satyr ever and I want to know where he is!'

'WOOF!'

Leneus's knees started knocking. 'I – I won't answer questions with this hellhound sniffing my tail!'

Nico looked like he was trying not to crack up. 'I'll walk the dog,' he volunteered.

He whistled and Mrs O'Leary bounded after him to the far end of the grove.

Leneus huffed indignantly and brushed the twigs off

his shirt. 'Now, as I was trying to explain, young lady, your boyfriend has not sent *any* reports since we voted him into exile.'

'You *tried* to vote him into exile,' I corrected. 'Chiron and Dionysus stopped you.'

'Bah! They are *honorary* council members. It wasn't a proper vote.'

'I'll tell Dionysus you said that.'

Leneus paled. 'I only meant – Now see here, Jackson. This is none of your business.'

'Grover's my friend,' I said. 'He wasn't lying to you about Pan's death. I saw it myself. You were just too scared to accept the truth.'

Leneus's lips quivered. 'No! Grover's a liar and good riddance. We're better off without him.'

I pointed at the withered thrones. 'If things are going so well, where are your friends? Looks like your council hasn't been meeting lately.'

'Maron and Silenus . . . I – I'm sure they'll be back,' he said, but I could hear the panic in his voice. 'They're just taking some time off to think. It's been a very unsettling year.'

'It's going to get a lot more unsettling,' I promised. 'Leneus, we *need* Grover. There's got to be a way you can find him with your magic.'

The old satyr's eye twitched. 'I'm telling you I've heard nothing. Perhaps he's dead.'

Juniper choked back a sob.

'He's not dead,' I said. 'I can feel that much.'

'Empathy links,' Leneus said disdainfully. 'Very unreliable.'

'So ask around,' I insisted. 'Find him. There's a war coming. Grover was preparing the nature spirits.'

'Without my permission! And it's not *our* war.'

I grabbed him by the shirt, which seriously wasn't like me, but the stupid old goat was making me mad. 'Listen, Leneus. When Kronos attacks, he's going to have *packs* of hellhounds. He's going to destroy everything in his path – mortals, gods, demigods. Do you think he'll let the satyrs go free? You're supposed to be a leader. So LEAD. Get out there and see what's happening. Find Grover and bring Juniper some news. Now GO!'

I didn't push him very hard, but he was kind of top-heavy. He fell on his furry rump, then scrambled to his hooves and ran away with his belly jiggling. 'Grover will never be accepted! He will die an outcast!'

When he'd disappeared into the bushes, Juniper wiped her eyes. 'I'm sorry, Percy. I didn't mean to get you involved. Leneus is still a Lord of the Wild. You don't want to make an enemy of him.'

'No problem,' I said. 'I've got worse enemies than overweight satyrs.'

Nico walked back to us. 'Good job, Percy. Judging from the trail of goat pellets, I'd say you shook him up pretty well.'

I was afraid I knew why Nico was here, but I tried for a smile. 'Welcome back. Did you come by just to see Juniper?'

He blushed. 'Um, no. That was an accident. I kind of . . . dropped into the middle of their conversation.'

'He scared us to death!' Juniper said. 'Right out of the shadows. But, Nico, you *are* the son of Hades and all. Are you sure you haven't heard anything about Grover?'

Nico shifted his weight. 'Juniper, like I tried to tell you . . . even if Grover died, he would reincarnate into something else in nature. I can't sense things like that, only mortal souls.'

'But if you *do* hear anything?' she pleaded, putting her hand on his arm. 'Anything at all?'

Nico's cheeks got even brighter red. 'Uh, you bet. I'll keep my ears open.'

'We'll find him, Juniper,' I promised. 'Grover's alive, I'm sure. There must be a simple reason why he hasn't contacted us.'

She nodded glumly. 'I hate not being able to leave the forest. He could be anywhere, and I'm stuck here waiting. Oh, if that silly goat has got himself hurt –'

Mrs O'Leary bounded back over and took an interest in Juniper's dress.

Juniper yelped. 'Oh, no you don't! I know about dogs and trees – I'm gone!'

She went *poof* into green mist. Mrs O'Leary looked disappointed, but she lumbered off to find another target, leaving Nico and me alone.

Nico tapped his sword on the ground. A tiny mound of animal bones erupted from the dirt. They knitted themselves together into a skeletal field mouse and scampered off. 'I was sorry to hear about Beckendorf.'

A lump formed in my throat. 'How did you –'

'I talked to his ghost.'

'Oh . . . right.' I'd never get used to the fact that this twelve-year-old kid spent more time talking with the dead than the living. 'Did he say anything?'

'He doesn't blame you. He figured you'd be beating yourself up, and he said you shouldn't.'

'Is he going to try for rebirth?'

Nico shook his head. 'He's staying in Elysium. Said he's waiting for someone. Not sure what he meant, but he seems okay with death.'

It wasn't much comfort, but it was something.

'I had a vision you were on Mount Tam,' I told Nico. 'Was that –'

'Real,' he said. 'I didn't mean to be spying on the Titans, but I was in the neighbourhood.'

'Doing what?'

Nico tugged at his sword belt. 'Following a lead on . . . you know, my family.'

I nodded. I knew his past was a painful subject. Until two years ago, he and his sister Bianca had been frozen in time at a place called the Lotus Casino. They'd been there for like seventy years. Eventually a mysterious lawyer rescued them and checked them into a boarding school, but Nico had no memories of his life before the casino. He didn't know anything about his mother. He didn't know who the lawyer was, or why they'd been frozen in time or allowed to go free. After Bianca died and left Nico alone, he'd been obsessed with finding answers.

'So how did it go?' I asked. 'Any luck?'

'No,' he murmured. 'But I may have a new lead soon.'

'What's the lead?'

Nico chewed his lip. 'That's not important right now. You know why I'm here.'

A feeling of dread started to build in my chest. Ever

since Nico first proposed his plan for beating Kronos last summer, I'd had nightmares about it. He would show up occasionally and press me for an answer, but I kept putting him off.

'Nico, I don't know,' I said. 'It seems pretty extreme.'

'You've got Typhon coming in what . . . a week? Most of the other Titans are unleashed now and on Kronos's side. Maybe it's time to think extreme.'

I looked back towards the camp. Even from this distance, I could hear the Ares and Apollo campers fighting again, yelling curses and spouting bad poetry.

'They're no match for the Titan army,' Nico said. 'You know that. This comes down to you and Luke. And there's only one way you can beat Luke.'

I remembered the fight on the *Princess Andromeda*. I'd been hopelessly outmatched. Kronos had almost killed me with a single cut to my arm, and I couldn't even wound him. Riptide had glanced right off his skin.

'We can give you the same power,' Nico urged. 'You heard the Great Prophecy. Unless you want to have your soul reaped by a cursed blade . . .'

I wondered how Nico had heard the prophecy – probably from some ghost.

'You can't prevent a prophecy,' I said.

'But you can fight it.' Nico had a strange, hungry light in his eyes. 'You can become invincible.'

'Maybe we should wait. Try to fight without –'

'No!' Nico snarled. 'It has to be now!'

I stared at him. I hadn't seen his temper flare like that in a long time. 'Um, you sure you're okay?'

He took a deep breath. 'Percy, all I mean . . . when the

fighting starts, we won't be able to make the journey. This is our last chance. I'm sorry if I'm being too pushy, but two years ago my sister gave her life to protect you. I want you to honour that. Do whatever it takes to stay alive and defeat Kronos.'

I didn't like the idea. Then I thought about Annabeth calling me a coward, and I got angry.

Nico had a point. If Kronos attacked New York, the campers would be no match for his forces. I had to do something. Nico's way was dangerous – maybe even deadly. But it might give me a fighting edge.

'All right,' I decided. 'What do we do first?'

His cold, creepy smile made me sorry I'd agreed. 'First we'll need to retrace Luke's steps. We need to know more about his past, his childhood.'

I shuddered, thinking about Rachel's picture from my dream – a smiling nine-year-old Luke. 'Why do we need to know about that?'

'I'll explain when we get there,' Nico said. 'I've already tracked down his mother. She lives in Connecticut.'

I stared at him. I'd never thought much about Luke's mortal parent. I'd met his dad, Hermes, but his mom . . .

'Luke ran away when he was really young,' I said. 'I didn't think his mom was alive.'

'Oh, she's alive.' The way he said it made me wonder what was wrong with her. What kind of horrible person could she be?

'Okay . . .' I said. 'So how do we get to Connecticut? I can call Blackjack –'

'No.' Nico scowled. 'Pegasi don't like me, and the feeling

is mutual. But there's no need for flying.' He whistled, and Mrs O'Leary came loping out of the woods.

'Your friend here can help.' Nico patted her head. 'You haven't tried shadow-travel yet?'

'Shadow-travel?'

Nico whispered in Mrs O'Leary's ear. She tilted her head, suddenly alert.

'Hop on board,' Nico told me.

I'd never considered riding a dog before, but Mrs O'Leary was certainly big enough. I climbed onto her back and held her collar.

'This will make her very tired,' Nico warned, 'so you can't do it often. And it works best at night. But all shadows are part of the same substance. There is only one darkness, and creatures of the Underworld can use it as a road, or a door.'

'I don't understand,' I said.

'No,' Nico said. 'It took me a long time to learn. But Mrs O'Leary knows. Tell her where to go. Tell her Westport, the home of May Castellan.'

'You're not coming?'

'Don't worry,' he said. 'I'll meet you there.'

I was a little nervous, but I leaned down to Mrs O'Leary's ear. 'Okay, girl. Uh, can you take me to Westport, Connecticut? May Castellan's place?'

Mrs O'Leary sniffed the air. She looked into the gloom of the forest. Then she bounded forward, straight into an oak tree.

Just before we hit, we passed into shadows as cold as the dark side of the moon.

6 MY COOKIES GET SCORCHED

I don't recommend shadow-travel if you're scared of:

a) the dark
b) cold shivers up your spine
c) strange noises or
d) going so fast you feel as if your face is peeling off.

In other words, I thought it was awesome. One minute I couldn't see anything. I could only feel Mrs O'Leary's fur and my fingers wrapped around the bronze links of her dog collar.

The next minute the shadows melted into a new scene. We were on a cliff in the woods of Connecticut. At least, it looked like Connecticut from the few times I'd been there – lots of trees, low stone walls, big houses. Down one side of the cliff, a highway cut through a ravine. Down the other side was someone's backyard. The property was huge – more wilderness than lawn. The house was a white colonial-style two-storey. Despite the fact that it was right on the other side of the hill from a highway, it felt like it was in the middle of nowhere. I could see a light glowing in the kitchen window. A rusty old swing set stood under an apple tree.

I couldn't imagine living in a house like this, with an

actual yard and everything. I'd lived in a tiny apartment or a school dorm my whole life. If this was Luke's home, I wondered why he'd ever wanted to leave.

Mrs O'Leary staggered. I remembered what Nico had said about shadow travel draining her, so I slipped off her back. She let out a huge toothy yawn that would've scared a T-rex, then turned in a circle and flopped down so hard the ground shook.

Nico appeared right next to me, like the shadows had darkened and created him. He stumbled but I caught his arm.

'I'm okay,' he managed, rubbing his eyes.

'How did you do that?'

'Practice. A few times running into walls. A few accidental trips to China.'

Mrs O'Leary started snoring. If it hadn't been for the roar of traffic behind us, I'm sure she would've woken up the whole neighbourhood.

'Are you going to take a nap, too?' I asked Nico.

He shook his head. 'The first time I shadow-travelled, I passed out for a week. Now it just makes me a little drowsy, but I can't do it more than once or twice a night. Mrs O'Leary won't be going anywhere for a while.'

'So we've got some quality time in Connecticut.' I gazed at the white colonial-style house. 'What now?'

'We ring the doorbell,' Nico said.

If I were Luke's mom, I would not have opened my door at night for two strange kids. But I wasn't *anything* like Luke's mom.

I knew that even before we reached the front door. The

sidewalk was lined with those little stuffed beanbag animals you see in gift shops. There were miniature lions, pigs, dragons, hydras, even a teeny Minotaur in a little Minotaur diaper. Judging from their sad shape, the beanbag creatures had been sitting out here a long time – since the snow melted last spring at least. One of the hydras had a tree sapling sprouting between its necks.

The front porch was infested with wind chimes. Shiny bits of glass and metal clinked in the breeze. Brass ribbons tinkled like water and made me realize I needed to use the bathroom. I didn't know how Ms Castellan could stand all the noise.

The front door was painted turquoise. The name CASTELLAN was written in English and below in Greek: Διοικητής Φρουρίου.

Nico looked at me. 'Ready?'

He'd barely tapped the door when it swung open.

'Luke!' the old lady cried happily.

She looked like someone who enjoyed sticking her fingers in electrical sockets. Her white hair stuck out in tufts all over her head. Her pink housedress was covered in scorch-marks and smears of ash. When she smiled, her face looked unnaturally stretched, and the high-voltage light in her eyes made me wonder if she were blind.

'Oh, my dear boy!' She hugged Nico. I was trying to figure out why she thought Nico was Luke (they looked absolutely nothing alike) when she smiled at me and said, 'Luke!'

She forgot all about Nico and gave me a hug. She smelled like burnt cookies. She was as thin as a scarecrow, but that didn't stop her from almost crushing me.

'Come in!' she insisted. 'I have your lunch ready!'

She ushered us inside. The living room was even weirder than the front lawn. Mirrors and candles filled every available space. I couldn't look anywhere without seeing my own reflection. Above the mantle, a little bronze Hermes flew around the second hand of a ticking clock. I tried to imagine the god of messengers ever falling in love with this old woman, but the idea was too bizarre.

Then I noticed the framed picture on the mantle, and I froze. It was exactly like Rachel's sketch – Luke around nine years old, with blond hair and a big smile and two missing teeth. The lack of a scar on his face made him look like a different person – carefree and happy. How could Rachel have known about that picture?

'This way, my dear!' Ms Castellan steered me towards the back of the house. 'Oh, I told them you would come back. I knew it!'

She sat us down at the kitchen table. Stacked on the counter were hundreds – I mean hundreds – of Tupperware boxes with peanut-butter-and-jam sandwiches inside. The ones on the bottom were green and fuzzy, like they'd been there for a long time. The smell reminded me of my sixth-grade locker – and that's not a good thing.

On top of the oven was a stack of cookie sheets. Each one had a dozen burnt cookies on it. In the sink was a mountain of empty plastic Kool-Aid pitchers. A beanbag Medusa sat by the faucet like she was guarding the mess.

Ms Castellan started humming as she got out peanut butter and jam and started making a new sandwich. Something was burning in the oven. I got the feeling more cookies were on the way.

Above the sink, taped all around the window, were dozens of little pictures cut from magazines and newspaper ads – pictures of Hermes from various company logos, pictures of the caduceus from medical ads.

My heart sank. I wanted to get out of that room, but Ms Castellan kept smiling at me as she made the sandwich, like she was making sure I didn't bolt.

Nico coughed. 'Um, Ms Castellan?'

'Mm?'

'We need to ask you about your son.'

'Oh, yes! They told me he would never come back. But I knew better.' She patted my cheek affectionately, giving me peanut-butter racing stripes.

'When did you last see him?' Nico asked.

Her eyes lost focus.

'He was so young when he left,' she said wistfully. 'Third grade. That's too young to run away! He said he'd be back for lunch. And I waited. He likes peanut-butter sandwiches and cookies and Kool-Aid. He'll be back for lunch very soon . . .' Then she looked at me and smiled. 'Why, Luke, there you are! You look so handsome. You have your father's eyes.'

She turned towards the pictures of Hermes above the sink. 'Now there's a good man. Yes, indeed. He comes to visit me, you know.'

The clock kept ticking in the other room. I wiped the peanut butter off my face and looked at Nico pleadingly, like *Can we get out of here now?*

'Ma'am,' Nico said. 'What, uh . . . what happened to your eyes?'

Her gaze seemed fractured – like she was trying to

focus on him through a kaleidoscope. 'Why, Luke, you know the story. It was right before you were born, wasn't it? I'd always been special, able to see through the . . . whatever they call it.'

'The Mist?' I said.

'Yes, dear.' She nodded encouragingly. 'And they offered me an important job. That's how special I was!'

I glanced at Nico, but he looked as confused as I was.

'What sort of job?' I asked. 'What happened?'

Ms Castellan frowned. Her knife hovered over the sandwich bread. 'Dear me, it didn't work out, did it? Your father warned me not to try. He said it was too dangerous. But I had to. It was my destiny! And now . . . I still can't get the images out of my head. They make everything seem so fuzzy. Would you like some cookies?'

She pulled a tray out of the oven and dumped a dozen lumps of chocolate-chip charcoal on the table.

'Luke was so kind,' Ms Castellan murmured. 'He left to protect me, you know. He said if he went away, the monsters wouldn't threaten me. But I told him the monsters are no threat! They sit outside on the sidewalk all day, and they never come in.' She picked up the little stuffed Medusa from the windowsill. 'Do they, Mrs Medusa? No, no threat at all.' She beamed at me. 'I'm so glad you came home. I knew you weren't ashamed of me!'

I shifted in my seat. I imagined being Luke, sitting at this table, eight or nine years old, and just beginning to realize that my mother wasn't all there.

'Ms Castellan,' I said.

'Mom,' she corrected.

'Um, yeah. Have you seen Luke since he left home?'

'Well, of course!'

I didn't know if she was imagining that or not. For all I knew, every time the mailman came to the door he was Luke. But Nico sat forward expectantly.

'When?' he asked. 'When did Luke visit you last?'

'Well, it was . . . oh goodness . . .' A shadow passed across her face. 'The last time, he looked so different. A scar. A terrible scar, and his voice so full of pain . . .'

'His eyes,' I said. 'Were they gold?'

'Gold?' She blinked. 'No. How silly. Luke has blue eyes. Beautiful blue eyes!'

So Luke really had been here, and this had happened before last summer – before he'd turned into Kronos.

'Ms Castellan?' Nico put his hand on the old woman's arm. 'This is very important. Did he ask you for anything?'

She frowned as if trying to remember. 'My – my blessing. Isn't that sweet?' She looked at us uncertainly. 'He was going to a river, and he said he needed my blessing. I gave it to him. Of course I did.'

Nico looked at me triumphantly. 'Thank you, ma'am. That's all the information we –'

Ms Castellan gasped. She doubled over and her cookie tray clattered to the floor. Nico and I jumped to our feet.

'Ms Castellan?' I said.

'*AHHHH.*' She straightened. I scrambled away and almost fell over the kitchen table because her eyes – her eyes were glowing green.

'*My child,*' she rasped in a much deeper voice. '*Must protect him! Hermes, help! Not my child! Not his fate – no!*'

She grabbed Nico by the shoulders and began to shake him as if trying to make him understand. '*Not his fate!*'

Nico made a strangled scream and pushed her away. He gripped the hilt of his sword. 'Percy, we need to get out –'

Suddenly Ms Castellan collapsed. I lurched forward and caught her before she could hit the edge of the table. I managed to get her into a chair.

'Ms C?' I asked.

She muttered something incomprehensible and shook her head. 'Goodness. I . . . I dropped the cookies. How silly of me.'

She blinked, and her eyes were back to normal – or, at least, what they had been before. The green glow was gone.

'Are you okay?' I asked.

'Well, of course, dear. I'm fine. Why do you ask?'

I glanced at Nico, who mouthed the word: *Leave.*

'Ms C, you were telling us something,' I said. 'Something about your son.'

'Was I?' she said dreamily. 'Yes, his blue eyes. We were talking about his blue eyes. Such a handsome boy!'

'We have to go,' Nico said urgently. 'We'll tell Luke . . . uh, we'll tell him you said hello.'

'But you can't leave!' Ms Castellan got shakily to her feet and I backed away. I felt silly being scared of a frail old woman, but the way her voice had changed, the way she'd grabbed Nico . . .

'Hermes will be here soon,' she promised. 'He'll want to see his boy!'

'Maybe next time,' I said. 'Thank you for –' I looked down at the burnt cookies scattered on the floor. 'Thanks for everything.'

She tried to stop us, to offer us Kool-Aid, but I had to get out of that house. On the front porch, she grabbed my wrist and I almost jumped out of my skin. 'Luke, at least be safe. Promise me you'll be safe.'

'I will . . . Mom.'

That made her smile. She released my wrist, and as she closed the front door, I could hear her talking to the candles: 'You hear that? He will be safe. I told you he would be!'

As the door shut, Nico and I ran. The little beanbag animals on the sidewalk seemed to grin at us when we passed.

Back at the cliff, Mrs O'Leary had found a friend.

A cosy campfire crackled in a ring of stones. A girl about eight years old was sitting cross-legged next to Mrs O'Leary, scratching the hellhound's ears.

The girl had mousy brown hair and a simple brown dress. She wore a scarf over her head so she looked like a pioneer kid – like the ghost of *Little House on the Prairie* or something. She poked the fire with a stick, and it seemed to glow more richly red than a normal fire.

'Hello,' she said.

My first thought was: monster. When you're a demigod and you find a sweet little girl alone in the woods – that's typically a good time to draw your sword and attack. Plus the encounter with Ms Castellan had rattled me pretty badly.

But Nico bowed to the little girl. 'Hello again, Lady.'

She studied me with eyes as red as the firelight. I decided it was safest to bow.

'Sit, Percy Jackson,' she said. 'Would you like some dinner?'

After staring at mouldy peanut-butter sandwiches and burnt cookies, I didn't have much of an appetite, but the girl waved her hand and a picnic appeared at the edge of the fire. There were plates of roast beef, baked potatoes, buttered carrots, fresh bread and a whole bunch of other foods I hadn't had in a long time. My stomach started to rumble. It was the kind of home-cooked meal people are supposed to have, but never do. The girl made a two-metre-long dog biscuit appear for Mrs O'Leary, who happily began tearing it to shreds.

I sat next to Nico. We picked up our food and I was about to dig in when I thought better of it.

I scraped part of my meal into the flames, the way we do at camp. 'For the gods,' I said.

The little girl smiled. 'Thank you. As tender of the flame, I get a share of every sacrifice, you know.'

'I recognize you now,' I said. 'The first time I came to camp, you were sitting by the fire, in the middle of the commons area.'

'You did not stop to talk,' the girl recalled sadly. 'Alas, most never do. Nico talked to me. He was the first in many years. Everyone rushes about. No time for visiting family.'

'You're Hestia,' I said. 'Goddess of the hearth.'

She nodded.

Okay . . . so she looked eight years old. I didn't ask. I'd learned that gods could look any way they pleased.

'My lady,' Nico asked, 'why aren't you with the other Olympians fighting Typhon?'

'I'm not much for fighting.' Her red eyes flickered. I realized they weren't just reflecting the flames. They were filled with flames — but not like Ares' eyes. Hestia's eyes were warm and cosy.

'Besides,' she said, 'someone has to keep the home fires burning while the other gods are away.'

'So you're guarding Mount Olympus?' I asked.

'"Guard" may be too strong a word. But if you ever need a warm place to sit and a home-cooked meal, you are welcome to visit. Now eat.'

My plate was empty before I knew it. Nico scarfed his down just as fast.

'That was great,' I said. 'Thank you, Hestia.'

She nodded. 'Did you have a good visit with May Castellan?'

For a moment, I'd almost forgotten the old lady with her bright eyes and her maniacal smile, the way she'd suddenly seemed possessed.

'What's wrong with her exactly?' I asked.

'She was born with a gift,' Hestia said. 'She could see through the Mist.'

'Like my mother,' I said. And I was also thinking, Like Rachel. 'But the glowing-eyes thing –'

'Some bear the curse of sight better than others,' the goddess said sadly. 'For a while, May Castellan had many talents. She attracted the attention of Hermes himself. They had a beautiful baby boy. For a brief time, she was happy. And then she went too far.'

I remembered what Mrs Castellan had said: *They offered*

me an important job. It didn't work out. I wondered what kind of job left you like that.

'One minute she was all happy,' I said. 'And then she was freaking out about her son's fate, like she knew he'd turned into Kronos. What happened to . . . to divide her like that?'

The goddess's face darkened. 'That is a story I do not like to tell. But May Castellan saw too much. If you are to understand your enemy Luke, you must understand his family.'

I thought about the sad little pictures of Hermes taped above May Castellan's sink. I wondered if Ms Castellan had been so crazy when Luke was little. That green-eyed fit could've seriously scared a nine-year-old kid. And if Hermes never visited, if he'd left Luke alone with his mom all those years . . .

'No wonder Luke ran away,' I said. 'I mean, it wasn't right to leave his mom like that, but still – he was just a kid. Hermes shouldn't have abandoned them.'

Hestia scratched behind Mrs O'Leary's ears. The hellhound wagged her tail and accidentally knocked over a tree.

'It's easy to judge others,' Hestia warned. 'But will you follow Luke's path? Seek the same powers?'

Nico set down his plate. 'We have no choice, my lady. It's the only way Percy stands a chance.'

'Mmm.' Hestia opened her hand and the fire roared. Flames shot ten metres into the air. Heat slapped me in the face. Then the fire died back down to normal.

'Not all powers are spectacular.' Hestia looked at me. 'Sometimes the hardest power to master is the power of yielding. Do you believe me?'

'Uh-huh,' I said. Anything to keep her from messing with her flame powers again.

The goddess smiled. 'You are a good hero, Percy Jackson. Not too proud. I like that. But you have much to learn. When Dionysus was made a god, I gave up my throne for him. It was the only way to avoid a civil war among the gods.'

'It unbalanced the council,' I remembered. 'Suddenly there were seven guys and five girls.'

Hestia shrugged. 'It was the best solution, not a perfect one. Now I tend the fire. I fade slowly into the background. No one will ever write epic poems about the deeds of Hestia. Most demigods don't even stop to talk to me. But that is no matter. I keep the peace. I yield when necessary. Can you do this?'

'I don't know what you mean.'

She studied me. 'Perhaps not yet. But soon. Will you continue your quest?'

'Is that why you're here – to warn me against going?'

Hestia shook her head. 'I am here because when all else fails, when all the other mighty gods have gone off to war, I am all that's left. Home. Hearth. I am the last Olympian. You must remember me when you face your final decision.'

I didn't like the way she said *final.*

I looked at Nico, then back at Hestia's warm glowing eyes. 'I have to continue, my lady. I have to stop Luke – I mean Kronos.'

Hestia nodded. 'Very well. I cannot be of much assistance, beyond what I have already told you. But since you sacrificed to me, I can return you to your own hearth. I will see you again, Percy, on Olympus.'

Her tone was ominous, like our next meeting would not be happy.

The goddess waved her hand, and everything faded.

Suddenly I was home. Nico and I were sitting on the couch in my mom's apartment on the Upper East Side. That was the good news. The bad news was that the rest of the living room was occupied by Mrs O'Leary.

I heard a muffled yell from the bedroom. Paul's voice said, 'Who put this wall of fur in the doorway?'

'Percy?' my mom called out. 'Are you here? Are you all right?'

'I'm here!' I shouted back.

'WOOF!' Mrs O'Leary tried to turn in a circle to find my mom, knocking all the pictures off the walls. She's only met my mom once before (long story), but she loves her.

It took a few minutes, but we finally got things worked out. After destroying most of the furniture in the living room and probably making our neighbours really mad, we got my parents out of the bedroom and into the kitchen, where we sat around the kitchen table. Mrs O'Leary still took up the entire living room, but she'd settled her head in the kitchen doorway so she could see us, which made her happy. My mom tossed her a five-kilogram pack of ground beef, which disappeared down her gullet. Paul poured lemonade for the rest of us while I explained about our visit to Connecticut.

'So it's true.' Paul stared at me like he'd never seen me before. He was wearing his white bathrobe, now covered in hellhound fur, and his salt-and-pepper hair was sticking up in every direction. 'All the talk about monsters, and being a demigod . . . it's really true.'

I nodded. Last autumn I'd explained to Paul who I was. My mom had backed me up. But until this moment I don't think he really believed us.

'Sorry about Mrs O'Leary,' I said, 'destroying the living room and all.'

Paul laughed like he was delighted. 'Are you kidding? This is awesome! I mean, when I saw the hoof prints on the Prius, I thought maybe. But this!'

He patted Mrs O'Leary's snout. The living room shook – *BOOM, BOOM, BOOM* – which either meant a SWAT team was breaking down the door or Mrs O'Leary was wagging her tail.

I couldn't help but smile. Paul was a pretty cool guy, even if he was my English teacher as well as my stepdad.

'Thanks for not freaking out,' I said.

'Oh, I'm freaking out,' he promised, his eyes wide. 'I just think it's awesome!'

'Yeah, well,' I said, 'you may not be so excited when you hear what's happening.'

I told Paul and my mom about Typhon, and the gods, and the battle that was sure to come. Then I told them Nico's plan.

My mom laced her fingers around her lemonade glass. She was wearing her old blue flannel bathrobe and her hair was tied back. Recently she'd started writing a novel like she'd wanted to do for years, and I could tell she'd been working on it late into the night, because the circles under her eyes were darker than usual.

Behind her at the kitchen window, silvery moonlace

glowed in the flowerbox. I'd brought the magical plant back from Calypso's island last summer, and it bloomed like crazy under my mother's care. The scent always calmed me down, but it also made me sad, because it reminded me of lost friends.

My mom took a deep breath, like she was thinking how to tell me no.

'Percy, it's dangerous,' she said. 'Even for you.'

'Mom, I know. I could die. Nico explained that. But if we don't try –'

'We'll all die,' Nico said. He hadn't touched his lemonade. 'Ms Jackson, we don't stand a chance against an invasion. And there *will* be an invasion.'

'An invasion of New York?' Paul said. 'Is that even possible? How could we not see the . . . the monsters?'

He said the word like he still couldn't believe this was real.

'I don't know,' I admitted. 'I don't see how Kronos could just march into Manhattan, but the Mist is strong. Typhon is trampling across the country right now and mortals think he's a storm system.'

'Ms Jackson,' Nico said, 'Percy needs your blessing. The process *has* to start that way. I wasn't sure until we met Luke's mom, but now I'm positive. This has only been done successfully twice before. Both times, the mother had to give her blessing. She had to be willing to let her son take the risk.'

'You want me to bless this?' She shook her head. 'It's crazy. Percy, please –'

'Mom, I can't do it without you.'

'And if you survive this – this *process*?'

'Then I go to war,' I said. 'Me against Kronos. And only one of us will survive.'

I didn't tell her the whole prophecy – about the soul reaping and the end of my days. She didn't need to know that I was probably doomed. I could only hope I'd stop Kronos and save the rest of the world before I died.

'You're my son,' she said miserably. 'I can't just . . .'

I could tell I'd have to push her harder if I wanted her to agree, but I didn't want to. I remembered poor Ms Castellan in her kitchen, waiting for her son to come home. And I realized how lucky I was. My mom had always been there for me, always tried to make things normal for me, even with the gods and monsters and stuff. She put up with me going off on adventures, but now I was asking her blessing to do something that would probably get me killed.

I locked eyes with Paul, and some kind of understanding passed between us.

'Sally.' He put his hand over my mother's hands. 'I can't claim to know what you and Percy have been going through all these years. But it sounds to me . . . it sounds like Percy is doing something noble. I wish I had that much courage.'

I got a lump in my throat. I didn't get compliments like that too much.

My mom stared at her lemonade. She looked like she was trying not to cry. I thought about what Hestia had said, about how hard it was to yield, and I figured maybe my mom was finding that out.

'Percy,' she said, 'I give you my blessing.'

I didn't feel any different. No magic glow lit the kitchen or anything.

I glanced at Nico.

He looked more anxious than ever, but he nodded. 'It's time.'

'Percy,' my mom said. 'One last thing. If you – if you survive this fight with Kronos, send me a sign.' She rummaged through her bag and handed me her cell phone.

'Mom,' I said, 'you know demigods and phones –'

'I know,' she said. 'But just in case. If you're not able to call . . . maybe a sign that I could see from anywhere in Manhattan. To let me know you're okay.'

'Like Theseus,' Paul suggested. 'He was supposed to raise white sails when he came home to Athens.'

'Except he forgot,' Nico muttered. 'And his father jumped off the palace roof in despair. But other than that it was a great idea.'

'What about a flag or a flare?' my mom said. 'From Olympus – the Empire State Building.'

'Something blue,' I said.

We'd had a running joke for years about blue food. It was my favourite colour, and my mom went out of her way to humour me. Every year my birthday cake, my Easter basket, my Christmas candy canes always had to be blue.

'Yes,' my mom agreed. 'I'll watch for a blue signal. And I'll try to avoid jumping off palace roofs.'

She gave me one last hug. I tried not to feel like I was saying goodbye. I shook hands with Paul. Then Nico and I walked to the kitchen doorway and looked at Mrs O'Leary.

'Sorry, girl,' I said. 'Shadow-travel time again.'

She whimpered and crossed her paws over her snout.

'Where now?' I asked Nico. 'Los Angeles?'

'No need,' he said. 'There's a closer entrance to the Underworld.'

We emerged in Central Park just north of the Pond. Mrs O'Leary looked pretty tired as she limped over to a cluster of boulders. She started sniffing around and I was afraid she might mark her territory, but Nico said, 'It's okay. She just smells the way home.'

I frowned. 'Through the rocks?'

'The Underworld has two major entrances,' Nico said. 'You know the one in L.A.'

'Charon's ferry.'

Nico nodded. 'Most souls go that way, but there's a smaller path, harder to find. The Door of Orpheus.'

'The dude with the harp.'

'Dude with the lyre,' Nico corrected. 'But, yeah, him. He used his music to charm the earth and open a new path into the Underworld. He sang his way right into Hades' palace and almost got away with his wife's soul.'

I remembered the story. Orpheus wasn't supposed to look behind him when he was leading his wife back to the world, but of course he did. It was one of those typical 'and-so-they-died/the-end' stories that always made us demigods feel warm and fuzzy.

'So this is the Door of Orpheus.' I tried to be impressed, but it still looked like a pile of rocks to me. 'How does it open?'

'We need music,' Nico said. 'How's your singing?'

'Um, no. Can't you just, like, tell it to open? You're the son of Hades and all.'

'It's not so easy. We need music.'

I was pretty sure if I tried to sing, all I would cause was an avalanche.

'I have a better idea.' I turned and called, 'GROVER!'

We waited for a long time. Mrs O'Leary curled up and took a nap. I could hear the crickets in the woods and an owl hooting. Traffic hummed along Central Park West. Horse hooves clopped down a nearby path, maybe a mounted police patrol. I was sure they'd love to find two kids hanging out in the park at one in the morning.

'It's no good,' Nico said at last.

But I had a feeling. My empathy link was really tingling for the first time in months, which either meant a whole lot of people had suddenly switched on the Nature Channel, or Grover was close.

I shut my eyes and concentrated. *Grover.*

I knew he was somewhere in the park. Why couldn't I sense his emotions? All I got was a faint hum in the base of my skull.

Grover, I thought more insistently.

Hmm-hmmmm, something said.

An image came into my head. I saw a giant elm tree deep in the woods, well off the main paths. Gnarled roots laced the ground, making a kind of bed. Lying in it with his arms crossed and his eyes closed was a satyr. At first I couldn't be sure it was Grover. He was covered in twigs and leaves like he'd been sleeping there a long time. The roots seemed to be shaping themselves around him, slowly pulling him into the earth.

Grover, I said. *Wake up.*

Unnnh — zzzzz.

Dude, you're covered in dirt. Wake up!

Sleepy, his mind murmured.

FOOD, I suggested. *PANCAKES!*

His eyes shot open. A blur of thoughts filled my head like he was suddenly on fast-forward. The image shattered and I almost fell over.

'What happened?' Nico asked.

'I got through. He's . . . yeah. He's on his way.'

A minute later, the tree next to us shivered. Grover fell out of the branches, right on his head.

'Grover!' I yelled.

'Woof!' Mrs O'Leary looked up, probably wondering if we were going to play fetch with the satyr.

'Blah-haa-haa!' Grover bleated.

'You okay, man?'

'Oh, I'm fine.' He rubbed his head. His horns had grown so much they poked right out of his curly hair. 'I was at the other end of the park. The dryads had this great idea of passing me through the trees to get here. They don't understand *height* very well.'

He grinned and got to his feet — well, his *hooves* actually. Since last summer, Grover had stopped trying to disguise himself as human. He never wore a cap or fake feet any more. He didn't even wear jeans, since he had furry goat legs from the waist down. His T-shirt had a picture from that book — *Where the Wild Things Are*. It was covered with dirt and tree sap. His goatee looked fuller, almost manly (or goatly?), and he was as tall as me now.

'Good to see you, G-man,' I said. 'You remember Nico.'

Grover nodded at Nico, then he gave me a big hug. He smelled like fresh-mown lawns.

'Perrrrcy!' he bleated. 'I missed you! I miss camp. They don't serve very good enchiladas in the wilderness.'

'I was worried,' I said. 'Where've you been the last two months?'

'The last two —' Grover's smile faded. 'The last *two months*? What are you talking about?'

'We haven't heard from you,' I said. 'Juniper's worried. We sent Iris-messages but —'

'Hold on.' He looked up at the stars, like he was trying to calculate his position. 'What month is this?'

'August.'

The colour drained from his face. 'That's impossible. It's June. I just lay down to take a nap and . . .' He grabbed my arms. 'I remember now! He knocked me out. Percy, we have to stop him!'

'Whoa,' I said. 'Slow down. Tell me what happened.'

He took a deep breath. 'I was . . . I was walking in the woods up by Harlem Meer. And I felt this tremble in the ground, like something powerful was near.'

'You can sense stuff like that?' Nico asked.

Grover nodded. 'Since Pan's death, I can feel when something is wrong in nature. It's like my ears and eyes are sharper when I'm in the wild. Anyway, I started following the scent. This man in a long black coat was walking through the park, and I noticed he didn't cast a shadow. Middle of a sunny day, and he cast no shadow. He kind of shimmered as he moved.'

'Like a mirage?' Nico asked.

'Yes,' Grover said. 'And whenever he passed humans —'

'The humans would pass out,' Nico said. 'Curl up and go to sleep.'

'That's right! Then after he was gone, they'd get up and go about their business like nothing happened.'

I stared at Nico. 'You know this guy in black?'

'Afraid so,' Nico said. 'Grover, what happened?'

'I followed the guy. He kept looking up at the buildings around the park like he was making estimates or something. This lady jogger ran by, and she curled up on the sidewalk and started snoring. The guy in black put his hand on her forehead like he was checking her temperature. Then he kept walking. By this time, I knew he was a monster or something even worse. I followed him into this grove, to the base of a big elm tree. I was about to summon some dryads to help me capture him when he turned and . . .'

Grover swallowed. 'Percy, his face. I couldn't make out his face because it kept shifting. Just looking at him made me sleepy. I said, "What are you doing?" He said, "Just having a look around. You should always scout a battlefield before the battle." I said something really smart like, "This forest is under my protection. You won't start any battles here!" And he laughed. He said, "You're lucky I'm saving my energy for the main event, little satyr. I'll just grant you a short nap. Pleasant dreams." And that's the last thing I remember.'

Nico exhaled. 'Grover, you met Morpheus, the god of dreams. You're lucky you *ever* woke up.'

[104]

'Two months,' Grover moaned. 'He put me to sleep for two months!'

I tried to wrap my mind around what this meant. Now it made sense why we hadn't been able to contact Grover all this time.

'Why didn't the nymphs try to wake you?' I asked.

Grover shrugged. 'Most nymphs aren't good with time. Two months for a tree – that's nothing. They probably didn't think anything was wrong.'

'We've got to figure out what Morpheus was doing in the park,' I said. 'I don't like this "main event" thing he mentioned.'

'He's working for Kronos,' Nico said. 'We know that already. A lot of the minor gods are. This just proves there's going to be an invasion. Percy, we have to get on with our plan.'

'Wait,' Grover said. 'What plan?'

We told him, and Grover started tugging at his leg fur.

'You're not serious,' he said. 'Not the Underworld again.'

'I'm not asking you to come, man,' I promised. 'I know you just woke up. But we need some music to open the door. Can you do it?'

Grover took out his reed pipes. 'I guess I could try. I know a few Nirvana tunes that can split rocks. But, Percy, are you sure you want to do this?'

'Please, man,' I said. 'It would mean a lot. For old times' sake?'

He whimpered. 'As I recall, in the old times we almost died a lot. But, okay, here goes nothing.'

He put his pipes to his lips and played a shrill, lively tune. The boulders trembled. A few more stanzas and they cracked open, revealing a triangular crevice.

I peered inside. Steps led down into the darkness. The air smelled of mildew and death. It brought back bad memories of my trip through the Labyrinth last year, but this tunnel felt even more dangerous. It led straight to the land of Hades, and that was almost always a one-way trip.

I turned to Grover. 'Thanks . . . I think.'

'Perrrrcy, is Kronos really going to invade?'

'I wish I could tell you better, but yeah. He will.'

I thought Grover might chew up his reed pipes in anxiety, but he straightened up and brushed off his T-shirt. I couldn't help thinking how different he looked from fat old Leneus. 'I've got to rally the nature spirits, then. Maybe we can help. I'll see if we can find this Morpheus!'

'Better tell Juniper you're okay, too.'

His eyes widened. 'Juniper! Oh, she's going to kill me!'

He started to run off, then scrambled back and gave me another hug. 'Be careful down there! Come back alive!'

Once he was gone, Nico and I roused Mrs O'Leary from her nap.

When she smelled the tunnel, she got excited and led the way down the steps. It was a pretty tight fit. I hoped she wouldn't get stuck. I couldn't imagine how much Drāno we'd need to unstick a hellhound wedged halfway down a tunnel to the Underworld.

'Ready?' Nico asked me. 'It'll be fine. Don't worry.'

He sounded like he was trying to convince himself.

I glanced up at the stars, wondering if I would ever see them again. Then we plunged into darkness.

The stairs went on forever — narrow, steep and slippery. It was completely dark except for the light of my sword. I tried to go slow, but Mrs O'Leary had other ideas. She bounded ahead, barking happily. The sound echoed through the tunnel like cannon shots, and I figured we would not be catching anybody by surprise once we reached the bottom.

Nico lagged behind, which I thought was strange.

'You okay?' I asked him.

'Fine.' What was that expression on his face — doubt? 'Just keep moving,' he said.

I didn't have much choice. I followed Mrs O'Leary into the depths. After another hour, I started to hear the roar of a river.

We emerged at the base of a cliff, on a plain of black volcanic sand. To our right, the River Styx gushed from the rocks and roared off in a cascade of rapids. To our left, far away in the gloom, fires burned on the ramparts of Erebos, the great black walls of Hades' kingdom.

I shuddered. I'd first been here when I was twelve, and only Annabeth and Grover's company had given me the courage to keep going. Nico wasn't going to be quite as helpful with the 'courage' thing. He looked pale and worried himself.

Only Mrs O'Leary acted happy. She ran along the beach, picked up a random human leg bone and romped back towards me. She dropped the bone at my feet and waited for me to throw it.

'Um, maybe later, girl.' I stared at the dark waters, trying to get up my nerve. 'So, Nico . . . how do we do this?'

'We have to go inside the gates first,' he said.

'But the river's right here.'

'I have to get something,' he said. 'It's the only way.'

He marched off without waiting.

I frowned. Nico hadn't mentioned anything about going inside the gates. But now that we were here I didn't know what else to do. Reluctantly, I followed him down the beach towards the big black gates.

Lines of the dead stood outside waiting to get in. It must've been a heavy day for funerals, because even the EZ-DEATH line was backed up.

'Woof!' Mrs O'Leary said. Before I could stop her she bounded towards the security checkpoint. Cerberus, the guard dog of Hades, appeared out of the gloom – a three-headed Rottweiler so big he made Mrs O'Leary look like a toy poodle. Cerberus was half-transparent, so he's really hard to see until he's close enough to kill you, but he acted like he didn't care about us. He was too busy saying hello to Mrs O'Leary.

'Mrs O'Leary, no!' I shouted at her. 'Don't sniff – oh, man.'

Nico smiled. Then he looked at me and his expression turned all serious again, like he'd remembered something unpleasant. 'Come on. They won't give us any trouble in the line. You're with me.'

I didn't like it, but we slipped through the security ghouls and into the Fields of Asphodel. I had to whistle for Mrs O'Leary three times before she left Cerberus alone and ran after us.

We hiked over black fields of grass dotted with black poplar trees. If I really died in a few days like the prophecy said, I might end up here forever, but I tried not to think about that.

Nico trudged ahead, bringing us closer and closer to the palace of Hades.

'Hey,' I said, 'we're inside the gates already. Where are we –'

Mrs O'Leary growled. A shadow appeared overhead – something dark, cold and stinking of death. It swooped down and landed in the top of a poplar tree.

Unfortunately, I recognized her. She had a shrivelled face, a horrible blue knitted hat and a crumpled velvet dress. Leathery bat wings sprang from her back. Her feet had sharp talons, and in her brass-clawed hands she held a flaming whip and a paisley handbag.

'Mrs Dodds,' I said.

She bared her fangs. 'Welcome back, honey.'

Her two sisters – the other Furies – swooped down and settled next to her in the branches of the poplar.

'You know Alecto?' Nico asked me.

'If you mean the hag in the middle, yeah,' I said. 'She was my maths teacher.'

Nico nodded, like this didn't surprise him. He looked up at the Furies and took a deep breath. 'I've done what my father asked. Take us to the palace.'

I tensed. 'Wait a second, Nico. What do you –'

'I'm afraid this is my new lead, Percy. My father promised me information about my family, but he wants to see you before we try the river. I'm sorry.'

'You *tricked* me?' I was so mad I couldn't think. I lunged

at him, but the Furies were fast. Two of them swooped down and plucked me up by the arms. My sword fell out of my hand and before I knew it I was dangling twenty metres in the air.

'Oh, don't struggle, honey,' my old maths teacher cackled in my ear. 'I'd hate to drop you.'

Mrs O'Leary barked angrily and jumped, trying to reach me, but we were too high.

'Tell Mrs O'Leary to behave,' Nico warned. He was hovering near me in the clutches of the third Fury. 'I don't want her to get hurt, Percy. My father is waiting. He just wants to talk.'

I wanted to tell Mrs O'Leary to attack Nico, but it wouldn't have done any good, and Nico was right about one thing: my dog could get hurt if she tried to pick a fight with the Furies.

I gritted my teeth. 'Mrs O'Leary, down! It's okay, girl.'

She whimpered and turned in circles, looking up at me.

'All right, traitor,' I growled at Nico. 'You've got your prize. Take me to the stupid palace.'

Alecto dropped me like a sack of turnips in the middle of the palace garden.

It was beautiful in a creepy way. Skeletal white trees grew from marble basins. Flowerbeds overflowed with golden plants and gemstones. A pair of thrones, one bone and one silver, sat on the balcony with a view of the Fields of Asphodel. It would've been a nice place to spend a Saturday morning except for the sulphurous smell and the cries of tortured souls in the distance.

Skeletal warriors guarded the only exit. They wore tattered U.S. Army desert combat fatigues and carried M16s.

The third Fury deposited Nico next to me. Then all three of them settled on the top of the skeletal throne. I resisted the urge to strangle Nico. They'd only stop me. I'd have to wait for my revenge.

I stared at the empty thrones, waiting for something to happen. Then the air shimmered. Three figures appeared – Hades and Persephone on their thrones and an older woman standing between them. They seemed to be in the middle of an argument.

'– told you he was a bum!' the older woman said.

'Mother!' Persephone replied.

'We have visitors!' Hades barked. 'Please!'

Hades, one of my least favourite gods, smoothed his black robes, which were covered with the terrified faces of the damned. He had pale skin and the intense eyes of a madman.

'Percy Jackson,' he said with satisfaction. 'At last.'

Queen Persephone studied me curiously. I'd seen her once before in the winter but now in the summer she looked like a totally different goddess. She had lustrous black hair and warm brown eyes. Her dress shimmered with colours. Flower patterns in the fabric changed and bloomed – roses, tulips, honeysuckle.

The woman standing between them was obviously Persephone's mother. She had the same hair and eyes, but looked older and sterner. Her dress was golden, the colour of a wheat field. Her hair was woven with dried grasses so it reminded me of a wicker basket. I figured if somebody lit a match next to her, she'd be in serious trouble.

'Hmmph,' the older woman said. 'Demigods. Just what we need.'

Next to me, Nico knelt. I wished I had my sword so I could cut his stupid head off. Unfortunately, Riptide was still out in the fields somewhere.

'Father,' Nico said. 'I have done as you asked.'

'Took you long enough,' Hades grumbled. 'Your sister would've done a better job.'

Nico lowered his head. If I hadn't been so mad at the little creep, I might've felt sorry for him.

I glared up at the god of the dead. 'What do you want, Hades?'

'To talk, of course.' The god twisted his mouth in a cruel smile. 'Didn't Nico tell you?'

'So this whole quest was a lie. Nico brought me down here to get me killed.'

'Oh, no,' Hades said. 'I'm afraid Nico was quite sincere about wanting to help you. The boy is as honest as he is dense. I simply convinced him to take a small detour and bring you here first.'

'Father,' Nico said, 'you promised that Percy would not be harmed. You said if I brought him, you would tell me about my past – about my mother.'

Queen Persephone sighed dramatically. 'Can we *please* not talk about *that woman* in my presence?'

'I'm sorry, my dove,' Hades said. 'I had to promise the boy something.'

The older lady harrumphed. 'I warned you, daughter. This scoundrel Hades is no good. You could've married the god of doctors or the god of lawyers, but *noooo*. You had to eat the pomegranate.'

'Mother –'

'And get stuck in the Underworld!'

'Mother, please –'

'And here it is August, and do you come home like you're supposed to? Do you ever think about your poor lonely mother?'

'DEMETER!' Hades shouted. 'That is enough. You are a guest in my house.'

'Oh, a house is it?' she said. 'You call this dump a house? Make my daughter live in this dark, damp –'

'I told you,' Hades said, grinding his teeth, 'there's a *war* in the world above. You and Persephone are better off here with me.'

'Excuse me,' I broke in, 'but if you're going to kill me, could you just get on with it?'

All three gods looked at me.

'Well, this one has an attitude,' Demeter observed.

'Indeed,' Hades agreed. 'I'd love to kill him.'

'Father!' Nico said. 'You promised!'

'Husband, we talked about this,' Persephone chided. 'You can't go around incinerating every hero. Besides, he's brave. I like that.'

Hades rolled his eyes. 'You liked that Orpheus fellow, too. Look how well that turned out. Let me kill him, just a little bit.'

'Father, you promised!' Nico said. 'You said you only wanted to talk to him! You said if I brought him, you'd explain.'

Hades glowered, smoothing the folds of his robes.

'And so I shall. Your mother — what can I tell you? She was a wonderful woman.' He glanced uncomfortably at Persephone. 'Forgive me, my dear. I mean for a mortal, of course. Her name was Maria di Angelo. She was from Venice, but her father was a diplomat in Washington, D.C. That's where I met her. When you and your sister were young, it was a bad time to be children of Hades. World War II was brewing. A few of my, ah, *other* children were leading the losing side. I thought it best to put you two out of harm's way.'

'That's why you hid us in the Lotus Casino?'

Hades shrugged. 'You didn't age. You didn't realize time was passing. I waited for the right time to bring you out.'

'But what happened to our mother? Why don't I remember her?'

'Not important,' Hades snapped.

'*What?* Of course it's important. And you had other children — why were we the only ones who were sent away? And who was the lawyer who got us out?'

Hades gritted his teeth. 'You would do well to listen more and talk less, boy. As for the lawyer . . .'

Hades snapped his fingers. On top of his throne, the Fury Alecto began to change until she was a middle-aged man in a pinstriped suit with a briefcase. She — he — looked strange crouching at Hades' shoulder.

'You!' Nico said.

The Fury cackled. 'I do lawyers and teachers very well!'

Nico was trembling. 'But why did you free us from the casino?'

'You know why,' Hades said. 'This idiot son of Poseidon cannot be allowed to be the child of the prophecy.'

I plucked a ruby off the nearest plant and threw it at Hades. It sank harmlessly into his robe. 'You should be helping Olympus!' I said. 'All the other gods are fighting Typhon, and you're just sitting here –'

'Waiting things out,' Hades finished. 'Yes, that's correct. When's the last time Olympus ever helped me, half-blood? When's the last time a child of *mine* was ever welcomed as a hero? Bah! Why should I rush out and help them? I'll stay here with my forces intact.'

'And when Kronos comes after you?'

'Let him try. He'll be weakened. And my son here, Nico –' Hades looked at him with distaste. 'Well, he's not much now, I'll grant you. It would've been better if Bianca had lived. But give him four more years of training. We can hold out that long, surely. Nico will turn sixteen, as the prophecy says, and then *he* will make the decision that will save the world. And I will be king of the gods.'

'You're crazy,' I said. 'Kronos will crush you, right after he finishes pulverizing Olympus.'

Hades spread his hands. 'Well, you'll get a chance to find out, half-blood. Because you'll be waiting out this war in my dungeons.'

'No!' Nico said. 'Father, that wasn't our agreement. And you haven't told me everything!'

'I've told you all you need to know,' Hades said. 'As for our agreement, I spoke with Jackson. I did not harm him. You got your information. If you wanted a better deal, you should've made me swear on the Styx. Now go to your room!' He waved his hand and Nico vanished.

'That boy needs to eat more,' Demeter grumbled. 'He's too skinny. He needs more cereal.'

Persephone rolled her eyes. 'Mother, enough with the cereal. My lord Hades, are you sure we can't let this little hero go? He's awfully brave.'

'No, my dear. I've spared his life. That's enough.'

I was sure she was going to stand up for me. The brave, beautiful Persephone was going to get me out of this.

She shrugged indifferently. 'Fine. What's for breakfast? I'm starving.'

'Cereal,' Demeter said.

'*Mother!*' The two women disappeared in a swirl of flowers and wheat.

'Don't feel too bad, Percy Jackson,' Hades said. 'My ghosts keep me well informed of Kronos's plans. I can assure you that you had no chance to stop him in time. By tonight, it will be too late for your precious Mount Olympus. The trap will be sprung.'

'What trap?' I demanded. 'If you know about it, do something! At least let me tell the other gods!'

Hades smiled. 'You are spirited. I'll give you credit for that. Have fun in my dungeon. We'll check on you again in – oh, fifty or sixty years.'

8   I TAKE THE WORST BATH EVER

My sword reappeared in my pocket.

Yeah, great timing. Now I could attack the walls all I wanted. My cell had no bars, no windows, not even a door. The skeletal guards shoved me straight through a wall and it became solid behind me. I wasn't sure if the room was airtight. Probably. Hades' dungeon was meant for dead people, and they don't breathe. So forget fifty or sixty years. I'd be dead in fifty or sixty minutes. Meanwhile, if Hades wasn't lying, some big trap was going to be sprung in New York by the end of the day, and there was absolutely nothing I could do about it.

I sat on the cold stone floor feeling miserable.

I don't remember dozing off. Then again it must've been about seven in the morning, mortal time, and I'd been through a lot.

I dreamed I was on the porch of Rachel's beach house in St Thomas. The sun was rising over the Caribbean. Dozens of wooded islands dotted the sea and white sails cut across the water. The smell of salt air made me wonder if I would ever see the ocean again.

Rachel's parents sat at the patio table while a personal chef fixed them omelettes. Mr Dare was dressed in a white linen suit. He was reading the *Wall Street Journal*. The lady across the table was probably Mrs Dare, though all I could

[117]

see of her were hot pink fingernails and the cover of *Condé Nast Traveller*. Why she'd be reading about vacations while she was on vacation, I wasn't sure.

Rachel stood at the porch railing and sighed. She wore Bermuda shorts and her van Gogh T-shirt. (Yeah, Rachel was trying to teach me about art, but don't get too impressed. I only remembered the dude's name because he cut his ear off.)

I wondered if she were thinking about me, and how much it sucked that I wasn't with them on vacation. I know that's what *I* was thinking.

Then the scene changed. I was in St Louis, standing downtown under the Arch. I'd been there before. In fact I'd almost fallen to my death there before.

Over the city, a thunderstorm boiled – a wall of absolute black with lightning streaking across the sky. A few blocks away, swarms of emergency vehicles gathered with their lights flashing. A column of dust rose from a mound of rubble, which I realized was a collapsed skyscraper.

A nearby reporter was yelling into her microphone: 'Officials are describing this as a structural failure, Dan, though no one seems to know if it is related to the storm conditions.'

Wind whipped her hair. The temperature was dropping rapidly – like ten degrees just since I'd been standing there.

'Thankfully the building had been abandoned for demolition,' she said. 'But police have evacuated all nearby buildings for fear the collapse might trigger –'

She faltered as a mighty groan cut through the sky. A blast of lightning hit the centre of the darkness. The entire city shook. The air glowed and every hair on my body stood up. The blast was so powerful I knew it could only be one thing: Zeus's master bolt. It should have vaporized its target, but the dark cloud only staggered backwards. A smoky fist appeared out of the clouds. It smashed another tower and the whole thing collapsed like children's blocks.

The reporter screamed. People ran through the streets. Emergency lights flashed. I saw a streak of silver in the sky – a chariot pulled by reindeer, but it wasn't Santa Claus driving. It was Artemis riding the storm, shooting shafts of moonlight into the darkness. A fiery golden comet crossed her path – maybe her brother, Apollo.

One thing was clear: Typhon had made it to the Mississippi River. He was halfway across the U.S., leaving destruction in his wake, and the gods were barely slowing him down.

The mountain of darkness loomed above me. A foot the size of Yankee Stadium was about to smash me when a voice hissed: '*Percy!*'

I lunged out blindly. Before I was fully awake, I had Nico pinned to the floor of the cell with the edge of my sword at his throat.

'Want – to – rescue,' he choked.

Anger woke me up fast. 'Oh, yeah? And why should I trust you?'

'No – choice?' he gagged.

I wished he hadn't said something logical like that. I let him go.

Nico curled into a ball and made retching sounds while his throat recovered. Finally he got to his feet, eyeing my sword warily. His own blade was sheathed. I suppose if he'd wanted to kill me, he could've done it while I slept. Still, I didn't trust him.

'We have to get out of here,' he said.

'Why?' I said. 'Does your dad want to *talk* to me again?'

He winced. 'Percy, I swear on the River Styx, I didn't know what he was planning.'

'You know what your dad is like!'

'He tricked me. He promised –' Nico held up his hands. 'Look . . . right now, we need to leave. I put the guards to sleep, but it won't last.'

I wanted to strangle him again. Unfortunately, he was right. We didn't have time to argue and I couldn't escape on my own. He pointed at the wall. A whole section vanished, revealing a corridor.

'Come on.' Nico led the way.

I wished I had Annabeth's invisibility hat, but as it turned out I didn't need it. Every time we came to a skeleton guard, Nico just pointed at it and its glowing eyes dimmed. Unfortunately, the more Nico did it, the more tired he seemed. We walked through a maze of corridors filled with guards. By the time we reached a kitchen staffed by skeletal cooks and servants, I was practically carrying Nico. He managed to put all the dead to sleep but nearly passed out himself. I dragged him out the servants' entrance and into the Fields of Asphodel.

I almost felt relieved until I heard the sound of bronze gongs high in the castle.

'Alarms,' Nico murmured sleepily.

'What do we do?'

He yawned then frowned like he was trying to remember. 'How about . . . run?'

Running with a drowsy child of Hades was more like doing a three-legged race with a life-sized rag doll. I lugged him along, holding my sword in front of me. The spirits of the dead made way like the celestial bronze was a blazing fire.

The sound of gongs rolled across the fields. Ahead loomed the walls of Erebos, but the longer we walked the further away they seemed. I was about to collapse from exhaustion when I heard a familiar 'WOOOOOF!'

Mrs O'Leary bounded out of nowhere and ran circles around us, ready to play.

'Good girl!' I said. 'Can you give us a ride to the Styx?'

The word 'Styx' got her excited. She probably thought I meant *sticks*. She jumped a few times, chased her tail just to teach it who was boss and then calmed down enough for me to push Nico onto her back. I climbed aboard and she raced towards the gates. She leaped straight over the EZ-DEATH line, sending guards sprawling and causing more alarms to blare. Cerberus barked, but he sounded more excited than angry, like: *Can I play, too?*

Fortunately, he didn't follow us, and Mrs O'Leary kept running. She didn't stop until we were far upriver and the fires of Erebos had disappeared in the murk.

Nico slid off Mrs O'Leary's back and crumpled in a heap on the black sand.

I took out a square of ambrosia – part of the emergency

god-food I always kept with me. It was a little bashed up, but Nico chewed it.

'Uh,' he mumbled. 'Better.'

'Your powers drain you too much,' I noted.

He nodded sleepily. 'With great power . . . comes great need to take a nap. Wake me up later.'

'Whoa, zombie dude.' I caught him before he could pass out again. 'We're at the river. You need to tell me what to do.'

I fed him the last of my ambrosia, which was a little dangerous. The stuff can heal demigods, but it can also burn us to ashes if we eat too much. Fortunately, it seemed to do the trick. Nico shook his head a few times and struggled to his feet.

'My father will be coming soon,' he said. 'We should hurry.'

The River Styx's current swirled with strange objects – broken toys, ripped-up college diplomas, wilted homecoming corsages – all the dreams people had thrown away as they'd passed from life into death. Looking at the black water, I could think of about three million places I'd rather swim.

'So . . . I just jump in?'

'You have to prepare yourself first,' Nico said, 'or the river will destroy you. It will burn away your body and soul.'

'Sounds fun,' I muttered.

'This is no joke,' Nico warned. 'There is only one way to stay anchored to your mortal life. You have to . . .'

He glanced behind me and his eyes widened. I turned and found myself face to face with a Greek warrior.

For a second, I thought he was Ares, because this guy looked exactly like the god of war – tall and buff, with a cruel scarred face and closely shaved black hair. He wore a white tunic and bronze armour. He held a plumed war helm under his arm. But his eyes were human – pale green like a shallow sea – and a bloody arrow stuck out of his left calf, just above the ankle.

I stunk at Greek names, but even I knew the greatest warrior of all time, who had died from a wounded heel.

'Achilles,' I said.

The ghost nodded. 'I warned the other one not to follow my path. Now I will warn you.'

'Luke? You spoke with Luke?'

'Do not do this,' he said. 'It will make you powerful. But it will also make you weak. Your prowess in combat will be beyond any mortal, but your weaknesses, your failings will increase as well.'

'You mean I'll have a bad heel?' I said. 'Couldn't I just, like, wear something besides sandals? No offence.'

He stared down at his bloody foot. 'The heel is only my *physical* weakness, demigod. My mother, Thetis, held me there when she dipped me in the Styx. What really killed me was my own arrogance. Beware! Turn back!'

He meant it. I could hear the regret and bitterness in his voice. He was honestly trying to save me from a terrible fate.

Then again, Luke had been here, and he hadn't turned back.

That's why Luke had been able to host the spirit of Kronos without his body disintegrating. This is how he'd prepared himself, and why he seemed impossible to kill.

He had bathed in the River Styx and taken on the powers of the greatest mortal hero, Achilles. He was invincible.

'I have to,' I said. 'Otherwise I don't stand a chance.'

Achilles lowered his head. 'Let the gods witness I tried. Hero, if you must do this, concentrate on your mortal point. Imagine one spot of your body that will remain vulnerable. This is the point where your soul will anchor your body to the world. It will be your greatest weakness, but also your only hope. No man may be completely invulnerable. Lose sight of what keeps you mortal, and the River Styx will burn you to ashes. You will cease to exist.'

'I don't suppose you could tell me Luke's mortal point?'

He scowled. 'Prepare yourself, foolish boy. Whether you survive this or not, you have sealed your doom!'

With that happy thought, he vanished.

'Percy,' Nico said, 'maybe he's right.'

'This was *your* idea.'

'I know, but now that we're here –'

'Just wait on the shore. If anything happens to me . . . Well, maybe Hades will get his wish, and you'll be the child of the prophecy after all.'

He didn't look pleased about that, but I didn't care.

Before I could change my mind, I concentrated on the small of my back – a tiny point just opposite my navel. It was well defended when I wore my armour. It would be hard to hit by accident, and few enemies would aim for it on purpose. No place was perfect, but this seemed right to me, and a lot more dignified than, like, my armpit or something.

I pictured a string – a bungee cord connecting me to the world from the small of my back. And I stepped into the river.

Imagine jumping into a pit of boiling acid. Now multiply that pain times fifty. You still won't be close to understanding what it felt like to swim in the Styx. I planned to walk in slow and courageous like a real hero. As soon as the water touched my legs, my muscles turned to jelly and I fell face first into the current.

I submerged completely. For the first time in my life, I couldn't breathe underwater. I finally understood the panic of drowning. Every nerve in my body burned. I was dissolving in the water. I saw faces – Rachel, Grover, Tyson, my mother – but they faded as soon as they appeared.

'Percy,' my mom said. 'I give you my blessing.'

'Be safe, brother!' Tyson pleaded.

'Enchiladas!' Grover said. I wasn't sure where that came from, but it didn't seem to help much.

I was losing the fight. The pain was too much. My hands and feet were melting into water, my soul being ripped from my body. I couldn't remember who I was. The pain of Kronos's scythe had been nothing compared to this.

The cord, a familiar voice said. *Remember your lifeline, dummy!*

Suddenly there was a tug in my lower back. The current pulled at me, but it wasn't carrying me away any more. I imagined the string in my back, keeping me tied to the shore.

'Hold on, Seaweed Brain.' It was Annabeth's voice, much clearer now. 'You're not getting away from me that easily.'

[125]

The cord strengthened.

I could see Annabeth now – standing barefoot above me on the canoe-lake pier. I'd fallen out of my canoe. That was it. She was reaching out her hand to haul me up, and she was trying not to laugh. She wore her orange camp T-shirt and jeans. Her hair was tucked up in her Yankees cap, which was strange, because that should have made her invisible.

'You are such an idiot sometimes.' She smiled. 'Come on. Take my hand.'

Memories came flooding back to me – sharper and more colourful. I stopped dissolving. My name was Percy Jackson. I reached up and took Annabeth's hand.

Suddenly I burst out of the river. I collapsed on the sand and Nico scrambled back in surprise.

'Are you okay?' he stammered. 'Your skin. Oh, gods. You're hurt!'

My arms were bright red. I felt like every inch of my body had been broiled over a slow flame.

I looked around for Annabeth, though I knew she wasn't here. It had seemed so real.

'I'm fine . . . I think.' The colour of my skin turned back to normal. The pain subsided. Mrs O'Leary came up and sniffed me with concern. Apparently, I smelled really interesting.

'Do you feel stronger?' Nico asked.

Before I could decide *what* I felt, a voice boomed, 'THERE!'

An army of the dead marched towards us. A hundred skeletal Roman legionnaires led the way with shields and spears. Behind them came an equal number of British redcoats with bayonets fixed. In the middle of the host, Hades himself rode a black-and-gold chariot pulled by nightmare horses, their eyes and manes smouldering with fire.

'You will not escape me this time, Percy Jackson!' Hades bellowed. 'Destroy him!'

'Father, no!' Nico shouted, but it was too late. The front line of Roman zombies lowered their spears and advanced.

Mrs O'Leary growled and got ready to pounce. Maybe that's what set me off. I didn't want them hurting my dog. Plus I was tired of Hades being a big bully. If I were going to die, I might as well go down fighting.

I yelled and the River Styx exploded. A black tidal wave smashed into the legionnaires. Spears and shields flew everywhere. Roman zombies began to dissolve, smoke coming off their bronze helmets.

The redcoats lowered their bayonets, but I didn't wait for them. I charged.

It was stupidest thing I've ever done. A hundred muskets fired at me – point blank. All of them missed. I crashed into their line and started hacking with Riptide. Bayonets jabbed. Swords slashed. Guns reloaded and fired. Nothing touched me.

I whirled through the ranks, slashing redcoats to dust one after the other. My mind went on autopilot: stab, dodge, cut, deflect, roll. Riptide was no longer a sword. It was an arc of pure destruction.

I broke through the enemy line and leaped into the black chariot. Hades raised his staff. A bolt of dark energy shot towards me, but I deflected it off my blade and slammed into him. The god and I both tumbled out of the chariot.

The next thing I knew, my knee was planted on Hades' chest. I was holding the collar of his royal robes in one fist, and the tip of my sword was poised right over his face.

Silence. The army did nothing to defend their master. I glanced back and realized why. There was nothing left of them but weapons in the sand and piles of smoking, empty uniforms. I had destroyed them all.

Hades swallowed. 'Now, Jackson, listen here . . .'

He was immortal. There was no way I could kill him, but gods can be wounded. I knew that firsthand, and I figured a sword in the face wouldn't feel too good.

'Just because I'm a nice person,' I snarled, 'I'll let you go. But first, tell me about that trap!'

Hades melted into nothing, leaving me holding empty black robes.

I cursed and got to my feet, breathing heavily. Now that the danger was over, I realized how tired I was. Every muscle in my body ached. I looked down at my clothes. They were slashed to pieces and full of bullet holes, but I was fine. Not a mark on me.

Nico's mouth hung open. 'You just . . . with a sword . . . you just –'

'I think the river thing worked,' I said.

'Oh, gee,' he said sarcastically. '*You think?*'

Mrs O'Leary barked happily and wagged her tail. She bounded around, sniffing empty uniforms and hunting for bones. I lifted Hades' robe. I could still see the tormented faces shimmering in the fabric.

I walked to the edge of the river. 'Be free.'

I dropped the robe in the water and watched as it swirled away, dissolving in the current.

'Go back to your father,' I told Nico. 'Tell him he owes me for letting him go. Find out what's going to happen to Mount Olympus and convince him to help.'

Nico stared at me. 'I – I can't. He'll hate me now. I mean . . . even more.'

'You have to,' I said. 'You owe me, too.'

His ears turned red. 'Percy, I told you I was sorry. Please . . . let me come with you. I want to fight.'

'You'll be more help down here.'

'You mean you don't trust me any more,' he said miserably.

I didn't answer. I didn't know what I meant. I was too stunned by what I'd just done in battle to think clearly.

'Just go back to your father,' I said, trying not to sound too harsh. 'Work on him. You're the only person who might be able to get him to listen.'

'That's a depressing thought.' Nico sighed. 'All right. I'll do my best. Besides, he's still hiding something from me about my mom. Maybe I can find out what.'

'Good luck. Now Mrs O'Leary and I have to go.'

'Where?' Nico said.

I looked at the cave entrance and thought about the long climb back to the world of the living. 'To get this war started. It's time I found Luke.'

9   TWO SNAKES SAVE MY LIFE

I love New York. You can pop out of the Underworld in Central Park, hail a taxi, head down Fifth Avenue with a giant hellhound loping along behind you and nobody even looks at you funny.

Of course, the Mist helped. People probably couldn't see Mrs O'Leary, or maybe they thought she was a large, loud, very friendly truck.

I took the risk of using my mom's cell phone to call Annabeth for the second time. I'd called her once from the tunnel, but only reached her voice mail. I'd had surprisingly good reception, seeing as I was at the mythological centre of the world and all, but I didn't want to see what my mom's roaming charges were going to be.

This time, Annabeth picked up.

'Hey,' I said. 'You get my message?'

'Percy, where have you been? Your message said almost nothing! We've been worried sick!'

'I'll fill you in later,' I said, though how I was going to do that I had no idea. 'Where are you?'

'We're on our way like you asked, almost to the Queens Midtown Tunnel. But, Percy, what are you planning? We've left the camp virtually undefended and there's no way the gods –'

'Trust me,' I said. 'I'll see you there.'

I hung up. My hands were trembling. I wasn't sure if it was a leftover reaction from my dip in the Styx, or anticipation of what I was about to do. If this didn't work, being invulnerable wasn't going to save me from getting blasted to bits.

It was late afternoon when the taxi dropped me at the Empire State Building. Mrs O'Leary bounded up and down Fifth Avenue, licking cabs and sniffing hot-dog carts. Nobody seemed to notice her, although people did swerve away and look confused when she came close.

I whistled her to heel as three white vans pulled up to the kerb. They said *Delphi Strawberry Service*, which was the cover name for Camp Half-Blood. I'd never seen all three vans in the same place at once, though I knew they shuttled our fresh produce into the city.

The first van was driven by Argus, our many-eyed security chief. The other two were driven by harpies, which are basically demonic human/chicken hybrids with bad attitudes. We used the harpies mostly for cleaning camp, but they did pretty well in midtown traffic, too.

The doors slid open. A bunch of campers climbed out, some of them looking a little green from the long drive. I was glad so many had come: Pollux, Silena Beauregard, the Stoll brothers, Michael Yew, Jake Mason, Katie Gardner and Annabeth, along with most of their siblings. Chiron came out of the van last. His horse half was compacted into his magic wheelchair, so he used the handicap lift. The Ares cabin wasn't here, but I tried not to get too angry about that. Clarisse was a stubborn idiot. End of story.

I did a head count: forty campers in all.

Not many to fight a war, but it was still the largest group of half-bloods I'd ever seen gathered in one place outside camp. Everyone looked nervous, and I understood why. We were probably sending out so much demigod aura that every monster in the north-east United States knew we were here.

As I looked at their faces – all these campers I'd known for so many summers – a nagging voice whispered in my mind: *One of them is a spy.*

But I couldn't dwell on that. They were my friends. I needed them.

Then I remembered Kronos's evil smile. *You can't count on friends. They will always let you down.*

Annabeth came up to me. She was dressed in black camouflage with her celestial bronze knife strapped to her arm and her laptop bag slung over her shoulder – ready for stabbing or surfing the internet, whichever came first.

She frowned. 'What is it?'

'What's what?' I asked.

'You're looking at me funny.'

I realized I was thinking about my strange vision of Annabeth pulling me out of the Styx River. 'It's, uh, nothing.' I turned to the rest of the group. 'Thanks for coming, everybody. Chiron, after you.'

My old mentor shook his head. 'I came to wish you luck, my boy. But I make it a point never to visit Olympus unless I am summoned.'

'But you're our leader.'

He smiled. 'I am your trainer, your teacher. That is not the same as being your leader. I will go gather what allies I can. It may not be too late to convince my brother centaurs

[132]

to help. Meanwhile, *you* called the campers here, Percy. *You* are the leader.'

I wanted to protest, but everybody was looking at me expectantly, even Annabeth.

I took a deep breath. 'Okay, like I told Annabeth on the phone, something bad is going to happen by tonight. Some kind of trap. We've got to get an audience with Zeus and convince him to defend the city. Remember, we can't take no for an answer.'

I asked Argus to watch Mrs O'Leary, which neither of them looked happy about.

Chiron shook my hand. 'You'll do well, Percy. Just remember your strengths and beware your weaknesses.'

It sounded eerily close to what Achilles had told me. Then I remembered Chiron had *taught* Achilles. That didn't exactly reassure me, but I nodded and tried to give him a confident smile.

'Let's go,' I told the campers.

A security guard was sitting behind the desk in the lobby, reading a big black book with a flower on the cover. He glanced up when we all filed in with our weapons and armour clanking. 'School group? We're about to close up.'

'No,' I said. 'Six-hundredth floor.'

He checked us out. His eyes were pale blue and his head was completely bald. I couldn't tell if he was human or not, but he seemed to notice our weapons, so I guess he wasn't fooled by the Mist.

'There is no six-hundredth floor, kid.' He said it like it was a required line he didn't believe. 'Move along.'

I leaned across the desk. 'Forty demigods attract an

awful lot of monsters. You really want us hanging out in your lobby?'

He thought about that. Then he hit a buzzer and the security gate swung open. 'Make it quick.'

'You don't want us going through the metal detectors,' I added.

'Um, no,' he agreed. 'Elevator on the right. I guess you know the way.'

I tossed him a golden drachma and we marched through.

We decided it would take two trips to get everybody up in the elevator. I went with the first group. Different elevator music was playing since my last visit – that old disco song 'Stayin' Alive'. A terrifying image flashed through my mind of Apollo in bellbottom trousers and a slinky silk shirt.

I was glad when the elevator doors finally dinged open. In front of us, a path of floating stones led through the clouds up to Mount Olympus, hovering two thousand metres over Manhattan.

I'd seen Olympus several times, but it still took my breath away. The mansions glittered gold and white against the sides of the mountain. Gardens bloomed on a hundred terraces. Scented smoke rose from braziers that lined the winding streets. And right at the top of the snow-capped crest rose the main palace of the gods. It looked as majestic as ever, but something seemed wrong. Then I realized the mountain was silent – no music, no voices, no laughter.

Annabeth studied me. 'You look . . . different,' she decided. 'Where exactly did you go?'

The elevator doors opened again and the second group of half-bloods joined us.

'Tell you later,' I said. 'Come on.'

We made our way across the sky bridge into the streets of Olympus. The shops were closed. The parks were empty. A couple of muses sat on a bench strumming flaming lyres, but their hearts didn't seem to be into it. A lone Cyclops swept the street with an uprooted oak tree. A minor godling spotted us from a balcony and ducked inside, closing his shutters.

We passed under a big marble archway with statues of Zeus and Hera on either side. Annabeth made a face at the queen of the gods.

'Hate her,' she muttered.

'Has she been cursing you or something?' I asked. Last year Annabeth had got on Hera's bad side, but Annabeth hadn't really talked about it since.

'Just little stuff so far,' she said. 'Her sacred animal is the cow, right?'

'Right.'

'So she sends cows after me.'

I tried not to smile. 'Cows? In San Francisco?'

'Oh, yeah. Usually I don't see them, but the cows leave me little presents all over the place – in our backyard, on the sidewalk, in the school hallways. I have to be careful where I step.'

'Look!' Pollux cried, pointing towards the horizon. 'What is *that*?'

We all froze. Blue lights were streaking across the evening sky towards Olympus like tiny comets. They seemed to be coming from all over the city, heading straight towards the mountain. As they got close, they fizzled out. We watched them for several minutes and they didn't seem to do any damage, but still it was strange.

'Like infrared scopes,' Michael Yew muttered. 'We're being targeted.'

'Let's get to the palace,' I said.

No one was guarding the hall of the gods. The gold-and-silver doors stood wide open. Our footsteps echoed as we walked into the throne room.

Of course, 'room' doesn't really cover it. The place was the size of Madison Square Garden. High above, the blue ceiling glittered with constellations. Twelve giant empty thrones stood in a U around a hearth. In one corner, a house-sized globe of water hovered in the air, and inside swam my old friend the Ophiotaurus – half-cow, half-serpent.

'Moooo!' he said happily, turning in a circle.

Despite all the serious stuff going on, I had to smile. Two years ago we'd spent a lot of time trying to save the Ophiotaurus from the Titans, and I'd got kind of fond of him. He seemed to like me, too, even though I'd originally thought he was a girl and named him Bessie.

'Hey, man,' I said. 'They treating you okay?'

'Mooo,' Bessie answered.

We walked towards the thrones and a woman's voice said, 'Hello again, Percy Jackson. You and your friends are welcome.'

Hestia stood by the hearth, poking the flames with a stick. She wore the same kind of simple brown dress as she had before, but she was a grown woman now.

I bowed. 'Lady Hestia.'

My friends followed my example.

Hestia regarded me with her red glowing eyes. 'I see you went through with your plan. You bear the curse of Achilles.'

The other campers started muttering among themselves: 'What did she say?' 'What about Achilles?'

'You must be careful,' Hestia warned me. 'You gained much on your journey. But you are still blind to the most important truth. Perhaps a glimpse is in order.'

Annabeth nudged me. 'Um . . . what is she talking about?'

I stared into Hestia's eyes and an image rushed into my mind: I saw a dark alley between red-brick warehouses. A sign above one of the doors read: RICHMOND IRON WORKS.

Two half-bloods crouched in the shadows – a boy about fourteen and a girl about twelve. I realized with a start that the boy was Luke. The girl was Thalia, daughter of Zeus. I was seeing a scene from back in the days when they were on the run, before Grover found them.

Luke carried a bronze knife. Thalia had her spear and shield of terror, Aegis. Luke and Thalia both looked hungry and lean, with wild animal eyes, like they were used to being attacked.

'Are you sure?' Thalia asked.

Luke nodded. 'Something down here. I sense it.'

A rumble echoed from the alley, like someone had banged on a sheet of metal. The half-bloods crept forward.

Old crates were stacked on a loading dock. Thalia and Luke approached with their weapons ready. A curtain of corrugated tin quivered as if something was behind it.

Thalia glanced at Luke. He counted silently: *One, two,*

three! He ripped away the tin and a little girl flew at him with a hammer.

'Whoa!' Luke said.

The girl had tangled blonde hair and was wearing flannel pyjamas. She couldn't have been more than seven, but she would've brained Luke if he hadn't been so fast.

He grabbed her wrist and the hammer skittered across the cement.

The little girl fought and kicked. 'No more monsters! Go away!'

'It's okay!' Luke struggled to hold her. 'Thalia, put your shield down. You're scaring her.'

Thalia tapped Aegis and it shrank into a silver bracelet. 'Hey, it's all right,' she said. 'We're not going to hurt you. I'm Thalia. This is Luke.'

'Monsters!'

'No,' Luke promised. 'But we know all about monsters. We fight them, too.'

Slowly, the girl stopped kicking. She studied Luke and Thalia with large intelligent grey eyes.

'You're like me?' she said suspiciously.

'Yeah,' Luke said. 'We're . . . well, it's hard to explain, but we're monster-fighters. Where's your family?'

'My family hates me,' the girl said. 'They don't want me. I ran away.'

Thalia and Luke locked eyes. I knew they both related to what she was saying.

'What's your name, kiddo?' Thalia asked.

'Annabeth.'

Luke smiled. 'Nice name. I tell you what, Annabeth — you're pretty fierce. We could use a fighter like you.'

Annabeth's eyes widened. 'You could?'

'Oh, yeah.' Luke turned his knife and offered her the handle. 'How'd you like a real monster-slaying weapon? This is celestial bronze. Works a lot better than a hammer.'

Maybe under most circumstances, offering a seven-year-old kid a knife would not be a good idea, but when you're a half-blood regular rules kind of go out of the window. Annabeth gripped the hilt.

'Knives are only for the bravest and quickest fighters,' Luke explained. 'They don't have the reach or power of a sword, but they're easy to conceal and they can find weak spots in your enemy's armour. It takes a clever warrior to use a knife. I have a feeling you're pretty clever.'

Annabeth stared at him with adoration. 'I am!'

Thalia grinned. 'We'd better get going, Annabeth. We have a safe house on the James River. We'll get you some clothes and food.'

'You're – you're not going to take me back to my family?' she said. 'Promise?'

Luke put his hand on her shoulder. 'You're part of *our* family now. And I promise I won't let anything hurt you. I'm *not* going to fail you like our families did us. Deal?'

'Deal!' Annabeth said happily.

'Now come on,' Thalia said. 'We can't stay put for long!'

The scene shifted. The three demigods were running through the woods. It must've been several days later, maybe even weeks. All of them looked beaten up like they'd seen some battles. Annabeth was wearing new clothes – jeans and an oversized army jacket.

'Just a little further!' Luke promised. Annabeth stumbled

and he took her hand. Thalia brought up the rear, brandishing her shield like she was driving back whatever pursued them. She was limping on her left leg.

They scrambled to a ridge and looked down the other side at a white colonial-style house – May Castellan's place.

'All right,' Luke said, breathing hard. 'I'll just sneak in and grab some food and medicine. Wait here.'

'Luke, are you sure?' Thalia asked. 'You swore you'd never come back here. If she catches you –'

'We don't have a choice!' he growled. 'They burned our nearest safe house. And you've got to treat that leg wound.'

'This is your house?' Annabeth said with amazement.

'It *was* my house,' Luke muttered. 'Believe me, if it wasn't an emergency –'

'Is your mom really horrible?' Annabeth asked. 'Can we see her?'

'No!' Luke snapped.

Annabeth shrank away from him, like his anger surprised her.

'I – I'm sorry,' he said. 'Just wait here. I promise everything will be okay. Nothing's going to hurt you. I'll be back –'

A brilliant golden flash illuminated the woods. The demigods winced, and a man's voice boomed: 'You should not have come home.'

The vision shut off.

My knees buckled, but Annabeth grabbed me. 'Percy! What happened?'

'Did – did you see that?' I asked.

'See what?'

I glanced at Hestia, but the goddess's face was expressionless. I remembered something she'd told me in the woods: *If you are to understand your enemy Luke, you must understand his family.* But why had she shown me those scenes?

'How long was I out?' I muttered.

Annabeth knitted her eyebrows. 'Percy, you weren't out at all. You just looked at Hestia for, like, one second and collapsed.'

I could feel everyone's eyes on me. I couldn't afford to look weak. Whatever those visions meant, I had to stay focused on our mission.

'Um, Lady Hestia,' I said, 'we've come on urgent business. We need to see —'

'We know what you need,' a man's voice said. I shuddered, because it was the same voice I'd heard in the vision.

A god shimmered into existence next to Hestia. He looked about twenty-five, with curly salt-and-pepper hair and elfin features. He wore a military pilot's flight suit, with tiny birds' wings fluttering on his helmet and his black leather boots. In the crook of his arm was a long staff entwined with two living serpents.

'I will leave you now,' Hestia said. She bowed to the aviator and disappeared into smoke. I understood why she was so anxious to go. Hermes, the god of messengers, did not look happy.

'Hello, Percy.' His brow furrowed like he was annoyed with me, and I wondered if he somehow knew about the vision I'd just had. I wanted to ask why he'd been at May

Castellan's house that night, and what had happened after he caught Luke. I remembered the first time I'd met Luke at Camp Half-Blood. I'd asked him if he'd ever met his father, and he looked at me bitterly and said: *Once*. But I could tell from Hermes' expression that this was not the time to ask.

I bowed awkwardly. 'Lord Hermes.'

Oh, sure, one of the snakes said in my mind. *Don't say hi to us. We're just reptiles.*

George, the other snake scolded. *Be polite.*

'Hello, George,' I said. 'Hey, Martha.'

Did you bring us a rat? George asked.

George, stop it, Martha said. *He's busy!*

Too busy for rats? George said. *That's just sad.*

I decided it was better not to get into it with George. 'Um, Hermes,' I said. 'We need to talk to Zeus. It's important.'

Hermes' eyes were steely cold. 'I am his messenger. May I take a message?'

Behind me, the other demigods shifted restlessly. This wasn't going as planned. Maybe if I tried to speak with Hermes in private . . .

'You guys,' I said. 'Why don't you do a sweep of the city? Check the defences. See who's left in Olympus. Meet Annabeth and me back here in thirty minutes.'

Silena frowned. 'But –'

'That's a good idea,' Annabeth said. 'Connor and Travis, you two lead.'

The Stolls seemed to like that – getting handed an important responsibility right in front of their dad. They usually never led anything except toilet-paper raids. 'We're on it!' Travis said. They herded the others out of the throne room, leaving Annabeth and me with Hermes.

'My lord,' Annabeth said. 'Kronos is going to attack New York. You must suspect that. My *mother* must have foreseen it.'

'Your mother,' Hermes grumbled. He scratched his back with his caduceus, and George and Martha muttered, *Ow, ow, ow.* 'Don't get me started on your mother, young lady. She's the reason I'm here at all. Zeus didn't want any of us to leave the front line. But your mother kept pestering him nonstop, "It's a trap, it's a diversion," blah, blah, blah. She wanted to come back herself, but Zeus was not going to let his number-one strategist leave his side while we're battling Typhon. And so, naturally, he sent *me* to talk to you.'

'But it *is* a trap!' Annabeth insisted. 'Is Zeus blind?'

Thunder rolled through the sky.

'I'd watch the comments, girl,' Hermes warned. 'Zeus is not blind *or* deaf. He has not left Olympus completely undefended.'

'But there are these blue lights –'

'Yes, yes. I saw them. Some mischief by that insufferable goddess of magic, Hecate, I'd wager, but you may have noticed they aren't doing any damage. Olympus has strong magical wards. Besides, Aeolus, the king of the winds, has sent his most powerful minions to guard the citadel. No one save the gods can approach Olympus from the air. They would be knocked out of the sky.'

I raised my hand. 'Um . . . what about that materializing/teleporting thing you guys do?'

'That's a form of air travel, too, Jackson. Very fast, but

the wind gods are faster. No – if Kronos wants Olympus, he'll have to march through the entire city with his army and take the elevators! Can you see him doing this?'

Hermes made it sound pretty ridiculous – hordes of monsters going up in the elevator twenty at a time, listening to 'Stayin' Alive'. Still, I didn't like it.

'Maybe just a few of you could come back,' I suggested.

Hermes shook his head impatiently. 'Percy Jackson, you don't understand. Typhon is our greatest enemy.'

'I thought that was Kronos.'

The god's eyes glowed. 'No, Percy. In the old days, Olympus was almost overthrown by Typhon. He is husband of Echidna –'

'Met her at the Arch,' I muttered. 'Not nice.'

'– and the father of all monsters. We can never forget how close he came to destroying us all – how he humiliated us! We were more powerful back in the old days. Now we can expect no help from Poseidon because he's fighting his own war. Hades sits in his realm and does nothing, and Demeter and Persephone follow his lead. It will take all our remaining power to oppose the storm giant. We can't divide our forces, nor wait until he gets to New York. We have to battle him now. And we're making progress.'

'Progress?' I said. 'He nearly destroyed St Louis.'

'Yes,' Hermes admitted. 'But he destroyed only *half* of Kentucky. He's slowing down. Losing power.'

I didn't want to argue, but it sounded like Hermes was trying to convince himself.

In the corner, the Ophiotaurus mooed sadly.

'Please, Hermes,' Annabeth said. 'You said my mother wanted to come. Did she give you any messages for us?'

'Messages,' he muttered. '"It'll be a great job," they told me. "Not much work. Lots of worshippers." Hmph. Nobody cares what *I* have to say. It's always about other people's *messages.*'

Rodents, George mused. *I'm in it for the rodents.*

Shhh, Martha scolded. *We care what Hermes has to say. Don't we, George?*

Oh, absolutely. Can we go back to the battle now? I want to do laser mode again. That's fun.

'Quiet, both of you,' Hermes grumbled.

The god looked at Annabeth, who was doing her 'big pleading grey eyes' thing.

'Bah,' Hermes said. 'Your mother said to warn you that you are on your own. You must hold Manhattan without the help of the gods. As if I didn't know that. Why they pay her to be the *wisdom* goddess, I'm not sure.'

'Anything else?' Annabeth asked.

'She said you should try plan twenty-three. She said you would know what that meant.'

Annabeth's face paled. Obviously, she knew what it meant, and she didn't like it. 'Go on.'

'Last thing.' Hermes looked at me. 'She said to tell Percy: "Remember the rivers." And, um – something about staying away from her daughter.'

I'm not sure whose face was redder: Annabeth's or mine.

'Thank you, Hermes,' Annabeth said. 'And I – I wanted to say . . . I'm sorry about Luke.'

The god's expression hardened like he'd turned to marble. 'You should've left that subject alone.'

Annabeth stepped back nervously. 'Sorry?'

'SORRY doesn't cut it!'

George and Martha curled around the caduceus, which shimmered and changed into something that looked suspiciously like a high-voltage cattle prod.

'You should've saved him when you had the chance,' Hermes growled at Annabeth. 'You're the only one who could have.'

I tried to step between them. 'What are you talking about? Annabeth didn't –'

'Don't defend her, Jackson!' Hermes turned the cattle prod towards me. 'She knows exactly what I'm talking about.'

'Maybe you should blame yourself!' I should've kept my mouth shut, but all I could think about was turning his attention away from Annabeth. This whole time – he hadn't been angry with me. He'd been angry with *her*. 'Maybe if you hadn't abandoned Luke and his mom!'

Hermes raised his cattle prod. He began to grow until he was three metres tall. I thought: *Well, that's it.*

But as he prepared to strike, George and Martha leaned in close and whispered something in his ear.

Hermes clenched his teeth. He lowered the cattle prod and it turned back to a staff.

'Percy Jackson,' he said, 'because you have taken on the curse of Achilles, I must spare you. You are in the hands of the Fates now. But you will *never* speak to me like that again. You have no idea how much I have sacrificed, how much –'

His voice broke, and he shrank back to human size. 'My son, my greatest pride . . . my poor May . . .'

He sounded so devastated I didn't know what to say. One minute he was ready to vaporize us. Now he looked like he needed a hug.

'Look, Lord Hermes,' I said. 'I'm sorry, but I need to know. What happened to May? She said something about Luke's fate, and her eyes –'

Hermes glared at me and my voice faltered. The look on his face wasn't really anger, though. It was pain. Deep, incredible pain.

'I will leave you now,' he said tightly. 'I have a war to fight.'

He began to shine. I turned away and made sure Annabeth did the same, because she was still frozen in shock.

Good luck, Percy, Martha the snake whispered.

Hermes glowed with the light of a supernova. Then he was gone.

Annabeth sat at the foot of her mother's throne and cried. I wanted to comfort her, but I wasn't sure how.

'Annabeth,' I said, 'it's not your fault. I've never seen Hermes act that way. I guess – I don't know – he probably feels guilty about Luke. He's looking for somebody to blame. I don't know why he lashed out at you. You didn't do anything to deserve that.'

Annabeth wiped her eyes. She stared at the hearth like it was her own funeral pyre.

I shifted uneasily. 'Um, you didn't, right?'

She didn't answer. Her celestial bronze knife was strapped to her arm – the same knife I'd seen in Hestia's vision. All these years, I hadn't realized it was a gift from

Luke. I'd asked her many times why she preferred to fight with a knife instead of a sword, and she'd never answered me. Now I knew.

'Percy,' she said. 'What did you mean about Luke's mother? Did you meet her?'

I nodded reluctantly. 'Nico and I visited her. She was a little . . . different.' I described May Castellan, and the weird moment when her eyes had started to glow and she talked about her son's fate.

Annabeth frowned. 'That doesn't make sense. But why were you visiting –' Her eyes widened. 'Hermes said you bear the curse of Achilles. Hestia said the same thing. Did you – did you bathe in the River Styx?'

'Don't change the subject.'

'Percy! Did you or not?'

'Um . . . maybe a little.'

I told her the story about Hades and Nico, and how I'd defeated an army of the dead. I left out the vision of her pulling me out of the river. I still didn't quite understand that part, and just thinking about it made me embarrassed.

She shook her head in disbelief. 'Do you have *any idea* how dangerous that was?'

'I had no choice,' I said. 'It's the only way I can stand up to Luke.'

'You mean . . . *di immortales*, of course! That's why Luke didn't die. He went to the Styx and – Oh no, Luke. What were you thinking?'

'So now you're worried about Luke again,' I grumbled.

She stared at me like I'd just dropped from space. 'What?'

'Forget it,' I muttered. I wondered what Hermes had meant about Annabeth not saving Luke when she'd had the chance. Clearly, she wasn't telling me something. But at the moment I wasn't in the mood to ask. The last thing I wanted to hear about was more of her history with Luke.

'The point is he didn't die in the Styx,' I said. 'Neither did I. Now I have to face him. We have to defend Olympus.'

Annabeth was still studying my face, like she was trying to see differences since my swim in the Styx. 'I guess you're right. My mom mentioned –'

'Plan twenty-three.'

She rummaged in her pack and pulled out Daedalus's laptop. The blue Delta symbol glowed on the top when she booted it up. She opened a few files and started to read.

'Here it is,' she said. 'Gods, we have a lot of work to do.'

'One of Daedalus's inventions?'

'A lot of inventions . . . dangerous ones. If my mother wants me to use this plan, she must think things are very bad.' She looked at me. 'What about her message to you: "Remember the rivers"? What does that mean?'

I shook my head. As usual, I had no clue what the gods were telling me. Which rivers was I supposed to remember? The Styx? The Mississippi?

Just then the Stoll brothers ran in to the throne room.

'You need to see this,' Connor said. '*Now.*'

The blue lights in the sky had stopped, so at first I didn't understand what the problem was.

The other campers had gathered in a small park at the

edge of the mountain. They were clustered at the guardrail, looking down at Manhattan. The railing was lined with those tourist binoculars, where you could deposit one golden drachma and see the city. Campers were using every single one.

I looked down at the city. I could see almost everything from here – the East River and the Hudson River carving the shape of Manhattan, the grid of streets, the lights of skyscrapers, the dark stretch of Central Park in the north. Everything looked normal, but something was wrong. I felt it in my bones before I realized what it was.

'I don't . . . hear anything,' Annabeth said.

That was the problem.

Even from this height, I should've heard the noise of the city – millions of people bustling around, thousands of cars and machines – the hum of a huge metropolis. You don't think about it when you live in New York, but it's always there. Even in the dead of night, New York is never silent.

But it was now.

I felt like my best friend had suddenly dropped dead.

'What did they do?' My voice sounded tight and angry. 'What did they do to my city?'

I pushed Michael Yew away from the binoculars and took a look.

In the streets below, traffic had stopped. Pedestrians were lying on the sidewalks, or curled up in doorways. There was no sign of violence, no wrecks, nothing like that. It was as if all the people in New York had simply decided to stop whatever they were doing and pass out.

'Are they dead?' Silena asked in astonishment.

Ice coated my stomach. A line from the prophecy rang in my ears: *And see the world in endless sleep.* I remembered Grover's story about meeting the god Morpheus in Central Park. *You're lucky I'm saving my energy for the main event.*

'Not dead,' I said. 'Morpheus has put the entire island of Manhattan to sleep. The invasion has started.'

10 I BUY SOME NEW FRIENDS

Mrs O'Leary was the only one happy about the sleeping city.

We found her pigging out at an overturned hot-dog stand while the owner was curled up on the sidewalk, sucking his thumb.

Argus was waiting for us with his hundred eyes wide open. He didn't say anything. He never does. I guess that's because he supposedly has an eyeball on his tongue. But his face made it clear he was freaking out.

I told him what we'd learned in Olympus, and how the gods would not be riding to the rescue. Argus rolled his eyes in disgust, which looked pretty psychedelic since it made his whole body swirl.

'You'd better get back to camp,' I told him. 'Guard it as best you can.'

He pointed at me and raised his eyebrow quizzically.

'I'm staying,' I said.

Argus nodded, like this answer satisfied him. He looked at Annabeth and drew a circle in the air with his finger.

'Yes,' Annabeth agreed. 'I think it's time.'

'For what?' I asked.

Argus rummaged around in the back of his van. He brought out a bronze shield and passed it to Annabeth. It looked pretty much standard issue – the same kind of round shield we always used in capture the flag. But when Annabeth set it on the ground, the reflection on the polished metal changed from sky and buildings to the Statue of Liberty – which wasn't anywhere close to us.

'Whoa,' I said. 'A video shield.'

'One of Daedalus's ideas,' Annabeth said. 'I had Beckendorf make this before –' She glanced at Silena. 'Um, anyway, the shield bends sunlight or moonlight from anywhere in the world to create a reflection. You can literally see any target under the sun or moon, as long as natural light is touching it. Look.'

We crowded around as Annabeth concentrated. The image zoomed and spun at first, so I got motion sickness just watching it. We were in the Central Park Zoo, then zooming down East Sixtieth past Bloomingdale's, then turning on Third Avenue.

'Whoa,' Connor Stoll said. 'Back up. Zoom in right there.'

'What?' Annabeth said nervously. 'You see invaders?'

'No, right there – Dylan's Candy Bar.' Connor grinned at his brother. 'Dude, it's open. And *everyone* is asleep. Are you thinking what I'm thinking?'

'Connor!' Katie Gardner scolded. She sounded like her mother Demeter. 'This is serious. You are not going to loot a candy store in the middle of a war!'

'Sorry,' Connor muttered, but he didn't sound very ashamed.

Annabeth passed her hand in front of the shield and another scene popped up: FDR Drive, looking across the river at Lighthouse Park.

'This will let us see what's going on across the city,' she

said. 'Thank you, Argus. Hopefully, we'll see you back at camp . . . someday.'

Argus grunted. He gave me a look that clearly meant *good luck — you'll need it*, then climbed into his van. He and the two harpy drivers swerved away, weaving around clusters of idle cars that littered the road.

I whistled for Mrs O'Leary and she came bounding over.

'Hey, girl,' I said. 'You remember Grover? The satyr we met in the park?'

'WOOF!'

I hoped that meant, *Sure I do!* And not, *Do you have more hot dogs?*

'I need you to find him,' I said. 'Make sure he's still awake. We're going to need his help. You got that? Find Grover!'

Mrs O'Leary gave me a sloppy wet kiss, which seemed kind of unnecessary. Then she raced off north.

Pollux crouched next to a sleeping policeman. 'I don't get it. Why didn't we fall asleep too? Why just the mortals?'

'This is a huge spell,' Silena Beauregard said. 'The bigger the spell, the easier it is to resist. If you want to sleep millions of mortals, you've got to cast a very thin layer of magic. Sleeping demigods is much harder.'

I stared at her. 'When did you learn so much about magic?'

Silena blushed. 'I don't spend *all* my time on my wardrobe.'

'Percy,' Annabeth called. She was still looking at the shield. 'You'd better see this.'

The bronze image showed Long Island Sound near La Guardia. A fleet of a dozen speedboats raced through the dark water towards Manhattan. Each boat was packed with demigods in full Greek armour. At the back of the lead boat, a purple banner emblazoned with a black scythe flapped in the night wind. I'd never seen that design before, but it wasn't hard to figure out: the battle flag of Kronos.

'Scan the perimeter of the island,' I said. 'Quick.'

Annabeth shifted the scene south to the harbour. A Staten Island ferry was ploughing through the waves near Ellis Island. The deck was crowded with *dracaenae* and a whole pack of hellhounds. Swimming in front of the ship was a pod of marine mammals. At first I thought they were dolphins. Then I saw their doglike faces and the swords strapped to their waists, and I realized they were telkhines.

The scene shifted again — the Jersey shore, right at the entrance to the Lincoln Tunnel. A hundred assorted monsters were marching past the lanes of stopped traffic — giants with clubs, rogue Cyclopes, a few fire-spitting dragons and, just to rub it in, a World War II-era Sherman tank, pushing cars out of its way as it rumbled into the tunnel.

'What's happening with the mortals outside Manhattan?' I said. 'Is the whole state asleep?'

Annabeth frowned. 'I don't think so, but it's strange. As far as I can tell from these pictures, Manhattan is totally asleep. Then there's, like, a fifty-mile radius around the island where time is running really, really slow. The closer you get to Manhattan, the slower it is.'

She showed me another scene – a New Jersey highway. It was Saturday evening, so the traffic wasn't as bad as it might've been on a weekday. The drivers looked awake, but the cars were moving at about one mile per hour. Birds flew overhead in slow motion.

'Kronos,' I said. 'He's slowing time.'

'Hecate might be helping,' Katie Gardner said. 'Look how the cars are all veering away from the Manhattan exits, like they're getting a subconscious message to turn back.'

'I don't know.' Annabeth sounded really frustrated. She *hated* not knowing. 'But somehow they've surrounded Manhattan in layers of magic. The outside world might not even realize something is wrong. Any mortals coming towards Manhattan will slow down so much they won't know what's happening.'

'Like flies in amber,' Jake Mason murmured.

Annabeth nodded. 'We shouldn't expect any help coming in.'

I turned to my friends. They looked stunned and scared, and I couldn't blame them. The shield had shown us at least three hundred enemies on the way. There were forty of us. And we were alone.

'All right,' I said. 'We're going to hold Manhattan.'

Silena tugged at her armour. 'Um, Percy, Manhattan is huge.'

'We *are* going to hold it,' I said. 'We have to.'

'He's right,' Annabeth said. 'The gods of the wind should keep Kronos's forces away from Olympus by air, so he'll try a ground assault. We have to cut off the entrances to the island.'

'They have boats,' Michael Yew pointed out.

An electric tingle went down my back. Suddenly I understood Athena's advice: *Remember the rivers.*

'I'll take care of the boats,' I said.

Michael frowned. 'How?'

'Just leave it to me,' I said. 'We need to guard the bridges and tunnels. Let's assume they'll try a midtown or downtown assault, at least on their first try. That would be the most direct way to the Empire State Building. Michael, take Apollo's cabin to the Williamsburg Bridge. Katie, Demeter's cabin takes the Brooklyn Battery Tunnel. Grow thorn bushes and poison ivy in the tunnel. Do whatever you have to do – but keep them out of there! Connor – take half of Hermes cabin and cover the Manhattan Bridge. Travis, you take the other half and cover the Brooklyn Bridge. And no stopping for looting or pillaging!'

'Awwww!' the whole Hermes cabin complained.

'Silena, take the Aphrodite crew to the Queens–Midtown Tunnel.'

'Oh, my gods,' one of her sisters said. 'Fifth Avenue is *so* on our way! We could accessorize, and monsters, like, *totally* hate the smell of Givenchy.'

'No delays,' I said. 'Well . . . the perfume thing, if you think it'll work.'

Six Aphrodite girls kissed me on the cheek in excitement.

'All right, enough!' I closed my eyes, trying to think what I'd forgotten. 'The Holland Tunnel. Jake – take Hephaestus cabin there. Use Greek fire, set traps. Whatever you've got.'

He grinned. 'Gladly. We've got a score to settle. For Beckendorf!'

The whole cabin roared in approval.

'The Fifty-ninth Street Bridge,' I said. 'Clarisse –'

I faltered. Clarisse wasn't here. The whole Ares cabin, curse them, was sitting back at camp.

'We'll take that.' Annabeth stepped in, saving me from an embarrassing silence. She turned to her siblings. 'Malcolm, take Athena cabin and activate plan twenty-three along the way, just like I showed you. Hold that position.'

'You got it.'

'I'll go with Percy,' she said. 'Then we'll join you – or we'll go wherever we're needed.'

Somebody in the back of the group said, 'No detours, you two.'

There were some giggles, but I decided to let it pass.

'All right,' I said. 'Keep in touch with cell phones.'

'We don't have cell phones,' Silena protested.

I reached down, picked up some snoring lady's BlackBerry and tossed it to Silena. 'You do now. You all know Annabeth's number, right? If you need us, pick up a random phone and call us. Use it once, drop it, then borrow another one if you have to. That should make it harder for the monsters to zero in on you.'

Everyone grinned like they liked this idea.

Travis cleared his throat. 'Uh, if we find a really nice phone –'

'No, you can't keep it,' I said.

'Aw, man.'

'Hold it, Percy,' Jake Mason said. 'You forgot the Lincoln Tunnel.'

I bit back a curse. He was right. A Sherman tank and a hundred monsters were marching through that tunnel right now, and I'd positioned our forces everywhere else.

Then a girl's voice called from across the street: 'How about you leave that to us?'

I'd never been happier to hear anyone in my life. A band of thirty adolescent girls crossed Fifth Avenue. They wore white shirts, silvery camouflage pants and combat boots. They all had swords at their sides, quivers on their backs and bows at the ready. A pack of white timber wolves milled around their feet, and many of the girls had hunting falcons on their arms.

The girl in the lead had spiky black hair and a black leather jacket. She wore a silver circlet on her head like a princess's tiara, which didn't match her skull earrings or her *Death to Barbie* T-shirt showing a little Barbie doll with an arrow through its head.

'Thalia!' Annabeth cried.

The daughter of Zeus grinned. 'The Hunters of Artemis, reporting for duty.'

There were hugs and greetings all around – or at least Thalia was friendly. The other Hunters didn't like being around campers, especially boys, but they didn't shoot any of us, which for them was a pretty warm welcome.

'Where have you been the last year?' I asked Thalia. 'You've got, like, twice as many Hunters now!'

She laughed. 'Long, *long* story. I bet my adventures were more dangerous than yours, Jackson.'

'Complete lie,' I said.

'We'll see,' she promised. 'After this is ~~

Annabeth and me: cheeseburgers and fries at that hotel on West Fifty-sixth.'

'Le Parker Meridien,' I said. 'You're on. And, Thalia – thanks.'

She shrugged. 'Those monsters won't know what hit them. Hunters, move out!'

She slapped her silver bracelet and the shield Aegis spiralled into full form. The golden head of Medusa moulded in the centre was so horrible the campers all backed away. The Hunters took off down the avenue, followed by their wolves and falcons, and I had a feeling the Lincoln Tunnel would be safe for now.

'Thank the gods,' Annabeth said. 'But if we don't blockade the rivers from those boats, guarding the bridges and tunnels will be pointless.'

'You're right,' I said.

I looked at the campers, all of them grim and determined. I tried not to feel like this was the last time I'd ever see them all together.

'You're the greatest heroes of this millennium,' I told them. 'It doesn't matter how many monsters come at you. Fight bravely, and we will win.' I raised Riptide and shouted, 'FOR OLYMPUS!'

They shouted in response, and our forty voices echoed off the buildings of midtown. For a moment, it sounded brave, but it died quickly in the silence of ten million sleeping New Yorkers.

Annabeth and I would've had our pick of cars, but they were all wedged in bumper-to-bumper traffic. None of the ⋯re running, which was weird. It seemed the drivers had had time to turn off the ignition before they got too sleepy. Or maybe Morpheus had the power to put engines to sleep as well. Most of the drivers had apparently tried to pull to the kerb when they felt themselves passing out, but still the streets were too clogged to navigate.

Finally we found an unconscious courier leaning against a brick wall, still straddling his red Vespa. We dragged him off the scooter and laid him on the sidewalk.

'Sorry, dude,' I said. With any luck, I'd be able to bring his scooter back. If I didn't, it would hardly matter, because the city would be destroyed.

I drove with Annabeth behind me, holding onto my waist. We zigzagged down Broadway with our engine buzzing through the eerie calm. The only sounds were occasional cell phones ringing – like they calling out to each other, as if New York had turned into a giant electronic aviary.

Our progress was slow. Every so often we'd come across pedestrians who'd fallen asleep right in front of a car, and we'd move them just to be safe. Once we stopped to extinguish a pretzel vendor's cart that had caught on fire. A few minutes later we had to rescue a baby carriage that was rolling aimlessly down the street. It turned out there was no baby in it – just somebody's sleeping poodle. Go figure. We parked it safely in a doorway and kept riding.

We were passing Madison Square Park when Annabeth said: 'Pull over.'

I stopped in the middle of East Twenty-third. Annabeth jumped off and ran towards the park. By the time I caught up with her, she was staring at a bronze statue on a red marble pedestal. I'd probably passed it a million times, but never really looked at it.

The dude was sitting in a chair with his legs crossed. He wore an old-fashioned suit – Abraham Lincoln style – with a bowtie and long coat-tails and stuff. A bunch of bronze books were piled under his chair. He held a writing quill in one hand and a big metal sheet of parchment in the other.

'Why do we care about . . .'. I squinted at the name on the pedestal. 'William H. Steward?'

'Seward,' Annabeth corrected. 'He was a New York governor. Minor demigod – son of Hebe, I think. But that's not important. It's the statue I care about.'

She climbed on a park bench and examined the base of the statue.

'Don't tell me he's an automaton,' I said.

Annabeth smiled. 'Turns out most of the statues in the city are automatons. Daedalus planted them here just in case he needed an army.'

'To attack Olympus or defend it?'

Annabeth shrugged. 'Either one. That was plan twenty-three. He could activate one statue and it would start activating its brethren all over the city, until there was an army. It's dangerous, though. You know how unpredictable automatons are.'

'Uh-huh,' I said. We'd had our share of bad experiences with them. 'You're seriously thinking about activating it?'

'I have Daedalus's notes,' she said. 'I think I can . . . Ah, here we go.'

She pressed the tip of Seward's boot and the statue stood up, its quill and paper ready.

'What's he going to do?' I muttered. 'Take a memo?'

'Shh,' said Annabeth. 'Hello, William.'

'Bill,' I suggested.

'Bill – oh, shut up,' Annabeth told me. The statue tilted its head, looking at us with blank metal eyes.

Annabeth cleared her throat. 'Hello, er, Governor Seward. Command sequence: Daedalus Twenty-three. Defend Manhattan. Begin Activation.'

Seward jumped off his pedestal. He hit the ground so hard his shoes cracked the sidewalk. Then he went clanking off towards the east.

'He's probably going to wake up Confucius,' Annabeth guessed.

'What?' I said.

'Another statue on Division. The point is, they'll keep waking each other up until they're all activated.'

'And then?'

'Hopefully, they defend Manhattan.'

'Do they know that we're not the enemy?'

'I think so.'

'That's reassuring.' I thought about all the bronze statues in the parks, plazas and buildings of New York. There had to be hundreds, maybe thousands.

Then a ball of green light exploded in the evening sky – Greek fire, somewhere over the East River.

'We have to hurry,' I said. And we ran for the Vespa.

We pulled over outside Battery Park, at the lower tip of Manhattan where the Hudson and East Rivers came together and emptied into the Bay.

'Wait here,' I told Annabeth.

'Percy, you shouldn't go alone.'

'Well, unless you can breathe underwater . . .'

She sighed. 'You are *so* annoying sometimes.'

'Like when I'm right? Trust me, I'll be fine. I've got the curse of Achilles now. I'm all invincible and stuff.'

Annabeth didn't look convinced. 'Just be careful. I don't want anything to happen to you. I mean – because we need you for the battle.'

I grinned. 'Back in a flash.'

I clambered down the shoreline and waded into the water.

Just for you non-sea-god types out there – don't go swimming in New York Harbor. It may not be as filthy as it was in my mom's day, but that water will still probably make you grow a third eye or have mutant children when you grow up.

I dived into the murk and sank to the bottom. I tried to find the spot where the two rivers' currents seemed equal – where they met to form the bay. I figured that was the best place to get their attention.

'HEY!' I shouted in my best underwater voice. The sound echoed in the darkness. 'I heard you guys are so polluted you're embarrassed to show your faces. Is that true?'

A cold current rippled through the Bay, churning up plumes of garbage and silt.

'I heard the East River is more toxic,' I continued, 'but the Hudson smells worse. Or is it the other way around?'

The water shimmered. Something powerful and angry was watching me now. I could sense its presence . . . or maybe *two* presences.

I was afraid I'd miscalculated with the insults. What if they just blasted me without showing themselves? But these were New York river gods. I figured their instinct would be to get in my face.

Sure enough, two giant forms appeared in front of me. At first they were just dark brown columns of silt, denser than the water around them. Then they grew legs, arms and scowling faces.

The creature on the left looked disturbingly like a telkhine. His face was wolfish. His body was vaguely like a seal's – sleek black with flipper hands and feet. His eyes glowed radiation green.

The dude on the right was more humanoid. He was dressed in rags and seaweed, with a chainmail coat made of bottle caps and old plastic six-pack holders. His face was blotchy with algae, and his beard was overgrown. His deep blue eyes burned with anger.

The seal, who had to be the god of the East River, said, 'Are you *trying* to get yourself killed, kid? Or are you just extra stupid?'

The bearded spirit of the Hudson scoffed. 'You're the expert on stupid, East.'

'Watch it, Hudson,' East growled. 'Stay on your side of the island and mind your business.'

'Or what? You'll throw another garbage barge at me?'

They floated towards each other, ready to fight.

'Hold it!' I yelled. 'We've got a bigger problem.'

'The kid's right,' East snarled. 'Let's both kill *him*, then we'll fight each other.'

'Sounds good,' Hudson said.

Before I could protest, a thousand scraps of garbage

surged off the bottom and flew straight at me from both directions – broken glass, rocks, cans, tyres.

I was expecting it, though. The water in front of me thickened into a shield. The debris bounced off harmlessly. Only one piece got through – a big chunk of glass that hit my chest and probably should've killed me, but it shattered against my skin.

The two river gods stared at me.

'Son of Poseidon?' East asked.

I nodded.

'Took a dip in the Styx?' Hudson asked.

'Yep.'

They both made disgusted sounds.

'Well, that's perfect,' East said. 'Now how do we kill him?'

'We could electrocute him,' Hudson mused. 'If I could just find some jumper cables –'

'Listen to me!' I said. 'Kronos's army is invading Manhattan!'

'Don't you think we know that?' East asked. 'I can feel his boats right now. They're almost across.'

'Yep,' Hudson agreed. 'I got some filthy monsters crossing my waters, too.'

'So stop them,' I said. 'Drown them. Sink their boats.'

'Why should we?' Hudson grumbled. 'So they invade Olympus. What do we care?'

'Because I can pay you.' I took out the sand dollar my father had given me for my birthday.

The river gods' eyes widened.

'It's mine!' East said. 'Give it here, kid, and I promise none of Kronos's scum are getting across the East River.'

'Forget that,' Hudson said. 'That sand dollar's mine, unless you want me to let all those ships cross the Hudson.'

'We'll compromise.' I broke the sand dollar in half. A ripple of clean fresh water spread out from the break, as if all the pollution in the Bay was being dissolved.

'You each get half,' I said. 'In exchange, you keep all of Kronos's forces away from Manhattan.'

'Oh, man,' Hudson whimpered, reaching out for the sand dollar. 'It's been so long since I was clean.'

'The power of Poseidon,' East River murmured. 'He's a jerk, but he sure knows how to sweep pollution away.'

They looked at each other, then spoke as one: 'It's a deal.'

I gave them each half of the sand dollar, which they held reverently.

'Um, the invaders?' I prompted.

East flicked his hand. 'They just got sunk.'

Hudson snapped his fingers. 'Bunch of hellhounds just took a dive.'

'Thank you,' I said. 'Stay clean.'

As I rose towards the surface, East called out, 'Hey, kid, any time you got a sand dollar to spend, come on back. Assuming you live.'

'Curse of Achilles,' Hudson snorted. 'They always think that'll save them, don't they?'

'If only he knew,' East agreed. They both laughed, dissolving into the water.

Back on the shore, Annabeth was talking on her cell phone, but she hung up as soon as she saw me. She looked pretty shaken.

'It worked,' I told her. 'The rivers are safe.'

'Good,' she said. 'Because we've got other problems. Michael Yew just called. Another army is marching over the Williamsburg Bridge. The Apollo cabin needs help. And, Percy, the monster leading the enemy . . . it's the Minotaur.'

11 WE BREAK A BRIDGE

Fortunately, Blackjack was on duty.

I did my best taxicab whistle, and within a few minutes two dark shapes circled out of the sky. They looked like hawks at first, but as they descended, I could make out the long galloping legs of pegasi.

Yo, boss. Blackjack landed at a trot, his friend Porkpie right behind him. *Man, I thought those wind gods were gonna knock us to Pennsylvania until we said we were with you!*

'Thanks for coming,' I told him. 'Hey, why do pegasi gallop as they fly, anyway?'

Blackjack whinnied. *Why do humans swing their arms as they walk? I dunno, boss. It just feels right. Where to?*

'We need to get to the Williamsburg Bridge,' I said.

Blackjack lowered his neck. *You're darn right, boss. We flew over it on the way here and it don't look good. Hop on!*

On the way to the bridge, a knot formed in the pit of my stomach. The Minotaur was one of the first monsters I'd ever defeated. Four years ago he'd nearly killed my mother on Half-Blood Hill. I still had nightmares about that.

I'd been hoping he would stay dead for a few centuries, but I should've known my luck wouldn't hold.

We saw the battle before we were close enough to make out individual fighters. It was well after midnight now, but the bridge blazed with light. Cars were burning. Arcs of fire streamed in both directions as flaming arrows and spears sailed through the air.

We came in for a low pass, and I saw the Apollo campers retreating. They would hide behind cars and snipe at the approaching army, setting off explosive arrows and dropping caltrops in the road, building fiery barricades wherever they could, dragging sleeping drivers out of their cars to get them out of harm's way. But the enemy kept advancing. An entire phalanx of *dracaenae* marched in the lead, their shields locked together, spear tips bristling over the top. An occasional arrow would connect with their snaky trunks, or a neck, or a chink in their armour, and the unlucky snake woman would disintegrate, but most of the Apollo arrows glanced harmlessly off their shield wall. About a hundred more monsters marched behind them.

Hellhounds leaped ahead of the line from time to time. Most were destroyed with arrows, but one got hold of an Apollo camper and dragged him away. I didn't see what happened to him next. I didn't want to know.

'There!' Annabeth called from the back of her pegasus.

Sure enough, in the middle of the invading legion was Old Beefhead himself.

The last time I'd seen the Minotaur, he'd been wearing nothing but his tighty whities. I don't know why. Maybe he'd been shaken out of bed to chase me. This time, he was prepared for battle.

From the waist down, he wore standard Greek battle gear – a kilt-like apron of leather and metal flaps, bronze greaves covering his legs and tightly wrapped leather sandals.

His top was all bull – hair and hide and muscle, leading to a head so large he should've toppled over just from the weight of his horns. He seemed larger than the last time I'd seen him – three metres tall at least. A double-bladed axe was strapped to his back, but he was too impatient to use it. As soon as he saw me circling overhead (or sniffed me more likely, since his eyesight was bad), he bellowed and picked up a white limousine.

'Blackjack, dive!' I yelled.

What? the pegasus asked. *No way could he – holy horse feed!*

We were at least thirty metres up, but the limo came sailing towards us, flipping fender over fender like a two-ton boomerang. Annabeth and Porkpie swerved madly to the left, while Blackjack tucked in his wings and plunged. The limo sailed over my head, missing by maybe five centimetres. It cleared the suspension lines of the bridge and fell towards the East River.

Monsters jeered and shouted, and the Minotaur picked up another car.

'Drop us behind the lines with the Apollo cabin,' I told Blackjack. 'Stay in earshot, but get out of danger!'

I ain't gonna argue, boss!

Blackjack swooped down behind an overturned school bus where a couple of campers were hiding. Annabeth and I leaped off as soon as our pegasi's hooves touched the pavement. Then Blackjack and Porkpie soared into the night sky.

Michael Yew ran up to us. He was definitely the shortest commando I'd ever seen. He had a bandaged cut on his arm. His ferrety face was smeared with soot and his quiver was almost empty, but he was smiling like he was having a great time.

'Glad you could join us,' he said. 'Where are the other reinforcements?'

'For now, we're it,' I said.

'Then we're dead,' he said.

'You still have your flying chariot?' Annabeth asked.

'Nah,' Michael said. 'Left it at camp. I told Clarisse she could have it. Whatever, you know? Not worth fighting about any more. But she said it was too late. We'd insulted her honour for the last time or some stupid thing.'

'Least you tried,' I said.

Michael shrugged. 'Yeah, well, I called her some names when she said she still wouldn't fight. I doubt that helped. Here come the uglies!'

He drew an arrow and launched it towards the enemy. The arrow made a screaming sound as it flew. When it landed, it unleashed a blast like a power chord on an electric guitar magnified through the world's largest speakers. The nearest cars exploded. Monsters dropped their weapons and clasped their ears in pain. Some ran. Others disintegrated on the spot.

'That was my last sonic arrow,' Michael said.

'A gift from your dad?' I asked. 'God of music?'

Michael grinned wickedly. 'Loud music can be bad for you. Unfortunately, it doesn't always kill.'

Sure enough, most monsters were regrouping, shaking off their confusion.

'We have to fall back,' Michael said. 'I've got Kayla and Austin setting traps further down the bridge.'

'No,' I said. 'Bring your campers forward to this position

and wait for my signal. We're going to drive the enemy back to Brooklyn.'

Michael laughed. 'How do you plan to do that?'

I drew my sword.

'Percy,' Annabeth said, 'let me come with you.'

'Too dangerous,' I said. 'Besides, I need you to help Michael coordinate the defensive line. I'll distract the monsters. You group up here. Move the sleeping mortals out of the way. Then you can start picking off monsters while I keep them focused on me. If anybody can do all that, you can.'

Michael snorted. 'Thanks a lot.'

I kept my eyes on Annabeth.

She nodded reluctantly. 'All right. Get moving.'

Before I could lose my courage, I said, 'Don't I get a kiss for luck? It's kind of a tradition, right?'

I figured she would punch me. Instead, she drew her knife and stared at the army marching towards us. 'Come back alive, Seaweed Brain. Then we'll see.'

I figured it was the best offer I would get, so I stepped out from behind the school bus. I walked up the bridge in plain sight, straight towards the enemy.

When the Minotaur saw me, his eyes burned with hate. He bellowed – a sound that was somewhere between a yell, a moo and a really loud belch.

'Hey, Beef Boy,' I shouted back. 'Didn't I kill you already?'

He pounded his fist into the hood of a Lexus and it crumpled like tinfoil.

A few *dracaenae* threw flaming javelins at me. I knocked

them aside. A hellhound lunged and I sidestepped. I could have stabbed it, but I hesitated.

This is not Mrs O'Leary, I reminded myself. *This is an untamed monster. It will kill me and all my friends.*

It pounced again. This time, I brought Riptide up in a deadly arc. The hellhound disintegrated into dust and fur.

More monsters surged forward – snakes and giants and telkhines – but the Minotaur roared at them and they backed off.

'One on one?' I called. 'Just like old times?'

The Minotaur's nostrils quivered. He seriously needed to keep a pack of Aloe Vera Kleenex in his armour pocket, because that nose was wet and red and pretty gross. He unstrapped his axe and swung it around.

It was beautiful in a harsh *I'm going to gut you like a fish* kind of way. Each of its twin blades was shaped like an omega – Ω – the last letter of the Greek alphabet. Maybe that was because the axe would be the last thing his victims ever saw. The shaft was about the same height as the Minotaur, bronze wrapped in leather. Tied around the base of each blade were lots of bead necklaces. I realized they were Camp Half-Blood beads – necklaces taken from defeated demigods.

I was so mad I imagined my eyes glowing just like the Minotaur's. I raised my sword. The monster army cheered for the Minotaur, but the sound died when I dodged his first swing and sliced his axe in half, right between the handholds.

'Moo?' he grunted.

'HAAA!' I spun and kicked him in the snout. He

staggered backwards, trying to regain his footing, then lowered his head to charge.

He never got the chance. My sword flashed – slicing off one horn, then the other. He tried to grab me. I rolled away, picking up half of his broken axe. The other monsters backed up in stunned silence, making a circle around us. The Minotaur bellowed in rage. He was never very smart to begin with, but now his anger made him reckless. He charged me and I ran for the edge of the bridge, breaking through a line of *dracaenae*.

The Minotaur must've smelled victory. He thought I was trying to get away. His minions cheered. At the edge of the bridge, I turned and braced the axe against the railing to receive his charge. The Minotaur didn't even slow down.

CRUNCH.

He looked down in surprise at the axe handle sprouting from his breastplate.

'Thanks for playing,' I told him.

I lifted him by his legs and tossed him over the side of the bridge. Even as he fell, he was disintegrating, turning back into dust, his essence returning to Tartarus.

I turned towards his army. It was now roughly one hundred and ninety-nine to one. I did the natural thing. I charged them.

You're going to ask how the 'invincible' thing worked – if I magically dodged every weapon, or if the weapons hit me and just didn't harm me. Honestly, I don't remember. All I knew was that I wasn't going to let these monsters invade my hometown.

I sliced through armour like it was made of paper.

Snake-women exploded. Hellhounds melted to shadow. I slashed and stabbed and whirled and I might have even laughed once or twice – a crazy laugh that scared me as much as it did my enemies. I was aware of the Apollo campers behind me shooting arrows, disrupting every attempt by the enemy to rally. Finally the monsters turned and fled – about twenty left alive out of two hundred.

I followed with the Apollo campers at my heels.

'Yes!' yelled Michael Yew. 'That's what I'm talking about!'

We drove them back towards the Brooklyn side of the bridge. The sky was growing pale in the east. I could see the toll stations ahead.

'Percy!' Annabeth yelled. 'You've already routed them. Pull back! We're overextended!'

Some part of me knew she was right, but I was doing so well. I wanted to destroy every last monster.

Then I saw the crowd at the base of the bridge. The retreating monsters were running straight towards their reinforcements. It was small group, maybe thirty or forty demigods in battle armour, mounted on skeletal horses. One of them held a purple banner with the black scythe design.

The lead horseman trotted forward. He took off his helm and I recognized Kronos himself, his eyes like molten gold.

Annabeth and the Apollo campers faltered. The monsters we'd been pursuing reached the Titan's line and were absorbed into the new force. Kronos gazed in our direction. He was a quarter of a mile away, but I swear I could see him smile.

'Now,' I said, 'we pull back.'

The Titan lord's men drew their swords and charged. The hooves of their skeletal horses thundered against the pavement. Our archers shot a volley, bringing down several of the enemy, but they just kept riding.

'Retreat!' I told my friends. 'I'll hold them!'

In a matter of seconds they were on me.

Michael and his archers tried to retreat, but Annabeth stayed right beside me, fighting with her knife and mirrored shield as we slowly backed up the bridge.

Kronos's cavalry swirled around us, slashing and yelling insults. The Titan himself advanced leisurely, like he had all the time in the world. Being the Lord of Time, I guess he did.

I tried to wound his men, not kill. That slowed me down, but these weren't monsters. They were demigods who'd fallen under Kronos's spell. I couldn't see faces under their battle helmets, but some of them had probably been my friends. I slashed the legs off their horses and made the skeletal mounts disintegrate. After the first few demigods took a spill, the rest figured out they'd better dismount and fight me on foot.

Annabeth and I stayed shoulder to shoulder, facing opposite directions. A dark shape passed over me and I dared to glance up. Blackjack and Porkpie were swooping in, kicking our enemies in the helmets and flying away like very large kamikaze pigeons.

We'd almost made it to the middle of the bridge when something strange happened. I felt a chill down my spine – like that old saying about someone walking on your grave. Behind me, Annabeth cried out in pain.

'Annabeth!' I turned in time to see her fall, clutching her arm. A demigod with a bloody knife stood over her.

In a flash, I understood what had happened. He'd been trying to stab me. Judging from the position of his blade, he would've taken me — maybe by sheer luck — in the small of my back, my only weak point.

Annabeth had intercepted the knife with her own body.

But why? She didn't know about my weak spot. No one did.

I locked eyes with the enemy demigod. He wore an eye patch under his war helm: Ethan Nakamura, the son of Nemesis. Somehow he'd survived the explosion on the *Princess Andromeda*. I slammed him in the face with my sword hilt so hard I dented his helm.

'Get back!' I slashed the air in a wide arc, driving the rest of the demigods away from Annabeth. 'No one touches her!'

'Interesting,' Kronos said.

He towered above me on his skeletal horse, his scythe in one hand. He studied the scene with narrowed eyes as if he could sense that I'd just come close to death, the way a wolf can smell fear.

'Bravely fought, Percy Jackson,' he said. 'But it's time to surrender — or the girl dies.'

'Percy, don't,' Annabeth groaned. Her shirt was soaked with blood. I had to get her out of here.

'Blackjack!' I yelled.

As fast as light, the pegasus swooped down and clamped his teeth on the straps of Annabeth's armour. They soared away over the river before the enemy could even react.

Kronos snarled. 'Some day soon, I am going to make

pegasus soup. But in the meantime . . .' He dismounted, his scythe glistening in the dawn light. 'I'll settle for another dead demigod.'

I met his first strike with Riptide. The impact shook the entire bridge, but I held my ground. Kronos's smile wavered.

With a yell, I kicked his legs out from under him. His scythe skittered across the pavement. I stabbed downward, but he rolled aside and regained his footing. His scythe flew back to his hands.

'So . . .' He studied me, looking mildly annoyed. 'You had the courage to visit the Styx. I had to pressure Luke in many ways to convince him. If only *you* had supplied my host body instead . . . but no matter. I am still more powerful. I am a *TITAN.*'

He struck the bridge with the butt of his scythe, and a wave of pure force blasted me backwards. Cars went careening. Demigods – even Luke's own men – were blown off the edge of the bridge. Suspension cords whipped around and I skidded halfway back to Manhattan.

I got unsteadily to my feet. The remaining Apollo campers had almost made it to the end of the bridge – except for Michael Yew, who was perched on one of the suspension cables a few metres away from me. His last arrow was notched in his bow.

'Michael, go!' I screamed.

'Percy, the bridge!' he called. 'It's already weak!'

At first I didn't understand. Then I looked down and saw fissures in the pavement. Patches of the road were half melted from Greek fire. The bridge had taken a beating from Kronos's blast and the exploding arrows.

'Break it!' Michael yelled. 'Use your powers!'

It was a desperate thought – no way it would work – but I stabbed Riptide into the bridge. The magic blade sank to its hilt in tarmac. Salt water shot from the crack like I'd hit a geyser. I pulled out my blade and the fissure grew. The bridge shook and began to crumble. Chunks the size of houses fell into the East River. Kronos's demigods cried out in alarm and scrambled backwards. Some were knocked off their feet. Within a few seconds, a twenty-metre chasm opened in the Williamsburg Bridge between Kronos and me.

The vibrations died. Kronos's men crept to the edge and looked at the forty-metre drop into the river.

I didn't feel safe, though. The suspension cables were still attached. The men could get across that way if they were brave enough. Or maybe Kronos had a magic way to span the gap.

The Titan lord studied the problem. He looked behind him at the rising sun, then smiled across the chasm. He raised his scythe in a mock salute. 'Until this evening, Jackson.'

He mounted his horse, whirled around and galloped back to Brooklyn followed by his warriors.

I turned to thank Michael Yew, but the words died in my throat. Five metres away, a bow lay in the street. Its owner was nowhere to be seen.

'No!' I searched the wreckage on my side of the bridge. I stared down at the river. Nothing.

I yelled in anger and frustration. The sound carried forever in the morning stillness. I was about to whistle for Blackjack to help me search when my mom's phone rang.

The LCD display said I had a call from Finklestein & Associates – probably a demigod calling on a borrowed phone.

I picked up, hoping for good news. Of course, I was wrong.

'Percy?' Silena Beauregard sounded like she'd been crying. 'Plaza Hotel. You'd better come quickly and bring a healer from Apollo's cabin. It's . . . it's Annabeth.'

12 RACHEL MAKES A BAD DEAL

I grabbed Will Solace from the Apollo cabin and told the rest of his siblings to keep searching for Michael Yew. We borrowed a Yamaha FZ1 from a sleeping biker and drove to the Plaza Hotel at speeds that would've given my mom a heart attack. I'd never driven a motorcycle before, but it wasn't any harder than riding a pegasus.

Along the way, I noticed a lot of empty pedestals that usually held statues. Plan twenty-three seemed to be working. I didn't know if that was good or bad.

It only took us five minutes to reach the Plaza – an old-fashioned white stone hotel with a gabled blue roof, sitting at the south-east corner of Central Park.

Tactically speaking, the Plaza wasn't the best place for a headquarters. It wasn't the tallest building in town or the most centrally located. But it had old-school style and had attracted a lot of famous demigods over the years, like the Beatles and Alfred Hitchcock, so I figured we were in good company.

I gunned the Yamaha over the kerb and swerved to a stop at the fountain outside the hotel.

Will and I hopped off. The statue at the top of the fountain called down, 'Oh, fine. I suppose you want me to watch your bike, too!'

She was a life-size bronze standing in the middle of a

granite bowl. She wore only a bronze sheet around her legs, and she was holding a basket of metal fruit. I'd never paid her too much attention before. Then again she'd never talked to me before.

'Are you supposed to be Demeter?' I asked.

A bronze apple sailed over my head.

'Everyone thinks I'm Demeter!' she complained. 'I'm Pompona, the Roman goddess of plenty, but why should *you* care? Nobody cares about the minor gods. If you cared about the minor gods, you wouldn't be losing this war! Three cheers for Morpheus and Hecate, I say!'

'Watch the bike,' I told her.

Pompona cursed in Latin and threw more fruit as Will and I ran towards the hotel.

I'd never actually been inside the Plaza. The lobby was impressive with the crystal chandeliers and the passed-out rich people, but I didn't pay much attention. A couple of Hunters gave us directions to the elevators, and we rode up to the penthouse suites.

Demigods had completely taken over the top floors. Campers and Hunters were crashed out on sofas, washing up in the bathrooms, ripping silk draperies to bandage their wounds and helping themselves to snacks and sodas from the mini-bars. A couple of timber wolves were drinking out of the toilets. I was relieved to see that so many of my friends had made it through the night alive, but everybody looked beaten up.

'Percy!' Jake Mason clapped me on the shoulder. 'We're getting reports —'

'Later,' I said. 'Where's Annabeth?'

'The terrace. She's alive, man, but . . .'

I pushed past him.

Under different circumstances, I would've loved the view from the terrace. It looked straight down onto Central Park. The morning was clear and bright – perfect for a picnic or a hike, or pretty much anything except fighting monsters.

Annabeth lay on a lounge chair. Her face was pale and beaded with sweat. Even though she was covered in blankets, she shivered. Silena Beauregard was wiping her forehead with a cool cloth.

Will and I pushed through a crowd of Athena kids. Will unwrapped Annabeth's bandages to examine the wound and I wanted to faint. The bleeding had stopped but the gash looked deep. The skin around the cut was a horrible shade of green.

'Annabeth . . .' I choked up. She'd taken that knife for me. How could I have let that happen?

'Poison on the dagger,' she mumbled. 'Pretty stupid of me, huh?'

Will Solace exhaled with relief. 'It's not so bad, Annabeth. A few more minutes and we would've been in trouble, but the venom hasn't gotten past the shoulder yet. Just lie still. Somebody hand me some nectar.'

I grabbed a flask. Will cleaned out the wound with the godly drink while I held Annabeth's hand.

'Ow,' she said. 'Ow, ow!' She gripped my fingers so tight they turned purple, but she stayed still like Will asked. Silena muttered words of encouragement. Will put some silver paste over the wound and hummed words in Ancient Greek – a hymn to Apollo. Then he applied fresh bandages and stood up shakily.

[184]

The healing must've taken a lot of his energy. He looked almost as pale as Annabeth.

'That should do it,' he said. 'But we're going to need some mortal supplies.'

He grabbed a piece of hotel stationery, jotted down some notes and handed it to one of the Athena guys. 'There's a pharmacy on Fifth. Normally, I would never steal —'

'I would,' Travis volunteered.

Will glared at him. 'Leave cash or drachmas to pay, whatever you've got, but this is an emergency. I've got a feeling we're going to have a lot more people to treat.'

Nobody disagreed. There was hardly a single demigod who hadn't already been wounded . . . except me.

'Come on, guys,' Travis Stoll said. 'Let's give Annabeth some space. We've got a pharmacy to raid — I mean, visit.'

The demigods shuffled back inside. Jake Mason grabbed my shoulder as he was leaving. 'We'll talk later, but it's under control. I'm using Annabeth's shield to keep an eye on things. The enemy withdrew at sunrise; not sure why. We've got a lookout at each bridge and tunnel.'

'Thanks, man,' I said.

He nodded. 'Just take your time.'

He closed the terrace doors behind him — leaving Silena, Annabeth and me alone.

Silena pressed a cool cloth to Annabeth's forehead. 'This is all my fault.'

'No,' Annabeth said weakly. 'Silena, how is it your fault?'

'I've never been any good at camp,' she murmured. 'Not like you or Percy. If I were a better fighter . . .'

Her mouth trembled. Ever since Beckendorf died she'd been getting worse, and every time I looked at her it made me angry about his death all over again. Her expression reminded me of glass — like she might break any minute. I swore to myself that if I ever found the spy who'd cost her boyfriend his life, I would give him to Mrs O'Leary as a chew toy.

'You're a great camper,' I told Silena. 'You're the best pegasus rider we have. And you get along with people. Believe me, anyone who can make friends with Clarisse has talent.'

She stared at me like I'd just given her an idea. 'That's it! We need the Ares cabin. I can talk to Clarisse. I *know* I can convince her to help us.'

'Whoa, Silena. Even if you could get off the island, Clarisse is pretty stubborn. Once she gets angry —'

'Please,' Silena said. 'I can take a pegasus. I *know* I can make it back to camp. Let me try.'

I exchanged looks with Annabeth. She nodded slightly.

I didn't like the idea. I didn't think Silena stood a chance of convincing Clarisse to fight. On the other hand, Silena was so distracted right now that she would just get herself hurt in battle. Maybe sending her back to camp would give her something else to focus on.

'All right,' I told her. 'I can't think of anybody better to try.'

Silena threw her arms around me. Then she pushed back awkwardly, glancing at Annabeth. 'Um — sorry. Thank you, Percy! I won't let you down!'

Once she was gone, I knelt next to Annabeth and felt her forehead. She was still burning up.

'You're cute when you're worried,' she muttered. 'Your eyebrows get all scrunched together.'

'You are *not* going to die while I owe you a favour,' I said. 'Why did you take that knife?'

'You would've done the same for me.'

It was true. I guess we both knew it. Still, I felt like somebody was poking my heart with a cold metal rod. 'How did you know?'

'Know what?'

I looked around to make sure we were alone. Then I leaned in close and whispered: 'My Achilles spot. If you hadn't taken that knife, I would've died.'

She got a faraway look in her eyes. Her breath smelled of grapes, maybe from the nectar. 'I don't know, Percy. I just had this feeling you were in danger. Where — where is the spot?'

I wasn't supposed to tell anyone. But this was Annabeth. If I couldn't trust her, I couldn't trust anyone.

'The small of my back.'

She lifted her hand. 'Where? Here?'

She put her hand on my spine and my skin tingled. I moved her fingers to the one spot that grounded me to my mortal life. A thousand volts of electricity seemed to arc through my body.

'You saved me,' I said. 'Thanks.'

She removed her hand but I kept holding it.

'So you owe me,' she said weakly. 'What else is new?'

We watched the sun come up over the city. The traffic

should've been heavy by now, but there were no cars honking, no crowds bustling along the sidewalks.

Far away, I could hear a car alarm echo through the streets. A plume of black smoke curled into the sky somewhere over Harlem. I wondered how many ovens had been left on when the Morpheus spell hit; how many people had fallen asleep in the middle of cooking dinner. Pretty soon there would be more fires. Everyone in New York was in danger – and all those lives depended on us.

'You asked me why Hermes was mad at me,' Annabeth said.

'Hey, you need to rest –'

'No, I want to tell you. It's been bothering me for a long time.' She moved her shoulder and winced. 'Last year, Luke came to see me in San Francisco.'

'In person?' I felt like she'd just hit me with a hammer. 'He came to your house?'

'This was before we went into the Labyrinth, before . . .' She faltered, but I knew what she meant: *before he turned into Kronos.* 'He came under a flag of truce. He said he only wanted five minutes to talk. He looked scared, Percy. He told me Kronos was going to use him to take over the world. He said he wanted to run away, like the old days. He wanted me to come with him.'

'But you didn't trust him.'

'Of course not. I thought it was a trick. Plus . . . well, a lot of things had changed since the old days. I told Luke there was no way. He got mad. He said – he said I might as well fight him right there, because it was the last chance I'd get.'

Her forehead broke out in sweat again. The story was taking too much of her energy.

'It's okay,' I said. 'Try to get some rest.'

'You don't understand, Percy. Hermes was right. Maybe if I'd gone with him, I could've changed his mind. Or – or I had a knife. Luke was unarmed. I could've –'

'Killed him?' I said. 'You know that wouldn't have been right.'

She squeezed her eyes shut. 'Luke said Kronos would use him *like a stepping stone*. Those were his exact words. Kronos would use Luke, and become even more powerful.'

'He did that,' I said. 'He possessed Luke's body.'

'But what if Luke's body is only a transition? What if Kronos has a plan to become even more powerful? I could've stopped him. The war is my fault.'

Her story made me feel like I was back in the Styx, slowing dissolving. I remembered last summer, when the two-headed god Janus had warned Annabeth she would have to make a major choice – and that had happened *after* she saw Luke. Pan had also said something to her: *You will play a great role, though it may not be the role you imagined.*

I wanted to ask her about the vision Hestia had shown me, about her early days with Luke and Thalia. I knew it had something to do with my prophecy, but I didn't understand what.

Before I could get up my nerve, the terrace door opened. Connor Stoll stepped through.

'Percy.' He glanced at Annabeth, like he didn't want to say anything bad in front of her, but I could tell he wasn't bringing good news. 'Mrs O'Leary just came back with Grover. I think you should talk to him.'

Grover was having a snack in the living room. He was dressed for battle in an armoured shirt made from tree bark and twist-ties, with his wooden cudgel and his reed pipes hanging from his belt.

The Demeter cabin had whipped up a whole buffet in the hotel kitchens – everything from pizza to pineapple ice cream. Unfortunately, Grover was eating the furniture. He'd already chewed the stuffing off a fancy chair and was now gnawing the armrest.

'Dude,' I said, 'we're only borrowing this place.'

'Blah-ha-ha!' He had stuffing all over his face. 'Sorry, Percy. It's just . . . Louis XVI furniture. *Delicious*. Plus I always eat furniture when I get –'

'When you get nervous,' I said. 'Yeah, I know. So what's up?'

He clopped on his hooves. 'I heard about Annabeth. Is she . . . ?'

'She's going to be fine. She's resting.'

Grover took a deep breath. 'That's good. I've mobilized most of the nature spirits in the city – well, the ones that will listen to me, anyway.' He rubbed his forehead. 'I had no idea acorns could hurt so much. Anyway, we're helping out as much as we can.'

He told me about the skirmishes they'd seen. Mostly they'd been covering uptown where we didn't have enough demigods. Hellhounds had appeared in all sorts of places, shadow-travelling inside our lines, and the dryads and satyrs had been fighting them off. A young dragon had appeared in Harlem and a dozen wood nymphs died before the monster was finally defeated.

As Grover talked, Thalia entered the room with two of her lieutenants. She nodded to me grimly, went outside to check on Annabeth and came back in. She listened while Grover completed his report – the details getting worse and worse.

'We lost twenty satyrs against some giants at Fort Washington,' he said, his voice trembling. 'Almost half my kinsmen. River spirits drowned the giants in the end, but . . .'

Thalia shouldered her bow. 'Percy, Kronos's forces are still gathering at every bridge and tunnel. And Kronos isn't the only Titan. One of my Hunters spotted a huge man in golden armour mustering an army on the Jersey shore. I'm not sure who he is, but he radiates power like only a Titan or god.'

I remembered the golden Titan from my dream – the one on Mount Othrys who erupted into flames.

'Great,' I said. 'Any good news?'

Thalia shrugged. 'We've sealed off the subway tunnels into Manhattan. My best trappers took care of it. Also, it seems like the enemy is waiting for tonight to attack. I think Luke –' she caught herself – 'I mean Kronos needs time to regenerate after each fight. He's still not comfortable with his new form. It's taking a lot of his power to slow time around the city.'

Grover nodded. 'Most of his forces are more powerful at night, too. But they'll be back after sundown.'

I tried to think clearly. 'Okay. Any word from the gods?'

Thalia shook her head. 'I know Lady Artemis would be here if she could. Athena, too. But Zeus has ordered them to stay at his side. The last I heard, Typhon was destroying the Ohio River Valley. He should reach the Appalachian Mountains by midday.'

'So at best,' I said, 'we've got another two days before he arrives.'

Jake Mason cleared his throat. He'd been standing there so silently I'd almost forgotten he was in the room.

'Percy, something else,' he said. 'The way Kronos showed up at the Williamsburg Bridge, like he knew you were going there. And he shifted his forces to our weakest points. As soon as we deployed, he changed tactics. He barely touched the Lincoln Tunnel, where the Hunters were strong. He went for our weakest spots, like he knew.'

'Like he had inside information,' I said. 'The spy.'

'What spy?' Thalia demanded.

I told her about the silver charm Kronos had shown me, the communication device.

'That's bad,' she said. 'Very bad.'

'It could be anyone,' Jake said. 'We were all standing there when Percy gave the orders.'

'But what can we do?' Grover asked. 'Frisk every demigod until we find a scythe charm?'

They all looked at me, waiting for a decision. I couldn't afford to show how panicked I felt, even if things seemed hopeless.

'We keep fighting,' I said. 'We can't obsess about this spy. If we're suspicious of each other, we'll just tear ourselves apart. You guys were awesome last night. I couldn't ask for a braver army. Let's set up a rotation for the watches. Rest up while you can. We've got a long night ahead of us.'

The demigods mumbled agreement. They went their separate ways to sleep or eat or repair their weapons.

'Percy, you too,' Thalia said. 'We'll keep an eye on things. Go lie down. We need you in good shape for tonight.'

I didn't argue too hard. I found the nearest bedroom and crashed on the canopied bed. I thought I was too wired to sleep, but my eyes closed almost immediately.

In my dream, I saw Nico di Angelo alone in the gardens of Hades. He'd just dug a hole in one of Persephone's flowerbeds, which I didn't figure would make the queen very happy.

He poured a goblet of wine into the hole and began to chant. 'Let the dead taste again. Let them rise and take this offering. Maria di Angelo, show yourself!'

White smoke gathered. A human figure formed, but it wasn't Nico's mother. It was a girl with dark hair, olive skin and the silvery clothes of a Hunter.

'Bianca,' Nico said. 'But –'

Don't summon our mother, Nico, she warned. *She is the one spirit you are forbidden to see.*

'Why?' he demanded. 'What's our father hiding?'

Pain, Bianca said. *Hatred. A curse that stretches back to the Great Prophecy.*

'What do you mean?' Nico said. 'I have to know!'

The knowledge will only hurt you. Remember what I said: holding grudges is a fatal flaw for children of Hades.

'I know that,' Nico said. 'But I'm not the same as I used to be, Bianca. Stop trying to protect me!'

Brother, you don't understand –

Nico swiped his hand through the mist, and Bianca's image dissipated.

'Maria di Angelo,' he said again. 'Speak to me!'

A different image formed. It was a scene rather than a single ghost. In the mist, I saw Nico and Bianca as little children, playing in the lobby of an elegant hotel, chasing each other around marble columns.

A woman sat on a nearby sofa. She wore a black dress, gloves and a black veiled hat like a star from an old 1940s movie. She had Bianca's smile and Nico's eyes.

On a chair next to her sat a large oily man in a black pinstripe suit. With a shock, I realized it was Hades. He was leaning towards the woman, using his hands as he talked like he was agitated.

'Please, my dear,' he said. 'You *must* come to the Underworld. I don't care what Persephone thinks! I can keep you safe there.'

'No, my love.' She spoke with an Italian accent. 'Raise our children in the land of the dead? I will not do this.'

'Maria, listen to me. The war in Europe has turned the other gods against me. A prophecy has been made. My children are no longer safe. Poseidon and Zeus have forced me into an agreement. None of us are to have demigod children ever again.'

'But you already *have* Nico and Bianca. Surely –'

'No! The prophecy warns of a child who turns sixteen. Zeus has decreed that the children I currently have must be turned over to Camp Half-Blood for *proper training*, but I know what he means. At best they'll be watched, imprisoned, turned against their father. Even more likely, he will not take a chance. He won't allow my demigod children to reach sixteen. He'll find a way to destroy them, and I won't risk that!'

'*Certamente*,' Maria said. 'We will stay together. Zeus is *un imbecille.*'

I couldn't help admiring her courage, but Hades glanced nervously at the ceiling. 'Maria, please. I told you, Zeus gave me a deadline of *last week* to turn over the children. His wrath will be horrible, and I cannot hide you forever. As long as you are with the children, you are in danger, too.'

Maria smiled, and again it was creepy how much she looked like her daughter. 'You are a god, my love. You will protect us. But I will not take Nico and Bianca to the Underworld.'

Hades wrung his hands. 'Then – there is another option. I know a place in the desert where time stands still. I could send the children there, just for a while, for their own safety, and we could be together. I will build you a golden palace by the Styx.'

Maria di Angelo laughed gently. 'You are a kind man, my love. A generous man. The other gods should see you as I do, and they would not fear you so. But Nico and Bianca need their mother. Besides, they are only children. The gods wouldn't really hurt them.'

'You don't know my family,' Hades said darkly. 'Please, Maria, I can't lose you.'

She touched his lips with her fingers. 'You will not lose me. Wait for me while I get my bag. Watch the children.'

She kissed the Lord of the Dead and rose from the sofa. Hades watched her walk upstairs as if her every step away caused him pain.

A moment later, he tensed. The children stopped playing as if they sensed something, too.

'No!' Hades said. But even his godly powers were too slow. He only had time to erect a wall of black energy around the children before the hotel exploded.

The force was so violent the entire mist image dissolved. When it came into focus again, I saw Hades kneeling in the ruins, holding the broken form of Maria di Angelo. Fires still burned all around him. Lightning flashed across the sky and thunder rumbled.

Little Nico and Bianca stared at their mother uncomprehendingly. The Fury Alecto appeared behind them, hissing and flapping her leathery wings. The children didn't seem to notice her.

'Zeus!' Hades shook his fist at the sky. 'I will crush you for this! I will bring her back!'

'My lord, you cannot,' Alecto warned. 'You of all immortals must respect the laws of death.'

Hades glowed with rage. I thought he would show his true form and vaporize his own children, but at the last moment he seemed to regain control.

'Take them,' he told Alecto, choking back a sob. 'Wash their memories clean in the Lethe and bring them to the Lotus Hotel. Zeus will not harm them there.'

'As you wish, my lord,' Alecto said. 'And the woman's body?'

'Take her as well,' he said bitterly. 'Give her the ancient rites.'

Alecto, the children and Maria's body dissolved into shadows, leaving Hades alone in the ruins.

'I warned you,' a new voice said.

Hades turned. A girl in a multicoloured dress stood by the smouldering remains of the sofa. She had short black hair and sad eyes. She was no more than twelve. I didn't know her, but she looked strangely familiar.

'You dare come here?' Hades growled. 'I should blast you to dust!'

'You cannot,' the girl said. 'The power of Delphi protects me.'

With a chill, I realized I was looking at the Oracle of Delphi, back when she was alive and young. Somehow seeing her like this was even spookier than seeing her as a mummy.

'You've killed the woman I loved!' Hades roared. 'Your prophecy brought us to this!'

He loomed over the girl but she didn't flinch.

'Zeus ordained the explosion to destroy the children,' she said, 'because you defied his will. I had nothing to do with it. And I did warn you to hide them sooner.'

'I couldn't! Maria would not let me! Besides, they were innocent.'

'Nevertheless, they are your children, which makes them dangerous. Even if you put them away in the Lotus Hotel, you only delay the problem. Nico and Bianca will never be able to rejoin the world lest they turn sixteen.'

'Because of your so-called Great Prophecy. And you have forced me into an oath to have no other children. You have left me with nothing!'

'I foresee the future,' the girl said. 'I cannot change it.'

Black fire lit the god's eyes, and I knew something bad was coming. I wanted to yell at the girl to hide or run.

'Then, Oracle, hear the words of Hades,' he growled.

'Perhaps I cannot bring back Maria. Nor can I bring you an early death. But your soul is still mortal, and I *can* curse you.'

The girl's eyes widened. 'You would not –'

'I swear,' Hades said, 'as long as my children remain outcasts, as long as I labour under the curse of your Great Prophecy, the Oracle of Delphi will never have another mortal host. You will never rest in peace. No other will take your place. Your body will wither and die, and still the Oracle's spirit will be locked inside you. You will speak your bitter prophecies until you crumble to nothing. The Oracle will die with you!'

The girl screamed, and the misty image was blasted to shreds. Nico fell to his knees in Persephone's garden, his face white with shock. Standing in front of him was the real Hades, towering in his black robes and scowling down at his son.

'And just what,' he asked Nico, 'do you think you're doing?'

A black explosion filled my dreams. Then the scene changed.

Rachel Elizabeth Dare was walking along a white sand beach. She wore a swimsuit with a T-shirt wrapped around her waist. Her shoulders and face were sunburnt.

She knelt and began writing in the surf with her finger. I tried to make out the letters. I thought my dyslexia was acting up until I realized she was writing in Ancient Greek.

That was impossible. The dream had to be false.

Rachel finished writing a few words and muttered, 'What in the world?'

I can read Greek, but I only recognized one word before the sea washed it away: Περσεύς. My name: *Perseus.*

Rachel stood abruptly and backed away from the surf.

'Oh, gods,' she said. '*That's* what it means.'

She turned and ran, kicking up sand as she raced back to her family's villa.

She pounded up the porch steps, breathing hard. Her father looked up from his *Wall Street Journal.*

'Dad.' Rachel marched up to him. 'We have to go back.'

Her dad's mouth twitched, like he was trying to remember how to smile. 'Back? We just got here.'

'There's trouble in New York. Percy's in danger.'

'Did he call you?'

'No . . . not exactly. But I *know.* It's a feeling.'

Mr Dare folded his newspaper. 'Your mother and I have been looking forward to this vacation for a long time.'

'No you haven't! You both hate the beach! You're just too stubborn to admit it.'

'Now, Rachel –'

'I'm telling you something is wrong in New York! The whole city . . . I don't know what exactly, but it's under attack.'

Her father sighed. 'I think we would've heard something like that on the news.'

'No,' Rachel insisted. 'Not this kind of attack. Have you had any calls since we got here?'

Her father frowned. 'No . . . but it is the weekend, in the middle of the summer.'

'You *always* get calls,' Rachel said. 'You've got to admit that's strange.'

Her father hesitated. 'We can't just leave. We've spent a lot of money.'

'Look,' Rachel said. 'Daddy . . . Percy needs me. I have to deliver a message. It's life or death.'

'What message? What are you talking about?'

'I can't tell you.'

'Then you can't go.'

Rachel closed her eyes like she was getting up her courage. 'Dad . . . let me go, and I'll make a deal with you.'

Mr Dare sat forward. Deals were something he understood. 'I'm listening.'

'Clarion Ladies' Academy. I'll – I'll go there in the autumn. I won't even complain. But you have to get me back to New York *right now*.'

He was silent for a long time. Then he opened his phone and made a call.

'Douglas? Prep the plane. We're leaving for New York. Yes . . . immediately.'

Rachel flung her arms around him, and her father seemed surprised, like she'd never hugged him before.

'I'll make it up to you, Dad!'

He smiled, but his expression was chilly. He studied her like he wasn't seeing his daughter – just the young lady he wanted her to be, once Clarion Academy got through with her.

'Yes, Rachel,' he agreed. 'You most certainly will.'

The scene faded. I mumbled in my sleep: 'Rachel, no!'

I was still tossing and turning when Thalia shook me awake.

'Percy,' she said. 'Come on. It's late afternoon. We've got visitors.'

I sat up, disoriented. The bed was too comfortable, and I hated sleeping in the middle of the day.

'Visitors?' I said.

Thalia nodded grimly. 'A Titan wants to see you, under a flag of truce. He has a message from Kronos.'

13 A TITAN BRINGS ME A PRESENT

We could see the white flag from half a mile away. It was as big as a football field, carried by a ten-metre-tall giant with bright blue skin and icy grey hair.

'A Hyperborean,' Thalia said. 'The giants of the north. It's a bad sign that they sided with Kronos. They're usually peaceful.'

'You've met them?' I said.

'Mmm. There's a big colony in Alberta. You do *not* want to get into a snowball fight with those guys.'

As the giant got closer, I could see three human-sized envoys with him — a half-blood in armour, an *empousa* demon with flaming hair in a black dress and a tall man in a tuxedo. The *empousa* held the tux dude's arm, so they looked like a couple on their way to a Broadway show or something — except for her flaming hair and fangs.

The group walked leisurely towards the Heckscher Playground. The swings and ball courts were empty. The only sound was the fountain on Umpire Rock.

I looked at Grover. 'The tux dude is the Titan?'

He nodded nervously. 'He looks like a magician. I hate magicians. They usually have rabbits.'

I stared at him. 'You're scared of bunnies?'

'Blah-hah-hah! They're big bullies. Always stealing celery from defenceless satyrs!'

Thalia coughed.

'What?' Grover demanded.

'We'll have to work on your bunny phobia later,' I said. 'Here they come.'

The man in the tux stepped forward. He was taller than an average human – well over two metres. His black hair was tied in a ponytail. Dark round glasses covered his eyes, but what really caught my attention was the skin on his face. It was covered in scratches, like he'd been attacked by a small animal – a really, *really* mad hamster, maybe.

'Percy Jackson,' he said in a silky voice. 'It's a great honour.'

His lady friend the *empousa* hissed at me. She'd probably heard how I'd destroyed two of her sisters last summer.

'My dear,' Tux Dude said to her. 'Why don't you make yourself comfortable over there, eh?'

She released his arm and drifted over to a park bench.

I glanced at the armed demigod behind Tux Dude. I hadn't recognized him in his new helmet, but it was my old backstabbing buddy Ethan Nakamura. His nose looked like a squashed tomato from our fight on the Williamsburg Bridge. That made me feel better.

'Hey, Ethan,' I said. 'You're looking good.'

Ethan glared at me.

'To business.' Tux Dude extended his hand. 'I am Prometheus.'

I was too surprised to shake. 'The fire-stealer guy? The chained-to-the-rock-with-the-vultures guy?'

Prometheus winced. He touched the scratches on his

face. 'Please, don't mention the vultures. But, yes, I stole fire from the gods and gave it to your ancestors. In return, the ever merciful Zeus had me chained to a rock and tortured for all eternity.'

'But –'

'How did I get free? Hercules did that, aeons ago. So you see, I have a soft spot for heroes. Some of you can be quite civilized.'

'Unlike the company you keep,' I noticed.

I was looking at Ethan, but Prometheus apparently thought I meant the *empousa*.

'Oh, demons aren't so bad,' he said. 'You just have to keep them well fed. Now, Percy Jackson, let us parley.'

He waved me towards a picnic table and we sat down. Thalia and Grover stood behind me.

The blue giant propped his white flag against a tree and began absently playing on the playground. He stepped on the monkey bars and crushed them, but he didn't seem angry. He just frowned and said, 'Uh-oh.' Then he stepped in the fountain and broke the concrete bowl in half. 'Uh-oh.' The water froze where his foot touched it. A bunch of stuffed animals hung from his belt – the huge kind you get for grand prizes at an arcade. He reminded me of Tyson, and the idea of fighting him made me sad.

Prometheus sat forward and laced his fingers. He looked earnest, kindly and wise. 'Percy, your position is weak. You know you can't stop another assault.'

'We'll see.'

Prometheus looked pained, like he really cared what happened to me. 'Percy, I'm the Titan of forethought. I know what's going to happen.'

'Also the Titan of crafty counsel,' Grover put in. 'Emphasis on *crafty*.'

Prometheus shrugged. 'True enough, satyr. But I supported the gods in the last war. I told Kronos: "You don't have the strength. You'll lose." And I was right. So you see I know how to pick the winning side. This time, I'm backing Kronos.'

'Because Zeus chained you to a rock,' I guessed.

'Partly, yes. I won't deny I want revenge. But that's not the only reason I'm supporting Kronos. It's the wisest choice. I'm here because I thought you might listen to reason.'

He drew a map on the table with his finger. Wherever he touched, golden lines appeared, glowing on the concrete. 'This is Manhattan. We have armies here, here, here and here. We know your numbers. We outnumber you twenty to one.'

'Your spy has been keeping you posted,' I guessed.

Prometheus smiled apologetically. 'At any rate, our forces are growing daily. Tonight, Kronos will attack. You will be overwhelmed. You've fought bravely, but there's just no way you can hold all of Manhattan. You'll be forced to retreat to the Empire State Building. There you'll be destroyed. I have seen this. It *will* happen.'

I thought about the picture Rachel had drawn in my dreams – an army at the base of the Empire State Building. I remembered the words of the young girl Oracle in my dream: *I foresee the future. I cannot change it.* Prometheus spoke with such certainty it was hard not to believe him.

'I won't let it happen,' I said.

Prometheus brushed a speck off his tux lapel. 'Understand, Percy. You are refighting the Trojan War here. Patterns repeat themselves in history. They reappear just as monsters do. A great siege. Two armies. The only difference is, this time you are defending. *You* are Troy. And you know what happened to the Trojans, don't you?'

'So you're going to cram a wooden horse into the elevator at the Empire State Building?' I asked. 'Good luck.'

Prometheus smiled. 'Troy was completely destroyed, Percy. You don't want that to happen here. Stand down, and New York will be spared. Your forces will be granted amnesty. I will personally assure your safety. Let Kronos take Olympus. Who cares? Typhon will destroy the gods anyway.'

'Right,' I said. 'And I'm supposed to believe Kronos would spare the city.'

'All he wants is Olympus,' Prometheus promised. 'The might of the gods is tied to their seats of power. You saw what happened to Poseidon once his undersea palace was attacked.'

I winced, remembering how old and decrepit my father looked.

'Yes,' Prometheus said sadly. 'I know that was hard for you. When Kronos destroys Olympus, the gods will fade. They will become so weak they will be easily defeated. Kronos would rather do this while Typhon has the Olympians distracted in the west. Much easier. Fewer lives lost. But, make no mistake, the best you can do is slow us down. The day after tomorrow, Typhon arrives in New York, and you will have no chance at all. The gods and Mount Olympus will still be destroyed, but it will be much messier. Much, much worse for you and your city. Either way, the Titans will rule.'

Thalia pounded her fist on the table. 'I serve Artemis. The Hunters will fight to our last breath. Percy, you're not seriously going to listen to this slimeball, are you?'

I figured Prometheus was going to blast her, but he just smiled. 'Your courage does you credit, Thalia Grace.'

Thalia stiffened. 'That's my mother's surname. I don't use it.'

'As you wish,' Prometheus said casually, but I could tell he'd got under her skin. I'd never even heard Thalia's last name before. Somehow it made her seem almost normal. Less mysterious and powerful.

'At any rate,' the Titan said, 'you need not be my enemy. I have always been a helper of mankind.'

'That's a load of Minotaur dung,' Thalia said. 'When mankind first sacrificed to the gods, you tricked them into giving you the best portion. You gave us fire to annoy the gods, not because you cared about us.'

Prometheus shook his head. 'You don't understand. I helped shape your nature.'

A wiggling lump of clay appeared in his hands. He fashioned it into a little doll with legs and arms. The lump man didn't have any eyes, but it groped around the table, stumbling over Prometheus's fingers. 'I have been whispering in man's ear since the beginning of your existence. I represent your curiosity, your sense of exploration, your inventiveness. Help me save you, Percy. Do this, and I will give mankind a new gift – a new revelation that will move you as far forward as fire did. You can't make that kind of advance under the gods. They would never allow it. But this could be a new golden age for you. Or . . .' He made a fist and smashed the clay man into a pancake.

The blue giant rumbled, 'Uh-oh.' Over at the park bench, the *empousa* bared her fangs in a smile.

'Percy, you know the Titans and their offspring are not all bad,' Prometheus said. 'You've met Calypso.'

My face felt hot. 'That's different.'

'How? Much like me, she did nothing wrong, and yet she was exiled forever simply because she was Atlas's daughter. We are not your enemies. Don't let the worst happen,' he pleaded. 'We offer you peace.'

I looked at Ethan Nakamura. 'You must hate this.'

'I don't know what you mean,' said Ethan.

'If we took this deal, you wouldn't get revenge. You wouldn't get to kill us all. Isn't that what you want?'

His good eye flared. 'All I want is respect, Jackson. The gods never gave me that. You wanted me to go to your stupid camp, spend my time crammed into the Hermes cabin because I'm not important? Not even recognized?'

He sounded just like Luke when he'd tried to kill me in the woods at camp four years ago. The memory made my hand ache where the pit scorpion had stung me.

'Your mom's the goddess of revenge,' I told Ethan. 'We should respect that?'

'Nemesis stands for balance! When people have too much good luck, she tears them down.'

'Which is why she took your eye?'

'It was payment,' he growled. 'In exchange, she swore to me that one day, *I* would tip the balance of power. I would bring the minor gods respect. An eye was a small price to pay.'

'Great mom.'

'At least she keeps her word, unlike the Olympians. She always pays her debts – good or evil.'

'Yeah,' I said. 'So I saved your life, and you repaid me by raising Kronos. That's fair.'

Ethan grabbed the hilt of his sword, but Prometheus stopped him.

'Now, now,' the Titan said. 'We're on a diplomatic mission.'

Prometheus studied me as if trying to understand my anger. Then he nodded like he'd just picked a thought from my brain.

'It bothers you what happened to Luke,' he decided. 'Hestia didn't show you the full story. Perhaps if you understood . . .'

The Titan reached out.

Thalia cried a warning, but before I could react Prometheus's index finger touched my forehead.

Suddenly I was back in May Castellan's living room. Candles flickered on the fireplace mantel, reflecting in the mirrors along the walls. Through the kitchen doorway I could see Thalia sitting at the table while Ms Castellan bandaged her wounded leg. Seven-year-old Annabeth sat next to her, playing with a Medusa beanbag toy.

Hermes and Luke stood apart in the living room.

The god's face looked liquid in the candlelight, like he couldn't decide what shape to adopt. He was dressed in a navy blue jogging outfit with winged Reeboks.

'Why show yourself now?' Luke demanded. His shoulders were tense as if he expected a fight. 'All these years I've been calling to you, praying you'd show up, and nothing. You left me with *her.*' He pointed towards the kitchen like he couldn't bear to look at his mother, much less say her name.

'Luke, do not dishonour her,' Hermes warned. 'Your mother did the best she could. As for me, I could not interfere with your path. The children of the gods must find their own way.'

'So it was for my own good. Growing up on the streets, fending for myself, fighting monsters.'

'You're my son,' Hermes said. 'I knew you had the ability. When I was only a baby, I crawled from my cradle and set out for –'

'I'm not a god! Just once, you could've said something. You could've helped when –' he took an unsteady breath, lowering his voice so no one in the kitchen could overhear '– when she was having one of her *fits*, shaking me and saying crazy things about my fate. When I used to hide in the closet so she wouldn't find me with those . . . those glowing eyes. Did you even *care* that I was scared? Did you even know when I finally ran away?'

In the kitchen, Ms Castellan chattered aimlessly, pouring Kool-Aid for Thalia and Annabeth as she told them stories about Luke as a baby. Thalia rubbed her bandaged leg nervously. Annabeth glanced into the living room and held up a burnt cookie for Luke to see. She mouthed, *Can we go now?*

'Luke, I care very much,' Hermes said slowly, 'but gods must not interfere directly in mortal affairs. It is one of our Ancient Laws. Especially when your destiny . . .' His voice trailed off. He stared at the candles as if remembering something unpleasant.

'What?' Luke asked. 'What about my destiny?'

'You should not have come back,' Hermes muttered. 'It only upsets you both. However, I see now that you are getting too old to be on the run without help. I'll speak with Chiron at Camp Half-Blood and ask him to send a satyr to collect you.'

'We're doing fine without your help,' Luke growled. 'Now what were you saying about my destiny?'

The wings on Hermes' Reeboks fluttered restlessly. He studied his son as if he were trying to memorize his face, and suddenly a cold feeling washed through me. I realized Hermes *knew* what May Castellan's mutterings meant. I wasn't sure how, but looking at his face I was absolutely certain. Hermes understood what would happen to Luke some day, how he would turn evil.

'My son,' he said, 'I'm the god of travellers, the god of roads. If I know anything, I know that you must walk your own path, even though it tears my heart.'

'You don't love me.'

'I promise I . . . I do love you. Go to camp. I will see that you get a quest soon. Perhaps you can defeat the hydra, or steal the apples of Hesperides. You will get a chance to be a great hero before . . .'

'Before what?' Luke's voice was trembling now. 'What did my mom see that made her like this? What's going to happen to me? If you love me, *tell* me.'

Hermes' expression tightened. 'I cannot.'

'Then you don't care!' Luke yelled.

In the kitchen, the talking died abruptly.

'Luke?' May Castellan called. 'Is that you? Is my boy all right?'

Luke turned to hide his face, but I could see the tears

in his eyes. 'I'm fine. I have a new family. I don't need either of you.'

'I'm your father,' Hermes insisted.

'A *father* is supposed to be around. I've never even *met* you. Thalia, Annabeth, come on! We're leaving!'

'My boy, don't go!' May Castellan called after him. 'I have your lunch ready!'

Luke stormed out of the door, Thalia and Annabeth scrambling after him. May Castellan tried to follow, but Hermes held her back.

As the screen door slammed, May collapsed in Hermes' arms and began to shake. Her eyes opened – glowing green – and she clutched desperately at Hermes' shoulders.

'*My son,*' she hissed in a dry voice. '*Danger. Terrible fate!*'

'I know, my love,' Hermes said sadly. 'Believe me, I know.'

The image faded. Prometheus pulled his hand away from my forehead.

'Percy?' Thalia asked. 'What – what was that?'

I realized I was clammy with sweat.

Prometheus nodded sympathetically. 'Appalling, isn't it? The gods know what is to come, and yet they do nothing, even for their children. How long did it take for them to tell you *your* prophecy, Percy Jackson? Don't you think your father knows what will happen to you?'

I was too stunned to answer.

'Perrrrcy,' Grover warned, 'he's playing with your mind. Trying to make you angry.'

Grover could read emotions, so he probably knew Prometheus was succeeding.

'Do you really blame your friend Luke?' the Titan asked me. 'And what about you, Percy? Will you be controlled by your fate? Kronos offers you a much better deal.'

I clenched my fists. As much as I hated what Prometheus had shown me, I hated Kronos a lot more. 'I'll give you a deal. Tell Kronos to call off his attack, leave Luke Castellan's body and return to the pits of Tartarus. Then maybe I won't have to destroy him.'

The *empousa* snarled. Her hair erupted in fresh flames, but Prometheus just sighed.

'If you change your mind,' he said, 'I have a gift for you.'

A Greek vase appeared on the table. It was about a metre high and thirty centimetres wide, glazed with black-and-white geometric designs. The ceramic lid was fastened with a leather harness.

Grover whimpered when he saw it.

Thalia gasped. 'That's not –'

'Yes,' Prometheus said. 'You recognize it.'

Looking at the jar, I felt a strange sense of fear, but I had no idea why.

'This belonged to my sister-in-law,' Prometheus explained. 'Pandora.'

A lump formed in my throat. 'As in Pandora's box?'

Prometheus shook his head. 'I don't know how this *box* business got started. It was never a box. It was a *pithos*, a storage jar. I suppose Pandora's *pithos* doesn't have the same ring to it, but never mind that. Yes, she did open this jar, which contained most of the demons that now haunt mankind – fear, death, hunger, sickness.'

'Don't forget me,' the *empousa* purred.

'Indeed,' Prometheus conceded. 'The first *empousa* was also trapped in this jar, released by Pandora. But what I find curious about the story — Pandora always gets the blame. She is punished for being curious. The gods would have you believe that this is the lesson: mankind should not explore. They should not ask questions. They should do what they are told. In truth, Percy, this jar was a trap designed by Zeus and the other gods. It was revenge on *me* and my entire family — my poor simple brother Epimetheus and his wife Pandora. The gods knew she would open the jar. They were willing to punish the entire race of humanity along with us.'

I thought about my dream of Hades and Maria di Angelo. Zeus had destroyed an entire hotel to eliminate two demigod children — just to save his own skin, because he was scared of a prophecy. He'd killed an innocent woman and probably hadn't lost any sleep over it. Hades was no better. He wasn't powerful enough to take his revenge on Zeus, so he cursed the Oracle, dooming a young girl to a horrible fate. And Hermes . . . why had he abandoned Luke? Why hadn't he at least warned Luke, or tried to raise him better so he wouldn't turn evil?

Maybe Prometheus was toying with my mind.

But what if he's right? part of me wondered. How are the gods any better than the Titans?

Prometheus tapped the lid of Pandora's jar. 'Only one spirit remained inside when Pandora opened it.'

'Hope,' I said.

Prometheus looked pleased. 'Very good, Percy. Elpis, the Spirit of Hope, would not abandon humanity. Hope does not leave without being given permission. She can only be released by a child of man.'

The Titan slid the jar across the table.

'I give you this as a reminder of what the gods are like,' he said. 'Keep Elpis, if you wish. But if you decide that you have seen enough destruction, enough futile suffering, then open the jar. Let Elpis go. Give up Hope, and I will know that you are surrendering. I promise Kronos will be lenient. He will spare the survivors.'

I stared at the jar and got a very bad feeling. I figured Pandora had been completely ADHD, like me. I could never leave things alone. I didn't like temptation. What if *this* was my choice? Maybe the prophecy all came down to me keeping this jar closed or opening it.

'I don't want the thing,' I growled.

'Too late,' Prometheus said. 'The gift is given. It cannot be taken back.'

He stood. The *empousa* came forward and slipped her arm through his.

'Morrain!' Prometheus called to the blue giant. 'We are leaving. Get your flag.'

'Uh-oh,' the giant said.

'We will see you soon, Percy Jackson,' Prometheus promised. 'One way or another.'

Ethan Nakamura gave me one last hateful look. Then the truce party turned and strolled up the lane through Central Park, like it was just a regular sunny Sunday afternoon.

14 PIGS FLY

Back at the Plaza, Thalia pulled me aside. 'What did Prometheus show you?'

Reluctantly, I told her about the vision of May Castellan's house. Thalia rubbed her thigh like she was remembering the old wound.

'That was a bad night,' she admitted. 'Annabeth was so little I don't think she really understood what she saw. She just knew Luke was upset.'

I looked out of the hotel windows at Central Park. Small fires were still burning in the north, but otherwise the city seemed unnaturally peaceful. 'Do you know what happened to May Castellan? I mean –'

'I know what you mean,' Thalia said. 'I never saw her have an, um, episode, but Luke told me about the glowing eyes, the strange things she would say. He made me promise never to tell. What caused it – I have no idea. If Luke knew, he never told me.'

'Hermes knew,' I said. 'Something caused May to see parts of Luke's future, and Hermes understood what would happen – how Luke would turn into Kronos.'

Thalia frowned. 'You can't be sure of that. Remember Prometheus was manipulating what you saw, Percy, showing you what happened in the worst possible light. Hermes *did* love Luke. I could tell just by looking at his face. And

Hermes was there that night because he was checking up on May, taking care of her. He wasn't all bad.'

'It's still not right,' I insisted. 'Luke was just a little kid. Hermes never helped him, never stopped him from running away.'

Thalia shouldered her bow. Again it struck me how much stronger she looked now that she'd stopped aging. You could almost see a silvery glow around her – the blessing of Artemis.

'Percy,' she said, 'you can't start feeling sorry for Luke. We all have tough things to deal with. All demigods do. Our parents are hardly ever around. But Luke made bad choices. Nobody forced him to do that. In fact –'

She glanced down the hall to make sure we were alone. 'I'm worried about Annabeth. If she has to face Luke in battle, I don't know if she can do it. She's always had a soft spot for him.'

Blood rose to my face. 'She'll do fine.'

'I don't know. After that night, after we left his mom's house? Luke was never the same. He got reckless and moody, like he had something to prove. By the time Grover found us and tried to get us to camp . . . well, part of the reason we had so much trouble was because Luke wouldn't be careful. He wanted to pick a fight with every monster we crossed. Annabeth didn't see that as a problem. Luke was her hero. She only understood that his parents had made him sad, and she got very defensive of him. She still *is* defensive. All I'm saying . . . Don't you fall into the same trap. Luke has given himself to Kronos now. We can't afford to be soft on him.'

I looked out at the fires in Harlem, wondering how

many sleeping mortals were in danger right now because of Luke's bad choices.

'You're right,' I said.

Thalia patted my shoulder. 'I'm going to check on the Hunters, then get some more sleep before nightfall. You should crash, too.'

'The last thing I need is more dreams.'

'I know, believe me.' Her dark expression made me wonder what she'd been dreaming about. It was a common demigod problem: the more dangerous our situation became, the worse and more frequent our dreams got. 'But, Percy, there's no telling when you'll get another chance for rest. It's going to be a long night – maybe our *last* night.'

I didn't like it, but I knew she was right. I nodded wearily and gave her Pandora's jar. 'Do me a favour. Lock this in the hotel vault, will you? I think I'm allergic to *pithos*.'

Thalia smiled. 'You got it.'

I found the nearest bed and passed out. But of course sleep only brought more nightmares.

I saw the undersea palace of my father. The enemy army was closer now, entrenched only a few hundred metres outside the palace. The fortress walls were completely destroyed. The temple my dad had used as his headquarters was burning with Greek fire.

I zoomed in on the armoury, where my brother and some other Cyclopes were on lunch break, eating from huge jars of extra-chunky peanut butter (and don't ask me how it tasted underwater, because I don't want to know). As I watched, the outer wall of the armoury exploded. A Cyclops warrior stumbled inside, collapsing on the lunch table.

Tyson knelt down to help, but it was too late. The Cyclops dissolved into sea silt.

Enemy giants moved towards the breech, and Tyson picked up the fallen warrior's club. He yelled something to his fellow blacksmiths – probably 'For Poseidon!' – but with his mouth full of peanut butter it sounded like, 'PUH PTEH BUN.' His brethren all grabbed hammers and chisels, yelled, 'PEANUT BUTTER!' and charged behind Tyson into battle.

Then the scene shifted. I was with Ethan Nakamura at the enemy camp. What I saw made me shiver, partly because the army was so huge, partly because I recognized the place.

We were in the backwoods of New Jersey, on a crumbling road lined with run-down businesses and tattered billboard signs. A trampled fence ringed a big yard full of cement statuary. The sign above the warehouse was hard to read because it was in red cursive, but I knew what it said: AUNTY EM'S GARDEN GNOME EMPORIUM.

I hadn't thought about the place in years. It was clearly abandoned. The statues were broken and spray-painted with graffiti. A cement satyr – Grover's Uncle Ferdinand – had lost his arm. Part of the warehouse roof had caved in. A big yellow sign pasted on the door read: CONDEMNED.

Hundreds of tents and fires surrounded the property. Mostly I saw monsters, but there were some human mercenaries in combat fatigues and demigods in armour, too. A purple-and-black banner hung outside the emporium, guarded by two huge blue Hyperboreans.

Ethan crouched at the nearest campfire. A couple of other demigods sat with him, sharpening their swords.

The doors of the warehouse opened and Prometheus stepped out.

'Nakamura,' he called. 'The master would like to speak to you.'

Ethan stood up warily. 'Something wrong?'

Prometheus smiled. 'You'll have to ask him.'

One of the other demigods snickered. 'Nice knowing you.'

Ethan readjusted his sword belt and headed into the warehouse.

Except for the hole in the roof, the place was just as I remembered. Statues of terrified people stood frozen in mid-scream. In the snack-bar area, the picnic tables had been moved aside. Right between the drink dispenser and pretzel warmer stood a golden throne. Kronos lounged on it, his scythe across his lap. He wore jeans and a T-shirt, and with his brooding expression he looked almost human – like the younger version of Luke I'd seen in the vision, pleading with Hermes to tell him his fate. Then Luke saw Ethan, and his face contorted into a very inhuman smile. His golden eyes glowed.

'Well, Nakamura. What did you think of the diplomatic mission?'

Ethan hesitated. 'I'm sure Lord Prometheus is better suited to speak –'

'But I asked *you*.'

Ethan's good eye darted back and forth, noting the guards that stood around Kronos. 'I . . . I don't think Jackson will surrender. Ever.'

Kronos nodded. 'Anything else you wanted to tell me?'

'N-no, sir.'

'You look nervous, Ethan.'

'No, sir. It's just . . . I heard this was the lair of –'

'Medusa? Yes, quite true. Lovely place, eh? Unfortunately, Medusa hasn't re-formed since Jackson killed her, so you needn't worry about joining her collection. Besides, there are much more dangerous forces in this room.'

Kronos looked over at a Laistrygonian giant who was munching noisily on some French fries. Kronos waved his hand and the giant froze. A French fry hung suspended in midair halfway between his hand and his mouth.

'Why turn them to stone,' Kronos asked, 'when you can freeze time itself?'

His golden eyes bored into Ethan's face. 'Now tell me one more thing. What happened last night on the Williamsburg Bridge?'

Ethan trembled. Beads of perspiration were popping up on his forehead. 'I – I don't know, sir.'

'Yes, you do.' Kronos rose from his seat. 'When you attacked Jackson, something happened. Something was not quite right. The girl, Annabeth, jumped in your way.'

'She wanted to save him.'

'But he is invulnerable,' Kronos said quietly. 'You saw that yourself.'

'I can't explain it. Maybe she forgot.'

'She forgot,' Kronos said. 'Yes, that must've been it. *Oh dear, I forgot my friend is invulnerable and took a knife for him. Oops.* Tell me, Ethan, where were you aiming when you stabbed at Jackson?'

Ethan frowned. He clasped his hand as if he were holding a blade and mimed a thrust. 'I'm not sure, sir. It all happened so fast. I wasn't aiming for any spot in particular.'

Kronos's fingers tapped the blade of his scythe.

'I see,' he said in a chilly tone. 'If your memory improves, I will expect —'

Suddenly the Titan lord winced. The giant in the corner unfroze and the French fry fell into his mouth. Kronos stumbled backwards and sank into his throne.

'My lord?' Ethan started forward.

'I —' The voice was weak, but just for a moment it was Luke's. Then Kronos's expression hardened. He raised his hand and flexed his fingers slowly as if forcing them to obey.

'It is nothing,' he said, his voice steely and cold again. 'A minor discomfort.'

Ethan moistened his lips. 'He's still fighting you, isn't he? Luke —'

'Nonsense,' Kronos spat. 'Repeat that lie, and I will cut out your tongue. The boy's soul has been crushed. I am simply adjusting to the limits of this form. It requires rest. It is annoying, but no more than a temporary inconvenience.'

'As — as you say, my lord.'

'You!' Kronos pointed his scythe at a *dracaena* with green armour and a green crown. 'Queen Sess, is it?'

'Yesssss, my lord.'

'Is our little surprise ready to be unleashed?'

The *dracaena* queen bared her fangs. 'Oh, yessss, my lord. Quite a lovely sssssurprissse.'

'Excellent,' Kronos said. 'Tell my brother Hyperion to move our main force south into Central Park. The half-bloods will be in such disarray they will not be able to defend themselves. Go now, Ethan. Work on improving your memory. We will talk again when we have taken Manhattan.'

Ethan bowed, and my dreams shifted one last time. I saw the Big House at camp, but it was a different era. The house was painted red instead of blue. The campers down at the volleyball pit had early 90s hairstyles, which were probably good for keeping monsters away.

Chiron stood by the porch, talking to Hermes and a woman holding a baby. Chiron's hair was shorter and darker. Hermes wore his usual jogging suit with his winged hi-tops. The woman was tall and pretty. She had blonde hair, shining eyes and a friendly smile. The baby in her arms squirmed in his blue blanket like Camp Half-Blood was the last place he wanted to be.

'It's an honour to have you here,' Chiron told the woman, though he sounded nervous. 'It's been a long time since a mortal was allowed at camp.'

'Don't encourage her,' Hermes grumbled. 'May, you *can't* do this.'

With a shock, I realized I was seeing May Castellan. She looked nothing like the old woman I'd met. She seemed full of life – the kind of person who could smile and make everyone around her feel good.

'Oh, don't worry so much,' May said, rocking the baby. 'You need an Oracle, don't you? The old one's been dead for what, twenty years?'

'Longer,' Chiron said gravely.

Hermes raised his arms in exasperation. 'I didn't tell you that story so you could *apply*. It's dangerous. Chiron, tell her.'

'It is,' Chiron warned. 'For many years, I have forbidden

anyone from trying. We don't know exactly what's happened. Humanity seems to have lost the ability to host the Oracle.'

'We've been through that,' May said. 'And I know I can do it. Hermes, this is my chance to do something good. I've been given the gift of sight for a reason.'

I wanted to yell at May Castellan to stop. I knew what was about to happen. I finally understood how her life had been destroyed. But I couldn't move or speak.

Hermes looked more hurt than worried. 'You couldn't marry if you became the Oracle,' he complained. 'You couldn't see *me* any more.'

May put her hand on his arm. 'I can't have you forever, can I? You'll move on soon. You're immortal.'

He started to protest, but she put her hand on his chest. 'You know it's true! Don't try to spare my feelings. Besides, we have a wonderful child. I can still raise Luke if I'm the Oracle, right?'

Chiron coughed. 'Yes, but in all fairness I don't know how that will affect the spirit of the Oracle. A woman who has already borne a child – as far as I know, this has never been done before. If the spirit does not take –'

'It will,' May insisted.

No, I wanted to shout. *It won't.*

May Castellan kissed her baby and handed the bundle to Hermes. 'I'll be right back.'

She gave them one last confident smile and climbed the steps.

Chiron and Hermes paced in silence. The baby squirmed.

A green glow lit the windows of the house. The campers

stopped playing volleyball and stared up at the attic. A cold wind rushed through the strawberry fields.

Hermes must've felt it, too. He cried, 'No! NO!'

He shoved the baby into Chiron's arms and ran for the porch. Before he reached the door, the sunny afternoon was shattered by May Castellan's terrified scream.

I sat up so fast I banged my head on somebody's shield.

'Ow!'

'Sorry, Percy.' Annabeth was standing over me. 'I was just about to wake you.'

I rubbed my head, trying to clear the disturbing visions. Suddenly a lot of things made sense to me: May Castellan had tried to become the Oracle. She hadn't known about Hades' curse preventing the spirit of Delphi from taking another host. Neither had Chiron or Hermes. They hadn't realized that by trying to take the job, May would be driven mad, plagued with fits during which her eyes would glow green and she would have shattered glimpses of her child's future.

'Percy?' Annabeth asked. 'What's wrong?'

'Nothing,' I lied. 'What – what are you doing in armour? You should be resting.'

'Oh, I'm fine,' she said, though she still looked pale. She was barely moving her right arm. 'That nectar and ambrosia fixed me up.'

'Uh-huh. You can't seriously go out and fight.'

She offered me her good hand and helped me up. My head was pounding. Outside, the sky was purple and red.

'You're going to need every person you have,' she said. 'I just looked in my shield. There's an army –'

'Heading south into Central Park,' I said. 'Yeah, I know.'

I told her part of my dreams. I left out the vision of May Castellan, because it was too disturbing to talk about. I also left out Ethan's speculation about Luke fighting Kronos inside his body. I didn't want to get Annabeth's hopes up.

'Do you think Ethan suspects about your weak spot?' she asked.

'I don't know,' I admitted. 'He didn't tell Kronos anything, but if he figures it out –'

'We can't let him.'

'I'll bonk him on the head harder next time,' I suggested. 'Any idea what surprise Kronos was talking about?'

She shook her head. 'I didn't see anything in the shield, but I don't like surprises.'

'Agreed.'

'So,' she said, 'are you going to argue about me coming along?'

'Nah. You'd just beat me up.'

She managed a laugh, which was good to hear. I grabbed my sword, and we went to rally the troops.

Thalia and the head counsellors were waiting for us at the reservoir. The lights of the city were blinking on at twilight. I guess a lot of them were on automatic timers. Streetlamps glowed around the shore of the lake, making the water and trees look even spookier.

'They're coming,' Thalia confirmed, pointing north with a silver arrow. 'One of my scouts just reported they've crossed the Harlem River. There was no way to hold them back. The army . . .' She shrugged. 'It's huge.'

'We'll hold them at the park,' I said. 'Grover, you ready?'

He nodded. 'As ready as we'll ever be. If my nature spirits can stop them anywhere, this is the place.'

'Yes, we will!' said another voice. A very old, fat satyr pushed through the crowd, stumbling over his own spear. He was dressed in wood-bark armour that only covered half of his belly.

'Leneus?' I said.

'Don't act so surprised,' he huffed. 'I *am* a leader of the council, and you *did* tell me to find Grover. Well, I found him, and I'm not going to let a mere *outcast* lead the satyrs without my help!'

Behind Leneus's back, Grover made gagging motions, but the old satyr grinned like he was the saviour of the day. 'Never fear! We'll show those Titans!'

I didn't know whether to laugh or be angry, but I managed to keep a straight face. 'Um . . . yeah. Well, Grover – you won't be alone. Annabeth and the Athena cabin will make their stand here. And me, and . . . Thalia?'

She patted me on the shoulder. 'Say no more. The Hunters are ready.'

I looked at the other counsellors. 'That leaves the rest of you with a job just as important. You have to guard the other entrances to Manhattan. You know how tricky Kronos is. He'll hope to distract us with this big army and sneak another force in somewhere else. It's up to you to make sure that doesn't happen. Has each cabin chosen a bridge or tunnel?'

The counsellors nodded grimly.

'Then let's do it,' I said. 'Good hunting, everybody!'

We heard the army before we saw it.

The noise was like a cannon barrage combined with a

football-stadium crowd – like every sports fan in New England was charging us with bazookas.

At the north end of the reservoir, the enemy vanguard broke through the woods – a warrior in golden armour leading a battalion of Laistrygonian giants with huge bronze axes. Hundreds of other monsters poured out behind them.

'Positions!' Annabeth yelled.

Her cabin mates scrambled. The idea was to make the enemy army break around the reservoir. To get to us, they'd have to follow the trails, which meant they'd be marching in narrow columns on either side of the water.

At first the plan seemed to work. The enemy divided and streamed towards us along the shore. When they were halfway across, our defences kicked in. The jogging trail erupted in Greek fire, incinerating many of the monsters instantly. Others flailed around, engulfed in green flames. Athena campers threw grappling hooks around the largest giants and pulled them to the ground.

In the woods on the right, the Hunters sent a volley of silver arrows into the enemy line, destroying twenty or thirty *dracaenae*, but more marched behind them. A bolt of lightning crackled out of the sky and fried a Laistrygonian giant to ashes, and I knew Thalia must be doing her 'daughter of Zeus' thing.

Grover raised his pipes and played a quick tune. A roar went up from the woods on both sides as every tree, rock and bush seemed to sprout a spirit. Dryads and satyrs raised their clubs and charged. The trees wrapped around the monsters, strangling them. Grass grew around the feet of the enemy archers. Stones flew up and hit *dracaenae* in the faces.

The enemy slogged forward. Giants smashed through the trees and naiads faded as their life sources were destroyed. Hellhounds lunged at the timber wolves, knocking them aside. Enemy archers returned fire and a Hunter fell from a high branch.

'Percy!' Annabeth grabbed my arm and pointed at the reservoir. The Titan in the gold armour wasn't waiting for his forces to advance around the sides. He was charging towards us, walking straight over the top of the lake.

A Greek fire bomb exploded right on top of him, but he raised his palm and sucked the flames out of the air.

'Hyperion,' Annabeth said in awe. 'The Lord of Light. Titan of the east.'

'Bad?' I guessed.

'Next to Atlas, he's the greatest Titan warrior. In the old days, four Titans controlled the four corners of the world. Hyperion was the east – the most powerful. He was the father of Helios, the first sun god.'

'I'll keep him busy,' I promised.

'Percy, even you can't –'

'Just keep our forces together.'

We'd set up at the reservoir for good reason. I concentrated on the water and felt its power surging through me.

I advanced towards Hyperion, running over the top of the water. *Yeah, buddy. Two can play that game.*

Six metres away, Hyperion raised his sword. His eyes were just like I'd seen in my dream – as gold as Kronos's but brighter, like miniature suns.

'The sea god's brat,' he mused. 'You're the one who trapped Atlas beneath the sky again?'

'It wasn't hard,' I said. 'You Titans are about as bright as my gym socks.'

Hyperion snarled. 'You want bright?'

His body ignited in a column of light and heat. I looked away, but I was still blinded.

Instinctively I raised Riptide – just in time. His blade slammed against mine. The shock wave sent a three-metre ring of water across the surface of the lake.

My eyes still burned. I had to shut off his light.

I concentrated on the tidal wave and forced it to reverse. Just before impact, I jumped upward on a jet of water.

'AHHHHH!' The waves smashed into Hyperion and he went under, his light extinguished.

I landed on the lake's surface just as Hyperion struggled to his feet. His golden armour was dripping wet. His eyes no longer blazed, but they still looked murderous.

'You will burn, Jackson!' he roared.

Our swords met again and the air charged with ozone.

The battle still raged around us. On the right flank, Annabeth was leading an assault with her siblings. On the left flank, Grover and his nature spirits were regrouping, entangling the enemies with bushes and weeds.

'Enough games,' Hyperion told me. 'We fight on land.'

I was about to make some clever comment, like 'No', when the Titan yelled. A wall of force slammed me through the air – just like the trick Kronos had pulled on the bridge. I sailed backwards about a hundred metres and smashed into the ground. If it hadn't been for my new invulnerability, I would've broken every bone in my body.

I got to my feet, groaning. 'I really *hate* it when you Titans do that.'

Hyperion closed on me with blinding speed.

I concentrated on the water, drawing strength from it.

Hyperion attacked. He was powerful and fast, but he couldn't seem to land a blow. The ground around his feet kept erupting in flames, but I kept dousing it just as quickly.

'Stop it!' the Titan roared. 'Stop that wind!'

I wasn't sure what he meant. I was too busy fighting.

Hyperion stumbled like he was being pushed away. Water sprayed his face, stinging his eyes. The wind picked up and Hyperion staggered backwards.

'Percy!' Grover called in amazement. 'How are you *doing* that?'

Doing what? I thought.

Then I looked down, and I realized I was standing in the middle of my own personal hurricane. Clouds of water vapour swirled around me, winds so powerful they buffeted Hyperion and flattened the grass in a twenty-metre radius. Enemy warriors threw javelins at me, but the storm knocked them aside.

'Sweet,' I muttered. 'But a little more!'

Lightning flickered around me. The clouds darkened and the rain swirled faster. I closed on Hyperion and blew him off his feet.

'Percy!' Grover called again. 'Bring him over here!'

I slashed and jabbed, letting my reflexes take over. Hyperion could barely defend himself. His eyes kept trying to ignite, but the hurricane quenched his flames.

I couldn't keep up a storm like this forever, though. I could feel my powers weakening. With one last effort, I propelled Hyperion across the field, straight to where Grover was waiting.

'I will not be toyed with!' Hyperion bellowed.

He managed to get to his feet again, but Grover put his reed pipes to his lips and began to play. Leneus joined him. Around the grove, every satyr took up the song – an eerie melody like a creek flowing over stones. The ground erupted at Hyperion's feet. Gnarled roots wrapped around his legs.

'What's this?' he protested. He tried to shake off the roots, but he was still weak. The roots thickened until he looked like he was wearing wooden boots.

'Stop this!' he shouted. 'Your woodland magic is no match for a Titan!'

But the more he struggled, the faster the roots grew. They curled about his body, thickening and hardening into bark. His golden armour melted into the wood, becoming part of a large trunk.

The music continued. Hyperion's forces backed up in astonishment as their leader was absorbed. He stretched out his arms and they became branches, from which smaller branches shot out and grew leaves. The tree grew taller and thicker, until only the Titan's face was visible in the middle of the trunk.

'You cannot imprison me!' he bellowed. 'I am Hyperion! I am –'

The bark closed over his face.

Grover took his pipes from his mouth. 'You are a very nice maple tree.'

Several of the other satyrs passed out from exhaustion, but they'd done their job well. The Titan lord was completely encased in an enormous maple. The trunk was at least seven metres in diameter, with branches as tall as any in the park. The tree might've stood there for centuries.

The Titans' army started to retreat. A cheer went up from the Athena cabin, but our victory was short-lived.

Because just then Kronos unleashed his surprise.

'REEEEET!'

The squeal echoed through upper Manhattan. Demigods and monsters alike froze in terror.

Grover shot me a panicked look. 'Why does that sound like — It can't be!'

I knew what he was thinking. Two years ago we'd got a 'gift' from Pan — a huge boar that carried us across the Southwest (after it tried to kill us). The boar had a similar squeal, but what we were hearing now seemed higher pitched, shriller, almost as if . . . as if the boar had an angry girlfriend.

'REEEEEET!' A huge pink creature soared over the reservoir — a Thanksgiving Day Parade nightmare blimp with wings.

'A sow!' Annabeth cried. 'Take cover!'

The demigods scattered as the winged lady pig swooped down. Her wings were pink like a flamingo's, which matched her skin beautifully, but it was hard to think of her as 'cute' when her hooves slammed into the ground, barely missing one of Annabeth's siblings. The pig stomped around and tore down half an acre of trees, belching a cloud of noxious gas. Then it took off again, circling around for another strike.

'Don't tell me that thing is from Greek mythology,' I complained.

'Afraid so,' Annabeth said. 'The Clazmonian Sow. It terrorized Greek towns back in the day.'

'Let me guess,' I said. 'Hercules beat it.'

'Nope,' Annabeth said. 'As far as I know, *no* hero has ever beaten it.'

'Perfect,' I muttered.

The Titans' army was recovering from its shock. I guess they realized the pig wasn't after them.

We only had seconds before they were ready to fight, and our forces were still in a panic. Every time the sow belched, Grover's nature spirits yelped and faded back into their trees.

'That pig has to go.' I grabbed a grappling hook from one of Annabeth's siblings. 'I'll take care of it. You guys hold the rest of the enemy. Push them back!'

'But, Percy,' Grover said, 'what if we can't?'

I saw how tired he was. The magic had really drained him. Annabeth didn't look much better from fighting with a bad shoulder wound. I didn't know how the Hunters were doing, but the right flank of the enemy army was now between them and us.

I didn't want to leave my friends in such bad shape, but that sow was the biggest threat. It would destroy everything – buildings, trees, sleeping mortals. It had to be stopped.

'Retreat if you need to,' I said. 'Just slow them down. I'll be back as soon as I can.'

Before I could change my mind, I swung the grappling hook like a lasso. When the sow came down for its next pass, I threw with all my strength. The hook wrapped around the base of the pig's wing. It squealed in rage and veered off, yanking the rope and me into the sky.

If you're heading downtown from Central Park, my advice is to take the subway. Flying pigs are faster, but way more dangerous.

The sow soared past the Plaza Hotel, straight into the canyon of Fifth Avenue. My brilliant plan was to climb the rope and get on the pig's back. Unfortunately, I was too busy swinging around dodging streetlamps and the sides of buildings.

Another thing I learned: it's one thing to climb a rope in gym class. It's a completely different thing to climb a rope attached to a moving pig's wing while you're flying at a hundred miles an hour.

We zigzagged along several blocks and continued south on Park Avenue.

Boss! Hey, boss! Out of the corner of my eye, I saw Blackjack speeding along next to us, darting back and forth to avoid the pig's wings.

'Watch out!' I told him.

Hop on! Blackjack whinnied. *I can catch you – probably.*

That wasn't very reassuring. Grand Central Station lay dead ahead. Above the main entrance stood the giant statue of Hermes, which I guess hadn't been activated because it was so high up. I was flying right towards him at the speed of demigod-smashing.

'Stay alert!' I told Blackjack. 'I've got an idea.'

Oh, I hate your ideas.

I swung outwards with all my might. Instead of smashing into the Hermes statue, I whipped around it, circling the rope under its arms. I thought this would tether the pig, but I'd underestimated the momentum of a thirty-ton sow in flight. Just as the pig wrenched the statue loose from its pedestal, I let go. Hermes went for a ride, taking my place as the pig's passenger, and I freefell towards the street.

In that split second, I thought about the days when

my mom used to work at the Grand Central Station candy shop. I thought how bad it would be if I ended up as a grease spot on the pavement.

Then a shadow swooped under me and *thump* – I was on Blackjack's back. It wasn't the most comfortable landing. In fact when I yelled, 'OW!' my voice was an octave higher than usual.

Sorry, boss, Blackjack murmured.

'No problem,' I squeaked. 'Follow that pig!'

The porker had taken a right at East Forty-second and was flying back towards Fifth Avenue. When it flew above the rooftops, I could see fires here and there around the city. It looked like my friends were having a rough time. Kronos was attacking on several fronts. But at the moment, I had my own problems.

The Hermes statue was still on its leash. It kept bonking into buildings and spinning around. The pig swooped over an office building and Hermes ploughed into a water tower on the roof, blasting water and wood everywhere.

Then something occurred to me.

'Get closer,' I told Blackjack.

He whinnied in protest.

'Just within shouting distance,' I said. 'I need to talk to the statue.'

Now I'm sure you've lost it, boss, Blackjack said, but he did what I asked. When I was close enough to see the statue's face clearly, I yelled, 'Hello, Hermes! Command sequence: Daedalus Twenty-three. Kill flying pigs! Begin Activation!'

Immediately the statue moved its legs. It seemed confused to find it was no longer on top of Grand Central Station. It was, instead, being given a sky-ride on the end of a rope by a large winged sow. It smashed through the side of a brick building, which I think made it a little mad. It shook its head and began to climb the rope.

I glanced down at the street. We were coming up on the main public library, with the big marble lions flanking the steps. Suddenly I had a weird thought – could *stone* statues be automatons, too? It seemed like a long shot, but . . .

'Faster!' I told Blackjack. 'Get in front of the pig. Taunt him!'

Um, boss –

'Trust me,' I said. 'I can do this – probably.'

Oh, sure. Mock the horse.

Blackjack burst through the air. He could fly pretty darned fast when we wanted to. He got in front of the pig, which now had a metal Hermes on its back.

Blackjack whinnied, *You smell like ham!* He kicked the pig in the snout with his back hooves and went into a steep dive. The pig screamed in rage and followed.

We barrelled straight for the front steps of the library. Blackjack slowed down just enough for me to hop off, then he kept flying towards the main doors.

I yelled out: 'Lions! Command sequence: Daedalus Twenty-three. Kill flying pigs! Begin Activation!'

The lions stood up and looked at me. They probably thought I was teasing them. But just then: 'REEEEEET!'

The massive pink pork monster landed with a thud, cracking the sidewalk. The lions stared at it, not believing their luck, and pounced. At the same time, a very beat-up Hermes statue leaped onto the pig's head and started banging it mercilessly with a caduceus. Those lions had

I drew Riptide, but there wasn't much for me to do. The pig disintegrated before my eyes. I almost felt sorry for it. I hoped it got to meet the boar of its dreams down in Tartarus.

When the monster had completely turned to dust, the lions and the Hermes statue looked around in confusion.

'You can defend Manhattan now,' I told them, but they didn't seem to hear. They went charging down Park Avenue, and I imagined they would keep looking for flying pigs until someone deactivated them.

Hey, boss, said Blackjack. *Can we take a doughnut break?*

I wiped the sweat off my brow. 'I wish, big guy, but the fight's still going on.'

In fact I could hear it getting closer. My friends needed help. I jumped on Blackjack and we flew north towards the sound of explosions.

15 CHIRON THROWS A PARTY

Midtown was a warzone. We flew over little skirmishes everywhere. A giant was ripping up trees in Bryant Park while dryads pelted him with nuts. Outside the Waldorf Astoria, a bronze statue of Benjamin Franklin was whacking a hellhound with a rolled-up newspaper. A trio of Hephaestus campers fought a squad of *dracaenae* in the middle of Rockefeller Center.

I was tempted to stop and help, but I could tell from the smoke and noise that the real action had moved further south. Our defences were collapsing. The enemy was closing on the Empire State Building.

We did a quick sweep of the surrounding area. The Hunters had set up a defensive line on Thirty-seventh, just three blocks north of Olympus. To the east on Park Avenue, Jake Mason and some other Hephaestus campers were leading an army of statues against the enemy. To the west, the Demeter cabin and Grover's nature spirits had turned Sixth Avenue into a jungle that was hampering a squadron of Kronos's demigods. The south was clear for now, but the flanks of the enemy army were swinging around. A few more minutes, and we'd be totally surrounded.

'We have to land where they need us most,' I muttered.

That's everywhere, boss.

I spotted a familiar silver owl banner in the southeast corner of the fight – Thirty-third at the Park Avenue tunnel. Annabeth and two of her siblings were holding back a Hyperborean giant.

'There!' I told Blackjack. He plunged towards the battle.

I leaped off his back and landed on the giant's head. When the giant looked up, I slid off his face, shield-bashing his nose on the way down.

'RAWWWR!' The giant staggered backwards, blue blood trickling from his nostrils.

I hit the pavement running. The Hyperborean breathed a cloud of white mist and the temperature dropped. The spot where I'd landed was now coated with ice, and I was covered in frost like a sugar doughnut.

'Hey, Ugly!' Annabeth yelled. I hoped she was talking to the giant, not me.

Blue Boy bellowed and turned towards her, exposing the unprotected back of his legs. I charged and stabbed him behind the knee.

'WAAAAH!' The Hyperborean buckled. I waited for him to turn, but he froze. I mean he *literally* turned to solid ice. From the point where I'd stabbed him, cracks appeared in his body. They got larger and wider until the giant crumbled in a mountain of blue shards.

'Thanks.' Annabeth winced, trying to catch her breath. 'The pig?'

'Pork chops,' I said.

'Good.' She flexed her shoulder. Obviously, the wound was still bothering her, but she saw my expression and rolled her eyes. 'I'm fine, Percy. Come on! We've got plenty of enemies left.'

She was right. The next hour was a blur. I fought like I'd never fought before — wading into legions of *dracaenae*, taking out dozens of telkhines with every strike, destroying *empousai* and knocking out enemy demigods. No matter how many I defeated, more took their place.

Annabeth and I raced from block to block, trying to shore up our defences. Too many of our friends lay wounded in the streets. Too many were missing.

As the night wore on and the moon got higher, we backed up metre by metre until we were only a block from the Empire State Building in any direction. At one point Grover was next to me, bonking snake-women over the head with his cudgel. Then he disappeared in the crowd, and it was Thalia at my side, driving the monsters back with the power of her magic shield. Mrs O'Leary bounded out of nowhere, picked up a Laistrygonian giant in her mouth and flung him into the air like a Frisbee. Annabeth used her invisibility cap to sneak behind the enemy lines. Whenever a monster disintegrated for no apparent reason with a surprised look on his face, I knew Annabeth had been there.

But it still wasn't enough.

'Hold your lines!' Katie Gardner shouted, somewhere off to my left.

The problem was there were too few of us to hold anything. The entrance to Olympus was six metres behind me. A ring of brave demigods, Hunters and nature spirits guarded the doors. I slashed and hacked, destroying everything in my path, but even I was getting tired, and I couldn't be everywhere at once.

Behind the enemy troops, a few blocks to the east, a bright light began to shine. I thought it was the sunrise. Then I realized Kronos was riding towards us on a golden chariot. A dozen Laistrygonian giants bore torches before him. Two Hyperboreans carried his black-and-purple banners. The Titan lord looked fresh and rested, his powers at full strength. He was taking his time advancing, letting me wear myself down.

Annabeth appeared next to me. 'We have to fall back to the doorway. Hold it at all costs!'

She was right. I was about to order a retreat when I heard the hunting horn.

It cut through the noise of the battle like a fire alarm. A chorus of horns answered from all around us, echoing off the buildings of Manhattan.

I glanced at Thalia, but she just frowned.

'Not the Hunters,' she assured me. 'We're all here.'

'Then who?'

The horns got louder. I couldn't tell where they were coming from because of the echo, but it sounded like an entire army was approaching.

I was afraid it might be more enemies, but Kronos's forces looked as confused as we were. Giants lowered their clubs. *Dracaenae* hissed. Even Kronos's honour guard looked uneasy.

Then, to our left, a hundred monsters cried out at once. Kronos's entire northern flank surged forward. I thought we were doomed, but they didn't attack. They ran straight past us and crashed into their southern allies.

A new blast of horns shattered the night. The air shimmered. In a blur of movement, an entire cavalry appeared as if dropping out of light speed.

'Yeah, baby!' a voice wailed. 'PARTY!'

A shower of arrows arced over our heads and slammed into the enemy, vaporizing hundreds of demons. But these weren't regular arrows. They made whizzy sounds as they flew, like WHEEEEEE! Some had pinwheels attached to them. Others had boxing gloves rather than points.

'Centaurs!' Annabeth yelled.

The Party Pony army exploded into our midst in a riot of colours — tie-dyed shirts, rainbow Afro wigs, oversized sunglasses and war-painted faces. Some had slogans scrawled across their flanks like: HORSEZ PWN or KRONOS SUX.

Hundreds of them filled the entire block. My brain couldn't process everything I saw, but I knew if I were the enemy, I'd be running.

'Percy!' Chiron shouted across the sea of wild centaurs. He was dressed in armour from the waist up, his bow in his hand, and he was grinning in satisfaction. 'Sorry we're late!'

'DUDE!' Another centaur yelled. 'Talk later. WASTE MONSTERS NOW!'

He locked and loaded a double-barrel paint gun and blasted an enemy hellhound bright pink. The paint must've been mixed with Celestial bronze dust or something, because as soon as it splattered the hellhound, the monster yelped and dissolved into a pink-and-black puddle.

'PARTY PONIES!' a centaur yelled. 'SOUTH FLORIDA CHAPTER!'

Somewhere across the battlefield, a twangy voice yelled back, 'HEART OF TEXAS CHAPTER!'

'HAWAII OWNS YOUR FACES!' a third one shouted.

It was the most beautiful thing I'd ever seen. The entire Titan army turned and fled, pushed back by a flood of paint balls, arrows, swords and NERF baseball bats. The centaurs trampled everything in their path.

'Stop running, you fools!' Kronos yelled. 'Stand and ACKK!'

That last part was because a panicked Hyperborean giant stumbled backwards and sat on top of him. The Lord of Time disappeared under a giant blue butt.

We pushed them for several blocks until Chiron yelled, 'HOLD! On your promise, HOLD!'

It wasn't easy, but eventually the order got relayed up and down the ranks of centaurs, and they started to pull back, letting the enemy flee.

'Chiron's smart,' Annabeth said, wiping the sweat off her face. 'If we pursue, we'll get too spread out. We need to regroup.'

'But the enemy —'

'They're not defeated,' she agreed. 'But the dawn is coming. At least we've bought some time.'

I didn't like pulling back, but I knew she was right. I watched as the last of the telkhines scuttled towards the East River. Then reluctantly I turned and headed back towards the Empire State Building.

We set up a two-block perimeter, with a command tent at the Empire State Building. Chiron informed us that the Party Ponies had sent chapters from almost every state in the Union – forty from California, two from Rhode Island, thirty from Illinois. Roughly five hundred total had answered his call, but even with that many, we couldn't defend more than a few blocks.

'Dude,' said a centaur named Larry. His T-shirt identified him as BIG CHIEF ÜBER GUY, NEW MEXICO CHAPTER. 'That was more fun than our last convention in Vegas!'

'Yeah,' said Owen from South Dakota. He wore a black leather jacket and an old World War II army helmet. 'We totally wasted them!'

Chiron patted Owen on the back. 'You did well, my friends, but don't get careless. Kronos should never be underestimated. Now why don't you visit the diner on West Thirty-third and get some breakfast? I hear the Delaware chapter found a stash of root beer.'

'Root beer!' They almost trampled each other as they galloped off.

Chiron smiled. Annabeth gave him a big hug and Mrs O'Leary licked his face.

'Ack,' he grumbled. 'Enough of that, dog. Yes, I'm glad to see you, too.'

'Chiron, thanks,' I said. 'Talk about saving the day.'

He shrugged. 'I'm sorry it took so long. Centaurs travel fast, as you know. We can bend distance as we ride. Even so, getting all the centaurs together was no easy task. The Party Ponies are not exactly organized.'

'How'd you get through the magic defences around the city?' Annabeth asked.

'They slowed us down a bit,' Chiron admitted, 'but I think they're intended mostly to keep mortals out. Kronos doesn't want puny humans getting in the way of his great victory.'

'So maybe other reinforcements can get through,' I said hopefully.

Chiron stroked his beard. 'Perhaps, though time is short. As soon as Kronos regroups, he will attack again. Without the element of surprise on our side . . .'

I understood what he meant. Kronos wasn't beaten. Not by a long shot. I half hoped Kronos had been squashed under that Hyperborean giant's butt, but I knew better. He'd be back, tonight at the latest.

'And Typhon?' I asked.

Chiron's face darkened. 'The gods are tiring. Dionysus was incapacitated yesterday. Typhon smashed his chariot and the wine god went down somewhere in the Appalachians. No one has seen him since. Hephaestus is out of action as well. He was thrown from the battle so hard he created a new lake in West Virginia. He will heal, but not soon enough to help. The others still fight. They've managed to slow Typhon's approach. But the monster cannot be stopped. He will arrive in New York by this time tomorrow. Once he and Kronos combine forces —'

'Then what chance do we have?' I said. 'We can't hold out another day.'

'We'll have to,' Thalia said. 'I'll see about setting some new traps around the perimeter.'

She looked exhausted. Her jacket was smeared in grime and monster dust, but she managed to get to her feet and stagger off.

'I will help her,' Chiron decided. 'I should make sure my brethren don't go too overboard with the root beer.'

I thought 'too overboard' pretty much summed up the Party Ponies, but Chiron cantered off, leaving Annabeth and me alone.

She cleaned the monster slime off her knife. I'd seen

her do that hundreds of times, but I'd never thought about why she cared so much about the blade.

'At least your mom is okay,' I offered.

'If you call fighting Typhon *okay*.' She locked eyes with me. 'Percy, even with the centaurs' help, I'm starting to think –'

'I know.' I had a bad feeling this might be our last chance to talk, and I felt like there were a million things I hadn't told her. 'Listen, there were some . . . some visions Hestia showed me.'

'You mean about Luke?'

Maybe it was just a safe guess, but I got the feeling Annabeth knew what I'd been holding back. Maybe she'd been having dreams of her own.

'Yeah,' I said. 'You and Thalia and Luke. The first time you met. And the time you met Hermes.'

Annabeth slipped her knife back into its sheath. 'Luke promised he'd never let me get hurt. He said . . . he said we'd be a new family, and it would turn out better than his.'

Her eyes reminded me of that seven-year-old girl in the alley – angry, scared, desperate for a friend.

'Thalia talked to me earlier,' I said. 'She's afraid –'

'That I can't face Luke,' she said miserably.

I nodded. 'But there's something else you should know. Ethan Nakamura seemed to think Luke was still alive inside his body, maybe even fighting Kronos for control.'

Annabeth tried to hide it, but I could almost see her mind working on the possibilities, maybe starting to hope.

'I didn't want to tell you,' I admitted.

She looked up at the Empire State Building. 'Percy, for

so much of my life, I felt like everything was changing, all the time. I didn't have anyone I could rely on.'

I nodded. That was something most demigods could understand.

'I ran away when I was seven,' she said. 'Then with Luke and Thalia I thought I'd found a family, but it fell apart almost immediately. What I'm saying . . . I *hate* it when people let me down, when things are temporary. I think that's why I want to be an architect.'

'To build something permanent,' I said. 'A monument to last a thousand years.'

She held my eyes. 'I guess that sounds like my fatal flaw again.'

Years ago in the Sea of Monsters, Annabeth had told me her biggest flaw was pride — thinking she could fix anything. I'd even seen a glimpse of her deepest desire, shown to her by the Sirens' magic. Annabeth had imagined her mother and father together, standing in front of a newly rebuilt Manhattan, designed by Annabeth. And Luke had been there, too — good again, welcoming her home.

'I guess I understand how you feel,' I said. 'But Thalia's right. Luke has already betrayed you so many times. He was evil even before Kronos. I don't want him to hurt you any more.'

Annabeth pursed her lips. I could tell she was trying not to get mad. 'And you'll understand if I keep hoping there's a chance you're wrong.'

I looked away. I felt like I'd done my best, but that didn't make me feel any better.

Across the street, the Apollo campers had set up a field hospital to tend the wounded — dozens of campers and almost as many Hunters. I was watching the medics work, and thinking about our slim chances for holding Mount Olympus . . .

And suddenly: I wasn't there any more.

I was standing in a long dingy bar with black walls, neon signs and a bunch of partying adults. A banner across the bar read, HAPPY BIRTHDAY, BOBBY EARL. Country music played on the speakers. Big guys in jeans and work shirts crowded the bar. Waitresses carried trays of drinks and shouted at each other. It was pretty much exactly the kind of place my mom would never let me go.

I was stuck in the very back of the room, next to the bathrooms (which didn't smell so great) and a couple of antique arcade games.

'Oh, good, you're here,' said the man at the Pac-Man machine. 'I'll have a Diet Coke.'

He was a pudgy guy in a leopard-skin Hawaiian shirt, purple shorts, red running shoes and black socks, which didn't exactly make him blend in with the crowd. His nose was bright red. A bandage was wrapped around his curly black hair like he was recovering from a concussion.

I blinked. 'Mr D?'

He sighed, not taking his eyes from the game. 'Really, Peter Johnson, how long will it take for you to recognize me on sight?'

'About as long as it'll take you to figure out my name,' I muttered. 'Where are we?'

'Why, Bobby Earl's birthday party,' Dionysus said. 'Somewhere in lovely rural America.'

'I thought Typhon swatted you out of the sky. They said you crash-landed.'

'Your concern is touching. I *did* crash-land. Very painfully. In fact part of me is still buried under fifty metres of rubble in an abandoned coalmine. It will be several more hours before I have enough strength to mend. But, in the meantime, part of my consciousness is *here*.'

'At a bar, playing Pac-Man.'

'Party time,' Dionysus said. 'Surely you've heard of it. Wherever there is a party, my presence is invoked. Because of this, I can exist in many different places at once. The only problem was finding a party. I don't know if you're aware how serious things are outside your safe little bubble of New York –'

'*Safe little bubble?*'

'– but, believe me, the mortals out here in the heartland are panicking. Typhon has terrified them. Very few are throwing parties. Apparently, Bobby Earl and his friends, bless them, are a little slow. They haven't yet figured out that the world is ending.'

'So . . . I'm not really here?'

'No. In a moment, I'll send you back to your normal insignificant life and it will be as if nothing had happened.'

'And *why* did you bring me here?'

Dionysus snorted. 'Oh, I didn't want you particularly. Any of you silly heroes would do. That Annie girl –'

'Annabeth.'

'The point is,' he said, 'I pulled you into party time to deliver a warning. We are in *danger*.'

'Gee,' I said. 'Never would've figured that out. Thanks.'

He glared at me and momentarily forgot his game. Pac-Man got eaten by the red ghost dude.

'*Erre es korakas, Blinky!*' Dionysus cursed. 'I will have your soul!'

'Um, he's a video-game character,' I said.

'That's no excuse! And you're ruining my game, Jorgenson!'

'Jackson.'

'Whichever! Now listen, the situation is graver than you imagine. If Olympus falls, not only will the gods fade, but everything that is connected to our legacy will also begin to unravel. The very fabric of your puny little civilization –'

The game played a song and Mr D progressed to level 254.

'Ha!' he shouted. 'Take that, you pixelated fiends!'

'Um, fabric of civilization,' I prompted.

'Yes, yes. Your entire society will dissolve. Perhaps not right away but, mark my words, the chaos of the Titans will mean the end of Western civilization. Art, law, wine tastings, music, video games, silk shirts, black-velvet paintings – all the things that make life worth living will disappear!'

'So why aren't the gods rushing back to help us?' I said. 'We should combine forces at Olympus. Forget Typhon.'

He snapped his fingers impatiently. 'You forgot my Diet Coke.'

'Gods, you're annoying.' I got the attention of a waitress and ordered the stupid soda. I put it on Bobby Earl's tab.

Mr D took a good long drink. His eyes never left the video game. 'The truth is, Pierre –'

'Percy.'

'– the other gods would *never* admit this, but we actually

need you mortals to rescue Olympus. You see, we are manifestations of your culture. If you don't care enough to save Olympus yourselves –'

'Like Pan,' I said, 'depending on the satyrs to save the wild.'

'Yes, quite. I will deny I ever said this, of course, but the gods *need* heroes. They always have. Otherwise we would not keep you annoying little brats around.'

'I feel so wanted. Thanks.'

'Use the training I have given you at camp.'

'*What* training?'

'You know. All those hero techniques and – No!' Mr D slapped the game console. '*Na pari i eychi!* The last level!'

He looked at me and purple fire flickered in his eyes. 'As I recall, I once predicted you would turn out to be as selfish as all the other human heroes. Well, here is your chance to prove me wrong.'

'Yeah, making you proud is real high on my list.'

'You must save Olympus, Pedro! Leave Typhon to the Olympians and save our seats of power. It must be done!'

'Great. Nice little chat. Now, if you don't mind, my friends will be wondering –'

'There is more,' Mr D warned. 'Kronos has not yet attained full power. The body of the mortal was only a temporary measure.'

'We kind of guessed that.'

'And did you also guess that within a day at most, Kronos will burn away that mortal body and take on the true form of a Titan king?'

'And that would mean . . .'

Dionysus inserted another coin. 'You know about the true forms of the gods.'

'Yeah. You can't look at them without burning up.'

'Kronos would be ten times more powerful. His very presence would incinerate you. And, once he achieves this, he will empower the other Titans. They are weak now, compared to what they will soon become unless you can stop them. The world will fall, the gods will die and I will never achieve a perfect score on this stupid machine.'

Maybe I should've been terrified, but, honestly, I was already about as scared as I could get.

'Can I go now?' I asked.

'One last thing. My son Pollux. Is he alive?'

I blinked. 'Yeah, last I saw him.'

'I would very much appreciate it if you could keep him that way. I lost his brother Castor last year –'

'I remember.' I stared at him, trying to wrap my mind around the idea that Dionysus could be a caring father. I wondered how many other Olympians were thinking about their demigod children right now. 'I'll do my best.'

'Your best,' Dionysus muttered. 'Well, isn't *that* reassuring. Go now. You have some nasty surprises to deal with, and I must defeat Blinky!'

'Nasty surprises?'

He waved his hand, and the bar disappeared.

I was back on Fifth Avenue. Annabeth hadn't moved. She didn't give any sign that I'd been gone or anything.

She caught me staring and frowned. 'What?'

'Um . . . nothing, I guess.'

I gazed down the avenue, wondering what Mr D had meant by nasty surprises. How much worse could it get?

My eyes rested on a beat-up blue car. The hood was badly dented, like somebody had tried to hammer out some huge craters. My skin tingled. Why did that car look so familiar? Then I realized it was a Prius.

Paul's Prius.

I bolted down the street.

'Percy!' Annabeth called. 'Where are you going?'

Paul was passed out in the driver's seat. My mom was snoring beside him. My mind felt like mush. How had I not seen them before? They'd been sitting here in traffic for over a day, the battle raging around them, and I hadn't even noticed.

'They — they must've seen those blue lights in the sky.' I rattled the doors but they were locked. 'I need to get them out.'

'Percy,' Annabeth said gently.

'I can't leave them here!' I sounded a little crazy. I pounded on the windshield. 'I have to move them. I have to —'

'Percy, just — just hold on.' Annabeth waved to Chiron, who was talking to some centaurs down the block. 'We can push the car to a side street, all right? They're going to be fine.'

My hands trembled. After all I'd been through over the last few days, I felt so stupid and weak, but the sight of my parents made me want to break down.

Chiron galloped over. 'What's — Oh, dear. I see.'

'They were coming to find me,' I said. 'My mom must've sensed something was wrong.'

'Most likely,' Chiron said. 'But, Percy, they will be fine. The best thing we can do for them is stay focused on our job.'

Then I noticed something in the backseat of the Prius, and my heart skipped a beat. Seat-belted behind my mother was a black-and-white Greek jar about a metre tall. Its lid was wrapped in a leather harness.

'No way,' I muttered.

Annabeth pressed her hand to the window. 'That's impossible! I thought you left that at the Plaza.'

'Locked in a vault,' I agreed.

Chiron saw the jar and his eyes widened. 'That isn't –'

'Pandora's jar.' I told him about my meeting with Prometheus.

'Then the jar is yours,' Chiron said grimly. 'It will follow you and tempt you to open it, no matter where you leave it. It will appear when you are weakest.'

Like now, I thought. *Looking at my helpless parents.*

I imagined Prometheus smiling, so anxious to help out us poor mortals. *Give up Hope, and I will know that you are surrendering. I promise Kronos will be lenient.*

Anger surged through me. I drew Riptide and cut through the driver's side window like it was made of plastic wrap.

'We'll put the car in neutral,' I said. 'Push them out of the way. And take that stupid jar to Olympus.'

Chiron nodded. 'A good plan. But, Percy . . .'

Whatever he was going to say, he faltered. A mechanical drumbeat grew loud in the distance – the *chop-chop-chop* of a helicopter.

On a normal Monday morning in New York, this

would've been no big deal, but after two days of silence, a mortal helicopter was the oddest thing I'd ever heard. A few blocks east, the monster army shouted and jeered as the helicopter came into view. It was a civilian model painted dark red, with a bright green 'DE' logo on the side. The words under the logo were too small to read, but I knew what they said: DARE ENTERPRISES.

My throat closed up. I looked at Annabeth and could tell she recognized the logo, too. Her face was as red as the helicopter.

'What is *she* doing here?' Annabeth demanded. 'How did she get through the barrier?'

'Who?' Chiron looked confused. 'What mortal would be insane enough —'

Suddenly the helicopter pitched forward.

'The Morpheus enchantment!' Chiron said. 'The foolish mortal pilot is asleep.'

I watched in horror as the helicopter careened sideways, falling towards a row of office buildings. Even if it didn't crash, the gods of the air would probably swat it out of the sky for coming near the Empire State Building.

I was too paralysed to move, but Annabeth whistled and Guido the pegasus swooped out of nowhere.

You rang for a handsome horse? he asked.

'Come on, Percy,' Annabeth growled. 'We have to save your *friend*.'

16 WE GET HELP FROM A THIEF

Here's my definition of *not fun*. Fly a pegasus towards an out-of-control helicopter. If Guido had been any less of a fancy flier, we would've been chopped to confetti.

I could hear Rachel screaming inside. For some reason, *she* hadn't fallen asleep, but I could see the pilot slumped over the controls, pitching back and forth as the helicopter wobbled towards the side of an office building.

'Ideas?' I asked Annabeth.

'You're going to have to take Guido and get out,' she said.

'What are *you* going to do?'

In response, she said, 'Hyah!' And Guido went into a nosedive.

'Duck!' Annabeth yelled.

We passed so close to the rotors I felt the force of the blades ripping at my hair. We zipped along the side of the helicopter and Annabeth grabbed the door.

That's when things went wrong.

Guido's wing slammed against the helicopter. He plummeted straight down with me on his back, leaving Annabeth dangling from the side of the aircraft.

I was so terrified I could barely think, but as Guido spiralled I caught a glimpse of Rachel pulling Annabeth inside the 'copter.

'Hang in there!' I yelled at Guido.

My wing, he moaned. *It's busted.*

'You can do it!' I desperately tried to remember what Silena used to tell us in pegasus-riding lessons. 'Just relax the wing. Extend it and glide.'

We fell like a rock – straight towards the pavement a hundred metres below. At the last moment, Guido extended his wings. I saw the faces of centaurs gaping up at us. Then we pulled out of our dive, sailed twenty metres and tumbled onto the pavement – Pegasus over demigod.

Ow! Guido moaned. *My legs. My head. My wings.*

Chiron galloped over with his medical pouch and began working on the pegasus.

I got to my feet. When I looked up, my heart crawled into my throat. The helicopter was only a few seconds away from slamming into the side of the building.

Then miraculously the helicopter righted itself. It spun in a circle and hovered. Very slowly, it began to descend.

It seemed to take forever, but finally the helicopter thudded to a landing in the middle of Fifth Avenue. I looked through the windshield and couldn't believe what I was seeing. Annabeth was at the controls.

I ran forward as the rotors spun to a stop. Rachel opened the side door and dragged out the pilot. Rachel was still dressed like she was on vacation, in beach shorts, a T-shirt and sandals. Her hair was tangled and her face was green from the helicopter ride.

Annabeth climbed out last.

I stared at her in awe. 'I didn't know you could fly a helicopter.'

'Neither did I,' she said. 'My dad's crazy into aviation. Plus Daedalus had some notes on flying machines. I just took my best guess on the controls.'

'You saved my life,' Rachel said.

Annabeth flexed her bad shoulder. 'Yeah, well . . . Let's not make a habit of it. What are you *doing* here, Dare? Don't you know better than to fly into a warzone?'

'I —' Rachel glanced at me. 'I had to be here. I knew Percy was in trouble.'

'Got that right,' Annabeth grumbled. 'Well, if you'll excuse me, I have some injured *friends* I've got to tend to. Glad you could stop by, Rachel.'

'Annabeth —' I called.

She stormed off.

Rachel plopped down on the kerb and put her head in her hands. 'I'm sorry, Percy. I didn't mean to . . . I always mess things up.'

It was kind of hard to argue with her, though I was glad she was safe. I looked in the direction Annabeth had gone, but she'd disappeared into the crowd. I couldn't believe what she'd just done — saved Rachel's life, landed a helicopter and walked away like it was no big deal.

'It's okay,' I told Rachel, though my words sounded hollow. 'So what's the message you wanted to deliver?'

She frowned. 'How did you know about that?'

'A dream.'

Rachel didn't look surprised. She tugged at her beach shorts. They were covered in drawings, which wasn't unusual for her, but these symbols I recognized: Greek letters, pictures from camp beads, sketches of monsters and faces of gods. I didn't understand how Rachel could have known

[259]

about some of that. She'd never been to Olympus or Camp Half-Blood.

'I've been seeing things, too,' she muttered. 'I mean not just through the Mist. This is different. I've been drawing pictures, writing lines –'

'In Ancient Greek,' I said. 'Do you know what they say?'

'That's what I wanted to talk to you about. I was hoping . . . well, if you had gone with us on vacation, I was hoping you could have helped me figure out what's happening to me.'

She looked at me pleadingly. Her face was sunburnt from the beach. Her nose was peeling. I couldn't get over the shock that she was here in person. She'd forced her family to cut short their vacation, agreed to go to a horrible school and flown a helicopter into a monster battle just to see me. In her own way, she was as brave as Annabeth.

But what was happening to her with these visions really freaked me out. Maybe it was something that happened to all mortals who could see through the Mist. But my mom had never talked about anything like that. And Hestia's words about Luke's mom kept coming back to me: *May Castellan went too far. She tried to see too much.*

'Rachel,' I said, 'I wish I knew. Maybe we should ask Chiron –'

She flinched like she'd got an electric shock. 'Percy, something is about to happen. A trick that ends in death.'

'What do you mean? Whose death?'

'I don't know.' She looked around nervously. 'Don't you feel it?'

'Is that the message you wanted to tell me?'

'No.' She hesitated. 'I'm sorry. I'm not making sense, but that thought just came to me. The message I wrote on the beach was different. It had your name in it.'

'Perseus,' I remembered. 'In Ancient Greek.'

Rachel nodded. 'I don't know its meaning. But I know it's important. You have to hear it. It said: *Perseus, you are not the hero.*'

I stared at her like she'd just slapped me. 'You came thousands of miles to tell me *I'm not the hero?*'

'It's important,' she insisted. 'It will affect what you do.'

'Not the hero of the prophecy?' I asked. 'Not the hero who defeats Kronos? What do you mean?'

'I'm — I'm sorry, Percy. That's all I know. I had to tell you because —'

'Well!' Chiron cantered over. 'This must be Miss Dare.'

I wanted to yell at him to go away, but of course I couldn't. I tried to get my emotions under control. I felt like I had another personal hurricane swirling around me.

'Chiron — Rachel Dare,' I said. 'Rachel — this is my teacher Chiron.'

'Hello,' Rachel said glumly. She didn't look at all surprised that Chiron was a centaur.

'You are not asleep, Miss Dare,' he noticed. 'And yet you are mortal?'

'I'm mortal,' she agreed, like it was a depressing thought. 'The pilot fell asleep as soon as we passed the river. I don't know why I didn't. I just knew I had to be here, to warn Percy.'

'Warn Percy?'

'She's been seeing things,' I said. 'Writing lines and making drawings.'

Chiron raised an eyebrow. 'Indeed? Tell me.'

She told him the same things she'd told me.

Chiron stroked his beard. 'Miss Dare . . . perhaps we should talk.'

'Chiron,' I blurted. I had a sudden terrible image of Camp Half-Blood in the 1990s, and May Castellan's scream coming from that attic. 'You – you'll *help* Rachel, right? I mean, you'll warn her that she's got to be careful with this stuff. Not go too far.'

His tail flicked like it does when he's anxious. 'Yes, Percy. I will do my best to understand what is happening and advise Miss Dare, but this may take some time. Meanwhile, you should rest. We've moved your parents' car to safety. The enemy seems to be staying put for now. We've set up bunks in the Empire State Building. Get some sleep.'

'Everybody keeps telling me to sleep,' I grumbled. 'I don't need sleep.'

Chiron managed a smile. 'Have you looked at yourself recently, Percy?'

I glanced down at my clothes, which were scorched, burnt, sliced and tattered from my night of constant battles. 'I look like death,' I admitted. 'But you think I can sleep after what just happened?'

'You may be invulnerable in combat,' Chiron chided, 'but that only makes your body tire faster. I remember Achilles. Whenever that lad wasn't fighting he was sleeping. He must've taken twenty naps a day. You, Percy, need your rest. You may be our only hope.'

I wanted to complain that I *wasn't* their only hope. According to Rachel, I wasn't even the hero. But the look in Chiron's eyes made it clear he wasn't going to take no for an answer.

'Sure,' I grumbled. 'Talk.'

I trudged towards the Empire State Building. When I glanced back, Rachel and Chiron were walking together in earnest conversation, like they were discussing funeral arrangements.

Inside the lobby, I found an empty bunk and collapsed, sure that I would never be able to sleep. A second later, my eyes closed.

In my dreams, I was back in Hades' garden. The Lord of the Dead paced up and down, holding his ears while Nico followed him, waving his arms.

'You *have* to!' Nico insisted.

Demeter and Persephone sat behind them at the breakfast table. Both of the goddesses looked bored. Demeter poured shredded wheat into four huge bowls. Persephone was magically changing the flower arrangement on the table, turning the blossoms from red to yellow to polka-dotted.

'I don't *have* to do anything!' Hades' eyes blazed. 'I'm a god!'

'Father,' Nico said, 'if Olympus falls, your own palace's safety doesn't matter. You'll fade, too.'

'I am not an Olympian!' he growled. 'My family has made that *quite* clear.'

'You are,' Nico said. 'Whether you like it or not.'

'You saw what they did to your mother,' Hades said.

'Zeus killed her. And you would have me *help* them? They deserve what they get!'

Persephone sighed. She walked her fingers across the table, absently turning the silverware into roses. 'Could we *please* not talk about that woman?'

'You know what would help this boy?' Demeter mused. 'Farming.'

Persephone rolled her eyes. 'Mother –'

'Six months behind a plough. Excellent character building.'

Nico stepped in front of his father, forcing Hades to face him. 'My mother understood about family. That's why she didn't want to leave us. You can't just abandon your family because they did something horrible. You've done horrible things to them, too.'

'Maria died!' Hades reminded him.

'You can't just cut yourself off from the other gods!'

'I've done very well at it for thousands of years.'

'And has that made you feel any better?' Nico demanded. 'Has that curse on the Oracle helped you at all? Holding grudges is a fatal flaw. Bianca warned me about that and she was right.'

'For demigods! I am immortal, all powerful! I would not help the other gods if they begged me, if Percy Jackson himself pleaded –'

'You're just as much an outcast as I am!' Nico yelled. 'Stop being angry about it and do something helpful for once. That's the only way they'll respect you!'

Hades' palm filled with black fire.

'Go ahead,' Nico said. 'Blast me. That's just what the other gods would expect from you. Prove them right.'

'Yes, please,' Demeter complained. 'Shut him up.'

Persephone sighed. 'Oh, I don't know. I would rather fight in the war than eat another bowl of cereal. This is boring.'

Hades roared in anger. His fireball hit a silver tree right next to Nico, melting it into a pool of liquid metal.

And my dream changed.

I was standing outside the United Nations, about a mile north-east of the Empire State Building. The Titan army had set up camp all around the UN complex. The flagpoles were hung with horrible trophies – helmets and armour pieces from defeated campers. All along First Avenue, giants sharpened their axes. Telkhines repaired armour at makeshift forges.

Kronos himself paced at the top of the plaza, swinging his scythe so his *dracaenae* bodyguards stayed way back. Ethan Nakamura and Prometheus stood nearby, out of slicing range. Ethan was fidgeting with his shield straps, but Prometheus looked as calm and collected as ever in his tuxedo.

'I hate this place,' Kronos growled. '*United Nations.* As if mankind could ever unite. Remind me to tear down this building after we destroy Olympus.'

'Yes, lord.' Prometheus smiled as if his master's anger amused him. 'Shall we tear down the stables in Central Park, too? I know how much horses can annoy you.'

'Don't mock me, Prometheus! Those cursed centaurs will be sorry they interfered. I will feed them to the hellhounds, starting with that son of mine – that weakling Chiron.'

Prometheus shrugged. 'That weakling destroyed an entire legion of telkhines with his arrows.'

Kronos swung his scythe and cut a flagpole in half. The national colours of Brazil toppled into the army, squashing a *dracaena*.

'We will destroy them!' Kronos roared. 'It is time to unleash the drakon. Nakamura – you will do this.'

'Y-yes, lord. At sunset?'

'No,' Kronos said. 'Immediately. The defenders of Olympus are badly wounded. They will not expect a quick attack. Besides, we know this drakon they cannot beat.'

Ethan looked confused. 'My lord?'

'Never you mind, Nakamura. Just do my bidding. I want Olympus in ruins by the time Typhon reaches New York. We will break the gods utterly!'

'But, my lord,' Ethan said. 'Your regeneration.'

Kronos pointed at Ethan and the demigod froze.

'Does it seem,' Kronos hissed, 'that I *need* to regenerate?'

Ethan didn't respond. Kind of hard to do when you're immobilized in time.

Kronos snapped his fingers and Ethan collapsed.

'Soon,' the Titan growled, 'this form will be unnecessary. I will not rest with victory so close. Now go!'

Ethan scrambled away.

'This is dangerous, my lord,' Prometheus warned. 'Do not be hasty.'

'Hasty? After festering for three thousand years in the depths of Tartarus, you call me hasty? I will slice Percy Jackson into a thousand pieces.'

'Thrice you've fought him,' Prometheus pointed out. 'And yet you've always said it is beneath the dignity of a

Titan to fight a mere mortal. I wonder if your mortal host is influencing you, weakening your judgement.'

Kronos turned his golden eyes on the other Titan. 'You call me weak?'

'No, my lord. I only meant –'

'Are your loyalties divided?' Kronos asked. 'Perhaps you miss your old friends, the gods. Would you like to join them?' Prometheus paled. 'I misspoke, my lord. Your orders will be carried out.' He turned to the armies and shouted: 'PREPARE FOR BATTLE!'

The troops began to stir.

From somewhere behind the UN compound, an angry roar shook the city – the sound of a drakon waking. The noise was so horrible it woke me, and I realized I could still hear it from a mile away.

Grover stood next to me, looking nervous. 'What was that?'

'They're coming,' I told him. 'And we're in trouble.'

The Hephaestus cabin was out of Greek fire. The Apollo cabin and the Hunters were scrounging for arrows. Most of us had already ingested so much ambrosia and nectar we didn't dare take any more.

We had sixteen campers, fifteen Hunters and half a dozen satyrs left in fighting shape. The rest had taken refuge on Olympus. The Party Ponies tried to form ranks, but they staggered and giggled and they all smelled like root beer. The Texans were head-butting the Coloradoans. The Missouri branch was arguing with Illinois. The chances were pretty good the whole army would end up fighting each other rather than the enemy.

Chiron trotted up with Rachel on his back. I felt a twinge of annoyance, because Chiron rarely gave anyone a ride, and never a mortal.

'Your friend here has some useful insights, Percy,' he said.

Rachel blushed. 'Just some things I saw in my head.'

'A drakon,' Chiron said. 'A Lydian drakon, to be exact. The oldest and most dangerous kind.'

I stared at her. 'How did you know that?'

'I'm not sure,' Rachel admitted. 'But this drakon has a particular fate. It will be killed by a child of Ares.'

Annabeth crossed her arms. 'How can you possibly know that?'

'I just saw it. I can't explain.'

'Well, let's hope you're wrong,' I said. 'Because we're a little short on children of Ares . . .'. A horrible thought occurred to me, and I cursed in Ancient Greek.

'What?' Annabeth asked.

'The spy,' I told her. 'Kronos said, "*We know they cannot beat this drakon.*" The spy has been keeping him updated. Kronos knows the Ares cabin isn't with us. He intentionally picked a monster we can't kill.'

Thalia scowled. 'If I ever catch your spy, he's going to be very sorry. Maybe we could send another messenger to camp –'

'I've already done it,' Chiron said. 'Blackjack is on his way. But if Silena wasn't able to convince Clarisse, I doubt Blackjack will be able –'

A roar shook the ground. It sounded *very* close.

'Rachel,' I said, 'get inside the building.'

'I want to stay.'

A shadow blotted out the sun. Across the street, the drakon slithered down the side of a skyscraper. It roared and a thousand windows shattered.

'On second thoughts,' Rachel said in a small voice, 'I'll be inside.'

Let me explain: there are dragons, and then there are *drakons*.

Drakons are several millennia older than dragons, and *much* larger. They look like giant serpents. Most don't have wings. Most don't breathe fire (though some do). All are poisonous. All are immensely strong, with scales harder than titanium. Their eyes can paralyse you – not the *turn you to stone* Medusa-type paralysis, but the *oh my gods that big snake is going to eat me* type of paralysis, which is just as bad.

We have drakon-fighting classes at camp, but there is no way to prepare yourself for a fifty-metre-long serpent as thick as a school bus slithering down the side of a building, its yellow eyes like searchlights and its mouth full of razor-sharp teeth big enough to chew elephants.

It almost made me long for the flying pig.

Meanwhile, the enemy army advanced down Fifth Avenue. We'd done our best to push cars out of the way to keep the mortals safe, but that just made it easier for our enemies to approach. The Party Ponies swished their tails nervously. Chiron galloped up and down their ranks, shouting encouragement to stand tough and think about victory and root beer, but I figured any second they would panic and run.

'I'll take the drakon.' My voice came out as a timid

squeak. Then I yelled louder: 'I'LL TAKE THE DRAKON! Everyone else, hold the line against the army!'

Annabeth stood next to me. She had pulled her owl helmet low over her face, but I could tell her eyes were red.

'Will you help me?' I asked.

'That's what I do,' she said miserably. 'I help my friends.'

I felt like a complete jerk. I wanted to pull her aside and explain that I didn't mean for Rachel to be here, that it wasn't my idea, but we had no time.

'Go invisible,' I said. 'Look for weak links in its armour while I keep it busy. Just be careful.'

I whistled. 'Mrs O'Leary, heel!'

'ROOOF!' My hellhound leaped over a line of centaurs and gave me a kiss that smelled suspiciously of pepperoni pizza.

I drew my sword and we charged the monster.

The drakon was three stories above us, slithering sideways along the building as it sized up our forces. Wherever it looked, centaurs froze in fear.

From the north, the enemy army crashed into the Party Ponies and our lines broke. The drakon lashed out, swallowing three Californian centaurs in one gulp before I could even get close.

Mrs O'Leary launched herself through the air – a deadly black shadow with teeth and claws. Normally, a pouncing hellhound is a terrifying sight, but next to the drakon Mrs O'Leary looked like a child's night-night doll.

Her claws raked harmlessly off the drakon's scales. She

bit the monster's throat, but couldn't make a dent. Her weight, however, was enough to knock the drakon off the side of the building. It flailed awkwardly and crashed to the sidewalk – hellhound and serpent twisting and thrashing. The drakon tried to bite Mrs O'Leary, but she was too close to the serpent's mouth. Poison spewed everywhere, melting centaurs into dust along with quite a few monsters, but Mrs O'Leary weaved around the serpent's head, scratching and biting.

'YAAAH!' I plunged Riptide deep into the monster's left eye. The spotlight went dark. The drakon hissed and reared back to strike, but I rolled aside.

It bit a swimming-pool-sized chunk out of the pavement. It turned towards me with its good eye and I focused on its teeth so I wouldn't get paralysed. Mrs O'Leary did her best to cause a distraction. She leaped onto the serpent's head and scratched and growled like a really angry black wig.

The rest of the battle wasn't going well. Centaurs panicked under the onslaught of giants and demons. An occasional orange camp T-shirt appeared in the sea of fighting, but it quickly disappeared. Arrows screamed. Fire exploded in waves across both armies, but the action was moving across the street to the entrance of the Empire State Building. We were losing ground.

Suddenly Annabeth materialized on the drakon's back. Her invisibility cap rolled off her head as she drove her bronze knife between a chink in the serpent's scales.

The drakon roared. It coiled around, knocking Annabeth off its back.

I reached her just as she hit the ground. I dragged her

out of the way as the serpent rolled, crushing a lamppost right where she'd been.

'Thanks,' she said.

'I told you to be careful!'

'Yeah, well – DUCK!'

It was her turn to save me. She tackled me as the monster's teeth snapped above my head. Mrs O'Leary body-slammed the drakon's face to get its attention and we rolled out of the way.

Meanwhile, our allies had retreated to the doors of the Empire State Building. The entire enemy army was surrounding them.

We were out of options. No more help was coming. Annabeth and I would have to retreat before we were cut off from Mount Olympus.

Then I heard a rumbling in the south. It wasn't a sound you hear much in New York, but I recognized it immediately: chariot wheels.

A girl's voice yelled, 'ARES!'

And a dozen war chariots charged into battle. Each flew a red banner with the symbol of the wild boar's head. Each was pulled by a team of skeletal horses with manes of fire. A total of thirty fresh warriors, armour gleaming and eyes full of hate, lowered their lances as one – making a bristling wall of death.

'The children of Ares!' Annabeth said in amazement. 'How did Rachel know?'

I didn't have an answer. But leading the charge was a girl in familiar red armour, her face covered by a boar's head helm. She held aloft a spear that crackled with electricity. Clarisse herself had come to the rescue. While half her chariots charged the monster army, Clarisse led the other six straight for the drakon.

The serpent reared back and managed to throw off Mrs O'Leary. My poor pet hit the side of the building with a yelp. I ran to help her, but the serpent had already zeroed in on the new threat. Even with only one eye, its glare was enough to paralyse two chariot drivers. They veered into a line of cars. The other four chariots kept charging. The monster bared its fangs to strike and got a mouthful of celestial bronze javelins.

'EEESSSSS!' it screamed, which was probably drakon for *OWWWW!*

'Ares, to me!' Clarisse screamed. Her voice sounded shriller than usual, but I guess that wasn't surprising given what she was fighting.

Across the street, the arrival of six chariots gave the Party Ponies new hope. They rallied at the doors of the Empire State Building, and the enemy army was momentarily thrown into confusion.

Meanwhile, Clarisse's chariots circled the drakon. Lances broke against the monster's skin. Skeletal horses breathed fire and whinnied. Two more chariots overturned, but the warriors simply leaped to their feet, drew their swords and went to work. They hacked at chinks in the creature's scales. They dodged poison spray like they'd been training for this all their lives, which of course they had.

No one could say the Ares campers weren't brave. Clarisse was right there in front, stabbing her spear at the drakon's face, trying to put out its other eye. But, as I watched, things started to go wrong. The drakon snapped up one Ares camper in a gulp. It knocked aside another and sprayed poison on a third, who retreated in a panic, his armour melting.

'We have to help,' Annabeth said.

She was right. I'd just been standing there frozen in amazement. Mrs O'Leary tried to get up but yelped again. One of her paws was bleeding.

'Stay back, girl,' I told her. 'You've done enough already.'

Annabeth and I jumped onto the monster's back and ran towards its head, trying to draw its attention away from Clarisse.

Her cabin mates threw javelins, most of which broke, but some lodged in the monster's teeth. It snapped its jaws together until its mouth was a mess of green blood, yellow foamy poison and splintered weapons.

'You can do it!' I screamed at Clarisse. 'A child of Ares is destined to kill it!'

Through her war helmet, I could only see her eyes – but I could tell something was wrong. Her blue eyes shone with fear. Clarisse never looked like that. And she didn't *have* blue eyes.

'ARES!' she shouted, in that strangely shrill voice. She levelled her spear and charged the drakon.

'No,' I muttered. 'WAIT!'

But the monster looked down at her – almost in contempt – and spat poison directly in her face.

She screamed and fell.

'Clarisse!' Annabeth jumped off the monster's back and ran to help while the other Ares campers tried to defend their fallen counsellor. I drove Riptide between two of the creature's scales and managed to turn its attention on me.

I got thrown but I landed on my feet. 'C'MON, you stupid worm! Look at me!'

For the next several minutes, all I saw were teeth. I retreated and dodged poison, but I couldn't hurt the thing.

At the edge of my vision, I saw a flying chariot land on Fifth Avenue.

Then someone ran towards us. A girl's voice, shaken with grief, cried, 'NO! Curse you, WHY?'

I dared to glance over, but what I saw made no sense. Clarisse was lying on the ground where she'd fallen. Her armour smoked with poison. Annabeth and the Ares campers were trying to unfasten her helmet. And kneeling next to them, her face blotchy with tears, was a girl in camp clothes. It was . . . Clarisse.

My head spun. Why hadn't I noticed before? The girl in Clarisse's armour was much thinner, not as tall. But why would someone pretend to be Clarisse?

I was so stunned the drakon almost snapped me in half. I dodged and the beast buried its head in a brick wall.

'WHY?' the real Clarisse demanded, holding the other girl in her arms while the campers struggled to remove the poison-corroded helmet.

Chris Rodriguez ran over from the flying chariot. He and Clarisse must've ridden it here from camp, chasing the Ares campers, who'd mistakenly been following the other girl, thinking she was Clarisse. But it still made no sense.

The drakon tugged its head from the brick wall and screamed in rage.

'Look out!' Chris warned.

Instead of turning towards me, the drakon whirled towards the sound of Chris's voice. It bared its fangs at the group of demigods.

The real Clarisse looked up at the drakon. Her face filled with absolute hate. I'd seen a look that intense only once before. Her father Ares had worn the same expression when I'd fought him in single combat.

'YOU WANT DEATH?' Clarisse screamed at the drakon. 'WELL, COME ON!'

She grabbed her spear from the fallen girl. With no armour or shield, she charged the drakon.

I tried to close the distance to help, but Clarisse was faster. She leaped aside as the monster struck, pulverizing the ground in front of her. Then she jumped onto the creature's head. As it reared up, she drove her electric spear into its good eye with so much force it shattered the shaft, releasing all of the magic weapon's power.

Electricity arced across the creature's head, causing its whole body to shudder. Clarisse jumped free, rolling safely to the sidewalk as smoke boiled from the drakon's mouth. The drakon's flesh dissolved, and it collapsed into a hollow scaly tunnel of armour.

The rest of us stared at Clarisse in awe. I had never seen anyone take down such a huge monster single-handedly. But Clarisse didn't seem to care. She ran back to the wounded girl who'd stolen her armour.

Finally Annabeth managed to remove the girl's helmet. We all gathered around – the Ares campers, Chris, Clarisse, Annabeth and me. The battle still raged along Fifth Avenue, but for that moment nothing existed except our small circle and the fallen girl.

Her features, once beautiful, were badly burned from poison. I could tell that no amount of nectar or ambrosia would save her.

Something is about to happen. Rachel's words rang in my ears. *A trick that ends in death.*

Now I knew what she meant, and I knew who had led the Ares cabin into battle.

I looked down at the dying face of Silena Beauregard.

17 I SIT ON THE HOT SEAT

'What were you thinking?' Clarisse cradled Silena's head in her lap.

Silena tried to swallow, but her lips were dry and cracked. 'Wouldn't . . . listen. Cabin would . . . only follow you.'

'So you stole my armour,' Clarisse said in disbelief. 'You waited until Chris and I went out on patrol, you stole my armour and pretended to be me.' She glared at her siblings. 'And NONE of you noticed?'

The Ares campers developed a sudden interest in their combat boots.

'Don't blame them,' Silena said. 'They wanted to . . . to believe I was you.'

'You *stupid* Aphrodite girl,' Clarisse sobbed. 'You charged a drakon? *Why?*'

'All my fault,' Silena said, a tear streaking the side of her face. 'The drakon, Charlie's death . . . camp endangered –'

'Stop it!' Clarisse said. 'That's not true.'

Silena opened her hand. In her palm was a silver bracelet with a scythe charm – the mark of Kronos.

A cold fist closed around my heart. 'You were the spy.'

Silena tried to nod. 'Before – before I liked Charlie, Luke was nice to me. He was so – charming. Handsome. Later, I wanted to stop helping him, but he threatened to tell. He promised . . . he promised I was saving lives. Fewer people would get hurt. He told me he wouldn't hurt – Charlie. He lied to me.'

I met Annabeth's eyes. Her face was chalky. She looked like somebody had just yanked the world out from under her feet.

Behind us, the battle raged.

Clarisse scowled at her cabin mates. 'Go, help the centaurs. Protect the doors. GO!'

They scrambled off to join the fight.

Silena took a heavy, painful breath. 'Forgive me.'

'You're not dying,' Clarisse insisted.

'Charlie . . .' Silena's eyes were a million miles away. 'See Charlie . . .'

She didn't speak again.

Clarisse held her and wept. Chris put a hand on her shoulder.

Finally Annabeth closed Silena's eyes.

'We have to fight.' Annabeth's voice was brittle. 'She gave her life to help us. We have to honour her.'

Clarisse sniffled and wiped her nose. 'She was a hero, understand? A hero.'

I nodded. 'Come on, Clarisse.'

She picked up a sword from one of her fallen siblings. 'Kronos is going to pay.'

I'd like to say I drove the enemy away from the Empire State Building. The truth was Clarisse did all the work. Even without her armour or spear, she was a demon. She rode her chariot straight into the Titans' army and crushed everything in her path.

She was so inspiring even the panicked centaurs started to rally. The Hunters scrounged arrows from the fallen and launched volley after volley into the enemy. The Ares cabin slashed and hacked, which was their favourite thing. The monsters retreated towards Thirty-fifth Street.

Clarisse drove to the drakon's carcass and looped a grappling line through its eye sockets. She lashed her horses and took off, dragging the drakon behind the chariot like a Chinese New Year dragon. She charged after the enemy, yelling insults and daring them to cross her. As she rode, I realized she was literally glowing. An aura of red fire flickered around her.

'The blessing of Ares,' Thalia said. 'I've never seen it in person before.'

For the moment, Clarisse was as invincible as I was. The enemy threw spears and arrows, but nothing hit her.

'I AM CLARISSE, DRAKON-SLAYER!' she yelled. 'I will kill you ALL! Where is Kronos? Bring him out! Is he a coward?'

'Clarisse!' I yelled. 'Stop it. Withdraw!'

'What's the matter, Titan lord?' she yelled. 'BRING IT ON!'

There was no answer from the enemy. Slowly, they began to fall back behind a *dracaenae* shield wall, while Clarisse drove in circles around Fifth Avenue, daring anyone to cross her path. The fifty-metre-long drakon carcass made a hollow scraping noise against the pavement, like a thousand knives.

Meanwhile, we tended our wounded, bringing them inside the lobby. Long after the enemy had retreated from sight, Clarisse kept riding up and down the avenue with her horrible trophy, demanding that Kronos meet her in battle.

Chris said, 'I'll watch her. She'll get tired eventually. I'll make sure she comes inside.'

'What about the camp?' I asked. 'Is anybody left there?'

Chris shook his head. 'Only Argus and the nature spirits. Peleus the dragon is still guarding the tree.'

'They won't last long,' I said. 'But I'm glad you came.'

Chris nodded sadly. 'I'm sorry it took so long. I tried to reason with Clarisse. I said there's no point in defending camp if you guys die. All our friends are here. I'm sorry it took Silena . . .'

'My Hunters will help you stand guard,' Thalia said. 'Annabeth and Percy, you should go to Olympus. I have a feeling they'll need you up there – to set up the final defence.'

The doorman had disappeared from the lobby. His book was face down on the desk and his chair was empty. The rest of the lobby, however, was jam-packed with wounded campers, Hunters and satyrs.

Connor and Travis Stoll met us by the elevators.

'Is it true?' Connor asked. 'About Silena?'

I nodded. 'She died a hero.'

Travis shifted uncomfortably. 'Um, I also heard –'

'That's it,' I insisted. 'End of story.'

'Right,' Travis mumbled. 'Listen, we figure the Titans' army will have trouble getting up the elevator. They'll have to go up a few at a time. And the giants won't be able to fit at all.'

'That's our biggest advantage,' I said. 'Any way to disable the elevator?'

'It's magic,' Travis said. 'Usually you need a key card, but the doorman vanished. That means the defences are crumbling. Anyone can walk into the elevator now and head straight up.'

'Then we have to keep them away from the doors,' I said. 'We'll bottle them up in the lobby.'

'We need reinforcements,' Travis said. 'They'll just keep coming. Eventually they'll overwhelm us.'

'There are no reinforcements,' Connor complained.

I looked outside at Mrs O'Leary, who was breathing against the glass doors and smearing them with hellhound drool.

'Maybe that's not true,' I said.

I went outside and put a hand on Mrs O'Leary's muzzle. Chiron had bandaged her paw, but she was still limping. Her fur was matted with mud, leaves, pizza slices and dried monster blood.

'Hey, girl.' I tried to sound upbeat. 'I know you're tired, but I've got one more big favour to ask you.'

I leaned next to her and whispered in her ear.

After Mrs O'Leary had shadow-travelled away, I rejoined Annabeth in the lobby. On the way to the elevator, we spotted Grover kneeling over a fat wounded satyr.

'Leneus!' I said.

The old satyr looked terrible. His lips were blue. There was a broken spear in his belly and his furry goat legs were twisted at a painful angle.

He tried to focus on us, but I don't think he saw us.

'Grover?' he murmured.

'I'm here, Leneus.' Grover was blinking back tears, despite all the horrible things Leneus had said about him.

'Did – did we win?'

'Um . . . yes,' Grover lied. 'Thanks to you, Leneus. We drove the enemy away.'

'Told you,' the old satyr mumbled. 'True leader. True . . .'

He closed his eyes for the last time.

Grover gulped. He put his hand on Leneus's forehead and spoke an ancient blessing. The old satyr's body melted, until all that was left was a tiny sapling in a pile of fresh soil.

'A laurel,' Grover said in awe. 'Oh, that lucky old goat.'

He gathered up the sapling in his hands. 'I – I should plant him. In Olympus, in the gardens.'

'We're going that way,' I said. 'Come on.'

Easy-listening music played as the elevator rose. I thought about the first time I'd visited Mount Olympus, back when I was twelve. Annabeth and Grover hadn't been with me then. I was glad they were with me now. I had a feeling it might be our last adventure together.

'Percy,' Annabeth said quietly. 'You were right about Luke.' It was the first time she'd spoken since Silena Beauregard's death. She kept her eyes fixed on the elevator floors as they blinked into the magical numbers – 400, 450, 500.

Grover and I exchanged glances.

'Annabeth,' I said. 'I'm sorry –'

'You tried to tell me.' Her voice was shaky. 'Luke is no

[283]

good. I didn't believe you until – until I heard how he'd used Silena. Now I know. I hope you're happy.'

'That doesn't make me happy.'

She put her head against the elevator wall and wouldn't look at me.

Grover cradled his laurel sapling in his hands. 'Well . . . sure good to be together again. Arguing. Almost dying. Abject terror. Oh, look. It's our floor.'

The doors dinged and we stepped onto the aerial walkway.

Depressing is not a word that usually describes Mount Olympus, but it looked that way now. No fires lit the braziers. The windows were dark. The streets were deserted and the doors were barred. The only movement was in the parks, which had been set up as field hospitals. Will Solace and the other Apollo campers scrambled around, caring for the wounded. Naiads and dryads tried to help, using nature magic songs to heal burns and poison.

As Grover planted the laurel sapling, Annabeth and I went around trying to cheer up the wounded. I passed a satyr with a broken leg, a demigod who was bandaged from head to toe and a body covered in the golden burial shroud of Apollo's cabin. I didn't know who was underneath. I didn't want to find out.

My heart felt like lead, but we tried to find positive things to say.

'You'll be up and fighting Titans in no time!' I told one camper.

'You look great,' Annabeth told another camper.

'Leneus turned into a shrub!' Grover told a groaning satyr.

I found Dionysus' son Pollux propped up against a tree. He had a broken arm, but otherwise he was okay.

'I can still fight with the other hand,' he said, gritting his teeth.

'No,' I said. 'You've done enough. I want you to stay here and help with the wounded.'

'But –'

'Promise me to stay safe,' I said. 'Okay? Personal favour.'

He frowned uncertainly. It wasn't like we were good friends or anything, but I wasn't going to tell him it was a request from his dad. That would just embarrass him. Finally he promised, and when he sat back down, I could tell he was kind of relieved.

Annabeth, Grover and I kept walking towards the palace. That's where Kronos would head. As soon as he made it up the elevator – and I had no doubt he would, one way or another – he would destroy the throne room, the centre of the gods' power.

The bronze doors creaked open. Our footsteps echoed on the marble floor. The constellations twinkled coldly on the ceiling of the great hall. The hearth was down to a dull red glow. Hestia, in the form of a little girl in brown robes, hunched at its edge, shivering. The Ophiotaurus swam sadly in his sphere of water. He let out a half-hearted *Moo* when he saw me.

In the firelight, the thrones cast evil-looking shadows, like grasping hands.

Standing at the foot of Zeus's throne, looking up at the stars, was Rachel Elizabeth Dare. She was holding a Greek ceramic vase.

'Rachel?' I said. 'Um, what are you doing with that?'

She focused on me as if she were coming out of a dream. 'I found it. It's Pandora's jar, isn't it?'

Her eyes were brighter than usual, and I had a bad flashback of mouldy sandwiches and burnt cookies.

'Please put down the jar,' I said.

'I can see Hope inside it.' Rachel ran her fingers over the ceramic designs. 'So fragile.'

'*Rachel.*'

My voice seemed to bring her back to reality. She held out the jar and I took it. The clay felt as cold as ice.

'Grover,' Annabeth mumbled. 'Let's scout around the palace. Maybe we can find some extra Greek fire or Hephaestus traps.'

'But –'

Annabeth elbowed him.

'Right!' he yelped. 'I love traps!'

She dragged him out of the throne room.

Over by the fire, Hestia was huddled in her robes, rocking back and forth.

'Come on,' I told Rachel. 'I want you to meet someone.'

We sat next to the goddess.

'Lady Hestia,' I said.

'Hello, Percy Jackson,' the goddess murmured. 'Getting colder. Harder to keep the fire going.'

'I know,' I said. 'The Titans are near.'

Hestia focused on Rachel. 'Hello, my dear. You've come to our hearth at last.'

Rachel blinked. 'You've been expecting me?'

Hestia held out her hands and the coals glowed. I saw

images in the fire: my mother, Paul and I eating Thanksgiving dinner at the kitchen table; my friends and me around the campfire at Camp Half-Blood, singing songs and roasting marshmallows; Rachel and me driving along the beach in Paul's Prius.

I didn't know if Rachel saw the same images, but the tension went out of her shoulders. The warmth of the fire seemed to spread across her.

'To claim your place at the hearth,' Hestia told her, 'you must let go of your distractions. It is the only way you will survive.'

Rachel nodded. 'I – I understand.'

'Wait,' I said. 'What is she talking about?'

Rachel took a shaky breath. 'Percy, when I came here . . . I thought I was coming for you. But I wasn't. You and me . . .' She shook her head.

'Wait. Now I'm a *distraction*? Is this because I'm "not the hero" or whatever?'

'I'm not sure I can put it into words,' she said. 'I was drawn to you because . . . because you opened the door to all of this.' She gestured at the throne room. 'I needed to understand my true sight. But you and me – that wasn't part of it. Our fates aren't intertwined. I think you've always known that, deep down.'

I stared at her. Maybe I wasn't the brightest guy in the world when it came to girls, but I was pretty sure Rachel had just dumped me, which was lame considering we'd never even been together.

'So . . . what,' I said. '"Thanks for bringing me to Olympus. See ya?" Is that what you're saying?'

Rachel stared at the fire.

'Percy Jackson,' Hestia said. 'Rachel has told you all she can. Her moment is coming, but your decision approaches even more rapidly. Are you prepared?'

I wanted to complain that, no, I wasn't even close to prepared.

I looked at Pandora's jar and for the first time, I had an urge to open it. Hope seemed pretty useless to me right now. So many of my friends were dead. Rachel was cutting me off. Annabeth was angry with me. My parents were asleep down in the streets somewhere while a monster army surrounded the building. Olympus was on the verge of falling, and I'd seen so many cruel things the gods had done: Zeus destroying Maria di Angelo, Hades cursing the last Oracle, Hermes turning his back on Luke even when he knew his son would become evil.

Surrender, Prometheus's voice whispered in my ear. *Otherwise your home will be destroyed. Your precious camp will burn.*

Then I looked at Hestia. Her red eyes glowed warmly. I remembered the images I'd seen in her hearth – friends and family, everyone I cared about.

I remembered something Chris Rodriguez had said: *There's no point in defending camp if you guys die. All our friends are here.* And Nico, standing up to his father Hades: *If Olympus falls,* he said, *your own palace's safety doesn't matter.*

I heard footsteps. Annabeth and Grover came back into the throne room and stopped when they saw us. I probably had a pretty strange look on my face.

'Percy?' Annabeth didn't sound angry any more – just concerned. 'Should we, um, leave again?'

Suddenly I felt like someone had injected me with steel. I understood what to do.

I looked at Rachel. 'You're not going to do anything stupid, are you? I mean . . . you talked to Chiron, right?'

She managed a faint smile. 'You're worried about *me* doing something stupid?'

'But I mean – will you be okay?'

'I don't know,' she admitted. 'That kind of depends on whether you save the world, hero.'

I picked up Pandora's jar. The spirit of Hope fluttered inside, trying to warm the cold container.

'Hestia,' I said, 'I give this to you as an offering.'

The goddess tilted her head. 'I am the least of the gods. Why would you trust me with this?'

'You're the last Olympian,' I said. 'And the most important.'

'And why is that, Percy Jackson?'

'Because Hope survives best at the hearth,' I said. 'Guard it for me, and I won't be tempted to give up again.'

The goddess smiled. She took the jar in her hands and it began to glow. The hearth fire burned a little brighter.

'Well done, Percy Jackson,' she said. 'May the gods bless you.'

'We're about to find out.' I looked at Annabeth and Grover. 'Come on, guys.'

I marched towards my father's throne.

The seat of Poseidon stood just to the right of Zeus's, but it wasn't nearly as grand. The moulded black leather seat was attached to a swivel pedestal, with a couple of iron rings on the side for fastening a fishing pole (or a trident). Basically it looked like a chair on a deep-sea boat that you would sit in if you wanted to hunt shark or marlin or sea monsters.

Gods in their natural state are about six metres tall, so I could just reach the edge of the seat if I stretched my arms.

'Help me up,' I told Annabeth and Grover.

'Are you crazy?' Annabeth asked.

'Probably,' I admitted.

'Percy,' Grover said, 'the gods *really* don't appreciate people sitting in their thrones. I mean, like, *turn you into a pile of ashes* don't appreciate it.'

'I need to get his attention,' I said. 'It's the only way.'

They exchanged uneasy looks.

'Well,' Annabeth said, 'this'll get his attention.'

They linked their arms to make a step then boosted me onto the throne. I felt like a baby with my feet so high off the ground. I looked around at the other gloomy, empty thrones, and I could imagine what it would be like sitting on the Olympian Council – so much power, but so much arguing, always eleven other gods trying to get their way. It would be easy to get paranoid, to look out only for my own interest, especially if I were Poseidon. Sitting in his throne, I felt like I had the entire sea at my command – vast cubic miles of ocean churning with power and mystery. Why should Poseidon listen to anyone? Why shouldn't he be the greatest of the twelve?

Then I shook my head. *Concentrate.*

The throne rumbled. A wave of gale-force anger slammed into my mind:

WHO DARES –

The voice stopped abruptly. The anger retreated, which was a good thing, because just those two words had almost blasted my mind to shreds.

Percy. My father's voice was still angry but more controlled. *What — exactly — are you doing on my throne?*

'I'm sorry, Father,' I said. 'I needed to get your attention.'

This was a very dangerous thing to do. Even for you. If I hadn't looked before I blasted, you would now be a puddle of seawater.

'I'm sorry,' I said again. 'Listen, things are rough up here.'

I told him what was happening. Then I told him my plan.

His voice was silent for a long time.

Percy, what you ask is impossible. My palace —

'Dad, Kronos sent an army against you on purpose. He wants to divide you from the other gods because he knows you could tip the scales.'

Be that as it may, he attacks my home.

'I'm *at* your home,' I said. 'Olympus.'

The floor shook. A wave of anger washed over my mind. I thought I'd gone too far, but then the trembling eased. In the background of my mental link, I heard underwater explosions and the sound of battle cries — Cyclopes bellowing, mermen shouting.

'Is Tyson okay?' I asked.

The question seemed to take my dad by surprise. *He's fine. Doing much better than I expected. Though 'peanut butter' is a strange battle cry.*

'You let him fight?'

Stop changing the subject! You realize what you are asking me to do? My palace will be destroyed.

'And Olympus might be saved.'

Do you have any idea how long I've worked on remodelling this palace? The game room alone took six hundred years.

'Dad –'

Very well! It shall be as you say. But, my son, pray this works.

'I am praying. I'm talking to you, right?'

Oh . . . yes. Good point. Amphitrite – incoming!

The sound of a large explosion shattered our connection.

I slipped down from the throne.

Grover studied me nervously. 'Are you okay? You turned pale and . . . you started smoking.'

'I did not!' Then I looked at my arms. Steam was curling off my shirtsleeves. The hair on my arms was singed.

'If you'd sat there any longer,' Annabeth said, 'you would've spontaneously combusted. I hope the conversation was worth it?'

Moo, said the Ophiotaurus in his sphere of water.

'We'll find out soon,' I said.

Just then the doors of the throne room swung open. Thalia marched in. Her bow was snapped in half and her quiver was empty.

'You've got to get down there,' she told us. 'The enemy is advancing. And Kronos is leading them.'

18 MY PARENTS GO COMMANDO

By the time we got to the street, it was too late.

Campers and Hunters lay wounded on the ground. Clarisse must've lost a fight with a Hyperborean giant, because she and her chariot were frozen in a block of ice. The centaurs were nowhere to be seen. Either they'd panicked and ran or they'd been disintegrated.

The Titan army ringed the building, standing maybe ten metres from the doors. Kronos's vanguard was in the lead – Ethan Nakamura, the *dracaena* queen in her green armour and two Hyperboreans. I didn't see Prometheus. The slimy weasel was probably hiding back at their headquarters. But Kronos himself stood right in front with his scythe in hand.

The only thing standing in his way was . . .

'Chiron,' Annabeth said, her voice trembling.

If Chiron heard us, he didn't answer. He had an arrow notched, aimed straight at Kronos's face.

As soon as Kronos saw me, his gold eyes flared. Every muscle in my body froze. Then the Titan lord turned his attention back to Chiron. 'Step aside, little son.'

Hearing Luke call Chiron his *son* was weird enough, but Kronos put contempt in his voice, like *son* was the worst word he could think of.

'I'm afraid not.' Chiron's tone was steely calm, the way he gets when he's really angry.

I tried to move, but my feet felt like concrete. Annabeth, Grover and Thalia were straining, too, like they were just as stuck.

'Chiron!' Annabeth said. 'Look out!'

The *dracaena* queen became impatient and charged. Chiron's arrow flew straight between her eyes and she vaporized on the spot, her empty armour clattering to the tarmac.

Chiron reached for another arrow, but his quiver was empty. He dropped the bow and drew his sword. I knew he hated fighting with a sword. It was never his favourite weapon.

Kronos chuckled. He advanced a step and Chiron's horse half skittered nervously. His tail flicked back and forth.

'You're a teacher,' Kronos sneered. 'Not a hero.'

'Luke was a hero,' Chiron said. 'He was a good one, until *you* corrupted him.'

'FOOL!' Kronos's voice shook the city. 'You filled his head with empty promises. You said the gods cared about me!'

'Me,' Chiron noticed. 'You said *me.*'

Kronos looked confused, and in that moment, Chiron struck. It was a good manoeuvre – a feint followed by a strike to the face. I couldn't have done better myself, but Kronos was quick. He had all of Luke's fighting skill, which was a lot. He knocked aside Chiron's blade and yelled, '*BACK!*'

A blinding white light exploded between the Titan and the centaur. Chiron flew into the side of the building with such force the wall crumbled and collapsed on top of him.

'No!' Annabeth wailed. The freezing spell broke. We ran towards our teacher, but there was no sign of him. Thalia and I pulled helplessly at the bricks while a ripple of ugly laughter ran through the Titans' army.

'YOU!' Annabeth turned on Luke. 'To think that I – that I thought –'

She drew her knife.

'Annabeth, don't.' I tried to take her arm, but she shook me off.

She attacked Kronos, and his smug smile faded. Perhaps some part of Luke remembered that he used to like this girl, used to take care of her when she was little. She plunged her knife between the straps of his armour, right at his collarbone. The blade should've sunk into his chest. Instead it bounced off. Annabeth doubled over, clutching her arm to her stomach. The jolt might've been enough to dislocate her bad shoulder.

I yanked her back as Kronos swung his scythe, slicing the air where she'd been standing.

She fought me and screamed, 'I HATE you!' I wasn't sure who she was talking to – me or Luke or Kronos. Tears streaked the dust on her face.

'I have to fight him,' I told her.

'It's my fight, too, Percy!'

Kronos laughed. 'So much spirit. I can see why Luke wanted to spare you. Unfortunately, that won't be possible.'

He raised his scythe. I got ready to defend, but before Kronos could strike, a dog's howl pierced the air somewhere behind the Titans' army. 'Arroooooooo!'

It was too much to hope, but I called, 'Mrs O'Leary?'

The enemy forces stirred uneasily. Then the strangest

thing happened. They began to part, clearing a path through the street like something behind them was forcing them to.

Soon there was a free aisle down the centre of Fifth Avenue. Standing at the end of the block was my giant dog and a small figure in black armour.

'Nico?' I called.

'ROWWF!' Mrs O'Leary bounded towards me, ignoring the growling monsters on either side. Nico strode forward. The enemy army fell back before him like he radiated death, which of course he did.

Through the face guard of his skull-shaped helmet, he smiled. 'Got your message. Is it too late to join the party?'

'Son of Hades.' Kronos spat on the ground. 'Do you love death so much you wish to experience it?'

'Your death,' Nico said, 'would be great for me.'

'I'm immortal, you fool! I have escaped Tartarus. You have no business here, and no chance to live.'

Nico drew his sword – a metre long of wicked sharp Stygian iron, black as a nightmare. 'I don't agree.'

The ground rumbled. Cracks appeared in the road, the sidewalks, the sides of the buildings. Skeletal hands grasped the air as the dead clawed their way into the world of the living. There were thousands of them, and as they emerged, the Titans' monsters got jumpy and started to back up.

'HOLD YOUR GROUND!' Kronos demanded. 'The dead are no match for us.'

The sky turned dark and cold. Shadows thickened. A harsh war horn sounded, and as the dead soldiers formed up ranks with their guns and swords and spears, an enormous chariot roared down Fifth Avenue. It came to a stop next to Nico. The horses were living shadows, fashioned from darkness. The chariot was inlaid with obsidian and gold, decorated with scenes of painful death. Holding the reins was Hades himself, Lord of the Dead, with Demeter and Persephone riding behind him.

Hades wore black armour and a cloak the colour of fresh blood. On top of his pale head was the helm of darkness: a crown that radiated pure terror. It changed shape as I watched – from a dragon's head to a circle of black flames to a wreath of human bones. But that wasn't the scary part. The helm reached into my mind and ignited my worst nightmares, my most secret fears. I wanted to crawl into a hole and hide, and I could tell the enemy army felt the same way. Only Kronos's power and authority kept his ranks from fleeing.

Hades smiled coldly. 'Hello, Father. You're looking . . . young.'

'Hades,' Kronos growled. 'I hope you and the ladies have come to pledge your allegiance.'

'I'm afraid not.' Hades sighed. 'My son here convinced me that perhaps I should prioritize my list of enemies.' He glanced at me with distaste. 'As much as I dislike certain *upstart* demigods, it would not do for Olympus to fall. I would miss bickering with my siblings. And if there is one thing we agree on – it is that you were a TERRIBLE father.'

'True,' muttered Demeter. 'No appreciation of agriculture.'

'Mother!' Persephone complained.

Hades drew his sword, a double-edged Stygian blade

etched with silver. 'Now fight me! For today the House of Hades will be called the saviours of Olympus.'

'I don't have time for this,' Kronos snarled.

He struck the ground with his scythe. A crack spread in both directions, circling the Empire State Building. A wall of force shimmered along the fissure line, separating Kronos's vanguard, my friends and me from the bulk of the two armies.

'What's he doing?' I muttered.

'Sealing us in,' Thalia said. 'He's collapsing the magic barriers around Manhattan – cutting off just the building, and us.'

Sure enough, outside the barrier, car engines revved to life. Pedestrians woke up and stared uncomprehendingly at the monsters and zombies all around them. No telling what they saw through the Mist, but I'm sure it was plenty scary. Car doors opened. And at the end of the block, Paul Blofis and my mom got out of their Prius.

'No,' I said. 'Don't . . .'

My mother could see through the Mist. I could tell from her expression that she understood how serious things were. I hoped she would have the sense to run. But she locked eyes with me, said something to Paul and they ran straight towards us.

I couldn't call out. The last thing I wanted to do was bring her to Kronos's attention.

Fortunately, Hades caused a distraction. He charged at the wall of force, but his chariot crashed against it and overturned. He got to his feet, cursing, and blasted the wall with black energy. The barrier held.

'ATTACK!' he roared.

The armies of the dead clashed with the Titans' monsters. Fifth Avenue exploded into absolute chaos. Mortals screamed and ran for cover. Demeter waved her hand and an entire column of giants turned into a wheat field. Persephone changed the *dracaenae's* spears into sunflowers. Nico slashed and hacked his way through the enemy, trying to protect the pedestrians as best he could. My parents ran towards me, dodging monsters and zombies, but there was nothing I could do to help them.

'Nakamura,' Kronos said. 'Attend me. Giants – deal with them.'

He pointed at my friends and me. Then he ducked into the lobby.

For a second, I was stunned. I'd been expecting a fight, but Kronos completely ignored me like I wasn't worth the trouble. That made me mad.

The first Hyperborean giant smashed at me with his club. I rolled between his legs and stabbed Riptide into his backside. He shattered into a pile of ice shards. The second giant breathed frost at Annabeth, who was barely able to stand, but Grover pulled her out of the way while Thalia went to work. She sprinted up the giant's back like a gazelle, sliced her hunting knives across his monstrous blue neck, and created the world's largest headless ice sculpture.

I glanced outside the magic barrier. Nico was fighting his way towards my mom and Paul, but they weren't waiting for help. Paul grabbed a sword from a fallen hero and did a pretty fine job keeping a *dracaena* busy. He stabbed her in the gut and she disintegrated.

'Paul?' I said in amazement.

He turned towards me and grinned. 'I hope that was a

monster I just killed. I was a Shakespearian actor in college! Picked up a little swordplay!'

I liked him even better for that, but then a Laistrygonian giant charged towards my mom. She was rummaging around in an abandoned police car — maybe looking for the emergency radio — and her back was turned.

'Mom!' I yelled.

She whirled when the monster was almost on top of her. I thought the thing in her hands was an umbrella until she cranked the pump and the shotgun blast blew the giant five metres backwards, right into Nico's sword.

'Nice one,' Paul said.

'When did you learn to fire a shotgun?' I demanded.

My mom blew the hair out of her face. 'About two seconds ago. Percy, we'll be fine. Go!'

'Yes,' Nico agreed, 'we'll handle the army. You have to get Kronos!'

'Come on, Seaweed Brain!' Annabeth said. I nodded. Then I looked at the rubble pile on the side of the building. My heart twisted. I'd forgotten about Chiron. How could I do that?

'Mrs O'Leary,' I said. 'Please — Chiron's under there. If anyone can dig him out, you can. Find him! Help him!'

I'm not sure how much she understood, but she bounded to the pile and started to dig. Annabeth, Thalia, Grover and I raced for the elevators.

19 WE TRASH THE ETERNAL CITY

The bridge to Olympus was dissolving. We stepped out of the elevator onto the white marble walkway and immediately cracks appeared at our feet.

'Jump!' Grover said, which was easy for him since he's part mountain goat.

He sprang to the next slab of stone while ours tilted sickeningly.

'Gods, I hate heights!' Thalia yelled as she and I leaped. But Annabeth was in no shape for jumping. She stumbled and yelled, 'Percy!'

I caught her hand as the pavement fell, crumbling into dust. For a second, I thought she was going to pull us both over. Her feet dangled in the open air. Her hand started to slip until I was holding her only by her fingers. Then Grover and Thalia grabbed my legs and I found extra strength. Annabeth was *not* going to fall.

I pulled her up and we lay trembling on the pavement. I didn't realize we had our arms around each other until she suddenly tensed.

'Um, thanks,' she muttered.

I tried to say *don't mention it*, but it came out as, 'Uh duh.'

'Keep moving!' Grover tugged my shoulder. We untangled ourselves and sprinted across the sky bridge as more stones disintegrated and fell into oblivion. We made it to the edge of the mountain just as the final section collapsed.

Annabeth looked back at the elevator, which was now completely out of reach – a polished set of metal doors hanging in space, attached to nothing, six hundred stories above Manhattan.

'We're marooned,' she said. 'On our own.'

'Blah-ha-ha!' Grover said. 'The connection between Olympus and America is dissolving. If it fails –'

'The gods won't move on to another country this time,' Thalia said. 'This will be the end of Olympus. The *final* end.'

We ran through streets. Mansions were burning. Statues had been hacked down. Trees in the parks were blasted to splinters. It looked like someone had attacked the city with a giant Weedwhacker.

'Kronos's scythe,' I said.

We followed the winding path towards the palace of the gods. I didn't remember the road being so long. Maybe Kronos was making time go slower, or maybe it was just dread slowing me down. The whole mountaintop was in ruins – so many beautiful buildings and gardens gone.

A few minor gods and nature spirits had tried to stop Kronos. What remained of them was strewn about the road – shattered armour, ripped clothing, swords and spears broken in half.

Somewhere ahead of us, Kronos's voice roared: 'Brick by brick! That was my promise. Tear it down BRICK BY BRICK!'

A white marble temple with a gold dome suddenly

exploded. The dome shot up like the lid of a teapot and shattered into a billion pieces, raining rubble over the city.

'That was a shrine to Artemis,' Thalia grumbled. 'He'll pay for that.'

We were running under the marble archway with the huge statues of Zeus and Hera when the entire mountain groaned, rocking sideways like a boat in a storm.

'Look out!' Grover yelped. The archway crumbled. I looked up in time to see a twenty-ton scowling Hera topple over on us. Annabeth and I would've been flattened, but Thalia shoved us from behind and we landed just out of danger.

'Thalia!' Grover cried.

When the dust cleared and the mountain stopped rocking, we found her still alive, but her legs were pinned under the statue.

We tried desperately to move it, but it would've taken several Cyclopes. When we tried to pull Thalia out from under it, she yelled in pain.

'I survive all those battles,' she growled, 'and I get defeated by a stupid chunk of rock!'

'It's Hera,' Annabeth said in outrage. 'She's had it in for me all year. Her statue would've killed me if you hadn't pushed us away.'

Thalia grimaced. 'Well, don't just stand there! I'll be fine. Go!'

We didn't want to leave her, but I could hear Kronos laughing as he approached the hall of the gods. More buildings exploded.

'We'll be back,' I promised.

'I'm not going anywhere,' Thalia groaned.

A fireball erupted on the side of the mountain, right near the gates of the palace.

'We've got to run,' I said.

'I don't suppose you mean *away*,' Grover murmured hopefully.

I sprinted towards the palace, Annabeth right behind me.

'I was afraid of that,' Grover sighed, and clip-clopped after us.

The doors of the palace were big enough to steer a cruise ship through, but they'd been ripped off their hinges and smashed like they weighed nothing. We had to climb over a huge pile of broken stone and twisted metal to get inside.

Kronos stood in the middle of the throne room, his arms wide, staring at the starry ceiling as if taking it all in. His laughter echoed even louder than it had from the pit of Tartarus.

'Finally!' he bellowed. 'The Olympian Council – so proud and mighty. Which seat of power shall I destroy first?'

Ethan Nakamura stood to one side, trying to stay out of the way of his master's scythe. The hearth was almost dead, just a few coals glowing deep in the ashes. Hestia was nowhere to be seen. Neither was Rachel. I hoped she was okay, but I'd seen so much destruction I was afraid to think about it. The Ophiotaurus swam in his water sphere in the far corner of the room, wisely not making a sound, but it wouldn't be long before Kronos noticed him.

Annabeth, Grover and I stepped forward into the torchlight. Ethan saw us first.

'My lord,' he warned.

Kronos turned and smiled through Luke's face. Except for the golden eyes, he looked just the same as he had four years ago when he'd welcomed me into the Hermes cabin. Annabeth made a painful sound in the back of her throat, like someone had just sucker-punched her.

'Shall I destroy you first, Jackson?' Kronos asked. 'Is that the choice you will make – to fight me and die instead of bowing down? Prophecies never end well, you know.'

'Luke would fight with a sword,' I said. 'But I suppose you don't have his skill.'

Kronos sneered. His scythe began to change, until he held Luke's old weapon – Backbiter, with its half-steel, half-celestial bronze blade.

Next to me, Annabeth gasped like she'd suddenly had an idea. 'Percy, the blade!' She unsheathed her knife. '*The hero's soul, cursed blade shall reap.*'

I didn't understand why she was reminding me of that prophecy line right now. It wasn't exactly a morale booster, but before I could say anything Kronos raised his sword.

'Wait!' Annabeth yelled.

Kronos came at me like a whirlwind.

My instincts took over. I dodged and slashed and rolled, but I felt like I was fighting a hundred swordsmen. Ethan ducked to one side, trying to get behind me until Annabeth intercepted him. They started to fight, but I couldn't focus on how she was doing. I was vaguely aware of Grover playing his reed pipes. The sound filled me with warmth and courage – thoughts of sunlight and a blue sky and a calm meadow, somewhere far away from the war.

Kronos backed me up against the throne of Hephaestus – a huge mechanical La-Z-Boy-type thing covered with bronze and silver gears. Kronos slashed and I managed to jump straight up onto the seat. The throne whirred and hummed with secret mechanisms. *Defence mode*, it warned. *Defence mode.*

That couldn't be good. I jumped straight over Kronos's head as the throne shot tendrils of electricity in all directions. One hit Kronos in the face, arcing down his body and up his sword.

'ARG!' He crumpled to his knees and dropped Backbiter.

Annabeth saw her chance. She kicked Ethan out of the way and charged Kronos. 'Luke, listen!'

I wanted to shout at her, to tell her she was crazy for trying to reason with Kronos, but there was no time. Kronos flicked his hand. Annabeth flew backwards, slamming into the throne of her mother and crumpling to the floor.

'Annabeth!' I screamed.

Ethan Nakamura got to his feet. He now stood between Annabeth and me. I couldn't fight him without turning my back on Kronos.

Grover's music took on a more urgent tune. He moved towards Annabeth, but he couldn't go any faster and keep up the song. Grass grew on the floor of the throne room. Tiny roots crept up between the cracks of the marble stones.

Kronos rose to one knee. His hair smouldered. His face was covered with electrical burns. He reached for his sword, but this time it didn't fly into his hands.

'Nakamura!' he groaned. 'Time to prove yourself. You know Jackson's secret weakness. Kill him, and you will have rewards beyond measure.'

Ethan's eyes dropped to my midsection, and I was sure that he knew. Even if he couldn't kill me himself, all he had to do was tell Kronos. There was no way I could defend myself forever.

'Look around you, Ethan,' I said. 'The end of the world. Is this the reward you want? Do you really want everything destroyed – the good with the bad? *Everything?*'

Grover was almost to Annabeth now. The grass thickened on the floor. The roots were almost half a metre long, like a stubble of whiskers.

'There is no throne to Nemesis,' Ethan muttered. 'No throne to my mother.'

'That's right!' Kronos tried to get up but stumbled. Above his left ear, a patch of blond hair still smouldered. 'Strike them down! They deserve to suffer.'

'You said your mom is the goddess of balance,' I reminded him. 'The minor gods deserve better, Ethan, but total destruction isn't *balance.* Kronos doesn't build. He only destroys.'

Ethan looked at the sizzling throne of Hephaestus. Grover's music kept playing, and Ethan swayed to it, as if the song were filling him with nostalgia – a wish to see a beautiful day, to be anywhere but here. His good eye blinked.

Then he charged – but not at me.

While Kronos was still on his knees, Ethan brought down his sword on the Titan lord's neck. It should have killed him instantly, but the blade shattered. Ethan fell back, grasping his stomach. A shard of his own blade had ricocheted and pierced his armour.

Kronos rose unsteadily, towering over his servant. 'Treason,' he snarled.

Grover's music kept playing and grass grew around Ethan's body. Ethan stared at me, his face tight with pain.

'Deserve better,' he gasped. 'If they just . . . had thrones —'

Kronos stomped his foot, and the floor ruptured around Ethan Nakamura. The son of Nemesis fell through a fissure that went straight through the heart of the mountain — straight into open air.

'So much for him.' Kronos picked up his sword. 'And now for the rest of you.'

My only thought was to keep him away from Annabeth. Grover was at her side now. He'd stopped playing and was feeding her ambrosia.

Everywhere Kronos stepped, the roots wrapped around his feet, but Grover had stopped his magic too early. The roots weren't thick or strong enough to do much more than annoy the Titan.

We fought through the hearth, kicking up coals and sparks. Kronos slashed an armrest off the throne of Ares, which was okay by me, but then he backed me up to my dad's throne.

'Oh, yes,' Kronos said. 'This one will make fine kindling for my new hearth!'

Our blades clashed in a shower of sparks. He was stronger than me, but for the moment I felt the power of the ocean in my arms. I pushed him back and struck again — slashing Riptide across his breastplate so hard I cut a gash in the celestial bronze.

He stamped his foot again and time slowed. I tried to attack but I was moving at the speed of a glacier. Kronos backed up leisurely, catching his breath. He examined the gash in his armour while I struggled forward, silently cursing him. He could take all the timeouts he wanted. He could freeze me in place at will. My only hope was that the effort was draining him. If I could wear him down . . .

'It's too late, Percy Jackson,' he said. 'Behold.'

He pointed to the hearth and the coals glowed. A sheet of white smoke poured from the fire, forming images like an Iris-message. I saw Nico and my parents down on Fifth Avenue, fighting a hopeless battle, ringed in enemies. In the background Hades fought from his black chariot, summoning wave after wave of zombies out of the ground, but the forces of the Titans' army seemed just as endless. Meanwhile, Manhattan was being destroyed. Mortals, now fully awake, were running in terror. Cars swerved and crashed.

The scene shifted, and I saw something even more terrifying.

A column of storm was approaching the Hudson River, moving rapidly over the Jersey shore. Chariots circled it, locked in combat with the creature in the cloud.

The gods attacked. Lightning flashed. Arrows of gold and silver streaked into the cloud like rocket tracers and exploded. Slowly, the cloud ripped apart, and I saw Typhon clearly for the first time.

I knew as long as I lived (which might not be that long) I would never be able to get the image out of my mind. Typhon's head shifted constantly. Every moment he was a different monster, each more horrible than the last. Looking at his face would've driven me insane, so I focused on his body, which wasn't much better. He was humanoid, but his skin reminded me of a meatloaf sandwich that had been in someone's locker all year. He was mottled green, with blisters the size of buildings and blackened patches from aeons of being stuck under a volcano. His hands were human, but with talons like an eagle's. His legs were scaly and reptilian.

'The Olympians are giving their final effort.' Kronos laughed. 'How pathetic.'

Zeus threw a thunderbolt from his chariot. The blast lit up the world. I could feel the shock even here on Olympus, but when the dust cleared, Typhon was still standing. He staggered a bit, with a smoking crater on top of his misshapen head, but he roared in anger and kept advancing.

My limbs began to loosen up. Kronos didn't seem to notice. His attention was focused on the fight and his final victory. If I could hold out a few more seconds, and if my dad kept his word . . .

Typhon stepped into the Hudson River and barely sank to mid-calf.

Now, I thought, imploring the image in the smoke. *Please, it has to happen now.*

Like a miracle, a conch horn sounded from the smoky picture. The call of the ocean. The call of Poseidon.

All around Typhon, the Hudson River erupted, churning

with twenty-metre waves. Out of the water burst a new chariot – this one pulled by massive hippocampi who swam in air as easily as in water. My father, glowing with a blue aura of power, rode a defiant circle around the giant's legs. Poseidon was no longer an old man. He looked like himself again – tan and strong with a black beard. As he swung his trident, the river responded, making a funnel cloud around the monster.

'No!' Kronos bellowed, after a moment of stunned silence. 'NO!'

'NOW, MY BRETHREN!' Poseidon's voice was so loud I wasn't sure if I was hearing it from the smoke image or from all the way across town. 'STRIKE FOR OLYMPUS!'

Warriors burst out of the river, riding the waves on huge sharks and dragons and seahorses. It was a legion of Cyclopes, and leading them into battle was . . .

'Tyson!' I yelled.

I knew he couldn't hear me, but I stared at him in amazement. He'd magically grown in size. He had to be ten metres tall, as big as any of his older cousins, and for the first time he was wearing full battle armour. Riding behind him was Briares, the Hundred-handed One.

All the Cyclopes held huge lengths of black iron chains – big enough to anchor a battleship – with grappling hooks at the ends. They swung them like lassos and began to ensnare Typhon, throwing lines around the creature's legs and arms, using the tide to keep circling, slowly tangling him. Typhon shook and roared and yanked at the chains, pulling some of the Cyclopes off their mounts, but there were too many chains. The sheer weight of the Cyclops battalion began to weigh Typhon down. Poseidon threw his trident and impaled the monster in the throat. Golden blood, immortal ichor, spewed from the wound, making a waterfall taller than a skyscraper. The trident flew back to Poseidon's hand.

The other gods struck with renewed force. Ares rode in and stabbed Typhon in the nose. Artemis shot the monster in the eye with a dozen silver arrows. Apollo shot a blazing volley of arrows and set the monster's loincloth on fire. And Zeus kept pounding the giant with lightning, until finally, slowly, the water rose, wrapping Typhon like a cocoon, and he began to sink under the weight of the chains. Typhon bellowed in agony, thrashing with such force that waves sloshed the Jersey shore, soaking five-storey buildings and splashing over the George Washington Bridge – but down he went as my dad opened a special tunnel for him at the bottom of the river – an endless water slide that would take him straight to Tartarus. The giant's head went under in a seething whirlpool, and he was gone.

'BAH!' Kronos screamed. He slashed his sword through the smoke, tearing the image to shreds.

'They're on their way,' I said. 'You've lost.'

'I haven't even started.'

He advanced with blinding speed. Grover – brave stupid satyr that he was – tried to protect me, but Kronos tossed him aside like a rag doll.

I sidestepped and jabbed under Kronos's guard. It was a good trick. Unfortunately, Luke knew it. He countered the strike and disarmed me using one of the first moves he'd ever taught me. My sword skittered across the ground and fell straight into the open fissure.

'STOP!' Annabeth came from nowhere.

Kronos whirled to face her and slashed with Backbiter, but somehow Annabeth caught the strike on her dagger hilt. It was a move only the quickest and most skilled knife fighter could've managed. Don't ask me where she found the strength, but she stepped in closer for leverage, their blades crossed, and for a moment she stood face to face with the Titan lord, holding him at a standstill.

'Luke,' she said, gritting her teeth, 'I understand now. You have to trust me.'

Kronos roared in outrage. 'Luke Castellan is dead! His body will burn away as I assume my true form!'

I tried to move but my body was frozen again. How could Annabeth, battered and half dead with exhaustion, have the strength to fight a Titan like Kronos?

Kronos pushed against her, trying to dislodge his blade, but she held him in check, her arms trembling as he forced his sword down towards her neck.

'Your mother,' Annabeth grunted. 'She saw your fate.'

'Service to Kronos!' the Titan roared. 'This is my fate.'

'No!' Annabeth insisted. Her eyes were tearing up, but I didn't know if it was from sadness or pain. 'That's not the end, Luke. The prophecy – she saw what you would do. It applies to you!'

'I will crush you, child!' Kronos bellowed.

'You won't,' Annabeth said. 'You promised. You're holding Kronos back even now.'

'LIES!' Kronos pushed again and this time Annabeth lost her balance. With his free hand, Kronos struck her face and she slid backwards.

I summoned all my will. I managed to rise, but it was like holding the weight of the sky again.

Kronos loomed over Annabeth, his sword raised.

Blood trickled from the corner of her mouth. She croaked, 'Family, Luke. You promised.'

I took a painful step forward. Grover was back on his feet, over by the throne of Hera, but he seemed to be struggling to move as well. Before either of us could get anywhere close to Annabeth, Kronos staggered.

He stared at the knife in Annabeth's hand, the blood on her face. '*Promise.*'

Then he gasped like he couldn't get air. 'Annabeth . . .' But it wasn't the Titan's voice. It was Luke's. He stumbled forward like he couldn't control his own body. 'You're bleeding . . .'

'My knife.' Annabeth tried to raise her dagger, but it clattered out of her hand. Her arm was bent at a funny angle. She looked at me, imploring, 'Percy, please . . .'

I could move again.

I surged forward and scooped up her knife. I knocked Backbiter out of Luke's hand and it spun into the hearth. Luke hardly paid me any attention. He stepped towards Annabeth, but I put myself between him and her.

'Don't touch her,' I said.

Anger rippled across his face. Kronos's voice growled: 'Jackson . . .' Was it my imagination, or was his whole body glowing, turning gold?

He gasped again. Luke's voice: 'He's changing. Help. He's – he's almost ready. He won't need my body any more. Please –'

'NO!' Kronos bellowed. He looked around for his sword, but it was in the hearth, glowing among the coals.

He stumbled towards it. I tried to stop him, but he

pushed me out of the way with such force I landed next to Annabeth and cracked my head on the base of Athena's throne.

'The knife, Percy,' Annabeth muttered. Her breath was shallow. 'Hero . . . cursed blade . . .'

When my vision came back into focus, I saw Kronos grasping his sword. Then he bellowed in pain and dropped it. His hands were smoking and seared. The hearth fire had grown red hot, like the scythe wasn't compatible with it. I saw an image of Hestia flickering in the ashes, frowning at Kronos with disapproval.

Luke turned and collapsed, clutching his ruined hands. 'Please, Percy . . .'

I struggled to my feet. I moved towards him with the knife. I should kill him. That was the plan.

Luke seemed to know what I was thinking. He moistened his lips. 'You can't . . . can't do it yourself. He'll break my control. He'll defend himself. Only my hand. I know where. I can . . . can keep him controlled.'

He was definitely glowing now, his skin starting to smoke.

I raised the knife to strike. Then I looked at Annabeth, at Grover cradling her in his arms, trying to shield her. And I finally understood what she'd been trying to tell me.

You are not the hero, Rachel had said. *It will affect what you do.*

'Please,' Luke groaned. 'No time.'

If Kronos evolved into his true form, there would be no stopping him. He would make Typhon look like a playground bully.

The line from the Great Prophecy echoed in my head:

A hero's soul, cursed blade shall reap. My whole world tipped upside down, and I gave the knife to Luke.

Grover yelped. 'Percy? Are you . . . um . . .'

Crazy. Insane. Off my rocker. Probably.

But I watched as Luke grasped the hilt.

I stood before him – defenceless.

He unlatched the side straps of his armour, exposing a small bit of his skin just under his left arm, a place that would be very hard to hit. With difficulty, he stabbed himself.

It wasn't a deep cut, but Luke howled. His eyes glowed like lava. The throne room shook, throwing me off my feet. An aura of energy surrounded Luke, growing brighter and brighter. I shut my eyes and felt a force like a nuclear explosion blister my skin and crack my lips.

It was silent for a long time.

When I opened my eyes, I saw Luke sprawled at the hearth. On the floor around him was a blackened circle of ash. Kronos's scythe had liquefied into molten metal and was trickling into the coals of the hearth, which now glowed like a blacksmith's furnace.

Luke's left side was bloody. His eyes were open – blue eyes, the way they used to be. His breath was a deep rattle.

'Good . . . blade,' he croaked.

I knelt next to him. Annabeth limped over with Grover's support. They both had tears in their eyes.

Luke gazed at Annabeth. 'You knew. I almost killed you, but you knew . . .'

'Shhh.' Her voice trembled. 'You were a hero at the end, Luke. You'll go to Elysium.'

He shook his head weakly. 'Think . . . rebirth. Try for three times. Isles of the Blest.'

Annabeth sniffled. 'You always pushed yourself too hard.'

He held up his charred hand. Annabeth touched his fingertips.

'Did you . . .' Luke coughed and his lips glistened red. 'Did you love me?'

Annabeth wiped her tears away. 'There was a time I thought . . . well, I thought . . .' She looked at me, like she was drinking in the fact that I was still here. And I realized I was doing the same thing. The world was collapsing, and the only thing that really mattered to me was that she was alive.

'You were like a brother to me, Luke,' she said softly. 'But I didn't love you.'

He nodded, as if he'd expected it. He winced in pain.

'We can get ambrosia,' Grover said. 'We can –'

'Grover,' Luke gulped. 'You're the bravest satyr I ever knew. But, no. There's no healing . . .' Another cough.

He gripped my sleeve, and I could feel the heat of his skin like a fire. 'Ethan. Me. All the unclaimed. Don't let it . . . Don't let it happen again.'

His eyes were angry, but pleading, too.

'I won't,' I said. 'I promise.'

Luke nodded, and his hand went slack.

The gods arrived a few minutes later in their full war regalia, thundering into the throne room and expecting a battle.

What they found were Annabeth, Grover and me

[317]

standing over the body of a broken half-blood, in the dim warm light of the hearth.

'Percy,' my father called, awe in his voice. 'What . . . what is this?'

I turned and faced the Olympians.

'We need a shroud,' I announced, my voice cracking. 'A shroud for the son of Hermes.'

20 WE WIN FABULOUS PRIZES

The Three Fates themselves took Luke's body.

I hadn't seen the old ladies in years, since I'd witnessed them snip a life thread at a roadside fruit stand when I was twelve. They'd scared me then, and they scared me now – three ghoulish grandmothers with bags of knitting needles and yarn.

One of them looked at me and, even though she didn't say anything, my life literally flashed before my eyes. Suddenly I was twenty. Then I was a middle-aged man. Then I turned old and withered. All the strength left my body, and I saw my own tombstone and an open grave, a coffin being lowered into the ground. All this happened in less than a second.

It is done, she said.

The Fate held up the snippet of blue yarn – and I knew it was the same one I'd seen four years ago, the lifeline I'd watched them snip. I had thought it was my life. Now I realized it was Luke's. They'd been showing me the life that would have to be sacrificed to set things right.

They gathered up Luke's body, now wrapped in a white-and-green shroud, and began carrying it out of the throne room.

'Wait,' Hermes said.

The messenger god was dressed in his classic outfit of

white Greek robes, sandals and helmet. The wings of his helm fluttered as he walked. The snakes George and Martha curled around his caduceus, murmuring, *Luke, poor Luke.*

I thought about May Castellan, alone in her kitchen, baking cookies and making sandwiches for a son who would never come home.

Hermes unwrapped Luke's face and kissed his forehead. He murmured some words in Ancient Greek – a final blessing.

'Farewell,' he whispered. Then he nodded, and allowed the Fates to carry away his son's body.

As they left, I thought about the Great Prophecy. The lines now made sense to me. *The hero's soul, cursed blade shall reap.* The hero was Luke. The cursed blade was the knife he'd given Annabeth long ago – cursed because Luke had broken his promise and betrayed his friends. *A single choice shall end his days.* My choice – to give him the knife, and to believe as Annabeth had, that he was still capable of setting things right. *Olympus to preserve or raze.* By sacrificing himself, he had saved Olympus. Rachel was right. In the end, I wasn't really the hero. Luke was.

And I understood something else: when Luke had descended into the River Styx, he would've had to focus on something important that would hold him to his mortal life. Otherwise he would've dissolved. I had seen Annabeth, and I had a feeling he had, too. He had pictured that scene Hestia showed me – of himself in the good old days with Thalia and Annabeth, when he promised that they would be a family. Hurting Annabeth in battle had shocked him into remembering that promise. It had allowed his mortal conscience to take over again, and defeat Kronos. His weak spot – his Achilles heel – had saved us all.

Next to me, Annabeth's knees buckled. I caught her but she cried out in pain, and I realized I'd grabbed her broken arm.

'Oh, gods,' I said. 'Annabeth, I'm sorry.'

'It's all right,' she said, as she passed out in my arms.

'She needs help!' I yelled.

'I've got this.' Apollo stepped forward. His fiery armour was so bright it was hard to look at, and his matching Ray-Bans and perfect smile made him look like a male model for battle gear. 'God of medicine, at your service.'

He passed his hand over Annabeth's face and spoke an incantation. Immediately the bruises faded. Her cuts and scars disappeared. Her arm straightened, and she sighed in her sleep.

Apollo grinned. 'She'll be fine in a few minutes. Just enough time for me to compose a poem about our victory: "Apollo and his friends save Olympus." Good, eh?'

'Thanks, Apollo,' I said. 'I'll, um, let you handle the poetry.'

The next few hours were a blur. I remembered my promise to my mother. Zeus didn't even blink an eye when I told him my strange request. He snapped his fingers and informed me that the top of the Empire State Building was now lit up blue. Most mortals would just have to wonder what it meant, but my mom would know: I had survived. Olympus was saved.

The gods set about repairing the throne room, which went surprisingly fast with twelve super-powerful beings at work. Grover and I cared for the wounded, and once the sky

[321]

bridge re-formed we greeted our friends who had survived. The Cyclopes had saved Thalia from the fallen statue. She was on crutches, but otherwise she was okay. Connor and Travis Stoll had made it through with only minor injuries. They promised me they hadn't even looted the city much. They told me my parents were fine, though they weren't allowed into Mount Olympus. Mrs O'Leary had dug Chiron out of the rubble and rushed him off to camp. The Stolls looked kind of worried about the old centaur, but at least he was alive. Katie Gardner reported that she'd seen Rachel Elizabeth Dare run out of the Empire State Building at the end of the battle. Rachel had looked unharmed, but nobody knew where she'd gone, which also troubled me.

Nico di Angelo came into Olympus to a hero's welcome, his father right behind him, despite the fact that Hades was only supposed to visit Olympus on winter solstice. The god of the dead looked stunned when his relatives clapped him on the back. I doubt he'd ever got such an enthusiastic welcome before.

Clarisse marched in, still shivering from her time in the ice block, and Ares bellowed, 'There's my girl!'

The god of war ruffled her hair and pounded her on the back, calling her the best warrior he'd ever seen. 'That drakon-slaying? THAT'S what I'm talking about!'

She looked pretty overwhelmed. All she could do was nod and blink, like she was afraid he'd start hitting her, but eventually she began to smile.

Hera and Hephaestus passed me, and while Hephaestus was a little grumpy about me jumping on his throne, he thought I'd done 'a pretty bang-up job, mostly'.

Hera sniffed in disdain. 'I suppose I won't destroy you and that little girl now.'

'Annabeth saved Olympus,' I told her. 'She convinced Luke to stop Kronos.'

'Hmm.' Hera whirled away in a huff, but I figured our lives would be safe, at least for a little while.

Dionysus' head was still wrapped in a bandage. He looked me up and down and said, 'Well, Percy Jackson. I see Pollux made it through, so I suppose you aren't completely inept. It's all thanks to my training, I suppose.'

'Um, yes, sir,' I said.

Mr D nodded. 'As thanks for my bravery, Zeus has cut my probation at that miserable camp in half. I now have only fifty years left instead of one hundred.'

'Fifty years, huh?' I tried to imagine putting up with Dionysus until I was an old man, assuming I lived that long.

'Don't get so excited, Jackson,' he said, and I realized he was saying my name correctly. 'I still plan on making your life miserable.'

I couldn't help smiling. 'Naturally.'

'Just so we understand each other.' He turned and began repairing his grapevine throne, which had been singed by fire.

Grover stayed at my side. From time to time he would break down in tears. 'So many nature spirits dead, Percy. So *many*.'

I put my arm around his shoulders and gave him a rag to blow his nose. 'You did a great job, G-man. We *will* come back from this. We'll plant new trees. We'll clean up the parks. Your friends will be reincarnated into a better world.'

He sniffled dejectedly. 'I – I suppose. But it was hard enough to rally them before. I'm still an outcast. I could barely get anyone to listen to me about Pan. Now will they ever listen to me again? I led them into a slaughter.'

'They will listen,' I promised. 'Because you care about them. You care about the wild more than anyone.'

He tried for a smile. 'Thanks, Percy. I hope . . . I hope you know I'm really proud to be your friend.'

I patted his arm. 'Luke was right about one thing, G-man. You're the bravest satyr I ever met.'

He blushed, but before he could say anything, conch horns blew. The army of Poseidon marched into the throne room.

'Percy!' Tyson yelled. He charged towards me with his arms open. Fortunately, he'd shrunk back to normal size, so his hug was like getting hit by a tractor, not the entire farm.

'You are not dead!' he said.

'Yeah!' I agreed. 'Amazing, huh?'

He clapped his hands and laughed happily. 'I am not dead, either. Yay! We chained Typhon. It was fun!'

Behind him, fifty other armoured Cyclopes laughed and nodded and gave each other high-fives.

'Tyson led us,' one rumbled. 'He is brave!'

'Bravest of the Cyclopes!' another bellowed.

Tyson blushed. 'Was nothing.'

'I saw you!' I said. 'You were incredible!'

I thought poor Grover would pass out. He's deathly

afraid of Cyclopes. But he steeled his nerves and said, 'Yes. Um . . . three cheers for Tyson!'

'YAAARRRRR!' the Cyclopes roared.

'Please don't eat me,' Grover muttered, but I don't think anyone heard him but me.

The conch horns blasted again. The Cyclopes parted, and my father strode into the throne room in his battle armour, his trident glowing in his hands.

'Tyson!' he roared. 'Well done, my son. And, Percy –' His face turned stern. He wagged his finger at me, and for a second I was afraid he was going to zap me. 'I even forgive you for sitting on my throne. You have saved Olympus!'

He held out his arms and gave me a hug. I realized, a little embarrassed, that I'd never actually hugged my dad before. He was warm – like a regular human, and he smelled of a salty beach and fresh sea air.

When he pulled away, he smiled kindly at me. I felt so good I'll admit I teared up a little. I guess until that moment I hadn't allowed myself to realize just how terrified I had been the last few days.

'Dad –'

'Shhh,' he said. 'No hero is above fear, Percy. And *you* have risen above every hero. Not even Hercules –'

'POSEIDON!' a voice roared.

Zeus had taken his throne. He glared across the room at my dad while all the other gods filed in and took their seats. Even Hades was present, sitting on a simple stone guest chair at the foot of the hearth. Nico sat cross-legged on the ground at his dad's feet.

'Well, Poseidon?' Zeus grumped. 'Are you too proud to join us in council, my brother?'

[325]

I thought Poseidon was going to get mad, but he just looked at me and winked. 'I would be honoured, Lord Zeus.'

I guess miracles do happen. Poseidon strode over to his fishing seat and the Olympian Council convened.

While Zeus was talking – some long speech about the bravery of the gods, blah, blah, blah – Annabeth walked in and stood next to me. She looked good for someone who'd recently passed out.

'Miss much?' she whispered.

'Nobody's planning to kill us, so far,' I whispered back.

'First time today.'

I cracked up, but Grover nudged me, because Hera was giving us a dirty look.

'As for my brothers,' Zeus said, 'we are thankful –' he cleared his throat, like the words were hard to get out – 'erm, thankful for the aid of Hades.'

The Lord of the Dead nodded. He had a smug look on his face, but I figure he'd earned the right. He patted his son Nico on the shoulders, and Nico looked happier than I'd ever seen him.

'And, of course,' Zeus continued, though he looked like his pants were smouldering, 'we must . . . um . . . thank Poseidon.'

'I'm sorry, brother,' Poseidon said. 'What was that?'

'We must thank Poseidon,' Zeus growled. 'Without whom . . . it would've been difficult –'

'Difficult?' Poseidon asked innocently.

'Impossible,' Zeus said. 'Impossible to defeat Typhon.'

The gods murmured agreement and pounded their weapons in approval.

'Which leaves us,' Zeus said, 'only the matter of thanking our young demigod heroes, who defended Olympus so well – even if there were a few dents in my throne.'

He called Thalia forward first, since she was his daughter, and promised her help in filling the Hunters' ranks.

Artemis smiled. 'You have done well, my lieutenant. You have made me proud, and all those Hunters who perished in my service will never be forgotten. They will achieve Elysium, I am sure.'

She glared pointedly at Hades.

He shrugged. 'Probably.'

Artemis glared at him some more.

'Okay,' Hades grumbled. 'I'll streamline their application process.'

Thalia beamed with pride. 'Thank you, my lady.' She bowed to the gods, even Hades, and then limped over to stand by Artemis's side.

'Tyson, son of Poseidon!' Zeus called. Tyson looked nervous, but he went to stand in the middle of the council, and Zeus grunted.

'Doesn't miss many meals, does he?' Zeus muttered. 'Tyson, for your bravery in the war, and for leading the Cyclopes, you are appointed a general in the armies of Olympus. You shall henceforth lead your brethren into war whenever required by the gods. And you shall have a new . . . um . . . what kind of weapon would you like? A sword? An axe?'

'Stick!' Tyson said, showing his broken club.

'Very well,' Zeus said. 'We will grant you a new, er, stick. The best stick that may be found.'

'Hooray!' Tyson cried, and all the Cyclopes cheered and pounded him on the back as he rejoined them.

'Grover Underwood of the satyrs!' Dionysus called.

Grover came forward nervously.

'Oh, stop chewing your shirt,' Dionysus chided. 'Honestly, I'm not going to blast you. For your bravery and sacrifice, blah, blah, blah, and since we have an unfortunate vacancy, the gods have seen fit to name you a member of the Council of Cloven Elders.'

Grover collapsed on the spot.

'Oh, wonderful,' Dionysus sighed, as several naiads came forward to help Grover. 'Well, when he wakes up, someone tell him that he will no longer be an outcast, and that all satyrs, naiads and other spirits of nature will henceforth treat him as a Lord of the Wild, with all rights, privileges, and honours, blah, blah, blah. Now, please, drag him off before he wakes up and starts grovelling.'

'FOOOOOD,' Grover moaned, as the nature spirits carried him away.

I figured he'd be okay. He would wake up a Lord of the Wild with a bunch of beautiful naiads taking care of him. Life could be worse.

Athena called, 'Annabeth Chase, my own daughter.'

Annabeth squeezed my arm, then walked forward and knelt at her mother's feet.

Athena smiled. 'You, my daughter, have exceeded all expectations. You have used your wits, your strength and your courage to defend this city, and our seat of power. It has come to our attention that Olympus is . . . well, trashed.

The Titan lord did much damage that will have to be repaired. We could rebuild it by magic, of course, and make it just as it was. But the gods feel that the city could be improved. We will take this as an opportunity. And you, my daughter, will design these improvements.'

Annabeth looked up, stunned. 'My – my lady?'

Athena smiled wryly. 'You *are* an architect, are you not? You have studied the techniques of Daedalus himself. Who better to redesign Olympus, and make it a monument that will last for another aeon?'

'You mean . . . I can design whatever I want?'

'As your heart desires,' the goddess said. 'Make us a city for the ages.'

'As long as you have plenty of statues of me,' Apollo added.

'And me,' Aphrodite agreed.

'Hey, and me!' Ares said. 'Big statues with huge wicked swords and –'

'All right!' Athena interrupted. 'She gets the point. Rise, my daughter – official architect of Olympus.'

Annabeth rose in a trance and walked back towards me.

'Way to go,' I told her, grinning.

For once, she was at a loss for words. 'I'll – I'll have to start planning . . . Drafting paper, and, um, pencils –'

'PERCY JACKSON!' Poseidon announced. My name echoed around the chamber.

All talking died down. The room was silent except for the crackle of the hearth fire. Everyone's eyes were on me – all the gods, the demigods, the Cyclopes, the spirits. I walked into the middle of the throne room. Hestia smiled at me reassuringly. She was in the form of a girl now, and she seemed happy and content to be sitting by her fire again. Her smile gave me courage to keep walking.

First I bowed to Zeus. Then I knelt at my father's feet.

'Rise, my son,' Poseidon said.

I stood uneasily.

'A great hero must be rewarded,' Poseidon said. 'Is there anyone here who would deny that my son is deserving?'

I waited for someone to pipe up. The gods never agreed on anything, and many of them still didn't like me, but not a single one protested.

'The council agrees,' Zeus said. 'Percy Jackson, you will have one gift from the gods.'

I hesitated. 'Any gift?'

Zeus nodded grimly. 'I know what you will ask. The greatest gift of all. Yes, if you want it, it shall be yours. The gods have not bestowed this gift on a mortal hero in many centuries, but Perseus Jackson – if you wish it, you shall be made a god. Immortal. Undying. You shall serve as your father's lieutenant for all time.'

I stared at him, stunned. 'Um . . . a god?'

Zeus rolled his eyes. 'A dim-witted god, apparently. But yes. With the consensus of the entire council, I can make you immortal. Then I will have to put up with you forever.'

'Hmm,' Ares mused. 'That means I can smash him to a pulp as often as I want, and he'll just keep coming back for more. I like this idea.'

'I approve as well,' Athena said, though she was looking at Annabeth.

I glanced back. Annabeth was trying not to meet my

eyes. Her face was pale. I flashed back to two years ago, when I'd thought she was going to take the pledge to Artemis and become a Hunter. I'd been on the edge of a panic attack, thinking that I'd lose her. Now she looked pretty much the same way.

I thought about the Three Fates, and the way I'd seen my life flash by. I could avoid all that. No aging, no death, no body in the grave. I could be a teenager forever, in top condition, powerful and immortal, serving my father. I could have power and eternal life.

Who could refuse that?

Then I looked at Annabeth again. I thought about my friends from camp – Charles Beckendorf, Michael Yew, Silena Beauregard, so many others who were now dead. I thought about Ethan Nakamura and Luke.

And I knew what to do.

'No,' I said.

The council was silent. The gods frowned at each other like they must have misheard.

'No?' Zeus said. 'You are . . . turning *down* our generous gift?'

There was a dangerous edge to his voice, like a thunderstorm about to erupt.

'I'm honoured and everything,' I said. 'Don't get me wrong. It's just . . . I've got a lot of life left to live. I'd hate to peak in my sophomore year.'

The gods were glaring at me, but Annabeth had her hands over her mouth. Her eyes were shining. And that kind of made up for it.

'I do want a gift, though,' I said. 'Do you promise to grant my wish?'

Zeus thought about this. 'If it is within our power.'

'It is,' I said. 'And it's not even difficult. But I need your promise on the River Styx.'

'What?' Dionysus cried. 'You don't trust us?'

'Someone once told me,' I said, looking at Hades, 'you should always get a solemn oath.'

Hades shrugged. 'Guilty.'

'Very well!' Zeus growled. 'In the name of the council, we swear by the River Styx to grant your *reasonable* request as long as it is within our power.'

The other gods muttered assent. Thunder boomed, shaking the throne room. The deal was made.

'From now on, I want you to properly recognize the children of the gods,' I said. 'All the children . . . of *all* the gods.'

The Olympians shifted uncomfortably.

'Percy,' my father said, 'what exactly do you mean?'

'Kronos couldn't have risen if it hadn't been for a lot of demigods who felt abandoned by their parents,' I said. 'They felt angry, resentful and unloved, and they had a good reason.'

Zeus's royal nostrils flared. 'You dare accuse –'

'No more undetermined children,' I said. 'I want you to promise to claim your children – all your demigod children – by the time they turn thirteen. They won't be left out in the world on their own at the mercy of monsters. I want them claimed and brought to camp so they can be trained right, and survive.'

'Now wait just a moment,' Apollo said, but I was on a roll.

'And the minor gods,' I said. 'Nemesis, Hecate, Morpheus,

Janus, Hebe – they all deserve a general amnesty and a place at Camp Half-Blood. Their children shouldn't be ignored. Calypso and the other peaceful Titan-kind should be pardoned, too. And Hades –'

'Are you calling me a *minor god*?' Hades bellowed.

'No, my lord,' I said quickly. 'But your children should not be left out. They should have a cabin at camp. Nico has proven that. No unclaimed demigods will be crammed into the Hermes cabin any more, wondering who their parents are. They'll have their own cabins, for all the gods. And no more pact of the Big Three. That didn't work anyway. You've got to stop trying to get rid of powerful demigods. We're going to train them and accept them instead. All children of the gods will be welcome and treated with respect. That is my wish.'

Zeus snorted. 'Is that all?'

'Percy,' Poseidon said, 'you ask much. You presume much.'

'I hold you to your oath,' I said. 'All of you.'

I got a lot of steely looks. Strangely, it was Athena who spoke up: 'The boy is correct. We have been unwise to ignore our children. It proved a strategic weakness in this war and almost caused our destruction. Percy Jackson – I have had my doubts about you, but perhaps –' she glanced at Annabeth, and then spoke as if the words had a sour taste – 'perhaps I was mistaken. I move that we accept the boy's plan.'

'Humph,' Zeus said. 'Being told what to do by a mere child. But I suppose . . .'

'All in favour,' Hermes said.

All the gods raised their hands.

'Um, thanks,' I said.

I turned, but before I could leave, Poseidon called, 'Honour guard!'

Immediately the Cyclopes came forward and made two lines from the thrones to the door – an aisle for me to walk through. They came to attention.

'All hail, Perseus Jackson,' Tyson said. 'Hero of Olympus . . . and my big brother!'

21 BLACKJACK GETS JACKED

Annabeth and I were on our way out when I spotted Hermes in a side courtyard of the palace. He was staring at an Iris-message in the mist of a fountain.

I glanced at Annabeth. 'I'll meet you at the elevator.'

'You sure?' Then she studied my face. 'Yeah, you're sure.'

Hermes didn't seem to notice me approach. The Iris-message images were going so fast I could hardly understand them. Mortal newscasts from all over the country flashed by – scenes of Typhon's destruction, the wreckage our battle had left across Manhattan, the president doing a news conference, the mayor of New York, some army vehicles riding down the Avenue of the Americas.

'Amazing,' Hermes murmured. He turned towards me. 'Three thousand years, and I will never get over the power of the Mist . . . and mortal ignorance.'

'Thanks, I guess.'

'Oh, not you. Although I suppose I should wonder, turning down immortality.'

'It was the right choice.'

Hermes looked at me curiously then returned his attention to the Iris-message. 'Look at them. They've already decided Typhon was a freak series of storms. Don't I wish. They haven't figured out how all the statues in Lower

Manhattan got removed from their pedestals and hacked to pieces. They keep showing a shot of Susan B. Anthony strangling Frederick Douglass. But I imagine they'll even come up with a logical explanation for that.'

'How bad is the city?'

Hermes shrugged. 'Surprisingly, not too bad. The mortals are shaken, of course. But this is New York. I've never seen such a resilient bunch of humans. I imagine they'll be back to normal in a few weeks and, of course, I'll be helping.'

'You?'

'I'm the messenger of the gods. It's my job to monitor what the mortals are saying and, if necessary, help them make sense of what's happened. I'll reassure them. Trust me, they'll put this down to a freak earthquake, or a solar flare. Anything but the truth.'

He sounded bitter. George and Martha curled around his caduceus, but they were silent, which made me think that Hermes was *really*, really angry. I probably should've kept quiet, but I said, 'I owe you an apology.'

Hermes gave me a cautious look. 'And why is that?'

'I thought you were a bad father,' I admitted. 'I thought you abandoned Luke because you knew his future and didn't do anything to stop it.'

'I *did* know his future,' Hermes said miserably.

'But you knew more than just the bad stuff – that he'd turn evil. You understood what he would do in the end. You knew he'd make the right choice. But you couldn't tell him, could you?'

Hermes stared at the fountain. 'No one can tamper with fate, Percy, not even a god. If I had warned him what was to come, or tried to influence his choices, I would've made things even worse. Staying silent, staying away from him . . . That was the hardest thing I've ever done.'

'You had to let him find his own path,' I said, 'and play his part in saving Olympus.'

Hermes sighed. 'I should not have got mad at Annabeth. When Luke visited her in San Francisco . . . Well, I knew she would have a part to play in his fate. I foresaw that much. I thought perhaps she could do what I could not and save him. When she refused to go with him, I could barely contain my rage. I should have known better. I was really angry with myself.'

'Annabeth did save him,' I said. 'Luke died a hero. He sacrificed himself to kill Kronos.'

'I appreciate your words, Percy. But Kronos isn't dead. You can't kill a Titan.'

'Then —'

'I don't know,' Hermes grumbled. 'None of us do. Blown to dust. Scattered to the wind. With luck, he's spread so thin that he'll never be able to form a consciousness again, much less a body. But don't mistake him for dead, Percy.'

My stomach did a queasy somersault. 'What about the other Titans?'

'In hiding,' Hermes said. 'Prometheus sent Zeus a message with a bunch of excuses for supporting Kronos. "I was just trying to minimize the damage," blah, blah. He'll keep his head low for a few centuries if he's smart. Krios has fled, and Mount Othrys has crumbled into ruins. Oceanus slipped back into the deep ocean when it was clear Kronos had lost. Meanwhile, my son Luke is dead.

He died believing I didn't care about him. I will never forgive myself.'

Hermes slashed his caduceus through the mist. The Iris-picture disappeared.

'A long time ago,' I said, 'you told me the hardest thing about being a god was not being able to help your children. You also told me that you couldn't give up on your family, no matter how tempting they made it.'

'And now you know I'm a hypocrite?'

'No, you were right. Luke loved you. At the end, he realized his fate. I think he realized why you couldn't help him. He remembered what was important.'

'Too late for him and me.'

'You have other children. Honour Luke by recognizing them. All the gods can do that.'

Hermes' shoulders sagged. 'They'll try, Percy. Oh, we'll all try to keep our promise. And maybe for a while things will get better. But we gods have never been good at keeping oaths. You were born because of a broken promise, eh? Eventually we'll become forgetful. We always do.'

'You can change.'

Hermes laughed. 'After three thousand years, you think the gods can change their nature?'

'Yeah,' I said. 'I do.'

Hermes seemed surprised by that. 'You think . . . Luke actually loved me? After all that happened?'

'I'm sure of it.'

Hermes stared at the fountain. 'I'll give you a list of my children. There's a boy in Wisconsin. Two girls in Los Angeles. A few others. Will you see that they get to camp?'

'I promise,' I said. 'And I won't forget.'

George and Martha twirled around the caduceus. I know snakes can't smile, but they seemed to be trying.

'Percy Jackson,' Hermes said, 'you might just teach us a thing or two.'

Another god was waiting for me on the way out of Olympus. Athena stood in the middle of the road with her arms crossed and a look on her face that made me think *uh-oh*. She'd changed out of her armour, into jeans and a white blouse, but she didn't look any less warlike. Her grey eyes blazed.

'Well, Percy,' she said. 'You will stay mortal.'

'Um, yes, ma'am.'

'I would know your reasons.'

'I want to be a regular guy. I want to grow up. Have, you know, a regular high-school experience.'

'And my daughter?'

'I couldn't leave her,' I admitted, my throat dry. 'Or Grover,' I added quickly. 'Or –'

'Spare me.' Athena stepped close to me, and I could feel her aura of power making my skin itch. 'I once warned you, Percy Jackson, that to save a friend you would destroy the world. Perhaps I was mistaken. You seem to have saved both your friends and the world. But think very carefully about how you proceed from here. I have given you the benefit of the doubt. Don't mess up.'

Just to prove her point, she erupted in a column of flame, charring the front of my shirt.

Annabeth was waiting for me at the elevator. 'Why do you smell like smoke?'

'Long story,' I said. Together we made our way down to the street level. Neither of us said a word. The music was awful – Neil Diamond or something. I should've made that part of my gift from the gods: better elevator tunes.

When we got into the lobby, I found my mother and Paul arguing with the bald security guy, who'd returned to his post.

'I'm telling you,' my mom yelled, 'we have to go up! My son –' Then she saw me and her eyes widened. 'Percy!'

She hugged the breath right out of me.

'We saw the building lit up blue,' she said. 'But then you didn't come down. You went up *hours* ago!'

'She was getting a bit anxious,' Paul said dryly.

'I'm all right,' I promised as my mom hugged Annabeth. 'Everything's okay now.'

'Mr Blofis,' Annabeth said, 'that was wicked sword work.'

Paul shrugged. 'It seemed like the thing to do. But, Percy, is this really . . . I mean, this story about the six-hundredth floor?'

'Olympus,' I said. 'Yeah.'

Paul looked at the ceiling with a dreamy expression. 'I'd like to see that.'

'Paul,' my mom chided. 'It's not for mortals. Anyway, the important thing is we're safe. All of us.'

I was about to relax. Everything felt perfect. Annabeth and I were okay. My mom and Paul had survived. Olympus was saved.

But the life of a demigod is never so easy. Just then

Nico ran in from the street, and his face told me something was wrong.

'It's Rachel,' he said. 'I just ran into her down on Thirty-second.'

Annabeth frowned. 'What's she done this time?'

'It's where she's gone,' Nico said. 'I told her she would die if she tried, but she insisted. She just took Blackjack and —'

'She took my *pegasus*?' I demanded.

Nico nodded. 'She's heading to Half-Blood Hill. She said she had to get to camp.'

22 I AM DUMPED

Nobody steals my pegasus. Not even Rachel. I wasn't sure if I was more angry or amazed or worried.

'What was she thinking?' Annabeth said as we ran for the river. Unfortunately, I had a pretty good idea, and it filled me with dread.

The traffic was horrible. Everybody was out on the streets gawking at the warzone damage. Police sirens wailed on every block. There was no possibility of catching a cab, and the pegasi had flown away. I would've settled for some Party Ponies, but they had disappeared along with most of the root beer in midtown. So we ran, pushing through mobs of dazed mortals that clogged the sidewalks.

'She'll never get through the defences,' Annabeth said. 'Peleus will eat her.'

I hadn't considered that. The Mist wouldn't fool Rachel like it would most people. She'd be able to find the camp no problem, but I'd been hoping the magical boundaries would just keep her out like a force field. It hadn't occurred to me that Peleus might attack.

'We've got to hurry.' I glanced at Nico. 'I don't suppose you could conjure up some skeleton horses.'

He wheezed as he ran. 'So tired . . . couldn't summon a dog bone.'

Finally we scrambled over the embankment to the shore and I let out a loud whistle. I hated doing it. Even with the sand dollar I'd given the East River for a magic cleaning, the water here was pretty polluted. I didn't want to make any sea animals sick, but they came to my call.

Three wake lines appeared in the grey water, and a pod of hippocampi broke the surface. They whinnied unhappily, shaking the river muck from their manes. They were beautiful creatures, with multicoloured fish tails and the heads and forelegs of white stallions. The hippocampus in front was much bigger than the others – a ride fit for a Cyclops.

'Rainbow!' I called. 'How's it going, buddy?'

He neighed a complaint.

'Yeah, I'm sorry,' I said. 'But it's an emergency. We need to get to camp.'

He snorted.

'Tyson?' I said. 'Tyson is fine! I'm sorry he's not here. He's a big general now in the Cyclops army.'

'NEEEEIGGGGH!'

'Yeah, I'm sure he'll still bring you apples. Now about that ride . . .'

In no time, Annabeth, Nico and I were zipping up the East River faster than jet skis. We sped under the Throgs Neck Bridge and headed for Long Island Sound.

It seemed like forever until we saw the beach at camp. We thanked the hippocampi and waded ashore only to find Argus waiting for us. He stood in the sand with his arms crossed, his hundred eyes glaring at us.

'Is she here?' I asked.

He nodded grimly.

'Is everything okay?' Annabeth said.

Argus shook his head.

We followed him up the trail. It was surreal being back at camp because everything looked so peaceful – no burning buildings, no wounded fighters. The cabins were bright in the sunshine and the fields glittered with dew. But the place was mostly empty.

Up at the Big House, something was definitely wrong. Green light was shooting out of all the windows, just like I'd seen in my dream about May Castellan. Mist – the magical kind – swirled around the yard. Chiron lay on a horse-sized stretcher by the volleyball pit, a bunch of satyrs standing around him. Blackjack cantered nervously in the grass.

Don't blame me, boss! he pleaded when he saw me. *The weird girl made me do it!*

Rachel Elizabeth Dare stood at the bottom of the porch steps. Her arms were raised like she was waiting for someone inside the house to throw her a ball.

'What's she doing?' Annabeth demanded. 'How did she get past the barriers?'

'She flew,' one of the satyrs said, looking accusingly at Blackjack. 'Right past the dragon, right through the magic boundaries.'

'Rachel!' I called, but the satyrs stopped me when I tried to go any closer.

'Percy, don't,' Chiron warned. He winced as he tried to move. His left arm was in a sling, his two back legs were in splints, and his head was wrapped in bandages. 'You can't interrupt.'

'I thought you explained things to her!'

'I did. And I invited her here.'

I stared at him in disbelief. 'You said you'd never let anyone try again! You said –'

'I know what I said, Percy. But I was wrong. Rachel had a vision about the curse of Hades. She believes it may be lifted now. She convinced me she deserves a chance.'

'And if the curse *isn't* lifted? If Hades hasn't got to that yet, she'll go crazy!'

The Mist swirled around Rachel. She shivered like she was going into shock.

'Hey!' I shouted. 'Stop!'

I ran towards her, ignoring the satyrs. I got within three metres and hit something like an invisible beach ball. I bounced back and landed in the grass.

Rachel opened her eyes and turned. She looked as if she were sleepwalking – as if she could see me, but only in a dream.

'It's all right.' Her voice sounded far away. 'This is why I've come.'

'You'll be destroyed!'

She shook her head. 'This is where I belong, Percy. I finally understand why.'

It sounded too much like what May Castellan had said. I had to stop her, but I couldn't even get to my feet.

The house rumbled. The door flew open and green light poured out. I recognized the warm musty smell of snakes.

Mist curled into a hundred smoky serpents, slithering up the porch columns, curling around the house. Then the Oracle appeared in the doorway.

The withered mummy shuffled forward in her rainbow dress. She looked even worse than usual, which is saying a lot. Her hair was falling out in clumps. Her leathery skin was cracking like the seat of a worn-out bus. Her glassy eyes stared blankly into space, but I got the creepiest feeling she was being drawn straight towards Rachel.

Rachel held out her arms. She didn't look scared.

'You've waited too long,' Rachel said. 'But I'm here now.'

The sun blazed more brightly. A man appeared above the porch, floating in the air – a blond dude in a white toga, with sunglasses and a cocky smile.

'Apollo,' I said.

He winked at me, but held up his finger to his lips.

'Rachel Elizabeth Dare,' he said. 'You have the gift of prophecy. But it is also a curse. Are you sure you want this?'

Rachel nodded. 'It's my destiny.'

'Do you accept the risks?'

'I do.'

'Then proceed,' the god said.

Rachel closed her eyes. 'I accept this role. I pledge myself to Apollo, god of oracles. I open my eyes to the future and embrace the past. I accept the spirit of Delphi, voice of the gods, speaker of riddles, seer of fate.'

I didn't know where she was getting the words, but they flowed out of her as the Mist thickened. A green column of smoke, like a huge python, uncoiled from the mummy's mouth and slithered down the stairs, curling affectionately around Rachel's feet. The Oracle's mummy crumbled, falling away until it was nothing but a pile of dust in an old tie-dyed dress. Mist enveloped Rachel in a column.

For a moment, I couldn't see her at all. Then the smoke cleared.

Rachel collapsed and curled into the foetal position. Annabeth, Nico and I rushed forward, but Apollo said, 'Stop! This is the most delicate part.'

'What's going on?' I demanded. 'What do you mean?'

Apollo studied Rachel with concern. 'Either the spirit takes hold, or it doesn't.'

'And if it doesn't?' Annabeth asked.

'Five syllables,' Apollo said, counting them on his fingers. '*That would be real bad.*'

Despite Apollo's warning, I ran forward and knelt over Rachel. The smell of the attic was gone. The Mist sank into the ground and the green light faded. But Rachel was still pale. She was barely breathing.

Then her eyes fluttered open. She focused on me with difficulty. 'Percy.'

'Are you okay?'

She tried to sit up. 'Ow.' She pressed her hands to her temples.

'Rachel,' Nico said, 'your life aura almost faded completely. I could *see* you dying.'

'I'm all right,' she murmured. 'Please, help me up. The visions – they're a little disorienting.'

'Are you sure you're okay?' I asked.

Apollo drifted down from the porch. 'Ladies and gentlemen, may I introduce the new Oracle of Delphi.'

'You're kidding,' Annabeth said.

Rachel managed a weak smile. 'It's a little surprising to

me, too, but this is my fate. I saw it when I was in New York. I know why I was born with true sight. I was meant to become the Oracle.'

I blinked. 'You mean you can tell the future now?'

'Not all the time,' she said. 'But there are visions, images, words in my mind. When someone asks me a question, I . . . oh no –'

'It's starting,' Apollo announced.

Rachel doubled over, as if someone had punched her. Then she stood up straight and her eyes glowed serpent green.

When she spoke, her voice sounded tripled – like three Rachels were talking at once:

> *'Seven half-bloods shall answer the call,*
> *To storm or fire the world must fall.*
> *An oath to keep with a final breath,*
> *And foes bear arms to the Doors of Death.'*

At the last word, Rachel collapsed. Nico and I caught her and helped her to the porch. Her skin was feverish.

'I'm all right,' she said, her voice returning to normal.

'What was that?' I asked.

She shook her head, confused. 'What was what?'

'I believe,' Apollo said, 'that we just heard the next Great Prophecy.'

'What does it mean?' I demanded.

Rachel frowned. 'I don't even remember what I said.'

'No,' Apollo mused. 'The spirit will only speak through you occasionally. The rest of the time, our Rachel will be much as she's always been. There's no point in grilling her, even if she has just issued the next big prediction for the future of the world.'

'What?' I said. 'But –'

'Percy,' Apollo said, 'I wouldn't worry too much. The last Great Prophecy about *you* took almost seventy years to complete. This one may not even happen in your lifetime.'

I thought about the lines Rachel had spoken in that creepy voice – about storm and fire and the Doors of Death. 'Maybe,' I said, 'but it didn't sound so good.'

'No,' said Apollo cheerfully. 'It certainly didn't. She's going to make a wonderful Oracle!'

It was hard to drop the subject, but Apollo insisted Rachel needed to rest, and she did look pretty disoriented.

'I'm sorry, Percy,' she said. 'Back on Olympus, I didn't explain everything to you, but the calling frightened me. I didn't think you'd understand.'

'I still don't,' I admitted. 'But I guess I'm happy for you.'

Rachel smiled. 'Happy probably isn't the right word. Seeing the future isn't going to be easy, but it's my destiny. I only hope my family . . .'

She didn't finish her thought.

'Will you still go to Clarion Academy?' I asked.

'I made a promise to my father. I guess I'll try to be a normal kid during the school year, but –'

'But right now you need sleep,' Apollo scolded. 'Chiron, I don't think the attic is the proper place for our new Oracle, do you?'

'No, indeed.' Chiron looked a lot better now that Apollo had worked some medical magic on him. 'Rachel may use a guest room in the Big House for now, until we give the matter more thought.'

'I'm thinking a cave in the hills,' Apollo mused. 'With torches and a big purple curtain over the entrance . . . really mysterious. But inside, a totally decked-out pad with a game room and one of those home-theatre systems.'

Chiron cleared his throat loudly.

'What?' Apollo demanded.

Rachel kissed me on the cheek. 'Goodbye, Percy,' she whispered. 'And I don't have to see the future to tell you what to do now, do I?'

Her eyes seemed more piercing than before.

I blushed. 'No.'

'Good,' she said. Then she turned and followed Apollo into the Big House.

The rest of the day was as strange as the beginning. Campers trickled in from New York by car, pegasus and chariot. The wounded were cared for. The dead were given proper funeral rites at the campfire.

Silena's shroud was hot pink, but embroidered with an electric spear. The Ares and Aphrodite cabins both claimed her as a hero, and lit the shroud together. No one mentioned the word *spy*. That secret burned to ashes as the designer perfume smoke drifted into the sky.

Even Ethan Nakamura was given a shroud – black silk, with a logo of swords crossed under a set of scales. As his shroud went up in flames, I hoped Ethan knew he had made a difference in the end. He'd paid a lot more than an eye, but the minor gods would finally get the respect they deserved.

Dinner at the pavilion was low-key. The only highlight was Juniper the tree nymph who screamed, 'Grover!' and gave her boyfriend a flying-tackle hug, making everybody cheer. They went down to the beach to take a moonlit walk, and I was happy for them, though the scene reminded me of Silena and Beckendorf, which made me sad.

Mrs O'Leary romped around happily, eating everybody's table scraps. Nico sat at the main table with Chiron and Mr D, and nobody seemed to think this was out of place. Everybody was patting Nico on the back, complimenting him on his fighting. Even the Ares kids seemed to think he was pretty cool. Hey, show up with an army of undead warriors to save the day, and suddenly you're everybody's best friend.

Slowly, the dinner crowd trickled away. Some went to the campfire for a singalong. Others went to bed. I sat at the Poseidon table by myself and watched the moonlight on Long Island Sound. I could see Grover and Juniper at the beach, holding hands and talking. It was peaceful.

'Hey.' Annabeth slid next to me on the bench. 'Happy birthday.'

She was holding a huge misshapen cupcake with blue icing.

I stared at her. 'What?'

'It's August eighteenth,' she said. 'Your birthday, right?'

I was stunned. It hadn't even occurred to me, but she was right. I had turned sixteen this morning – the same morning I'd made the choice to give Luke the knife. The prophecy had come true right on schedule, and I hadn't even thought about the fact that it was my birthday.

'Make a wish,' she said.

'Did you bake this yourself?' I asked.

'Tyson helped.'

'That explains why it looks like a chocolate brick,' I said. 'With extra-blue cement.'

Annabeth laughed.

I thought for a second then blew out the candle.

We cut it in half and shared, eating with our fingers. Annabeth sat next to me and we watched the ocean. Crickets and monsters were making noise in the woods, but otherwise it was quiet.

'You saved the world,' she said.

'We saved the world.'

'And Rachel is the new Oracle, which means she won't be dating anybody.'

'You don't sound disappointed,' I noticed.

Annabeth shrugged. 'Oh, I don't care.'

'Uh-huh.'

She raised an eyebrow. 'You got something to say to me, Seaweed Brain?'

'You'd probably kick my butt.'

'You *know* I'd kick your butt.'

I brushed the cake off my hands. 'When I was at the River Styx, turning invulnerable . . . Nico said I had to concentrate on one thing that kept me anchored to the world, that made me want to stay mortal.'

Annabeth kept her eyes on the horizon. 'Yeah?'

'Then up on Olympus,' I said, 'when they wanted to make me a god and stuff, I kept thinking –'

'Oh, you *so* wanted to.'

'Well, maybe a little. But I didn't, because I thought

[352]

– I didn't want things to stay the same for eternity, because things could always get better. And I was thinking . . .' My throat felt really dry.

'Anyone in particular?' Annabeth asked, her voice soft.

I looked over and saw that she was trying not to smile.

'You're laughing at me,' I complained.

'I am not!'

'You are *so* not making this easy.'

Then she laughed for real, and she put her hands around my neck. 'I am never, *ever* going to make things easy for you, Seaweed Brain. Get used to it.'

When she kissed me, I had the feeling my brain was melting right through my body.

I could've stayed that way forever, except a voice behind us growled, 'Well, it's about time!'

Suddenly the pavilion was filled with torchlight and campers. Clarisse led the way as the eavesdroppers charged and hoisted us both onto their shoulders.

'Oh, come on!' I complained. 'Is there no privacy?'

'The lovebirds need to cool off!' Clarisse said with glee.

'The canoe lake!' Connor Stoll shouted.

With a huge cheer, they carried us down the hill, but they kept us close enough to hold hands. Annabeth was laughing, and I couldn't help laughing, too, even though my face was completely red.

We held hands right up to the moment they dumped us in the water.

Afterwards, I had the last laugh. I made an air bubble

at the bottom of the lake. Our friends kept waiting for us to come up, but hey — when you're the son of Poseidon, you don't have to hurry.

And it was pretty much the best underwater kiss of all time.

23 WE SAY GOODBYE, SORT OF

Camp went late that summer. It lasted two more weeks, right up to the start of a new school year, and I have to admit they were the best two weeks of my life.

Of course, Annabeth would kill me if I said anything different, but there was a lot of other great stuff going on, too. Grover had taken over the satyr seekers and was sending them out across the world to find unclaimed half-bloods. So far, the gods had kept their promise. New demigods were popping up all over the place – not just in America, but in a lot of other countries as well.

'We can hardly keep up,' Grover admitted one afternoon as we were taking a break at the canoe lake. 'We're going to need a bigger travel budget, and I could use a hundred more satyrs.'

'Yeah, but the satyrs you *have* are working super hard,' I said. 'I think they're scared of you.'

Grover blushed. 'That's silly. I'm not scary.'

'You're a Lord of the Wild, dude. The chosen one of Pan. A member of the Council of –'

'Stop it!' Grover protested. 'You're as bad as Juniper. I think she wants me to run for president next.'

He chewed on a tin can as we stared across the pond at the line of new cabins under construction. The U-shape would soon be a complete rectangle, and the demigods had really taken to the new task with gusto.

Nico had some undead builders working on the Hades cabin. Even though he was still the only kid in it, it was going to look pretty cool – solid obsidian walls with a skull over the door and torches that burned with green fire twenty-four hours a day. Next to that were the cabins of Iris, Nemesis, Hecate and several others I didn't recognize. They kept adding new ones to the blueprints every day. It was going so well Annabeth and Chiron were talking about adding an entirely new wing of cabins just so they could have enough room.

The Hermes cabin was a lot less crowded now, because most of the unclaimed kids had received signs from their godly parents. It happened almost every night, and every night more demigods straggled over the property line with the satyr guides, usually with some nasty monsters pursuing them, but almost all of them made it through.

'It's going to be a lot different next summer,' I said. 'Chiron's expecting we'll have twice as many campers.'

'Yeah,' Grover agreed, 'but it'll be the same old place.'

He sighed contentedly.

I watched as Tyson led a group of Cyclops builders. They were hoisting huge stones in place for the Hecate cabin, and I knew it was a delicate job. Each stone was engraved with magical writing, and if they dropped one, it would either explode or turn everyone within half a mile into a tree. I figured nobody but Grover would like that.

'I'll be travelling a lot,' Grover warned, 'between protecting nature and finding half-bloods. I may not see you as much.'

'Won't change anything,' I said. 'You're still my best friend.'

He grinned. 'Except for Annabeth.'

'That's different.'

'Yeah,' he agreed. 'It sure is.'

In the late afternoon, I was taking one last walk along the beach when a familiar voice said, 'Good day for fishing.'

My dad, Poseidon, was standing knee-deep in the surf, wearing his typical Bermuda shorts, beat-up cap and a real subtle pink-and-green tropical shirt. He had a deep-sea fishing rod in his hands, and when he cast it, the line went way out – like halfway across Long Island Sound.

'Hey, Dad,' I said. 'What brings you here?'

He winked. 'Never really got to talk in private on Olympus. I wanted to thank you.'

'Thank me? You came to the rescue.'

'Yes, and I got my palace destroyed in the process, but you know – palaces can be rebuilt. I've had so many thank-you cards from the other gods. Even Ares wrote one, though I think Hera forced him to. It's rather gratifying. So thank you. I suppose even the gods can learn new tricks.'

The Sound began to boil. At the end of my dad's line, a huge green sea serpent erupted from the water. It thrashed and fought, but Poseidon just sighed. Holding his fishing pole with one hand, he whipped out his knife and cut the line. The monster sank below the surface.

'Not eating size,' he complained. 'I have to release the little ones or the game wardens will be all over me.'

'Little ones?'

He grinned. 'You're doing well with those new cabins,

by the way. I suppose this means I can claim all those other sons and daughters of mine and send you some siblings next summer.'

'Ha-ha.'

Poseidon reeled in his empty line.

I shifted my feet. 'Um, you *were* kidding, right?'

Poseidon gave me one of his inside-joke winks, and I still didn't know whether he was serious or not. 'I'll see you soon, Percy. And remember – know which fish are big enough to land, eh?'

With that he dissolved in the sea breeze, leaving a fishing pole lying in the sand.

That evening was the last night of camp – the bead ceremony. The Hephaestus cabin had designed the bead this year. It showed the Empire State Building, and etched in tiny Greek letters, spiralling around the image, were the names of all the heroes who had died defending Olympus. There were too many names, but I was proud to wear the bead. I put it on my camp necklace – four beads now. I felt like an old-timer. I thought about the first campfire I'd ever attended, back when I was twelve, and how I'd felt so at home. That at least hadn't changed.

'Never forget this summer!' Chiron told us. He had healed remarkably well, but he still trotted in front of the fire with a slight limp. 'We have discovered bravery and friendship and courage this summer. We have upheld the honour of the camp.'

He smiled at me, and everybody cheered. As I looked at the fire, I saw a little girl in a brown dress tending the flames. She winked at me with red glowing eyes. No one else seemed to notice her, but I realized maybe she preferred it that way.

'And now,' Chiron said, 'early to bed! Remember you must vacate your cabins by noon tomorrow unless you've made arrangements to stay the year with us. The cleaning harpies will eat any stragglers, and I'd hate to end the summer on a sour note!'

The next morning, Annabeth and I stood at the top of Half-Blood Hill. We watched the buses and vans pull away, taking most of the campers back to the real world. A few old-timers would be staying behind, and a few of the newcomers, but I was heading back to Goode High School for my sophomore year – the first time in my life I'd ever done two years at the same school.

'Goodbye,' Rachel said to us as she shouldered her bag. She looked pretty nervous, but she was keeping a promise to her father and attending Clarion Academy in New Hampshire. It would be next summer before we got our Oracle back.

'You'll do great.' Annabeth hugged her. Funny, she seemed to get along fine with Rachel these days.

Rachel bit her lip. 'I hope you're right. I'm a little worried. What if somebody asks what's on the next maths test and I start spouting a prosphecy in the middle of geometry class? *The Pythagorean theorem shall be problem two . . .* Gods, that would be embarrassing.'

Annabeth laughed, and to my relief it made Rachel smile.

'Well,' she said, 'you two be good to each other.' Go figure, but she looked at *me* like I was some kind of troublemaker. Before I could protest, Rachel wished us well and ran down the hill to catch her lift.

Annabeth, thank goodness, would be staying in New York. She'd got permission from her parents to attend a boarding school in the city so she could be close to Olympus and oversee the rebuilding efforts.

'And close to me?' I asked.

'Well, someone's got a big sense of his own importance.' But she laced her fingers through mine. I remembered what she'd told me in New York, about building something permanent, and I thought – just maybe – we were off to a good start.

The guard dragon Peleus curled contentedly around the pine tree underneath the Golden Fleece and began to snore, blowing steam with every breath.

'You've been thinking about Rachel's prophecy?' I asked Annabeth.

She frowned. 'How did you know?'

'Because I know you.'

She bumped me with her shoulder. 'Okay, so I have. *Seven half-bloods shall answer the call.* I wonder who they'll be. We're going to have so many new faces next summer.'

'Yep,' I agreed. 'And all that stuff about the world falling in storm or fire.'

She pursed her lips. 'And foes at the Doors of Death. I don't know, Percy, but I don't like it. I thought . . . well, maybe we'd get some *peace* for a change.'

'Wouldn't be Camp Half-Blood if it was peaceful,' I said.

'I guess you're right . . . or maybe the prophecy won't happen for years.'

'Could be a problem for another generation of demigods,' I agreed. 'Then we can kick back and enjoy.'

She nodded, though she still seemed uneasy. I didn't blame her, but it was hard to feel too upset on a nice day, with her next to me, knowing that I wasn't really saying goodbye. We had lots of time.

'Race you to the road?' I said.

'You are so going to lose.' She took off down Half-Blood Hill and I sprinted after her.

For once, I didn't look back.

HOMEWORK OR
FIGHTING MONSTERS
TOUGH CHOICE . . .